"I have been sick and tired and lost. I have tripped and fallen on my face. I have shivered—and sweated—with fear. My heart has been broken, my will bridled, my spirit battered and bruised. . . .

"But all this has validated my statement of faith: I know that my Redeemer lives!

"God's plans are much better than mine. He has given me the honor—the great honor—of presenting this true story, which is written so that you, too, may believe—and serve."

—Mary Jane Chambers

HERE AM I! SEND ME

MARY JANE CHAMBERS

SPIRE BOOKS

Fleming H. Revell Company   •   Old Tappan, New Jersey

Unless otherwise noted, scripture quotations are from the *Revised Standard Version of the Bible*, copyright 1946, 1952 and © 1971 by the Division of Christian Education of the National Council of the Churches of Christ in the U.S.A. and used by permission.

The Bible verses marked *The Living Bible* are taken from *The Living Bible, Paraphrased* (Wheaton: Tyndale House Publishers, 1971) and are used by permission.

AUTHOR'S NOTE

This is a true story. However, some of the names, places, and circumstances have beeen disguised to protect the privacy of those involved.

Mary Jane Chambers

Contents

*And I heard the voice of the Lord saying,
"Whom shall I send, and who will go for us?"
Then I said, "Here am I! Send me."*
                                        Isaiah 6:8 RSV

One of God's Unemployed

I was never really an atheist—or even an agnostic. I have always believed in God. My problem was that I could not seem to get in touch with him. For years, I looked for him in the church—and outside of it. I called out to him; I even offered to serve him in ways which I thought would please him. But I never seemed to receive an answer.

This problem first came to light in my Sunday School class when I was eleven.

The Junior High Class of about a dozen girls was taught by Miss Mary Timmings in a corner of the basement of the Westminster Presbyterian Church of Gary, Indiana. In the late 1930's there was no such thing as an education building. Sunday School was conducted in small groups in the church basement (which also doubled as a social hall) and even in the sanctuary itself. Each teacher had to shout to make herself heard above the cacophony of the other classes—and by raising her voice she contributed to the uproar.

Miss Timmings was what was politely called a "maiden lady" and more commonly called an "old maid." She was medium sized, with graying dark hair and glasses which did nothing to enhance her features. She wore drab two-piece wool suits and sensible oxfords. But the most memorable thing about her was her facial expression, which said quite plainly that we all have our cross to bear in this life—and that part of her cross was the Junior High Class. The rest of her burden was the classes she taught during the week at the nearby high school.

At that time, I was searching very hard to find God, and I assumed that Miss Timmings already knew where he was. It puzzled me that this knowledge seemed to give her so little comfort. In those days we sang "Brighten the Corner Where You Are" and "I Love to Tell the Story," but I always had my doubts that Miss Timmings enjoyed anything about Sunday School or church.

My problem was exhibited to the whole church school on a lovely Sunday morning in May. I was wearing a new dress of my favorite shade—the color of deep pink roses. Like most 11-year-olds, I felt shapeless, clumsy, and self-conscious much of the time. But I was convinced that the pink dress made up for all deficiencies of nature, and I was happier than usual when I set out on the short walk from my house to Sunday School.

The windows of the church basement were open to a soft, flower-scented breeze, and the neighborhood birds seemed to be having their own choir practice in the background. Six groups of assorted Sunday School students were discussing their various lessons. Miss Timmings stood before the Junior High girls, addressing us on the subject of "Doing God's Work."

"Our abilities come from God," she informed us as she scowled at two girls who were whispering in the third row.

"God expects us to use these gifts to make the world a better place to live," she insisted.

Then she stepped to one side of the class and asked if anybody had any plans for doing God's work. I slumped down into my chair and looked at my shoes, fearing that if I met her eyes, she would know my secret.

I was average size for an eleven-year-old and was very thankful not to be bigger. At that moment I would have been happy had I been a midget. And, as the class members revealed their plans, I longed to disappear completely.

Phyllis Whitman, a tiny blonde who always said and did what was expected of her, promptly raised her hand.

12

"I've always wanted to be a teacher," she announced. "Maybe I can go to Africa and teach the heathen."

"Very good," said Miss Timmings with one of her rare half-smiles. "Has anyone else got any ideas?"

"Since I'm going to be a nurse," said Mary Alice Moffatt grandly, "I'll be doing God's work, too. He wants us to care for the sick."

I could see through this right away. Athletic Mary Alice was always talking about being a nurse and evidently had decided to put her ambition to a double purpose. But Miss Timmings nodded her head approvingly.

Joanne Phillips, who played the flute for every occasion whether or not it was an occasion, spoke up. "I'm going to major in music and perhaps I can play the organ."

"Those are all very good plans," Miss Timmings said. "Anybody else? How about you, Mary Jane?"

They all looked at me and waited for my answer. I squirmed in my chair, hoping that the crack in the cement floor would suddenly expand and swallow me up. Finally, the silence grew embarrassing and I just blurted out: "Well, I guess I'm going to be one of God's unemployed."

The class dissolved in screams of girlish laughter, disturbing all of the other classes in the basement. Even deaf old Mr. Bond turned around and glared at us. The Men's Bible Class considered the Junior High girls to be unnecessarily boisterous as it was.

Miss Timmings, her face flushed with embarrassment, did the only thing her school-teacher mind could think of to punish me: She kept me after class. However, she must have realized at once that if she kept me very long she would be late taking her place in the choir. So my punishment had to be brief.

"You know that you disrupted the whole church school, don't you, Mary Jane?"

"Yes, ma'am, and I'm very sorry." Sorry? I stood there, knee-deep in anguish and wondered how Miss Timmings could fail to realize that my confession had been far more painful to me than to anybody else.

"I didn't mean to say it," I murmured, "but I was only telling the truth."

13

"Mary Jane, don't be flippant. That's a terrible way to talk and you ought to ask God to forgive you for it."

I was getting ready to ask her if she knew where God was these days, but she dismissed me with a quick wave of her hand and headed for the choir room.

A few months later, Miss Timmings' class and Mr. Whitman's class of Junior High boys were organized into a preparatory class for church membership. We were to meet for an hour every Saturday morning for eight weeks before taking our formal membership vows. I felt like one of those hypocrites Jesus was always mentioning in the Bible, but I went along with the plans because I didn't know what else to do.

I had tried to talk to our minister about my problem, but his attitude was that adolescent problems were something that would soon be outgrown. I suppose he had grown-up problems requiring his attention. He did give me one ray of hope, though.

"Have you found anything that you like to do?" he asked me.

"Yes, I love music," I told him. "I've been learning to play the piano."

"Well, then," he said, seeming relieved, "why don't you plan to become a church organist or even a choir soloist?"

Joanne Phillips had already thought of this, but I decided that God would probably need more than one church organist anyway. So I went home and practiced the piano and sang hymns at the top of my voice.

For several years I practiced the piano and sang with little apparent improvement. I had a number of real handicaps—I was practically tone deaf, and I had little sense of rhythm. Music came hard to me, and I battled my way through each new piano book. Years later I realized that if God had wanted me to become a church organist, he would surely have given me some natural musical ability.

I remained in the preparatory class only because the minister persuaded me I was as well prepared as any of the youngsters. After all, he and I had decided that I was going to be a church organist. The class consisted of eighteen boys and girls in various stages of adolescence. We looked all the more awkward because of our clothes. They were

"Sunday best" finery, but in the days before permanent-pressed clothes, they were wrinkled when we sat down after the first hymn.

On membership Sunday the minister asked the preparatory class to come forward. As the group began walking slowly down the aisle, I considered bolting for the door. But Miss Timmings caught me with her eyes, and I meekly followed Phyllis Whitman to the altar. I stood there smoothing my wrinkled dress with my damp hands, wishing that I could smooth out my conscience as well. Then I promised God—the God I didn't know and couldn't find—that I would support and serve the church which, without him, meant little to me. I almost choked on the words.

I attended church all through high school even though my problem persisted. There was a joke which emerged about a little boy who asked his mother what church was. She told him it was God's house. The next Sunday when he was sitting in his pew, the little boy said in a loud voice, "I sure wish God would show up!" Most people thought this story was hilarious, but it wasn't funny to me because I wished the same thing so desperately.

At about this time I began to examine the other parishioners to see if any appeared to know God. I'm sure that some of them did.

Old Mrs. Burton, who walked with a cane, managed to be there in the second pew, left of the aisle, every Sunday regardless of the weather. She also gave a considerable amount of her money to the church, a fact which was mentioned by various church officials from time to time. I decided that no one in her position would bother to limp her way to church each Sunday, bringing a lot of money, if she didn't know that God expected it of her.

Then there was Mr. Johnson, who taught the class of Senior High boys. His wife had been killed in an automobile accident, leaving him with four sons and considerable domestic difficulties Despite these obstacles, he always arrived a bit early for Sunday School, with all of his boys scrubbed and neatly dressed. He carried a notebook full of carefully-prepared comments about the current lesson. He had offers of help from a number of single ladies, including Miss Timmings, but he seemed to delight in meeting life's

15

challenges by himself. He seemed to have no bitterness whatsoever toward God.

Maybe a dozen others out of the congregation demonstrated what I thought were the necessary qualifications for knowing God—service, monetary contributions, and a noble attitude. The rest, most of them much older than I, slouched down in the pews Sunday after Sunday, eyes glassy with boredom. Their prayers seemed to have a hollow sound as though the words were directed to nobody in particular. And sometimes during the sermon, the women looked as though they were thinking about cooking dinner, and the men's minds seemed to be wandering off to some business problem. They acted as though they were waiting for God to show up, but doubted that he ever would

One of the hymns we sang frequently was "True-Hearted, Whole-Hearted." The words always affected me: "True-hearted, whole-hearted, faithful and loyal, King of our lives, by Thy grace we will be . . . ."

Nobody in the entire congregation expressed that much enthusiasm for God.

I kept attending Sunday School during my high school years although the class dwindled until only Mary Alice, Phyllis, and I showed up regularly. Then I went off to college in another town and, in my newfound freedom, attended the Presbyterian church only when I felt like it. During these college years I sought out other churches occasionally under the guise of rounding out my education. Actually, I was hoping to meet a wider variety of young men than the Presbyterians seemed to offer.

On one of my visits to the University Methodist Church in Bloomington, Indiana, I met a young graduate student. Randall Chambers was tall and handsome with curly, sandy-colored hair and startling blue eyes. Like most graduate students, he was in no position to marry. But every time I looked into those blue eyes, marriage seemed more and more sensible. Eventually love triumphed over reason completely and we were married back home in my Presbyterian church.

This was in September, 1949—just in time for Randy to start his first term at the University of Missouri at Columbia.

For the next few years we went to church only when we felt like it—and avoided Sunday School almost entirely. He was busy with graduate school, and I had a newspaper job along with the apartment housework. Church didn't seem to have as much priority with either of us as it once had.

After two years in Missouri, we moved to Cleveland, Ohio, where Randy completed his doctorate in psychology at Western Reserve University. Our next move was to Bar Harbor, Maine, where Randy received a post-doctoral fellowship at a research laboratory.

Our first son, Mark, was born in Maine in March, 1954. We dutifully had him baptized in the Methodist Church. Mark was a quiet, sandy-haired boy with deep blue eyes I had seen before.

When Mark was fifteen months old, Randy was called to active duty with the Air Force Reserves. With characteristic insensitivity, the government moved us from Maine to San Antonio, Texas, in the midst of an August heat wave.

I was much busier than I had been in earlier days, but the emptiness persisted in the realm of religion. My "solution" was to attend church less and less and try to ignore my spiritual ache.

Then suddenly I was searching for God again. In the ninth month of my second pregnancy, I developed a stubborn case of pneumonia. I was scheduled to undergo my second Caesarean section, but the doctors were trying very hard to clear up the pneumonia first. Time simply ran out. The pneumonia had not responded to the bombardment of antibiotics. Now that my pregancy was full term, the doctors were afraid to wait any longer. An emergency Caesarean would only add to the risk.

I doubt that there is any condition more miserable than that of being nine months pregnant. The skin that once fit perfectly without any special attention now seems to be too tight and pinches every time you move. Moreover, there is no stationary position, either lying down or sitting up, that is comfortable for more than five minutes. And standing up —unable to see your feet—makes you feel like a basketball with legs. The only reason this condition is bearable at all is that it is temporary. Being nine months pregnant makes you look forward to giving birth. Perilous as the birth process

17

seems, it is infinitely preferable to being nine months pregnant the rest of your life.

In addition to being normally miserable, I coughed in a continual staccato as a result of the pneumonia. I coughed so thoroughly, as a matter of fact, that the doctors sent me to have my chest X-rayed to check the possibility that I had developed TB. They didn't come to any conclusions about this largely because, as the X-ray technician explained to his friend, "We had a hard time finding her chest."

As I lay on my hospital bed on the eve of the Caesarean, my room seemed to be the center of activity. Randy was there, of course. He had been spending most of his time with me, leaving Mark with his grandmother. Randy was "dismissed" for the night when a dozen doctors appeared at my bedside, speaking in hushed tones, and scribbling in their notebooks. I was in an Air Force hospital, and I found out that the doctors comprised a class for anesthesiologists. When my obstetrician arrived, I demanded to know why the whole class was interested in my case.

"I guess I'd better tell you," the doctor began. "Since we haven't been able to clear up your pneumonia, we're worried about the shock of major surgery. We can't give you a general anesthetic because your breathing is already difficult. So you'll have to stay awake during the operation, relying on a spinal anesthetic. These are just precautions," he added. "I'm sure you'll be fine."

The doctor didn't sound overly convincing. And as if to emphasize this doubt, the chaplains arrived. The Jewish and Catholic chaplains, obviously doing their duty, remained briefly and said hurried prayers. Then the Protestant chaplain entered my room in a cheery, optimistic manner. He was, he told me, a Christian Scientist.

It would have been laughable if it had not been so serious. As I looked at this smiling little man who was to be my chaplain, my comforter, I thought of an old Jimmy Stewart movie I had seen years earlier. Jimmy Stewart was getting ready to jump off a bridge for some reason that has since eluded me. Just as he got ready to jump, a brokendown old man appeared. "I'm your guardian angel," he said in a creaky voice.

And Jimmy Stewart said with dismay, "Wouldn't you know that's the kind of guardian angel I'd get!"

This chaplain affected me the same way. He talked to me about faith for awhile and then prayed one of his mind-over-matter prayers. However, when he learned of my total predicament, he became quite nervous about recommending his denomination to me. He backed out of the room before I had time to ask him any questions.

After he left, I faced the fact: I was on my own spiritually. Well, that was all right. After all those years in Sunday School, I could surely find some comfort in the scriptures on my own. So I started reciting the 23rd Psalm.

The Lord is my shepherd, I shall not want; he makes me lie down in green pastures. He leads me beside still waters; he restores my soul. He leads me in paths of righteousness for his name's sake. Even though I walk through the valley of the shadow of. . . .

I stopped abruptly. I couldn't bring myself to say the word "death." I was 31 years old, but I was still searching for the God of my Sunday School days. I was physically sick and spiritually confused. As sincerely as I had ever prayed in my life, I began: "Dear God, please give me the courage to die."

Then I cried bitter, terrified tears into my pillow. This made my eyes red and puffy, only adding to the wretchedness of my appearance.

I tried once more to pull myself together. I had heard of people who found courage in the Bible simply by opening it at random. I decided to try it.

I took my Bible from the nightstand beside the bed. It was the one Miss Timmings had given me when I joined the church. Slowly, I separated the pages with my thumbs, and read the passage which first caught my eye. It began with Matthew 7:21—

Not every one who says to me, 'Lord, Lord,' shall enter the kingdom of heaven, but he who does the will of my Father who is in heaven.

On that day many will say to me, 'Lord, Lord, did we not prophesy in your name, and cast out demons in your name, and do many mighty works in your name?' And then will I declare to them, 'I never knew you. . . .'

Those four words, "I never knew you," stood out on that page as though they were three feet high. It was true. God had ignored me in my youth and had failed to comfort me when I faced a medical crisis. Worse still, when I prayed for the courage to die, he seemed to be seeing how far he could go to be ludicrous. All of us have spiritual highlights in our lives—and spiritual depressions. That night I touched the bottom.

The next morning, when the hospital corpsmen brought their stretcher to take me to surgery, they found that the whimpering wretch, cowering in a heap of hopelessness, had disappeared. In her place was a wounded tigress, furious over the events of the previous night and smoldering with the determination to live.

In the operating room I was surrounded by men in surgical gowns and masks. At least half of the anesthesiologists' class were assisting the surgical team. I lay there, fully conscious, watching them pit their knowledge and skill against my crisis.

For three hours they fought for my life and that of my infant with blood transfusions, oxygen masks, and glucose injections. And I waged a mental battle which was equally hard-fought. By sheer will power, I marshaled every bone, muscle, and nerve of my body into an attitude of cooperation. The Christian Science chaplain would have been proud of me.

When it was all over and the baby—a big, healthy boy —was sleeping in the nursery, the doctor took my hand.

"You were just great," he said. "Last night I was worried about your attitde of resignation. It seemed to me that you had given up the fight. But you certainly made up for it this morning!"

I didn't even consider the possibility that God really had answered my prayers—in his own way. The words "I never knew you" continued to haunt me.

Chapter 2

The Blind Leading The Blind

Eighteen months later, I had shoved the entire medical crisis—and my search for God—into a little-used, attic corner of my mind. Randy had left the Air Force and we had moved first to New Jersey and then to Jonestown, Pennsylvania, all within a year. He traveled a great deal in his new job. I was very busy taking care of the house, the baby, and four-year-old Mark.

Both boys were active and mischievous, and I had difficulty keeping up with them. Mark refused to stay in the yard and Craig, at age one and a half, roamed the house getting into everything. But he was always properly penitent for his crimes and gazed at me so sincerely with dark eyes, a reflection of my own, that I was prevented from punishing him as he deserved.

Whatever importance we had attached to church attendance had disappeared. We tried to send Mark to Sunday School almost every Sunday, but Sunday School and church had lost any relevance they had ever had for either of us.

Customarily, Randy stayed at home with the baby while I drove Mark down to Sunday School and dropped him off in the church parking lot.

The church was a comfortable old building made of graying white stucco. A steeple cast its shadow over the

21

parking lot, and mellow chimes reminded the entire neighborhood that it was time to come to God's house. I deliberately closed my ears and turned my back on the invitation
and drove down to the corner drugstore instead.

Then I bought a big fat Sunday newspaper and went
home where I read it leisurely over a second cup of coffee.
I did this for six months and kept telling myself that this
was the best way to enjoy Sunday morning. I would never
attend Sunday School again!

However, one Sunday morning I took Mark to Sunday
School during a downpour. The small church parking lot
was a hodge-podge of children, umbrellas, and cars with fu-
riously flapping windshield wipers. Instead of dropping
Mark off, I had to park the car and escort him around the
puddles to his classroom. When I returned, I found my car
was boxed into a corner by several abandoned automobiles
whose owners obviously were not going to return for at
least an hour. So I went back into the education building
and inquired about an adult class.

The Christian Service Class for adult women met in the
church sanctuary and had already begun its session when I
arrived. About fifty women of assorted ages and sizes sat in
the last four or five rows of pews, surrounded by dripping
umbrellas and plastic rain hats. I was wearing an old dress,
but it was covered by my new raincoat. A nondescript
gray-haired woman in a dark suit—reminiscent of Miss
Timmings of my girlhood—stood in front of the class,
reading from the lesson quarterly which was propped up on
a lectern.

The lesson, from the Old Testament, concerned the rebellion of the ancient Hebrews to God's plans. The scripture, which was called the "golden text" for the morning,
was Leviticus 26:12: *And I will walk among you, and will
be your God, and you shall be my people.*

It was a variation of the theme which had been plaguing
me for years, so at first I thought it was going to be an interesting lesson. But Mrs. Barrett, the teacher, didn't relate
the scripture to present-day living. She droned on and on
about the ancient Jews and their problems.

"The first covenant relationship between the Hebrews

and God was found in the Ten Commandments," Mrs. Barrett said.

"God also promised land to Abraham and his descendants," Mrs. Barrett continued, "and God even delivered Abraham's descendants from bondage in Egypt. When they were wandering in the wilderness, God renewed his covenant relationship with them."

From my seat in the back row, near the door, I cast a look around at the rest of the class. They sat motionless—from boredom rather than intrigue. The steady plop, plop, plop of rain on the roof lulled some of the class into a state of near-sleep. The problems of the ancient Hebrews were not an overriding concern to any of us. Once again I found myself asking the question I had asked so often in the Sunday School of my childhood. What was being accomplished here this morning? I had been right all along, I decided. The best plan was to observe Sunday mornings with the newspaper and leisurely cups of coffee.

At the end of the lecture, Mrs. Barrett dropped what was evidenly a bombshell to the regular members of the class. "As some of you may know," she said, "I will have to give up teaching your class at the end of this month. Joe has taken a new job in Pittsburgh and we plan to move there. I hope you will join me in praying that we can find a good teacher to replace me."

There was an excited murmur as six or eight of the class "regulars" jumped up and grouped themselves around Faye Barrett, clamoring for more details. I slipped out the door. If they were going to pray for a teacher, I certainly wished them well. Personally, I thought the whole situation was hopeless.

I didn't give the Christian Service Class another thought until Tuesday afternoon. The baby was taking his nap and Mark was playing with a neighbor boy in the backyard, so I tackled the ironing. I was applying the iron to the sleeve of a white shirt when I first heard it—an inner voice which said to me, "You can do it. You can teach the class. Tell them you will do it."

At first I thought it was some bizarre twist of my conscience prodding me. But the conscience is a part of one's

23

mind, and the idea of teaching that class had never occurred to me at all. I was as guilt-free about that class as I was about passing by the hospital without offering my services in surgery. Then I realized that this voice, this absurd suggestion, had originated outside of my mind. Slowly, the knowledge came to me with a certainty which remains unshakable: It was the voice of God.

During all the years I had been seeking him, I had never wondered what form a confrontation with him would take. If I had considered the possibilities, I would have imagined him speaking with a mighty voice out of an earth-shaking clap of thunder—or a blinding light forcing me to my knees in awe. But this was merely a soft, compelling voice whispering orders into my ear. And instead of falling on my knees, I stood there at the ironing board, pressing the same shirt sleeve over and over.

After seeking him for so long, one would have thought that I would have obeyed him immediately. But I seemed to have a lot of the stiffnecked tendencies of the ancient Israelites.

My first reaction was that my teaching that class was a preposterous idea. Teach it? I wasn't even planning to attend it!

"You can do it. Tell them that you will teach the class," the voice commanded me again.

It was startling to think that God would be interested in personally recruiting such a lowly worker as a Sunday School teacher. I had no doubt that over the centuries he had been recruiting workers for the big jobs. The Apostle Paul, as Saul of Tarsus, was confronted by Christ on the road to Damascus. But Paul was needed to help establish the Christian Church! I also believed that such men as John Wesley, David Livingstone, Albert Schweitzer, and Billy Graham had been called by God to do the work he wanted done. But theirs were big undertakings—not an indifferent Sunday School class in a sleepy church in an obscure town in Pennsylvania.

These were also ten-talent men. Saul was a Jew by birth, a Roman citizen, a resident of Greece, and a tentmaker by profession—ideal qualifications for traveling around preaching the gospel to Jews, Romans, and Greeks. Albert

Schweitzer ran his hospital during the week, and conducted a worship service on Sunday, when he both preached and played the organ. And if the organ broke down there in the wilds of Africa, he could also repair it.

But I wasn't even a one-talent person—so far as I could tell. I didn't like Sunday School. It was either dull or frustrating—or both. I was raised in the Presbyterian Church and had only joined the Methodists after my marriage. I had never known a Sunday School teacher of any denomination who seemed to enjoy the job. I had never taught a class of any kind, and I didn't want the responsibility.

"God, I know you don't make mistakes," I said, "at least not very often. But, Sir, I have no desire to be a Sunday School teacher. I know I promised that I would become a church organist, and I intend to get back to practicing when the children are older. I would also like to sing solos in the choir when I learn to sing better. But I have no inclination whatsoever to teach that class!"

I thought the matter settled. But all during the rest of the week, every time I was in a quiet room, the voice commanded me to teach the class. I tried to block it out. Randy was out of town, and I fought the quiet with the radio, the stereo, the TV. I frantically struck up a conversation with anyone who came by. The milkman, the paper boy, and the mailman began to look at me quizzically when I grabbed each one by the arm and tried to engage him in lengthy small talk.

I couldn't tell anybody that I was having an argument with God. I feared I would be referred to the nearest mental institution—or, worse yet, be branded a religious fanatic. Now there was a ridiculous thought: a Sunday School drop-out becoming a religious fanatic.

But, ridiculous or not, the situation remained unchanged. The voice kept prodding me, commanding me in that quiet, yet imperative, way. I couldn't eat and I had trouble sleeping. By the end of the week I had the hunted look of a criminal on the "most wanted" posters.

On Sunday morning I drove Mark to the far edge of the church parking lot. I let him out as quietly as possible, wishing that I could somehow make my car tiptoe past the classrooms. I drove down to the drugstore and bought *two*

25

bulky Sunday papers. Then I went home to put on the coffee pot. I spread the papers out and tried to read, but for some reason they didn't seem to be as interesting as usual. My mind wandered to the Christian Service Class. Surely they already had a volunteer. A class with eighty members on the roll and an average attendance of fifty should have no trouble finding a teacher. Maybe somebody was volunteering at this very moment! I forced my attention back to the papers—but they contained mostly advertising this morning. And, to make matters worse, my coffee was bitter.

The voice subsided somewhat the next week and I began to think that I had won the argument. Aside from an occasional burst of encouragement ("You can do it") the voice had reduced the pressure. So the next Sunday I decided it would be safe to go back to the class once more—just to make sure that they did have a teacher.

I was greeted at the door of the sanctuary by a pleasant young woman with long brown hair. She introduced herself as Vicky Peterson and gave me a name tag which said "Visitor" on it. I sat on the back row, close to the door, and watched the assorted women gather. The sanctuary, their classroom, had three doors and class members converged from all three directions. They greeted each other and exchanged private bits of gossip like school girls.

A middle-aged woman finally arose and walked to the lectern. She was petite with well-groomed salt-and-pepper hair. I learned later that her name was Joy Werner—one of the pillars of the church.

"For the devotion this morning," Mrs. Werner announced, "I will read Psalm 100."

Make a joyful noise to the Lord, all the lands! Serve the Lord with gladness!
Come into his presence with singing!
Know that the Lord is God! It is he that made us, and we are his; we are his people, and the sheep of his pasture.
Enter his gates with thanksgiving and his courts with praise! Give thanks to him, bless his name! For the Lord is good; his steadfast love endures for ever, and his faithfulness to all generations

Two phrases fairly jumped out at me: "Serve the Lord with gladness" and "his steadfast love endures forever."

While I was still pondering these words, Joy Werner sat down and Faye Barrett spread her notes out on the lectern.

"Our scripture lesson this morning is very appropriate, considering that we're having so much trouble finding a teacher. It is Matthew 9:37: *Then he said to his disciples, "The harvest is plentiful, but the laborers are few."*

"I guess the truth of this verse doesn't hit people who have never tried serving God," Faye Barrett continued. "It probably looks like very unrewarding work, but I want you all to know that teaching this Sunday School class has been the most rewarding experience of my life.

"The only disappointment about this work is our inability to recruit more help. People sitting on the sidelines don't seem to take our word for it. It's like saying 'Come on in, the water's fine' to a group of non-swimmers.

"Well, I haven't given up hope. For the past two weeks I've been stopping by the chapel every chance I had, praying for a fine teacher. I even prayed that God would recruit someone and haunt her until she said 'yes.' "

My heart fluttered and then seemed to stop beating. My hands were clammy. I was trembling with the realization: I was the one whom God had chosen.

Faye Barrett continued, sounding to me as though she were off in the distance somewhere: "The Commission on Education is going to have an emergency meeting right after Sunday School to decide what to do. We may have to be combined with another class for awhile."

The class members groaned. Then a small group engulfed Faye Barrett to discuss the problem further.

As soon as my weak knees could support me, I stumbled out the door. I stood for a moment on the sidewalk, only dimly aware that I was obstructing the traffic of children and adults rushing by in different directions. I completely forgot that Mark would be waiting for me.

I asked a tall young man if he knew where the Commission on Education was meeting. He pointed to a nearby basement door. I ran to the door, pushed it open, and burst into the room as though somebody or something was chasing me

27

Six or seven men and women, all total strangers to me, were sitting around a long narrow table discussing their problems in low tones. I interrupted them without hesitation.

"I'll do it. I'll teach the class!" I announced breathlessly.

They looked at me for a long moment with a mixture of surprise, puzzlement, and even a trace of suspicion. Then the chairman, who introduced himself as Frank Finley, asked me to sit down and discuss the possibilities with the group.

"Are you a member of this church?" asked one of the women.

"Well, no," I hedged, "but we've been thinking of transferring our membership here."

"That's a basic requirement," Frank Finley said. "We also require that our Sunday School teachers abstain from alcohol and preferably cigarettes."

"There's no problem with me," I assured them.

It was ironic, I thought, that the requirements were so superficial. A person could attend church every Sunday and remain sober all his life and still not know God. I wanted to tell the committee that I had recently made God's acquaintance, but the interview continued along other lines.

One of the men who had been silent up until now gave voice to a suspicion that hovered over the group like a cloud.

"You say you just moved here. Is your husband setting up a business by any chance?"

"No, my husband works for the government."

They had suspected that I wanted to use a Sunday School affiliation for business reasons! Insulting as it was, I found I couldn't get angry at them. When I considered my wild-eyed entrance, I knew that I would have been suspicious, too.

"My husband travels a lot," I told the committee, "and I have an eighteen-month-old baby. So if he gets sick on a Sunday morning when my husband is away, you'll have to get a substitute teacher."

"We can do that," Mr. Finley assured me. "Just call George Marvin here. He's the church school superintendent, and he'll find a substitute."

Chapter 3

The Girls

I made my debut as a Sunday School teacher on a bright April morning when the hyacinths were in bloom. I wanted to present a pot of hyacinths to the class as an eloquent witness to the glory of God, but the International Sunday School Lesson was on the subject of Jonah and the whale.

I had begun studying the lesson on Monday afternoon. By Tuesday night I had read the two journals, the quarterly, and the lesson annual containing various interpretations of the lesson. On Wednesday I went to the library. On Thursday I went shopping and bought a new dress in a rose Italian print with a hat to match. On Friday I went to the hairdresser who thinned out my shaggy dark hair and subdued the curls until they actually behaved.

I had never been overly interested in clothes and had become even more careless of my appearance since the birth of my second baby. But I couldn't stand up in front of a group of strange women without making an effort to improve my appearance. Randy was still incredulous, but he seemed to approve of my new finery.

When The Sunday arrived, I was awake by 5:30 a.m. I don't know why I thought teaching Sunday School would preclude my having a second cup of coffee. On that morning I had had four cups by 6:30! Four-year-old Mark had

31

always looked well-scrubbed when I got him ready for Sunday School—but on this day he was outdone by his mother, who was bathed, perfumed, combed, brushed, and polished to near-perfection. When I checked myself in the bedroom mirror, I had to admit that Sunday School teaching had already improved me on the outside. I was an unglamorous thirtyish housewife and mother—but I was holding my shoulders back with the assumed grace of a model.

By 9:00 a.m. Mark and I were en route to the church. Vicky Peterson greeted me at the door of the sanctuary and handed me a name tag with freshly-printed letters on it.

"Ordinarily, you have to be a visitor for four Sundays before we make a name tag," she said laughingly, "but we made an exception in your case since you're going to be our teacher."

I sat near the aisle, about six rows from the back of the sanctuary. By turning my head half way around, I could see the women as they came in the door.

Most of them were strangers to me so I was relieved to see my good friend, Allison Crandall, entering the room. Allison, tall and graceful with long black hair and a mischievous smile, was one of the first people I had met when my family moved to Jonestown last year. Her children, Andrea, aged five, and Hobart, aged three, attended the day nursery school with Mark. Allison and I had formed a nursery school car pool. Allison's husband, Hobart, Sr., was principal of an elementary school. An amiable, blond giant of a man, Hobart was even more popular with adults than he was with kids. When he was busy with his planning sessions and my husband was traveling, Allison and I often took the children on picnics or fixed a light supper together. Somehow, everything was more fun when Allison was there.

Next to arrive was Martha Koontz, a five by five woman about ten years my senior. I recognized her only by sight —and by her horrible horse laugh. I tried not to cringe as she pumped my hand heartily and said, "Nice morning, ain't it?" This was followed by her laugh which grated on my nerves like a fingernail against a blackboard.

Following Martha into the room, I saw with dismay, was Bernice Oglethorpe. Bulldog Bernice is what I had mentally called her when I first encountered her in church. She was short and sturdily built with a prominent lower jaw jutting out in defiance of the world. Bernice had never been known for her sunny disposition. And after the problems with her daughter. Brenda, several months before, Bernice was in a state of perpetual irritation.

Until Brenda Oglethorpe reached the age of eighteen, she had been a model daughter. Pretty in a pale, listless way, she had taken her father's path to domestic harmony—never disagreeing with her mother in even the slightest matter. However, during her first year of college, Brenda fell in love with a Korean graduate student. She began making plans to fly to Seoul where he was setting up a business.

"Forget him," ordered Bernice. And Brenda packed her bags.

"He's a different race, religion, and nationality. Find a nice Methodist boy—or even a Baptist," her mother dictated.

"I love him" was Brenda's answer to this and all other arguments.

The airline ticket did not arrive promptly and Bernice hoped that it never would. Perhaps the young Oriental man was having difficulty with his family. Perhaps he was not interested in marrying Brenda after all. And then, just as Bernice dared hope he had jilted Brenda, the tickets arrived, along with a letter of instructions and encouragement —with love stated or implied in every line.

Pete Oglethorpe drove his daughter to the airport. Bernice had refused to give her blessings to the venture.

"If you ever want to come back home, Honey, just let me know," her father had said.

Bernice never mentioned her daughter these days, but her negative approach to life had intensified. I felt that my teaching the class was a mistake, and Bernice Bulldog only reinforced this feeling. By this time, the sanctuary-classroom was filled with fifty or sixty women of various shapes, sizes, and ages. Joy Werner was trying to quiet them down in order to begin the lesson. She gave devotions from the Psalms: *This is the day which the Lord has made; let us rejoice and be glad in it.*

Then Joy began a typical prayer, asking for help for our

33

nation's leaders, help for our church and Sunday School leaders, and healing for those in the hospital. While she was praying, I said one of my own—more to the point.

"Dear God," I whispered, "you got me into this so please don't desert me now."

Joy called for announcements. Martha Koontz stood up and urged everyone to come to the church on Monday morning to help with the soup project. Once a month the group made and sold homemade soup, netting several hundred dollars which they used for various charitable causes.

Then the big moment came. Joy said simply, "We are very pleased to have Jane Chambers as our new teacher and she will now present the lesson."

Somehow I managed to stand up and force my legs to walk me up to the front where a lectern held my notebook. I was glad that I had made such extensive notes—I fully realized that there were sixty pairs of eyes watching me and sixty pairs of ears waiting for me to say something important. Sunday School teaching certainly looked different from up front. I took a deep breath and plunged into the lesson.

"Our lesson today concerns the story of Jonah and the whale. Most of us first heard this story as children, but actually it's not as simple as it sounds. Bible scholars disagree as to whether it's a true story or a myth used to make a point. Actually, it's not really important whether the story is true or not—it's the moral of the story which counts."

"I disagree!" interrupted Bernice, the bulldog. "I think it makes sense to interpret the Bible literally wherever possible. I don't care what your Bible scholars say—the Bible says that Jonah was swallowed by a whale and I believe it."

For a moment I felt like bolting for the door and leaving the lectern to Bernice. But then a new feeling of determination surged over me: God had recuited me to teach this class and I had spent many hours preparing for it. I was going to do it!

"We'll have a discussion period later, Bernice," I said as pleasantly as possible, "but we need to get a few basic facts presented first. As I was saying, the important thing about the story is that Jonah was trying to run away from God."

Bernice still wore a scowl, but she settled back in her seat and I continued the lesson, feeling like a veteran teacher.

"God had told Jonah to go and warn the people of Nineveh that they had better reform. However, Jonah decided, all on his own, that the people of Nineveh were so wicked that they deserved to perish. So he ran in the opposite direction and climbed aboard a boat.

"A storm came up, threatening to capsize the boat. The sailors became so frightened that they all began to pray—but the storm increased in fury. Then they noticed the sleeping Jonah. When they woke him up, he admitted that God was displeased with him.

"The sailors didn't really want to throw Jonah overboard —but human nature being what it is, they eventually had to do that in order to save their own skins. And, sure enough, as soon as Jonah was tossed out of the boat, the storm subsided. Jonah was then swallowed by a large fish, and coughed up on dry land three days later.

"This may sound, if you will pardon the expression, like a 'fish story.'" (To my great relief the class laughed out loud. I was almost afraid I had put them to sleep—but now I could see that they hung intently upon every word I was saying.)

"But whether you believe this or not, take note of what the Bible says in Chapter 3, beginning with verse 1: *Then the word of the Lord came to Jonah the second time, saying, "Arise, go to Nineveh, that great city, and proclaim to it the message that I tell you." So Jonah arose and went to Nineveh, according to the word of the Lord.*

"That part of it sounds very plausible to me. After such an experience, Jonah no doubt was convinced that it is impossible to run away from God."

I had decided in advance that I was going to make the lessons relevant. I had been a journalist, not a teacher, and I wasn't content just to present the biblical material. Nobody was going to get bored in my class, if I could help it!

So after I had presented the story, I asked some questions to spark a discussion, even though it meant dealing with Bernice.

"What do you think about this question of doing God's will? Elsewhere in the Bible we are told that we are free to choose whether to obey God's will or not. Did Jonah really have a choice?"

"I think Jonah was right in refusing to go to Nineveh." Bernice, the bulldog, had returned to the discussion. "If they were as wicked as they were described, they deserved to be punished."

Vicky Peterson's sweet, lilting voice cut in.

"I disagree with Bernice," she said. "We have to accept whatever assignments or burdens God sends us and do the best we can with them. I think that's God's way of testing us."

"I don't know how you can say that," said a class member named Mavis Folger. "When I lost my child some years ago, I decided that it had just happened—that God was not to blame. Why, if I thought God had had anything to do with it, I would never set foot in the church again!"

"I agree with Mavis," announced Allison Crandall. "I think we read too much into what is God's will and what isn't. My favorite verse tells me what I have to do: *What does the Lord require of you but to do justice, and to love kindness, and to walk humbly with your God?* (Micah 6:8)"

I had no way of knowing then how often the words of Vicky and Allison were to re-echo in my ears. I had never realized how important our beliefs and our philosophies are to our lives—that we literally become what we believe. But as I look back, I can see that Vicky's attitude toward burdens enabled her to carry the staggering burden that was thrust upon her. Allison had chosen a postive, rather lighthearted verse to live by, and the phrase "to do justice" must have really haunted her in the years ahead.

Nor did I know that Mavis and I, each in our own way, were candidates for enlightenment concerning this whole question of doing God's will: One of God's unemployed and one of God's doubters were each to receive an assignment!

The discussion was lively right up to the dismissal bell. Then I pronounced the benediction: "May the Lord watch between me and thee while we are absent one from the other."

After a scramble for purses and gloves, the girls trooped

36

out in groups of two and three. A number of them paused to say that they had enjoyed the lesson. I was startled to realize that I also had been enjoying myself. For the first time in my life I had gotten something out of a Sunday School lesson.

Even though I had told the 'hiring' committee that I couldn't participate in the activities, I joined the soup-making project the next morning. There had been some talk about building a new church and that project would need a great deal of money.

When we arrived at the church kitchen, five huge kettles were already beginning to boil on the big, black, old-fashioned gas stove. Mark and Craig ran off with the other children, racing around the cavernous social hall under the inept tutelage of "Pops" Carter. Pops, in addition to his duties as sexton, played the role of grandfather to all the children who would allow it.

About fifteen or tweny class members were hard at work in the big kitchen, peeling carrots, potatoes, and onions, and opening large cans of other vegetables. I had to look twice in order to recognize some of them—instead of Sunday clothes they were wearing slacks, sweaters, and aprons.

Martha Koontz was the indisputable queen of the kitchen. On Sunday morning she annoyed me with her grating laugh and her ungrammatical speech—and complete lack of interest in philosophy. But here in the kitchen she seemed to come alive—the kitchen was her *milieu*.

"What can I do to help, Martha?" I asked.

"How about cleaning the celery?" she asked, guiding me toward one of the sinks. And celery there was—about a bushel basket full. While I stood there trying to decide how to attack such a job, Martha reached over and turned on the water faucet. Then she dunked the whole basketful into the sink with one swift, sure motion.

I picked up a stalk and chopped away at it with a little paring knife.

"We need this stuff today—not day after tomorrow," Martha chided me. "Here, you can use this food chopper if you can keep your pinkies out of the way." She guffawed at her own joke and added, "Your trouble is that you've got too much education."

37

Everybody laughed at that—and I found myself joining them. The peeling, chopping, sorting, and good-natured teasing continued for several hours as the spicy aroma wafting from the kettles smelled more and more like soup.

"We were talking about the lesson just before you came in," Vicky called out from her post at the stove. "You said some things which really set us thinking."

"Yes, Jane, I like your style of presenting the lesson and then calling for discussion," added Joy, with several others nodding in agreement. "You make the lesson interesting."

On Sunday morning I was their teacher, but here in the kitchen I was a sort of backward apprentice. For some reason, I enjoyed both roles very much.

When lunchtime came, Martha put on the coffee pot. She pulled out a cake she had whipped up the night before, and dispatched several women to the kosher delicatessen for lunch meat and bread.

After making sandwiches for the children—and the exhausted "Pops"—we sat or stood around the kitchen eating our lunch. With Martha's special applesauce cake for dessert, we decided that we had never had a better lunch.

After we cleared away the lunch remnants, it was time to ladle the soup into waiting quart jars. Customers arrived soon and Gerry Bass, who had assumed the role of bookkeeper when the business expanded, checked off names in her notebook.

Allison breezed in just in time to collect her soup order. She had been shopping and had found, she informed me, three new dresses and a darling leather coat.

"What's Hobe going to say?" I asked her.

"Oh, he told me to go shopping," she said. "He's been working so hard lately that we haven't been going out together at all—so he suggested that I get a sitter this afternoon and go on a shopping spree.

"I'd really like to stay awhile and help with the dishes," Allison continued, "but I'd better get home and look after Hobe. He's been so tired lately; I'm going to try to persuade him to take a nap before dinner."

I had spent the day working in the church kitchen while Allison had been out enjoying herself. And yet, for some reason, I couldn't get angry with her. And the startling thing was that nobody else seemed to be annoyed with her, either—even though we all knew that her offer to help was only a gesture. She just wasn't the type one would expect to find in the kitchen peeling onions.

Hobe often laughed about this. "It took me years to get used to seeing Allison in the kitchen," he told me once. "When we were first married, it was a startling sight to watch her risking a fingernail to turn the roast. She reminded me of those movie glamor girls who are cast as farmers' wives and look so out of place gathering the eggs."

Allison and Hobe had been married for nine years and appeared to be still very much in love. Even though Hobe did most of the work and Allison seemed to provide only the laughter and the frivolity, they were partners in life and I knew that one would be lost without the other.

Allison liked pretty clothes, fast cars, dry sherry, extra-long cigarettes, and loud parties. She also enjoyed mother-hood—as long as she could get a sitter periodically. She attended Sunday School and church regularly, but seemed to feel no obligation to support any other church or community activity.

Hobe, on the other hand, took his responsibilities seriously. He was never too busy to talk to a parent who asked to see him. This lengthened his working day considerably, but he felt it was a principal's job.

"It's not fair for school officials to be too busy to talk to parents—and then turn around and blame the parents for not taking an interest in their child's education," he said.

Hobe was a big man both physically and philosophically. He was 6 feet, 3 inches tall with heavy bones. Even though he weighed more than the doctor's charts allowed, he did not look fat. He loved life and people, especially children. Despite his serious approach to work, he had a keen sense of humor. He loved to quote the comments he overheard at school. His favorite story was about the first grader who pointed him out in the cafeteria and announced, "There's the owner."

His own children were enthralled with him, particularly on festive occasions. My children and I attended Andrea's fifth birthday party right after we moved into the community. Hobe arrived home in time to participate in some of the

39

games and to demand that his piece of the cake include part of the words "Happy Birthday, Andrea." He deliberately failed at the games, managing somehow to pin the tail squarely on the donkey's nose—to the wild delight of the other players.

Randy and I and Hobe and Allison also discovered that we had a mutual interest in the community theater. So we all bought season tickets and about once a month the four of us attended a play and then met at our house—or theirs—for dessert and coffee. Hobe enjoyed discussing the plays, but too much serious talk bored Allison. She preferred big gatherings with small talk, loud music, and stronger drinks.

Many people undoubtedly wondered how Allison and I could be such good friends, since we are so different. What can I say about friendship—except that it transcends differences? When I had told Allison I was going to teach the Sunday School class, she thought I was foolish to tie myself down to such an unexciting responsibility.

"Here I had plans to reform you," she said. "I was going to teach you to drink and smoke and become the life of the party—and you spoil it all by becoming a Sunday School teacher."

"You had six months and you didn't make much progress," I said, and we both laughed.

Allison paid Gerry for her soup and headed home, no doubt feeling that she had met her obligations. I took my children home at 3:30 and felt somewhat guilt-ridden because there were still some dishes to be washed. Only Martha seemed to be undaunted by the demands of such a project. I couldn't remember when I had worked so hard—or had enjoyed the companionship of other women so much.

I decided that since I was teaching the class I should also attend their monthly business meetings. These were held on the third Monday night of each month and were a combination of business, devotions, and special programs. I went to my first one with the attitude of a faculty member who is sponsor of a sorority, but before long I succumbed to the ladies-night-out atmosphere.

About thirty-five class members sat in a large circle in the middle of the church social hall. They wore casual clothes, mostly skirts and blouses or suits. Martha and Gerry, along with several other thoroughly-domestic types, knitted. Vicky tried to check her attendance report while Bernice tapped impatiently on the treasurer's notebook with her pencil. The noise level was just under a roar, and snatches of various conversations filled the room.

"She had been having pains for several months" . . . "I feel like going over to that school and telling that teacher" . . . "I'm going to ask for the recipe" . . . "You should see what a lovely fabric I found for my drapes" . . . "George says we won't be able to go till October" . . . "My mother-in-law almost makes me lose my religion" . . . "Gloria lost ten pounds in one week with that grapefruit diet."

Finally, slim, red-headed Patty Bedford, the president, quieted the group and Donna Pearce, wife of our young associate minister, began the devotions. Donna was a small, energetic young woman who loved the outdoors and had short, curly blonde hair which was usually windblown. Her movements were quick and graceful like the birds she enjoyed watching. And like the birds, she was slender without being frail.

"I would like to read from the 25th chapter of Matthew," Donna began in her loud clear voice.

I was hungry and you gave me food, I was thirsty and you gave me drink, I was a stranger and you welcomed me, I was naked and you clothed me, I was sick and you visited me, I was in prison and you came to me.

. . . as you did it to one of the least of these my brethren, you did it to me.

"Since Matt and I came here last year, we have been very pleased with the efforts of this class to carry out Christ's command to look after the needy and the unfortunate. Let's continue with these efforts to the glory of God. We will now sing 'I Would be True' on page eighty-five of the old hymnal."

Jackie Willard began pounding on the old piano and the group sang. We were not the choir—which was undoubtedly a good thing. I was sitting clear across the room from Martha, but even at that distance I could hear her tenor monotone amidst the more tuneful voices. We all had difficulty keeping together, and we raced each other to the end of the last stanza.

Patty did her best to preside over the business meeting—but the fact of the matter was that this class was not a business organization.

Just because the class was not business-like is not to say they didn't accomplish anything. When Patty asked for reports, there was a long list of accomplishments.

"We made 368 quarts of soup last week," Martha reported, "and that gave us a profit of almost $200."

"The exact amount was $192.45," Gerry added.

"I have sent a monthly check to our Korean orphan, and I'm now collecting money for his birthday present," announced Mavis. "So see me if you haven't contributed."

Joy Werner was chairman of our project to help a local children's home. "We bought Easter shoes for forty-two children at the home this year," she announced, "and those of you who were unable to drive to the shoe store with us really missed a treat! Some of those children have never had any new clothes and they were really thrilled to be able to pick out new shoes."

Ardith Winston announced that the group had collected, packed, and shipped 380 pounds of good used clothing to the church world service program for overseas relief.

"We had to go through and sort out a few rags this time," she said, "but it was much better than last time. I think we're finally getting through to people that we are not trying to collect rags for refugees—they probably have enough rags."

"The needlework committee wants me to tell you that we are still working on the altar cloths for the church sanctuary. We're finished with the embroidery work on the green and the white sets, and now all we have to do is the fine sewing." This announcement came from Joanna Neilson, who was the church's leading seamstress. "Martha and I are also making layettes for the city hospital's maternity ward for babies whose mothers have no clothing for them."

"Thank you all," said the president. "Is there any new business?"

Donna Pearce spoke up. "Madam chairman, I would like

to add another project to the long list of projects of this class. I have been asked by the Methodist Children's Home near Philadelphia if we would sponsor a girl. It would cost us $100 a year for her basic needs, and they would like us also to send her presents for her birthday and for Christmas."

"I don't think we can afford it," said Bernice.

"We seemed to have a lot of money in the treasury when you read the report awhile ago, Bernice," the president said.

"Well, it's just that I think we've got enough to do. We don't want to spread ourselves too thin."

"I don't like to see money sitting there doing nothing when some child could be using it," Donna added.

"Come on, Bernice, it's not your money—just because you're the treasurer don't make you in charge," Martha guffawed. "Let's vote."

So we voted and the Methodist orphanage project was approved with one dissenting vote—Bernice's.

Then it was time to close the business session. We stood in a circle, holding hands.

"Say a prayer for the girl on your left," said Patty. "Now say a prayer for the girl on your right." Then, with heads bowed and still holding hands, we sang softly, "Into my heart, into my heart, come into my heart, Lord Jesus. Come in today. Come in to stay. Come into my heart, Lord Jesus."

Despite their lamentations over calories and their talk about trying to lose weight, the class always had an abundance of rich refreshments after each business meeting. Each month the refreshment committee seemed to be trying to serve the fanciest desserts and decorate the finest table.

The refreshment table was magnificent that night. It was decorated with daffodils and other spring flowers. The noise level steadily crescendoed as the girls gathered around the table and filled their trays with coffee cups, mints, nuts, and large pieces of pineapple upside down cake topped with huge blobs of whipped cream.

At that first meeting my head swam trying to keep up with everything that was being reported. I had always thought of church groups as do-nothing organizations. For years I had read that "faith without works is dead" (James 2:20), and thought that it described most church groups very well. But the Christian Service Class had more good works than any group of similar size that I had ever heard about. A good slogan for them, from the first chapter of James, would have been: *But be doers of the word, and not hearers only.* . . .

Almost from the beginning, I realized that the girls were not interested in the intellectual ramblings of the Bible scholars which filled the lesson material. Consequently, the teacher-student roles soon were reversed and they began teaching me about the application of religion to life.

Like Jonah, I had a lot to learn.

Chapter 4

On This Rock

I had been teaching for only six months when I encountered a lesson that I didn't think I could present. I had learned from the beginning that the teacher has to know what she's talking about or the class will immediately find her out.

The lesson was from Acts 1, relating to Christ's ascension into heaven. It says that Jesus showed himself to be alive "by many proofs" and that he traveled around speaking to his followers for forty days after the crucifixion and resurrection.

It was verse 9 that got me: *And when he had said this, as they were looking on, he was lifted up, and a cloud took him out of their sight.*

I was a college graduate, living in the technologically advanced twentieth century, and I was supposed to stand in front of a group of adults and read that verse. It was too much to ask!

The whole story was suspect. I was familiar with the crucifixion and resurrection stories from lessons given by my own Sunday School teachers. But they, too, must have shied away from the ascension story, because I didn't even know that it was in the Bible.

As I tried to study, I realized that the basic problem was

my attitude toward death. Intellectually, I had accepted the story of Jesus' resurrection. Theoretically, I had accepted the possibility that there is life after death, even for us mortals. But the practical, doubting-Thomas side of my nature refused to believe it. My own brush with death was still close to the surface of my memory. I remembered facing death with a feeling of empty blackness: Death was the end. The end of life, hope, sunshine, love. The night before my surgery, I would have welcomed the sight of a cloud ready to take me to heaven. But the fact was, I saw no sign of such a phenomenon.

I struggled all week with preparing the lesson. But when Sunday morning came, I still wasn't ready.

My usual procedure was to put the scripture lesson into its context, describing the surrounding circumstances. I followed this plan with Acts. I had no idea what I was going to do after that.

Joy Werner unwittingly rescued me. "I thought a lot about this last year when my husband died," she said. "I concluded that the Christian religion is, as they say in advertising, a 'package deal.' You can't just pick out some things to believe and other things to reject. You either believe in life after death or you don't. And if you don't, then you're saying that you don't believe that Jesus Christ arose from the dead."

"Why do we carry on so when people die if we really believe they've gone to heaven?" Vicky asked.

I waited, hoping Joy would answer.

"I'm doing a lot of the talking," said Joy, "but to answer your question, I think we grieve for ourselves. It's so hard to say good-by to a loved one, and we look ahead, seeing long years without him. We feel sorry for ourselves."

"It's also the mystery," said Patty. "Death is something we don't understand, and it frightens us."

The discussion continued in this vein until the end of the session with very little guidance from me. They failed to notice my shortcomings because their attention was focused on a congregational meeting. Called for that afternoon, it was to discuss plans for building a new church. My class had been anticipating this for months, so the members were as excited as a group of ten-year-olds on the eve of summer vacation.

I was also eager to build a new sanctuary. When I began teaching Sunday School, the church service began to mean more to me. It was as though the ritual had been in a foreign language that I had just learned to translate. Occasionally, a word or phrase in a hymn caught at my throat and I couldn't finish singing. "How Great Thou Art" choked me up so I didn't even attempt it. One time, with tears running down my cheeks, I chanced to look up in the choir loft to see Patty and Joy with tears in their eyes, too. After that, I never looked toward the choir when we sang that hymn.

My new understanding of the worship service whetted my appetite for a new church building. The old sanctuary, which doubled as a classroom for my Sunday School class, was seventy-five years old. It was made of graying white stucco which contrasted with the lovely old stained-glass windows. A faded rose-colored carpet went up the center aisle between well-worn mahogany pews. The floor sagged and some pews rocked precariously. There were reports that the foundation had been declared unsafe, but some discounted this as being a rumor started by proponents of building a new sanctuary.

The social hall was already full that afternoon when I arrived for the congregational meeting. Some of the men were helping "Pops" Carter set up extra chairs, while others rigged up a microphone.

Joe Townsend, who was chairman of the church's official board, sat at a table in front of the hall, flanked by the ministers, Reverend Pearce and Reverend Donald Marsden. Joe was a lanky man of forty-five, with graying black hair and snapping blue eyes. A successful businessman, he conducted meetings in a precise, no-nonsense manner.

"We will open our meeting this afternoon with some appropriate words by our senior pastor, Reverend Marsden," Joe announced.

"There are two passages that I think seem to be written for this occasion," said Reverend Marsden. "The first is from the 16th chapter of Matthew:

Now when Jesus came into the district of Caesarea Philippi, he asked his disciples, "Who do men say that the Son of man is?"
And they said, "Some say John the Baptist, others say Elijah, and others Jeremiah or one of the prophets."
He said to them, "But who do you say that I am?" Simon Peter replied, "You are the Christ, the Son of the living God."
And Jesus answered him, "Blessed are you, Simon Bar-Jona! For flesh and blood has not revealed this to you, but my Father who is in heaven.
And I tell you, you are Peter, and on this rock I will build my church, and the powers of death shall not prevail against it.

"And the other verse I want to read is from Psalm 127: *Unless the Lord builds the house, those who build it labor in vain.* And so we pray, O God, that thou wilt be with us this afternoon while we make plans to build thy house. Amen."

Joe Townsend rose to his full 6-foot stature and began: "Last year this congregation voted to proceed with plans to build a new sanctuary. We now have architect's drawings and we are meeting here this afternoon to get your approval to begin a building fund campaign. Do I hear a motion to this effect?"

"I move that this congregation begin a building fund campaign for the purpose of building a new sanctuary." The speaker was Hobart Crandall, Allison's husband.

Someone seconded the motion. Then the chairman asked for discussion.

"Mr. Chairman," said Jonathan Day, who headed the church music committee, "our choir director is very disturbed about the plans. He doesn't think the choir will like facing the center instead of facing the congregation. Nobody can see them back there behind the altar. And when he asked the architect to include a podium for him to use in directing, the architect refused."

"A podium?" sneered George Willard. "What does the director think we're building, a concert hall?"

"Well, no, but since the music is such an important part of the service. . . ."

"Important part of the service, my eye! As far as I'm concerned, you can do away with the choir and the director, too, for all they add to the service!" George said.

Murmurs of surprise and dismay filled the room.

"You're just bitter because your wife didn't make it as the soprano soloist!" Jonathan Day exploded.

"That's not true. It's your loss if you don't recognize talent when you hear it, and I don't think you do! Jack Beach, who was the choir director before Mr. Fancy Pants came along, was a lot better at playing the organ, but you ran him off."

There was embarrassed silence. Reverend Marsden, sitting facing the crowd, flushed. Generally, he hid his feelings behind a mask of smiling impartiality, but this ugly scene was painful to him.

Typical of the Methodist minister of the 1960's, Donald Marsden worked very hard. He arose early and filled his day with visitation, counseling, study, sermon preparation, and other activities. He rarely missed a meeting either in his own church or in the district. He was also active in the ministerial association. When the district superintendent announced that he felt it important for ministers to be community-minded, Reverend Marsden joined the Rotary Club and became active in the Community Chest campaign.

Some of his parishioners had glimpsed the tenderness of this man of God. He stayed all night at the bedside of Jeremy Hall as the child fought for his life against meningitis. And Leonora Webb, whose husband suffered a fatal heart attack at a race track—in the company of another woman —vowed that the prayers and concern of Reverend Marsden were all that sustained her. Most of the time, however, he was stoic and reserved, his mask firmly in place.

Donald and Francine Marsden were parents of four teen-aged daughters. On Sunday mornings, he was proud of his family, sitting together—like a cheering section—on the left, half way back. His daughters were pretty, black-haired girls and were well-dressed because Francine and Meredith, the oldest, were skilled seamstresses. Sometimes, though,

49

their manner of dress embarrassed him. Diane, who was fifteen, was a cheerleader in high school, and several times Mr. Marsden overheard ladies in the church discussing the brevity of Diane's skirt. He couldn't understand why Diane should wear long skirts just because she was a minister's daughter, but some of the ladies obviously believed in a different standard for residents of the parsonage.

The minister's workload made it difficult for him to give his family the time they needed. This was particularly true of the twins, Joanie and Janet, who were thirteen years old. They complained that they saw their father only in church and at breakfast. Francine also complained about his long hours, particulary now that he was involved in the building program.

Reverend Marsden had tried to explain to Francine how important his new building was to him professionally. For several years, both the district superintendent and the bishop had mentioned the need of a new building to him every chance they got. If a congregation chose to worship in an old building, the hierarchy regarded their decision as a lack of ministerial leadership.

So the discussion of the building project was a great strain to Reverend Marsden. The stakes were high.

Finally, the chairman made himself heard over the angry voices. "Gentlemen! Gentlemen! Let's have this meeting restored to order. I think Reverend Marsden has something he wants to say."

"I can see no good purpose in arguing over the merits of the choir and where they will sit," Reverend Marsden said calmly. "I don't like to see such fine Christian men as Jon Day and George Willard here saying petty things they don't really mean. The Bible says we are all brothers—and sometimes I think we really act like brothers!" (There was light laughter.) "Let's get on with the business at hand and keep away from personalities."

"All right," Joe said, "our purpose is to discuss whether or not the board shall be authorized to conduct a building fund drive for a new sanctuary. The meeting is open to discussion, but only on the subject of the building. Anyone who introduces any other issue will be out of order."

"Why can't we just remodel the old sanctuary?" someone in the back asked.

"I can answer that," said Reverend Marsden. "The old sanctuary is structurally unsound and would take a great deal of work. When finished, it would still be too small. Do you realize that we have to conduct two services each Sunday now—and three on Christmas and Easter? If we're to continue to grow, we need more room."

"That architect's drawing that you have up there, is that the way the new building would look?"

"Yes, we chose that plan in order to get the most for our money," said Frank Finley, whom I had met on the education committee. He was to head up the building fund. "We don't feel that we should spend more than $400,000."

"Do you mean to tell me that this—this barn—is going to cost $400,000?" The speaker was Bernice the bulldog. "Personally, I think it's ugly.

"The Baptists have a new building which didn't cost that much and it's really beautiful," she continued. "Even the Lutheran church, which looks like a factory from the outside, is lovely inside. If we go ahead with these plans, people are going to call our church the 'Methodist Barn'!"

"It's those small, clear windows that make it look so barn-like," offered Mavis Folger. "Now, if we could have stained-glass windows, it might not look so bad."

"Stained-glass windows are out of the question financially," Frank Finley said. "They cost a great deal more nowadays."

"Besides, we couldn't put money into stained-glass windows when it would be better spent feeding the hungry," said Vicky Peterson, as if she thought everyone would agree with her.

"The Bible says the poor you will have with you always," countered Mavis Folger. "I think if we spend $400,000 for a church, it ought to look like a church. Is there going to be room for a pipe organ?"

"That's out of the question, too," Frank Finley said, apologetically. "The building will cost $400,000, not including an organ."

Then there were several more rounds among the various

factions: One group held out for remodeling, another group insisted on a prettier building, and another wanted stained-glass windows and/or a pipe organ. A few thought we should hold off and do nothing for a while at least. Vociferous choir members insisted that the choir lofts be made to face the congregation.

I sat dumfounded. I had never before been involved in the building of a church. I was unprepared for the vitriolic attacks and the unchristian attitudes. I had been naive enough to think that everybody would be in favor of building the finest church possible.

"Mr. Chairman," said Hobe Crandall, "let's consider our purpose in coming here this afternoon. As the principal of an elementary school, I work with and for children, so I guess that's why I look at the business of building a church the way I do. As I see it, we're not building a church for ourselves. For all we know, the old sanctuary may outlive us all. If we build a church, let's build it as a witness to our faith in God and leave it as a legacy to future generations. Building costs are rising and interest rates will undoubtedly rise above 5½% soon. I don't see what we can possibly gain by waiting."

For a moment there was silence and I could tell that Hobe's common-sense approach had had an impact on the meeting. He sat down quickly before questions could be hurled at him.

"Thank you, Hobe," said Joe. "You've heard the motion, the second, and the discussion. All in favor signify by saying 'Aye.' "

A goodly number shouted "Aye!"

"Those opposed, signify by saying 'No.' "

There were, I thought, a considerable number of "Noes."

"The 'ayes' have it," Joe announced. "We can now begin our building fund. I would personally like to start the fund off with a pledge of $500. Reverend Marsden, will you please close the meeting?"

"Let's rise and sing 'Praise God from Whom All Blessings Flow,' " Mr. Marsden said. The words seemed appropriate: "Praise God from whom all blessings flow. Praise Him all creatures here below. . . ."

As I stood looking around me, I marveled that such a diverse set of "creatures here below" could finally pull themselves together enough to embark upon such a magnificent undertaking.

I had trouble sleeping that night. The dissension had shaken me. I had encouraged discussion—even disagreement—in my class, convinced that it would stimulate the women to think. But my theories didn't have a price tag as the new building did. It was startling how much more bitter an argument over the practical, bread-and-butter issues could become. I was still tossing restlessly at 6 o'clock the next morning when the phone rang.

The voice was so low and pinched that I scarcely recognized it as Allison Crandall's.

"It's Hobe," she said. "Hobe's dead!"

"What happened?" I gasped.

"He complained of indigestion when he came home from the meeting. He took some of his medicine and went to bed. Well, I soon realized that something was terribly wrong. I went into the bedroom and he didn't seem to be breathing. I called an ambulance, but it was too late."

"I'll be right over."

I knelt by my bed like a child. "Dear God," I said, "please help me to console Allison and the children. Help me to know what to say to them."

And then, in a voice which was almost a reprimand, I added, "Oh, God! Of all the people I know, Allison is the least likely to make it as a widow."

I had promised myself that I would go to Allison as a friend, not as her Sunday School teacher. Faye Barrett, who had taught the Christain Service Class previously, had been very good at consoling the bereaved. But I couldn't imagine how anyone could console Allison. I kept thinking what a waste it was. Hobe Crandall was a fine man. His wife and children needed him. He was a worker in his church and his community. He had spent the last day of his life helping to build a new church. Why should he be dead at the age of forty-one when there were thousands of other men who were just taking up space in the world?

Randy was away on a trip to Houston, and Mark and

Craig were still asleep. I tiptoed out of the house and closed the door softly, so as not to awaken them. I hurried over to Allison's on leaden feet which kept trying to postpone the ordeal.

Chapter 5

Aftermath of Death

Even before Allison opened the door, I felt the cold hand of death gripping her house. When I saw her, I realized the impact had been much worse than I had feared. Her face had collapsed under the weight of grief like a papier-mâché mask crushed under the heel of a heavy boot.

As we cried on each other's shoulder, I could only imagine her loss. Then we sat in her sewing room and she talked for a long time, as if she were trying to pour out all of her bewilderment and pain. She told me about the sadness in her life—beginning when her father deserted his family when Allison was five. She had met Hobe at college when she was a freshman and he a graduate student. From the beginning, it was a delicately balanced relationship—Allison, frivolous, impractical, self-indulgent; and Hobe, nine years her senior, hard-working, serious, stable.

Even though Randy had always given me more independence and responsibility than Hobe had given Allison, I knew that if I ever lost my husband, my life would be both empty and difficult. For Allison, life without Hobe would be nearly impossible.

Allison finished each verbal sortie with the agonized question, "What am I going to do?"

I was dismayed that I had no answers to give her—neither philosophical nor practical. I thought I had learned a lot as a Sunday School teacher—but I had really been going around in circles. I had gone from where (where is God?) to what (what do I really believe?) and now I was asking why (why do these things happen?). When I tried to console Allison, I found that I had lost all the ground I had gained in the past six months—and maybe more.

In an effort to divert her I asked, "Where are the children?"

"Joy Werner came and picked them up," Allison replied. "She wanted to take them to the park. She also called Hobe's parents in Columbus, and they'll be here tonight."

Just then the door opened and Andrea and Hobie came bouncing into the room, followed by Joy.

"We've been talking about heaven," said Andrea, with the directness of a five-year-old. "Mrs. Werner says that Daddy's gone there to be with Jesus."

"We've been singing some songs," Hobie added and began to demonstrate his new skill. "Jesus loves me this I know, for the Bible tells me so. Little ones to him belong, they are weak but he is strong. *Yes,* Jesus loves me! *Yes,* Jesus love me! *Yes,* Jesus loves me, the Bible tells me so." Each time Hobie came to the word "yes," he shouted it.

I thought to myself: This is too sad to be believed! But Allison was saying to Joy, "I've been thinking about what you said this morning—that God wouldn't have sent for Hobe if God hadn't really wanted him—and it makes me feel a lot better."

How could Hobie accept the fact that Jesus loves him and, at the same time, has deprived him of a father? How could Allison believe in a God who would do such a terrible thing? I could imagine what the class could have done with this argument. At least a half-dozen in the class would have said that God didn't send for Hobe—that he had died because he had heart disease—as simple as that. And there were others—myself among them—who would have said they just didn't know any of the answers. As a matter of fact, very few class members had reached Joy's state of certainty.

I turned to Joy. She pressed my hand and whispered, "It's part of that package deal we were talking about last

Sunday. We have to accept these things even if we don't understand them. It's a matter of trusting God."

Just then Reverend Marsden arrived and I took the opportunity to leave. I wanted to go off to myself to think. As I circled the block in my car, I decided I either had to straighten out my thinking or give up teaching the class.

Ironically, I had just had a call the previous week from George Marvin, the Sunday School superintendent. He reminded me that I had taken the class on a six-month-trial basis.

"We've been hearing a lot of good things about the way you teach the class and we hope you'll continue," he said. I had assured him that I was enjoying it far more than I ever thought possible. Now I wasn't so sure.

The answer still eluded me as I reached home and climbed out of my car. I numbly fixed lunch for Mark and Craig and absent-mindedly performed my household chores. Then I called Mr. Marvin and asked him to get a substitute teacher for awhile, since I wanted to spend a great deal of time with Allison. This was certainly true enough.

The substitute teacher arrived a bit early the following Sunday morning. She was Annalee Farrell, a no-nonsense student of the Bible, who attended the Women's Bible Class every Sunday—and smiled once a year, usually when she had proved herself to be right. She was tall and gaunt with a pained expression that suggested she was afflicted with permanent indigestion. Her dresses were drab and somber —as though cheerfulness was somehow sinful. A sensible hat always covered her mousey hair, even after hats went out of style. To her, hats represented the formality that she felt Sunday School required.

The Women's Bible Class had been engaged for years in an ongoing competition with the Christian Service Class. The former had started out as a class for "older" ladies, while the latter was said to be for younger women. However, nobody ever "graduated" into the older group, regardless of birthdays. Consequently, by the time I started teaching the Christian Service Class, the members were divided by philosophy rather than age.

The Women's Bible Class, true to its name, used only the

Bible as its lesson material, eyeing the Methodist Publishing House with a great suspicion. They had heard about my discussion periods, the little playlets that I wrote from time to time to help illustrate a lesson, and my efforts to relate the Bible to present times. They couldn't decide whether this was merely disgraceful—or subversive as well.

Nor were the Bible class devotees impressed with the many activities and good works of the Christian Service Class. They frequently expressed the opinion that the Christian Service Class should read the Bible more and socialize less.

Mrs. Farrell came to our class with the air of a missionary arriving in darkest Africa. She handled all of the preliminaries herself, not trusting the Christian Service Class with the devotions or the prayer. She omitted the announcements and ignored the visitors in her haste to present the lesson. The teaching consisted of reading the Bible word-for-word in a monotone, while fixing us in our seats with a series of severe glances. Those stares implied that the Bible was unpleasant medicine to taste, but was good for what ailed us. She took us through several of Paul's missionary journeys, managing somehow to render them uneventful and unrelated to the Christian church. She read up to—and beyond—the dismissal bell, giving no one else a chance to say a word.

After only one session, the girls began clamoring for me to resume teaching. Under the circumstances, this wasn't particularly flattering—especially when Mavis Folger said, "It's enough to make a Unitarian out of me."

But I was in no condition emotionally to teach. I had tired to console Allison and found I had none of the answers. I felt like a chemistry student who has botched up an experiment and messed up the lab. At any moment the professor would come in and dismiss me—or at least give me an "F" on my report card.

Meanwhile, I was still trying to help Allison—as a friend, not as a spiritual advisor. She seemed to go through many different stages in her new role as a widow.

When I went over to her house, I never knew which Allison I would find. One day, Allison the merry widow, dressed in her flashiest outfit, would be putting candles on the table for dinner. A short while later, I would meet an Allison who was in the depths of depression. Dressed completely in black, including thick black stockings, she would feed the children on bread and cheese, evidently symbolic of the Spartan life they were to lead. Then there was Allison the sleep walker, who did the ironing at 3:00 a.m. because she couldn't sleep in that "cold, empty bed." And Allison the flirt, who imagined that every male—including the paper boy—was eyeing her with interest.

Sometimes I saw unmistakable signs that Allison had been drinking. I reacted to this with the scorn that only a total abstainer can show towards the over-imbiber. I had been a teetotaler long before I became a Methodist, and the church's rule against alcoholic beverages had been one which I upheld with verve. And yet my reaction to Allison's drinking was mostly bluster. I was startled to discover that my chief objection to alcohol at this point was that it seemed to be such a temporary anesthetic.

Like many abstainers I had always felt somewhat ill-at-ease around drinkers. However, I had never before experienced this awkwardness with Allison. She had always joked about what I was missing and I had responded with a light-hearted retort, such as: "You know I have a hard enough time driving!"

We all reached a low point the day I arrived and found Allison and both children in tears. Allison had scolded Andrea, who had responded with "You wouldn't treat me this way if Daddy was here!" And all three of them had clung together crying. I cried with them, disgusted with myself for being unable to help.

Several weeks later a much happier day arrived. Allison and the children pulled into my driveway in a compact car, resplendent with chrome and aquamarine paint, the assembly-line freshness still clinging to its upholstery. Allison had traded in Hobe's big powerful car and her own unreliable old clunker to obtain a more sensible automobile.

My children climbed into the back seat with Andrea and Hobie, and I sat beside Allison. She drove us around a countryside still vivid with the bronze, gold, and red leaves of autumn. We stopped at a roadside stand and bought candied apples on sticks and laughed at the antics of two squirrels chasing each other up and down trees. A hint of our old gaiety returned. The feeling lingered until we started for home, and we all realized that their home was incomplete without Hobe.

I resumed teaching the next week. I still had not reconciled my feelings about death with the basic doctrine of the Christian church. But I was plagued by a feeling that I had left my work unfinished. Even though I had botched up the job, my Boss had not relieved me of it—and until he did, it was my responsibility.

I returned none too soon. Annalee Farrell's dreary Bible reading and I'm-the-only-Christian-in-the-room approach had cut the attendance nearly in half and had decreased any interest in the Bible that her audience may have had.

I returned to teaching just in time to prepare a lesson which was to be the most memorable one of my life. It was on that old familiar subject: serving God. This time, however, the International Lesson material had given the theme a new twist. The scripture was from Acts 9 which describes Saul's confrontation with Jesus on the Damascus road. The lesson material pointed out that Saul became the Apostle Paul merely by saying a simple sentence to Jesus: "What wilt thou have me to do?"

The theme of the lesson was that few people—even the most dedicated Christians—actually take their directions from God. Most of the prayers that are sent heavenward are requests for help and blessing upon plans made on earth.

"Don't ask God to put his rubber stamp of approval on your project," one Bible scholar wrote. "Instead, try offering yourself as a servant who will do whatever God commands."

The girls entered into the discussion period with the joyful abandon of inmates released from prison. They all talked at once, including Martha, who hadn't even realized in the pre-Annalee Farrell days that she liked discussions. Finally, Mavis got carried away completely and tossed off a challenge: "As you know, I've never really gone along with the idea that God has personal errands he wants each of us to do. So I think it would be interesting to test out today's les-

60

son. Let's all go home and pray, offering to do his work as today's lesson recommends."

There was a murmur of surprise—and then approval—from the class. They continued to talk about the possibilities and even whispered about them during the morning worship service. My own reaction to Mavis' challenge was mixed. On the one hand, I asked myself, what can I lose? I'm already carrying out one of his assignments. It's true I hadn't asked for it; I had, in fact, fought accepting it for two weeks. But the beauty of getting involved is that once you are involved, you no longer have to worry about it.

On the other hand, suppose I offered to serve God and he wanted me to do something I didn't want to do—or something that was impossible? I could think of something in this category. Our bedroom was a large room with a big empty corner which I thought, sooner or later, would probably contain a sewing machine. I had disliked sewing since childhood when my mother had tried to make a seamstress out of me. At the same time, I felt guilty about not sewing, as if somehow this were an indisputable sign of laziness.

I decided finally to accept the challenge—a teacher has to at least follow her puplis! So I knelt down by the bed and prayed. "Dear God, I offer myself as your humble servant. Guide me and direct me to the work that you want me to do." Then, in a grand dramatic finale I added, "I say with Isaiah, 'Here am I! Send me.'"

I half expected to hear the Voice again—or to open my eyes just in time to see a sewing machine take shape in the corner. But nothing happened right away. Then the answer came in an idea which was so far-fetched that I knew it had not originated with me. God wanted me to write a book!

My first reaction was that I must be mistaken. So I tried to dismiss it from my mind and go about my business. One of my errands for the day was to take some church publicity down to the local newspaper. When I handed my story to the editor, he complimented me.

"I used to work on a newspaper," I explained, "and I really did enjoy it. As a matter of fact, sometimes I miss it very much."

"Why don't you write a book?" he asked, as though it were the most logical suggestion in the world.

61

This startled me, but I refused to accept it as anything more than a coincidence. I needed another opinion. I would ask the first acquaintance I met on the way home—and this time I would give no hints at all. As I parked my car, I encountered one of my neighbors working in her rose garden.

"You'd never guess what I'm thinking about doing," I called to her, trying to sound casual.

"No, I can't guess—I never know what you're going to do," she said, "but I know what you ought to do. You ought to write a book."

So it was official.

My willingness to do his bidding had lasted about twenty-four hours. Now I found myself arguing in that Dear-God-let's-be-sensible vein that I had perfected when he urged me to teach Sunday School.

It is true that I had been writing practically all of my life. Starting at the age of six or seven, I had filled numerous notebooks with words and phrases that caught my fancy. And when I wasn't trying to develop my minuscule musical talents by practicing on the piano, I was writing stories, plays, and poems. When I was fifteen, my piano teacher had suggested that I become a writer, but I had ignored her advice. I was determined to be a church organist! At college, though, I soon realized that I would never even gain admittance to the music school, much less graduate from it. So I enrolled in the school of journalism. I had enjoyed working on newspapers, and they had provided valuable experience in putting words together. But that was a far cry from writing a whole book.

Now there was a real riddle: What, in heaven's name, could I write about? I could certainly understand why God would want someone to write a religious book, but that was out of the question for me. In matters of theology, I was only one step ahead of my pupils—and in matters of basic doctrine, I was several steps behind some of them. Besides, the church library was full of weighty volumes written by Bible scholars who had devoted their whole lives to the task.

I remembered the words of my journalism professor: "Write about a subject you know something about." Well, that really narrows it down, I thought. The only subject I really know anything about is my own life.

In considering that idea, I realized that my situation did have interest. My husband, Randy, was setting up the first astronaut-training programs, and my sons were showing unmistakable scientific leanings, also. I could write about life among the scientists. But it was a baffling assignment.

I went out and bought a new typewriter and set it on a table in the empty corner of the bedroom. This part of the plan made sense: The typewriter was a great improvement over a sewing machine.

Chapter 6

These Are My Sisters

On the following Sunday morning we compared notes on the outcome of our prayers. The results were not very remarkable for God—but were quite noteworthy for mortals. Martha arrived with a fist full of church pledge envelopes.

"He reminded me that I had not been keeping up with my pledge," she told us simply.

Bernice told of making peace with one of her neighbors. "We hadn't spoken to each other for two years," she said. "So I knocked on her door and told her it was time that we started acting like Christians. She invited me in, put the teakettle on, and we talked for three hours."

Mavis never came to our class again. The skeptic who doubted that God had "errands" to be done had found herself with an assignment. She sent word that henceforth she could be contacted in the seventh grade department where she was going to teach.

No one else admitted having anything to report. So I don't know whether they actually prayed the way we had planned and received no answer—or whether they had chickened out somewhere along the way.

After hearing Bernice's story, I vowed to pray more often for Allison. I seemed to have a one-track mind: When I sought to know God's will for my life, I neglected the simple things I already knew I was supposed to be doing. Being a Christian, I told myself, was like trying to fight a war simultaneously on several fronts.

I finally told the class about my startling book-writing assignment. They reacted to my news with such unimpressed silence that I felt compelled to beef up my plans.

"And if my book is a success," I added grandly, "I'm going to give ten percent of my royalties to the church building fund. I'll give ten percent right off the top—before taxes. And if it becomes a best seller, I'll be able to buy a pipe organ."

Our lesson for the morning was still part of the series on serving God. I pointed out that serving God doesn't have to be a grim business—that it can be enjoyable.

"For example," I told them, "I have found that teaching this class is very rewarding. When I was a child, I thought that Sunday School teachers were pitiful, broken-down creatures who were trying to get somebody—anybody—to listen to them. I remember one Rally Day when Mr. Foster received a gold tie pin and a new Bible for having taught Sunday School forty years. The poor old fellow could hardly hobble up to the platform, and I felt sorry for him. He had sacrificed practically all of his weekends, and those tokens were all he had to show for it.

"However, since I've been teaching I realize that Mr. Foster had his compensations in the knowledge that he was serving God. I've come to the point where I don't mind spending Sunday mornings here. I'll never go on any glamorous weekend trips with the jet set—but Sunday School teachers shouldn't expect a vacation with pay anyway!" (This statement wasn't entirely accurate. The truth was that while I had resigned myself to the fact that I couldn't have long, glamorous weekends, I still felt that I was missing something.)

As I made this last statement, I glanced at my wristwatch: The time was 10:15 a.m. I remember this well because on the following morning I was aboard a Pan-American jet clipper en route to Puerto Rico for a glamorous three-day, all-expense-paid trip. The plane took off at exactly 10:15.

A large insurance corporation was planning to entertain its

top salesmen in Puerto Rico and, as was its custom, had arranged for an outside speaker to talk about some timely subject. The speaker, however, had cancelled at the last minute.

Where to find a replacement? One of the vice presidents had told us that he was trying to think of someone when his eye fell upon a brochure from the Franklin Institute. It featured a picture of my husband, who had recently given a speech at the Institute about space travel and astronaut training. So Randy was invited as speaker, and I was urged to come along. All expenses were paid—plus an honorarium of $500.

The accommodations were luxurious. We flew first class where they served an eight-course luncheon of gourmet dishes, including exotic fruits, filet mignon, French pastries, and champagne. I didn't drink the champagne, but it gave the trip a glamorous send-off, anyway.

A large room, which cost $40 a day, had been reserved for us in a beautiful resort hotel. A private balcony overlooked the turquoise bay with its border of white sand and gently-swaying palm trees. A maid unpacked our clothes and turned down the bed sheets. Bellhops, doormen, elevator operators, chauffeurs, and guides were at our beck and call. In the dining room atop the hotel, our own waiter hovered over us, anticipating every wish, and a group of strolling troubadours sang our favorite songs. I felt like a princess in a castle by the sea!

For two days I enjoyed the glamorous life of the jet set. We walked the beach and swam alternately in both the ocean and the pool. We went sightseeing and shopping at antique and souvenir shops. We danced under the stars to the exotic beat of a calypso band. I wore a giant orchid, the largest I had ever seen.

On the third day an unbelievable thing happened: I grew tired of this paradise! I had relaxed so thoroughly that further relaxation was impossible. The scenery, at first so spectacularly beautiful, now began to look faded. And I was tired of filet mignon!

Then I looked more closely at some of the regular jet set members, wrapped in mink and ermine, bedecked with diamonds and emeralds. I was startled to see that while their

67

huge jewels were sparkling—they were not. They looked, unseeing, at the azure ocean and laughed without mirth at tasteless jokes. They dined on three-pound lobsters, flaming cherries jubilee, and huge goblets of champagne—and came away from the table still empty.

It reminded me of Jesus' words to the Samaritan woman at the well in the 4th chapter of John:

Every one who drinks of this water will thirst again, but whoever drinks of the water that I shall give him will never thirst. . . .

I came home from the trip certain of one thing: On Sunday morning I would rather be in my Father's house doing his work than any other place in the world. The trip settled that question for me, once and for all.

When Randy and I returned, it was time to prepare for Christmas. I soon discovered that the Christian Service Class had a lot to teach me about "keeping Christmas."

The first order of business was planning for those less fortunate. We had "adopted" a twelve-year-old girl named Joyce at the Methodist Children's Home. All during the first part of December the class members wrapped little gifts and signed cards for Joyce.

The church had the names of some twenty families in the community who needed food baskets. The Christian Service Class took the biggest challenge: a family with seven young children whose father was in prison. Our class put out a call for canned goods—and received enough to see the family well into spring. Then they solicited enough outgrown school clothing to outfit each of the children. After exhausting the supply of donations, they dipped into the class treasury, still fat from soup-making and other projects, and bought a turkey, ham, fruitcake, candy, and a Christmas tree with some trimmings. They also circulated a list of the names and ages of the children in the hope of acquiring some suitable toys.

Books, games, dolls, and trucks soon began to accumulate in the box placed near the front doors. Some of the children of the class members donated their toys. Were these the spoiled, over-indulged children of affluence? It was difficult to recognize them as such at that moment. My younger son, Craig, donated one of his favorite toys, a small wooden train, and I was very proud of him.

Patty Bedford, our president, challenged Annalee Farrell and the other members of the Women's Bible Class to donate a food basket to the needy. That class finally took the names of two elderly ladies who lived alone. Annalee Farrell promptly sent word to our class:

"Not only are we going to send food for Christmas dinner, we are going over to visit and read the Bible to them."

I always tried to remain aloof from this petty bickering between the two classes, but I couldn't help laughing when Martha replied, "That woman with the seven kids and the husband in jail doesn't know how lucky she is!"

Vicky Peterson, who had been the leader of a Girl Scout troop for several years, put the scouts to work gathering good used toys to be sent to a school for mentally-retarded children. The Girl Scouts' favorite job was fixing up dolls and sewing new clothes for them, assisted by our members. Martha and Joanna Neilsen were experts with needle and thread and could be seen at odd moments rescuing a doll's dress from the inept fingers of a novice seamstress.

One Sunday morning in mid-December, Rachel Anderson, who was class representative to the Methodist Home for the Aged, made an announcement.

"I hope nobody objects," she began, "but I took it upon myself to spend some extra money from our treasury. When I visited the Home the other day, I discovered a sad thing. Somebody had stolen a radio from an elderly blind man. That radio was his only link to the outside world, and he was lost and bewildered without it. So I took some of the class's money and bought him a new radio—without taking time to go through the proper channels. He was very touched—kept asking me why a group of strangers would do this for him."

We were so moved that we didn't even put that expenditure to a vote.

This, then, was rule Number One for keeping Christmas: Spread the spirit of giving as far as possible, to those who are to receive help and to those who are in the position to give help—and at the same time set an example for the young. The next step for the Christian Service Class was to plan a celebration. They took the attitude that if Christ is your Savior, Christmas is a day for celebration. In this modern, super-sophisticated world where Christmas is celebrated in department stores and at cocktail parties, the class declared that Jesus' birthday should be observed with love, joy, and wholesome festivity.

The class Christmas party was set for the third Monday night of December, the regular meeting date. Many organizations have their Christmas meetings in late November because they want to spend the holiday elsewhere. Our class felt that there was no better place to celebrate than at church.

The program began with a banquet in the church social hall, which had been decorated by an enthusiastic committee. Boughs of evergreens, tied with red ribbons, beautified the high window sills of the large room. The banquet tables were made festive with centerpieces of red candles, nestling in evergreen wreaths. A party favor, a small holiday corsage, was placed by each plate.

The corsages had been made by the clever fingers of some of the class members who could take a piece of velvet ribbon, twist it deftly, and turn it into a rose. They had worked at odd moments for weeks so that each person could have one of the lovely creations. I had been dismissed from the project—laughingly—when it was discovered that the only thing I could make from a twisted piece of ribbon was a tattered, wrinkled remnant. Although it was generally brought up in good-natured banter, this was continually being pointed out to me: There are many hands more clever than mine to sew, knit, mend, arrange flowers, cook, and decorate. Somewhere along the way, those of us who call ourselves intellectuals tend to forget that we, too, have our limitations. Whatever left-over feelings of superiority I had after my experience in the soup kitchen with Martha were wiped out in the needlework and handicraft projects.

On the night of the banquet, the girls arrived dressed in party finery with their hair freshly coiffured. None of them was to set foot in the church kitchen that night. A catering firm was preparing the food and the Methodist Men's Club served as waiters.

The menu consisted of prime ribs of beef and assorted delicacies, topped off with lemon cream pie. I learned that in a previous year, the class had argued for three and a half hours over the menu, finally agreeing on roast beef. So, in order to reserve their business meetings for worthier problems, the menu became a tradition. The food was served with exaggerated courtliness by the men, many of whom were husbands of the members. The waiters were resplendent in dark trousers, white shirts, green bow ties and dazzling red velvet cummerbunds.

The entertainment was to be a production of "The Night Before Christmas" starring some of the class members. They entered into it with the special enthusiasm of amateurs entertaining their peers. The rehearsal had gone well and had been pronounced humorous by the cast. It turned out, however, that the unrehearsed fiascos which crept into the production were to render it much more comical.

The stage of the social hall was set sparsely with furniture. A flimsy red cardboard fireplace occupied the back wall, just to the left of the center, and next to it was a window, which was in reality only a frame with no glass. I was to be the narrator and was to stand to one side and read the poem while various characters enacted the roles.

We started out soberly enough.

Twas the night before Christmas when all through the house
Not a creature was stirring, not even a mouse.

At this point, Gerry Bass, who was about five feet two inches tall and weighed 175 pounds, appeared in a mouse costume—possibly the biggest mouse in the world.

I was supposed to repeat the second line and shoo the mouse away.

I did this and Gerry started to make her exit through the fireplace. However, when she had crawled half way through, she became stuck and could go neither forward nor backward. With her long tail and chubby derriere pointed toward the audience, she squirmed, wiggled, and heaved.

"Not a creature was stirring, not even a mouse," I repeated for the third time and Gerry pushed so hard the whole fireplace trembled. She was finally able to back out. With great dignity she left the stage by another exit.

The children were nestled all snug in their beds
While visions of sugar plums danced through their
heads.

A group of four or five "children," ranging in age from thirty-five to fifty, came out on stage wearing flannel nighties and old-fashioned night caps, with some wisps of gray hair poking through. They sat down on the stage and rested their innocent-looking heads on large pillows.

Valerie Cross, who had studied ballet as a girl, was supposed to dance to the "Dance of the Sugar Plum Fairy," while Bernice Oglethorpe managed the record player. Valerie, who was still lithe and slender in middle age, danced forth. In her costume of purple net and silver sequins, she really looked like a sugar plum fairy.

Valerie whirled and twirled and bowed—and whirled and twirled and bowed again. A dozen times she went through all of the steps in her repertoire—but the music continued. The needle was stuck and Bernice, who was unfamiliar with Tschaikovsky, failed to notice it. Finally, the exhausted Sugar Plum Fairy staggered behind the curtains, while the "children" on stage whispered instructions that could be heard in the back row.

To dramatize the middle of the poem, Bernice was equipped with a large bag of artificial snow to scatter when I read the appropriate lines. It hardly seemed possible that something else could go wrong in such a short space of time, but when the Christian Service Class takes to the stage—and behind the stage—anything can happen.

Away to the window I flew like a flash
Tore open the shutters and threw up the sash.
The moon on the breast of the new-fallen snow,
Gave a luster of midday to objects below.

This was Bernice's cue to give the audience a view of a wild snowstorm through the fake, pane-less window at the back of the stage. However, she threw the snowflakes at an angle which sent them whirling into the room—pelting the sleeping children and flinging drifts into the corners. Unaware that her aim had gone wrong—and spurred on by the laughter of the audience—she doubled her efforts until she had created a veritable indoor bilzzard.

I was relieved to see Santa Claus arrive, appropriately dressed, right on schedule—and through the fireplace without mishap. Patty Bedford was playing the role and looked very authentic in a bright new suit. However, Patty was rather lean for a Santa Claus and had padded herself all over. On top of the other padding, she had wrapped a large pillow around her middle and fastened it in place with a belt.

Santa bounded into the room and opened a bulging bag of toys as I read:

*He was dressed all in fur from his head to his foot
And his clothes were all tarnished with ashes and soot.*

At this point the audience laughed so hard I had to quit reading because no one could hear me. I realized that "The Night Before Christmas" wasn't really that funny. So I sneaked a look behind me—and saw the crowning unplanned event of the production.

Santa Claus had placed his bag of toys (in reality, a pillowcase) on the floor and was bending over it, pulling out toys. The string holding his bright new pants in place had untied, and each time he delved into the toy bag, the pants rolled down a little more, like a flag unfurling. The pants were down around his ankles by the time he became aware of it.

When Santa discovered this predicament, he pulled up his pants, grasped them by the strings, and ran out through the chimney, dragging the bag of toys behind him. When he yelled as an afterthought from back stage "Happy Christmas to all and to all a good night!" it was with such an evident mixture of relief and embarrassment that the audience again fell into fits of laughter. Reverend Marsden, usually so proper and reserved, laughed so hard he almost fell off his chair. And he could never be persuaded that the humorous catastrophes were unplanned.

Santa returned and began distributing candy to all of the "good girls" in the audience. Then he called me up to the front and handed me a dozen red roses ("because we love you") and a gift certificate to a local dress shop. Close to tears, I began to protest that I really didn't expect a gift and Martha blurted out: "We want you to get a new dress so we won't have to look at the same one every Sunday."

Everybody laughed at this, including me.

When I started teaching the class, I was a rather formal, introverted young woman. I had never had a sister or a daughter and had lost my mother at an early age. Although I had heard ministers talk about "Christian fellowship" all my life, I had never known the real meaning of this phrase, and I fear that many people never experience it.

I found Christian fellowship with that Sunday School class. We worked and played and worshiped God together. We exchanged ideas on life, death, world affairs—and child care. We comforted each other through disasters: The newborn infant who gulped three breaths of life and decided it wasn't worth the struggle; the beautiful little girl on her way to catch the school bus, shot between the eyes by an over-eager hunter; the sons who went to Vietnam, or to the hospital—or to jail. There was, inevitably, the faithless husband who left town with the young secretary and the handsome young teenager who told his mother, "I'll be home early," and went out and jumped over a cliff.

Through these terrible events—and many more—each class member bled a little, cried a little, and prayed a lot. Although tragedy appeared far too often, the accompanying feelings of hopelessness and despair did not linger. It was because of this closeness that we could laugh together over such foolishness as our unbelievable Christmas production.

That night I realized: These are my sisters, my daughters, my mother. And the Lord knew—before I did—that I had need of these things.

Chapter 7

A Parting Of The Ways

The first Christmas after the death of a loved one is always an agonized tug-of-war between remembering and forgetting. For Allison, this anguish was deepened by the arrival of her in-laws who came from the Midwest to "cheer up" their only son's widow and did just the opposite. They countermanded all of her instructions and ignored all of her house rules. By Christmas Eve the children were unruly and Allison was on the verge of exploding.

I persuaded Allison to let the grandparents baby-sit while she attended the midnight Christmas Eve service with me. (My father-in-law was visiting us, and he and my husband had agreed to baby-sit with our boys and assemble some of the toys.)

Allison brightened when we closed the door on her domestic problems, but when we arrived at the gaily-decorated church, she began to cry. Every carol and every candle seemed to bring back some different memory, each more poignant than the last. I inadvertently made her laugh at one point by sitting down on my purse after we had stood to sing. But this levity slipped back into despair when the Christmas chimes sounded at midnight. She sobbed as though her partly-healed wounds were torn open and bleeding again.

When we returned to Allison's house—so quiet and unfestive despite the Christmas trappings—she seemed almost hysterical.

"I can't do it," she sobbed. "I can't go on living alone. I can't and I won't!"

I had been an independent young woman with an admiration for men of strong character. And I had always assumed that if I were ever widowed, I would revert to that philosophy—a strong man or no man at all. But Allison gauged realistically the slim chances of a widow with two small children in a suburb as paired-off as Noah's Ark. She wanted a man—and almost any man would do.

Along in April I began to hear rumors that Allison was seeing a man. A woman, whose daughter worked as Allison's baby-sitter, was spreading the news that "young widow Crandall" was staying out so late that the mother had to forbid her daughter to sit for Allison on school nights. Allison herself talked of attending several parties, but always hedged when I brought up the subject of her escort. I didn't press her for information. I thought she would tell me when the time came.

Actually, Hobie and my son Mark innocently revealed the man's identity. I drove over to Allison's early one morning to take her children to nursery school. Hobie came bounding out the door and dragged Mark back into the house to see his new steam shovel. They stayed so long that I ran into the house to get them. There was Doug Bryant, very much at home, sitting at Allison's breakfast table drinking coffee.

I waved my hand in a feeble greeting, rounded up the children, and hurried them to the car. En route to nursery school, I felt compelled to ask the question which I was almost afraid to ask. Finally, hating myself for the thoughts which kept nibbling away at my mind, I asked Andrea, "Did your Uncle Doug just come over this morning, or was he here last night?"

"He just came this morning," she said. "I like Uncle Doug—he fixed my doll buggy."

I was only slightly relieved. The fact was that Doug Bryant was an unsuitable companion for Allison. Unfortunately, he looked very suitable: He was lean and good-looking with wheat-colored hair and an appealing little-boy expression in his eyes. He was of medium height for a man, thus making him only slightly taller than Allison, but he moved with the grace of a tiger and seemed to generate an animal magnetism.

The members of my class knew him well. His wife, Heather, had been injured in an automobile accident the previous year and was paralyzed from the waist down. They lived near the church and after the accident Patty and Joy had gone over to see if they could help. But they could never get Doug Bryant to address himself to the problems of his wife and three young daughters. He kept feeling sorry for himself and seemed bitter that the accident had ruined his plans for going into the automatic laundry business. The little girls were dirty and hungry, but their father did nothing beyond complaining about his "bad luck."

Joy had stayed with the girls while their father went to visit his wife in the hospital. She had bathed them, dressed them in clean clothes, finished five huge loads of laundry, and fixed the girls a good hot meal.

Doug still had not returned though hospital visiting hours were long over. At midnight he finally came through the door, reeking of booze and mumbling about "having to get away from it all." He never thanked Joy or concerned himself that she had to drive home by herself at such a late hour.

Several months later Patty had stopped by the Bryants to visit Heather, who was sitting in a wheelchair.

"This is awfully hard on Doug," Heather had said. "He's never been around an invalid before, and he says he just isn't able to stay in the house very long. He doesn't know how to do much for the girls, either. He never did learn much about taking care of them."

"It's you I worry about," Patty said. "After all, you're the one who's been having such a hard time."

"Oh, I'm tough!" Heather had answered. "I just grit my teeth and take whatever comes along."

Patty, Joy, and I had discussed the Bryants' situation some time later. We decided that Doug Bryant was the most conceited, self-centered, spoiled brat who had ever attained the age of thirty-eight.

When I brought the children home from nursery school, Allison was waiting for me, girded for battle. She greeted all four children with her usual warmth, but her eyes blazed with anger when she looked at me. Her words were controlled, deliberately low key because of the children, but laced with significance: "Doug tells me that he knows some of the ladies from the class," she began.

Then, smoothly, she turned to Andrea and Hobie. "It's such a nice day I thought you two, and Mark and Craig, would enjoy a picnic," she said, ushering them out to a table in the backyard where she had arranged sandwiches, fruit, milk, and cookies. Then we stood in her kitchen, facing each other like two contenders in a boxing match.

It was such a corny situation that writers of soap operas would have hesitated to borrow it; yet here it was in real life: the lonely, vulnerable young widow and the man with a roving eye and an invalid wife.

Watching this drama from a box seat was the devoted friend who was, of all things, a Sunday School teacher.

Allison fired the first volley. "I know *you* won't approve," she said, her voice unsteady, "but I'm enjoying his company very much. He comes over for a cup of coffee in the morning before he goes to work. And he stops by here on his way home and we talk about all kinds of things. It's wonderful to have a man around the house again!"

"Where did you meet him?" I asked mildly.

"One of my former neighbors, Janet Forsythe, had a party and insisted that it would do me good to get out for an evening, even though she didn't know any suitable single men to invite to be my escort. Both Doug and Heather were supposed to come, but at the last minute Heather decided that it was too much trouble for Doug to haul her and the wheelchair around. So Doug came alone. We came back here after the party and talked till four in the morning."

"When was that?"

"It was the first part of February. I'm sure Heather must know about it. We've taken all the children out several times and you know how they tell everything. We took them to a Walt Disney movie one Saturday afternoon and to the zoo one Sunday. Andrea and Marilyn are about the

78

same age and get along famously. Carol is eight and I don't think she likes me very well. Lisa is three and fights with Hobie—like one big happy family," she chuckled.

Her laugh unnerved me. I loved her like a sister and she had shed so many tears that I should have been happy to hear her laugh. But did it have to be at the expense of a poor broken woman in a wheelchair?

"Allison," I pleaded, "can't you see that there's no future with this man?"

"Janey girl," she said, trying to laugh, "after you've been through what I've been through you don't worry about the future. All I know is that he has improved my present." She moved away from me but her eyes were defiant. "Besides, he keeps saying that he's thinking of asking Heather for a divorce."

"Oh, come on now, Allison! Can't you see a judge giving a divorce to a man on the grounds that his wife is a helpless invalid?"

"You don't like Doug Bryant, do you?"

"There's no use for me to deny it. So I'll tell you the truth: No!"

"Why not? He's handsome, charming, and lots of fun to be with. He's a wonderful dancer, knows all the latest steps."

"That's fine as long as his partner can *do* the latest steps. But what does he do when she is relegated to a wheelchair?"

"Well, what do you expect him to do—sit around the house moping? She's the one who's an invalid, not he! If you were an invalid, would you expect Randy to give up his social life?" she challenged.

I hesitated before I answered. "Yes, I guess I would. I know it sounds overly sentimental, but we married each other 'in sickness and in health,' and that's the way I look at it."

Her long fingers gripped the back of a chair. "Boy, are you ever naive about men. Do you know any who don't seek female companionship when they are lonely?"

I had an answer ready. "I certainly do. You probably know Cliff Madison from our church. His wife had multiple sclerosis and was bedridden for about seven or eight years before she died. When she became an invalid, he hired a practical nurse to look after her in the daytime and took over the night shift himself. He put up a cot in the corner of her bedroom and slept there so he could hear if she called for anything. He stayed right there for at least five years, leaving her only to go to work and to church." I felt a glow of victory, but she lifted her pointed chin.

"Didn't he remarry within a short time after she died?"

"That's right."

"Aha! See what I told you about men!"

"It's not the same thing and you know it!" I knew my frustration showed in my voice. "The point you refuse to acknowledge is that he was faithful to her as long as she lived—and that's what Doug Bryant can't seem to fathom, either."

"I can't see that visiting with me is being unfaithful to her," she cried. "She admits that she doesn't feel comfortable being carted around in a wheelchair—she just doesn't like parties anymore. When I enjoy Doug's companionship, I'm not taking anything away from Heather that she needs or wants now."

We were interrupted by a call from Hobie and Mark for more milk. Allison went out to the backyard with a pitcher and then returned to resume our talk.

"No, Janey girl," she challenged, "you can't convince me that I'm doing anything wrong. If you think so, just spell it out."

The question—the whole argument—was so distorted that I didn't know where to begin to answer. So I sputtered around, fumbling for words, and finally stammered, "Well, what about the Ten Commandments?"

"What about them?" she shot back.

"There's one that says 'thou shalt not commit adultery' and another one that says "thou shalt not covet anything that is thy neighbor's.' "

"Haven't you heard, Janey girl? The Ten Commandments are no longer practical in this modern age." Her tone was mocking now, as though she were scoffing at some slight infraction of a rule in a high school study hall.

I had controlled my temper until the mockery crept in. "The Ten Commandments are still the most practical guide for happy living that you can find anywhere!" I shouted.

"I'm beginning to see your trouble, Janey girl," she flared. "The reason you don't sympathize with Doug and me is that you are a cold fish—a cold fish and a Sunday School teacher!"

Rage welled up from somewhere deep inside my brain and boiled over like lava from a volcano. It wasn't until I heard the resounding smack that I realized I had slapped her face.

Then I ran out the back door, scooped up Mark in one arm and Craig in the other, and, ignoring their protests, pulled them to the car. Through lips which seemed to be made of wood, I told them that it was time to go home.

I was still shaking when I sat down at home to try to piece together the fragments of a friendship smashed like a crystal vase. My first thought was to apologize to her for having lost my temper. But the more I reviewed the facts, the more convinced I became that I was right.

When Hobart Crandall died, I had experienced great difficulty in accepting the Christian doctrine about life after death. But this time the doctrine was clear. Besides the Ten Commandments, there were Doug Bryant's marriage vows and the golden rule. No matter how she rationalized it, Allison was doing wrong.

After that day, I discontinued the nursery school car pool, telling my children that Andrea and Hobie were going to ride in their own new car. I refused to be a chauffeur while Allison had morning coffee with Doug! Allison didn't return to the Sunday School class, although she brought her children to Sunday School and dropped them off in the parking lot. Occasionally I got a glimpse of her at the church service, but we made no attempt to speak.

I had once been wholeheartedly sorry for Allison, but now I was just as thoroughly enraged. I was furious with both her and Doug Bryant for breaking the rules that I was pledged to uphold. I began to think of myself as a modern defender of the faith. I had always wondered where the Catholic Church had found its biblical justification for excommunicating those who broke the rules. If the church is for sinners, I had reasoned, why did the church throw the sinners out? Now I could understand the Catholic point of view. In the Methodist Church, you could flaunt the rules and still be welcomed on Sunday morning—and nobody seemed to be doing anything about it.

There are only two aspects of this whole ugly affair of which I can be proud. The first was that from that day on I prayed for Allison, asking God to guide her and to help her set a good example for her children. The second was that I vowed not to join in the gossip.

For quite awhile, the town buzzed with speculation and insinuation. Allison and Doug were seen together early and late. They were seen with the children—and without them. There was a rumor that they were planning to take a vacation trip together. And there was another rumor that Heather Bryant was so dispirited by the situation that she had lost all interest in living.

People who knew that I had been one of Allison's closest friends tried to pump me for information. But when any innuendos reached my ears, I quickly changed the subject. I wish I could say that I refrained from gossiping out of Christian kindness, but this is not the case. Actually, the whole situation had shaken me so badly that I couldn't talk about it. So far as I could see, it was a dilemma from which none of the principals could emerge unscathed.

Chapter 8

The Book

After my friendship with Allison exploded, I threw myself into church work with even more vigor. I spent at least three hours each week preparing the Sunday School lesson, and I participated in most of the class activities. In addition, I had agreed to serve on the building committee which was organized to expedite the erection of the new sanctuary. And there, in the corner of the bedroom, was the new typewriter upon which God wanted me to write a book.

Every time I glanced at that typewriter I was eleven years old again and Miss Timmings was talking about using our God-given abilities. Why did I have so much trouble with this business of doing God's will? Other people seemed to have settled the matter easily, if indeed they had considered it at all. One day I asked Martha if she ever longed to work anywhere else in the church besides the kitchen and she guffawed.

"Sure," she laughed, "but I can't decide whether I should sing a solo or preach a sermon—so I just go on peeling potatoes."

Martha never seemed to question God on the subject of her endowments—or lack of them. Her face was more than plain—it was downright homely. Each of her features was purely utilitarian, like a stripped-down model of an economy car. Framing this ordinary face was stringy brown hair which had begun to turn gray in a haphazard way. Her figure was large-boned and square with the exception of her legs. These, for some unaccountable reason, were spindly, giving her the overall appearance of a box supported by match sticks. And her loud, harsh voice still made me cringe.

But Martha had gifted hands to accomplish God's work. She stood for hours at a time in the church kitchen, turning out brown-velvet gravy, cakes that were captive clouds, and centerpieces that were the envy of the local florist. Many times she missed the program out front because she was left alone to wash the dishes. Childless during thirty years of marriage, Martha sewed layettes for the local hospital to give to babies born into a world of poverty. Many people would have sent plain, patched-up clothes for these unfortunates—but not Martha. She bought pretty flannelette by the bolt and added bits of embroidery and even ribbon and lace. The fine embroidery on the altar cloths in the church was largely Martha's work also.

On the other hand, I had almost as much difficulty accepting my gifts as I had in acknowledging my limitations. I was quite uneasy about allowing myself to become a writer. I was born with a passion for language and, at first, I showed my ardor as unashamedly as a young lover. As soon as I could hold a pencil, I succumbed to an innate urge to observe and record the scenes around me. I read constantly, in school and out. When my grammar school teacher assigned a little composition, I submitted twenty pages.

The penalties for this devotion accrued during my entire school career. My classmates began calling me "walking dictionary" and "teacher's pet." My history teacher punished me for hiding a rhyming dictionary inside my history notebook. My math teachers despaired of ever pulling me through. My eye seemed to be so permanently focused upon describing life that I was totally unable to think quantitatively. The first time a teacher queried, "How much is two and two?" I asked, "Two what?" She said, "Two of anything—it doesn't matter what." I spent grueling, torturous years after that trying to understand how math could, at the same time, be an exact science and equate two elephants with two mosquitoes.

To be different in childhood is tantamount to being a target for wanton insults. I suffered all the more at the hands of my classmates because I was cursed with the writer's supersensitive nature. A reprimand from a teacher struck my ears as though she had wielded a stick. A jeer from a friend was an arrow piercing the heart. And even though they teased me unmercifully, I could not retaliate. Instead of being smug and superior over a classmate who couldn't tell "cheery" from "cherry" or "through" from "though," I felt like crying for him.

In high school I won all the prizes for poetry, essays, and oratory. I was the salutatorian and the poet laureate, but I would have traded it all to be the prom queen. (I was also suspicious that the poet laureate business was a title invented by my English teacher as compensation for the misfit.)

I went to college encased in a tougher skin. I liked journalism because it gave me the opportunity to work with words without involving much of my own emotion. One of my professors was not fooled.

"You're like a Cadillac chugging down the highway on one cylinder," he told me. "If you don't express your feelings more freely, you're going to be nothing but a dilettante."

I looked up the word "dilettante" and found that it means "one who follows an art superficially."

Better superficially than deeply, I thought. To me, the word "dilettante" had a lovely sound—almost like debutante.

Ten years later, though, the problem had surfaced again. I had always assumed that we had an option—that we could either use the abilities God gave us or not. But it had begun to look as though I had about as much choice as Jonah caught between a sinking ship and a whale.

Since I was planning to write about my life among the scientists, I began reading other books dealing with the influence of a man's occupation upon the household. Then I went to the library and checked out a pile of books about how to write a book. The librarians began regarding me quizzically as though I were preparing to fill my own teeth or take out my own appendix.

It might have been easier to try those things. The advice on book writing, which came mostly from unsuccessful writers, was to a large extent contradictory, redundant, and unclear. The two pieces of advice which impressed me most were: "Use the language sparingly—make every word count," and, "Just tell the story." Many times over the next three years I had the urge to search out those two advisers and knock their heads together!

Finally, it came to putting words on paper. Haltingly, I wrote an introduction. Then I tore it up and wrote another. After several false starts, I finished the first chapter. Eventually, I developed a routine: Every morning after the boys had gone to school I sat down at the typewriter and worked until they came home early in the afternoon.

I had never worked so hard. There were times when I thought my brain would burst from so much unaccustomed exertion. But, strangely enough, I also found that I had never enjoyed anything quite so much, either. It wasn't until I had written about five chapters that I realized there was a serious problem: I had no one who knew anything about editing to advise me. It was then that Lenore Brock came into my life.

I realized that many people—in the church and outside of it—will scoff at the idea that God sends help to those who are trying to do his will and really need assistance. But I am convinced that Lenore Brock was sent to help me.

Our meeting came about in an unexpected way. My husband had been installed as president of the elementary school PTA. I had always been lukewarm to the PTA, preferring to put my efforts into the church, but Randy feels that education is very important. When he took over the presidency, he was distressed to discover that the treasury was practically empty—and there were no plans for raising funds.

The principal, Rayford Jackson, suggested having a book fair. "I have a friend who operates a book store, and she would be glad to work with us. In addition to making some money, the book fair would be an educational experience for the children."

After the call for a volunteer to head up the book fair committee was unsuccessful, Ray Jackson and Randy looked at me. So, like all loyal wives whose husbands are president of something, I agreed to take the most distasteful job: ways and means chairman.

In preparation for the book fair, Ray Jackson and I drove over to "Book Haven," which was operated by Miss Lenore Brock. En route Ray told me that Miss Brock was a retired editor, having worked in New York book publishing houses for almost forty years. Last year, she had grown tired of life in New York and had decided that her experience in selecting reading material to be published would give her the background she needed for operating a successful bookstore.

I probably would never have had enough courage to mention my book to an editor of such impressive qualifications as Miss Brock, but Ray Jackson did it for me. I had been chattering away about my endeavor to everyone I knew, so when he introduced me to Miss Brock he added, "Mrs. Chambers is a writer—she's writing a book!"

"How interesting!" said Miss Brock. "I'd like to see it some time." I thought she was just being polite and I had no intention of bringing up the subject again.

I soon found that a book fair is much more complicated than it sounds. When you turn 600 elementary school children loose with 150 books, the bookkeeping problems are enormous. So I had to make numerous extra trips to Book Haven for replacements and exchanges. On one of these trips, Miss Brock and I found ourselves all alone surrounded by books.

"What are you writing about, Mrs. Chambers?" she asked.

"Well, my husband is a space scientist and I'm writing about my life with him."

"That sounds intriguing. Does his work affect your household?"

"It certainly does—we have two young sons and they're both showing scientific leanings. As a matter of fact, I'm the only normal one in the group."

Miss Brock laughed. "Now I insist that you bring me what you've done so far."

On my next trip, I carried the first five chapters of my book in a big brown envelope. Miss Brock was busy with a publisher's representative so, after much hesitation, I left the envelope on her desk and departed.

Ray Jackson had told me that Miss Brock had been inundated with manuscripts from local amateur writers, so I didn't really expect to hear from her very soon. However, she called me at ten o'clock that night, her voice high with excitement.

"You're a born writer," she said, "and I think you've got a best seller there! I'm sending your chapters to New York to a friend of mine to see if he agrees—and you hurry up and get it finished."

About a week later Miss Brock forwarded a letter from the New York editor in which he also expressed great optimism for the book. However, he had also sent a detailed list of changes which he felt should be made. Instead of being grateful, I was annoyed. In my experience as a newspaper writer, I had never had much time for rewriting. With four deadlines a day, I snatched the story from the typewriter and turned it in without any reworking at all. I had never had any patience for making extensive revisions.

For several months I wrote and rewrote under the tutelage of Miss Brock and her editorial friends, detesting it more and more. I felt like a little boy who has been happily playing with his marbles, placing them in patterns, rolling them around to suit himself. Suddenly, a big bully comes along and insists on playing by the rules—and playing for keeps. Then something happened which changed all this.

It was July 4th and the temperature was close to 100 degrees. Randy and the boys were clamoring to go on a picnic and I had packed a basket of food. My head had ached for two or three weeks, and as I put the cupcakes into the basket I realized that they looked very unappetizing. As a matter of fact, none of the food was appealing.

We got into the car, but I asked them to wait a minute. I went back into the house and appeared again—wearing my coat! I huddled in a corner of the car most of the day and finally had to admit that something was drastically wrong with my health.

Later in the week, the diagnosis was completed: I had that most miserable of diseases, hepatitis.

For months I was engulfed with nausea, filled with pain, and unable to get out of bed. My skin was jaundiced and I was covered with big red blotches. Inactivity made my muscles ache so much that sometimes I felt as though I had been run over by a truck. For awhile I didn't care whether I lived or died. I was so wretched that death would have been a relief.

The girls from my class, along with some of my neighbors, took turns at preparing our dinner and sending it to our house. Most of them were afraid of the disease and had scant knowledge of how viruses are transmitted. Martha fixed a delicious tuna fish casserole, complete with vegetables, salad, rolls, and a cake. She put it in a cardboard box and gingerly deposited it at the very edge of the front yard: Chirstian charity from a distance.

The ministers came to see me from time to time, bringing me communion from a portable communion service. I had never expected to be partaking of that—I had always thought of the portable communion service as being for invalids and death-bed cases.

On these occasions when Reverend Pearce arrived, he was his usual brusque, irritable self and departed as soon as he could possibly manage it. However, I saw a side of Reverend Marsden that I had rarely glimpsed. He prayed aloud for me and pressed my hand in a firm, warm grip. With the air of a father bringing a surprise to a child, he usually gave me some little token—an inspirational booklet, or a picture taken at some church activity. Once, with a twinkle in his steel-blue eyes, he handed me an elaborate "get well" card which had been designed and constructed by his twin daughters—at his suggestion, no doubt.

Another visitor who came—even before it was safe—was Frank Finley. I had met Frank that frantic day I had volunteered to teach the class. He was a short, plump man in his early sixties with a thatch of white hair and a ruddy complexion. He smiled at me over the top of a huge bouquet of long-stemmed red roses.

"How are you feeling, Janey?" he asked. Then he prayed aloud, asking God to heal and comfort me. I felt better.

"Where did you get the flowers?" I asked.

"Well, Janey, I'll tell you my secret. I have a friend who's a florist and he gives me his leftovers. I visit the sick in our church and community every Wednesday night, you know."

I hadn't known about his visiting and I still didn't understand how he could serve on the education committee, head up the building fund, teach a Sunday School class of young people, and serve as treasurer of the Methodist Men's Club. Last Christmas he had also helped my glass distribute some coats to needy children. Most of us would have dropped the coats on the doorstep, but this dear man went into each house and helped to fit the child with a coat which was not only the right size, but also a favorite color.

Frank Finley visited me every Wednesday night for several months, always clutching some flowers and offering a short but sincere prayer. I had always thought of an angel as a cherub with golden hair and wings. But now I know this isn't necessarily the case—an angel can have hair, a bouquet of wilted orchids, and a carload of warm, used children's coats.

I received nearly 100 "get well" cards but, sad to say, I did not hear from Allison. I felt that I had done what I could to comfort her when she needed it most, but evidently it was a one-sided relationship. My children reported having seen Andrea and Hobie with their "Uncle" Doug, so I knew that he and Allison were still a twosome. I couldn't help wondering what kind of life they could have together. Can two such weak people prop up each other—or will both collapse when one begins to lean heavily?

One of my cards came from Annalee Farrell, who had scrawled across the bottom, "Be still and know that I am God." I felt like poking her in the nose, but gave up the idea as soon as I realized I couldn't even get out of bed. I didn't really know whether to blame God for my illness or not. But the very least I could say about it is that since God is all-powerful, he certainly could have prevented it if he had chosen to. (I was the only one for miles around to have the disease that summer, so it could hardly be called an epidemic.)

Miserable as I was, I found that I was not bitter toward God. In fact, I felt quite close to him, especially in the morning after a night of pain and nausea. A ray of sunshine would touch my pillow, or a bird would sing sweetly outside my window, or a flower on my nightstand would open its petals and I would think of that Bible verse, *I know that my Redeemer lives. . . .*

I thought all along that that verse was somewhere in the book of Isaiah. But when I began to recover enough to read the Bible, I was startled to find it was from Job 19—Job, the most patient man in the history of the world!

When I resumed work on my book, I found that I did, indeed, have more patience than I had ever thought possible. I was able to write, rewrite, redo, and rework the manuscript as much as necessary without even becoming irritated.

I recovered from hepatitis just in time to participate in the groundbreaking ceremony for the new sanctuary. On a cold, blustery morning in March the congregation trooped outside after the morning worship service. We stood there—men, women, children, and mothers with infants-in-arms—looking heavenward at an uncertain sun, trying to visualize a new church building standing in what was now a patch of dead weeds.

The district superintendent, our church's immediate supervisor, gave a little talk about erecting a sanctuary "to the glory of God." Then he dug into the hard dirt with a well-worn spade and turned over a shovel full of Pennsylvania clay. He was followed by our ministers, first Reverend Marsden and then Reverend Pearce, and then by officials of the local church and members of the building committee. I was about tenth in line and was struck by how little dirt had actually been moved by the ceremonious shoveling. It was going to take a lot of people working together, with God's help, to build that church.

I thought of Hobe, who had undoubtedly precipitated the building of the new church. Just a short time ago Hobe had had a lovely wife, devoted children, a challenging job, and a church which needed and valued his service. He was gone now, missing from the scene, but life and the church were continuing without him.

We stood there, shivering with cold and excitement, while the choir, huddled in a group near one side of the excavation site, sang: "The church's one foundation is Jesus Christ her Lord. . . ."

They sang spontaneously, without musical accompaniment or direction, but it was the most moving rendition I have ever heard.

Chapter 9

The Fund Raisers

The groundbreaking ceremony spurred the Christian Service Class into new activities. As a group, we had pledged $1500 a year to the building fund for a three-year period even though we had a nucleus of only 20-30 faithful workers. The members thought up a variety of ways to make money.

To my surprise, the first thing they did was to drop the soup project. Although this had been very lucrative, it had reached a point where it was too much work and was too big an operation for the kitchen. The great demand for our soup was requiring several days of work a month, and the girls were tired of peeling and chopping vegetables.

At the next business meeting, Martha and Gerry quoted some estimates prompting them to predict that the class could cater weddings and make more than we had been making on the soup. Like real caterers, we would offer several kinds of receptions. Our repertoire included: punch, coffee, and wedding cake; or fancy tea sandwiches, cookies, ice cream, and cake; or a buffet with ham, chicken salad, potato chips, etc.; or a sit-down roast beef dinner. Each type was served quite elegantly in the church social hall, decorated by the clever members of the class. Seasonal flowers brightened each table. Wedding bells hung from the ceiling. The serving table was decorated with bouquets of vegetables-turned-into-flowers. A "wedding ring" of ice, complete with pineapple and cherry "gems," floated in the punch bowl.

The brides—and their mothers—loved these extra little touches. And the fathers liked the modest prices.

Colored bread for fancy sandwiches was ordered from the bakery, and a team of women usually lined up and put the sandwiches together, assembly line fashion. Once again, my lack of manual skill came to light: For some reason, my checkerboard sandwiches turned out to be striped instead. Even Martha couldn't figure out what had gone wrong, so we ate my batch of sandwiches for our lunch— and I was reassigned to mixing the fillings.

On the day of a wedding, the girls came down and put the finishing touches on the reception hall. Shortly before the ceremony was to begin, they opened the side door and slipped into front seats in the chapel. This opened into the church at right angles to the altar. From this vantage point, they sighed over the scene: the organ music, the white runner unfolded down the center aisle, the young bridesmaids marching slowly, bouquets trembling. When the bride appeared, the caterers always shed a few tears.

At one afternoon ceremony, Patty, wiping the tears from her eyes, leaned over and asked Gerry, "Who are the bride and groom, anyway?"

Immediately following the ceremony, the caterers jumped up from their box seats, ran out the side door, and took their stations in the kitchen.

The class soon discovered a way to increase our earnings. We could take the same menus, the same kind of decorations, and cater anniversary celebrations. In rapid succession we served a fiftieth anniversary party, a fortieth celebration, and a twenty-fifth one.

I didn't know that the ways and means committee had other plans for expanding the business until one Saturday afternoon, Martha called me and asked if I could come down and help serve a buffet.

It was a small group—only about twenty-five guests— and I noticed immediately that they were very solemn. Several even looked as though they had been crying. The decorations, too, were very austere—one floral centerpiece. And for some reason there didn't seem to be an honoree in sight. Finally, during a pause in the serving, I confronted Martha in the kitchen.

"What kind of an occasion is this?" I asked.

"Well, it's a funeral," she confessed. "They wanted someone to feed the out-of-town guests."

Another fund-raising project called "Luncheon for Milady" was sponsored by various food processors to provide a luncheon for a group of at least 100 women. We would have to set the tables, serve the food, and wash the dishes —but we could sell tickets for $1 each and the money would be clear profit.

Nobody enjoys going out to lunch more than housewives who usually eat a sandwich in solitude. They came early, stayed late, and read the piles of recipes, booklets, and coupons beside their plates. Martha was a case to consider. She sat near the front of the hall and listened with great concentration while the young home economist, our hostess, gave us tips on cooking, table setting, and meal planning. Martha also feigned great pleasure when she won a box of cake mix, one of the door prizes donated by the sponsors. None of the strangers present could have guessed that Martha never used cake mixes. She was a great actress regarding all of the products demonstrated, until the luncheon was over and our faithful crew was out in the kitchen washing the dishes.

"I was going to point out that the powdered milk was flavored with vanilla and sugar," she chuckled, "but that little gal was working so hard I decided not to shake her up! Besides, we made $119 for the building fund."

I don't remember who first told the class about the tours —but they seemed to be made to order for our group. The area was peppered with small factories which offered tours and treats to women's groups. The tours were free and we could sell the tickets for any amount we chose.

We had a fifty-cent tour of a local baking company where we watched the production of crackers and cookies on an automated assembly line. Each person received two sample boxes of cookies, making the tour worthwhile even to those uninterested in the baking business.

The local spaghetti factory was our prize find. They offered daily tours and luncheons in a special dining room in their lovely new plant. Any civic or church group which could provide thirty-five to fifty persons could take the tour, devour all the spaghetti they could eat—and earn a profit of a dollar a head. Understandably, the luncheons were booked up for two years in advance.

We had to wait only a week. Patty Bedford's cousin was the factory's reservation secretary, and she called us to fill in for the first cancellation. We toured the factory, fifty strong, and then consumed the mountains of spaghetti and meat balls, green salad, and hard bread provided by our hosts. They also gave us samples of their lasagna, pizza, and macaroni—finished off with some Italian cookies they were testing.

The day was pronounced an unconditional success. The only problems were that the food sent the dieters into a decline—and nobody in the group had much interest in preparing her family's dinner that night.

After that, we received frequent calls from Patty's cousin to fill in for cancellations. When the call came, everybody would drop what she was doing, don her going-out-to-lunch clothes and her comfortable factory-touring shoes, and rush over to the spaghetti plant. One time we even responded to a call that came at ten o'clock on the morning of the luncheon. We arrived like a bunch of volunteer firemen.

Before long we knew as much about the manufacture of pasta products as our guide did—and any one of us could have taken a visitor around the place. We appeared more frequently than the ladies' sodality from the nearby Catholic church, which was comprised largely of Italians and was also trying to build a new church.

The meat balls were plump and delicately seasoned and the spaghetti was cooked to perfection. Even so, I began to grow tired of it. Unfortunately, Martha and Gerry discovered that the factory was also having a contest: A $100 savings bond would be awarded on a certain date to the organization which turned in the most package coupons.

Martha did everything but add spaghetti to our wedding menus. She announced every Sunday morning that she was collecting those coupons. Soon she was receiving them from friends of friends—from as far away as East Orange, New Jersey. She demanded that we do our part also. We all served so much spaghetti, macaroni, and pizza to our families that they thought, as Patty's son expressed it, "We're all in training to be Italians."

Finally, the contest deadline approached and Martha announced that she had 850 coupons. This was twenty-one more than the Catholics had collected—and we won the bond. The architect's drawings of the proposed church building had led Bernice to nickname the new structure "The Methodist Barn." Another nickname came to my mind: "The Spaghetti Cathedral."

It was probably the need for a change in diet that led to the advent of the "Tasting Tea." The idea was that each woman of the church would prepare her favorite dish plus copies of the recipe. Then everybody would taste and buy the recipes of the dishes they liked.

Another brainstorm of the ways and means committee was a white elephant sale, held after one of the business meetings. Each girl was to bring some good item that was no longer useful to her, and it would be auctioned off.

About thirty-five members of the group were seated in a circle with a like number of oddly-shaped packages on the floor in front of them. Each member drew a number. When her turn came, she could either open a new package or bid on one that someone else had already opened. Everything went fine until Patty and Gerry both liked the same cookie jar. Patty tried to interest Gerry in a ceramic vase, but Gerry roared, "I wouldn't have it as a gift!"

This remark incensed Bernice. She had recently given a similar vase as a wedding present for a niece. "It was a lot more expensive than that cookie jar," Bernice snapped.

Whereupon Martha, who had donated the cookie jar, rose to its defense. And what had started out as good-natured banter was fast becoming petty bickering.

"All right, girls," shouted Donna Pearce, "let's call it quits. Every girl keeps what she has in her possession at the moment. If you don't like it, put it in your attic and bring it back next year."

Then Gerry and Martha decided we should have a rummage sale, and after much discussion the group agreed.

The sale was scheduled for Friday in the church hall. The announcement in the church bulletin had urged people to bring their items in any time from Monday to Thursday. By Thursday the hall looked as though it had been hit by a giant tidal wave which had washed over at least fifty attics, basements, and garages. The contents had formed dunes of shoes, dresses, coats, hats, books, toys, vases, dishes, lamps, and small electrical appliances. There also were a few large items such as a tooth-marked crib and a battered chest of drawers. We offered some highly unusual relics too, such as a souvenir plate from the 1933 Chicago World's Fair and a gadget to remove seeds from cherries.

The committee was comprised of the faithful few: Martha, Gerry, Joy, Patty, Vicky, Miriam Jackson, Valerie Cross, and Bernice, who grumbled mightily about the entire enterprise. After resisting the urge to faint, the committee tried to bring order to the big room, an undertaking somewhat like trying to straighten up after an avalanche.

Five hours later the dresses, coats, and suits hung neatly on racks borrowed from the church vestibule. The smaller items were placed on the long banquet tables. A coffee and cupcake concession was set up in one corner and a check-out table was placed near the back door. After much discussion, it was decided that it would be impossible to put price tags on the items, so a price schedule was drawn up instead. A sweater, blouse, shirt, or pair of shoes in good condition would cost a quarter; a "good" dress or pair of slacks, fifty cents; and coats, $1 to $1.25. Larger, one-of-a-kind items would go to the highest bidder.

We all went home that Thursday afternoon wondering if our venture would be successful.

When Martha arrived early the next morning, nearly forty people were waiting. As soon as she unlocked the door, the group surged forward and fairly ran into the hall. They hurried around to each rack and table, tossing wanted items into bags or boxes. Then, triumphant as a runner winning a cross-country race, each shopper dumped his chosen items at the check-out table to be tabulated by the cashiers.

The atmosphere was that of a shopper's carnival, a pack rat's heaven. From early morning till late afternoon, the "patrons" fingered the fantastic array of odds and ends.

Then, as a respite from such solemn responsibility, they gathered in the coffee and cupcake corner for a coffee break.

Class members who were brave enough to volunteer as cashiers found themselves making Solomon-like decisions. Yes, that cord could have belonged to that waffle iron. No, that dress probably is not washable. That snowsuit might fit a five-year-old, if he were of average size.

The reputation of various cashiers soon spread among the patrons. Patty was too high, Martha was a soft touch, and Jane couldn't add. Some of the customers simply chose the cashier with whom they wanted to deal. Others tried to bargain.

Our customers ranged from the very poor, who came to these sales out of necessity, to those wealthy enough to live in a swanky apartment house nearby. Gerry swears that one customer, wearing a mink stole as she rummaged through the sale items, had a big car and chauffeur awaiting her in the parking lot. No one else noticed the chauffeur, but with such a cross section of humanity, no one doubted the story, either.

Many of our customers were professional rummagers who made a practice of attending all of the sales in the area. Their ethics were as jaded as our merchandise. An elderly gentleman with a kindly, grandfatherly face played a sort of one-for-me, one-for-you game as he pocketed many small items, but paid for others with a great show of honesty. A teenaged girl arrived wearing a pair of navy blue slacks, and left wearing a pair of green and red plaid ones over them. And a sweet little old lady taught us a new meaning for the term "wearing two hats" after she paid for only one.

While we were trying to regain our faith in human nature, a slender, dark-haired woman of about 40 began checking out countless armloads of boys' clothes.

"I'm trying to help my poor, motherless nephews," she told us with a sob in her voice. "Their mother died last month and when I went to see them, I found they had nothing to wear. There are six of them, poor little tykes, ranging in age from 2 to 14."

For a moment we forgot we were trying to make money, and we became the Christian Service Class, doers of the word. Gerry and Bernice scouted around and helped find some more bargains in jeans and sneakers. And, after a conference, we decided to give the woman the clothes for half price.

She thanked us profusely, assured us that God's blessing was on us all, and departed—an operation which required at least five trips to her battered old car.

After she left, one of the other customers, a professional rummager, asked, "Is Florence giving you a hard luck story about her poor, fatherless neighbors again?"

"Well, no," I said. "She's trying to help her motherless nephews."

"That's this week. Last week it was the neighbors. Next rummage sale it'll be her cousins. She sure gets some bargains that way!" she said drily.

Patty, who regarded these petty shoplifters as a challenge, said, "It's too bad we can't bring some of them back here on Sunday." This is undoubtedly the proper Christian attitude, but I wasn't at all sure we could have coped with them.

In addition to having something for everyone who attended, the rummage sale also had items that appealed to the help. Martha latched onto the gadget which seeded cherries. Valerie bought up the odds and ends of jewelry that she was going to use to make Christmas ornaments. And Bernice stubbornly insisted she could refinish that chest of drawers like new.

Patty, who wore a size ten, found several almost-new dresses that had been donated by Vicky. Vicky seemed happy that the clothes no longer fit, so Martha pursued the subject.

"I might as well tell you," Vicky exclaimed. "Yes, it is true—I'm pregnant. We've been waiting eight years for this and we're so pleased!" The room buzzed with the news. We agreed that Vicky would be a perfect mother.

"Are you hoping for a boy or a girl?" Patty asked.

"It doesn't matter in the least," Vicky said, and we knew she meant it. "Just as long as it's healthy."

Many prospective mothers make similar remarks that are soon forgotten. However, in Vicky's case, the words were tragically memorable.

Toward the end of the day, Joy and I carried boxes around the tables and racks and collected some of the remaining clothing to send to the overseas relief program sponsored by Church World Service. Then we called a local mission to send a truck and clear out all the leftovers. Still dizzy with the events of the day, we counted our money and found we had made a clear profit of $375.

Despite the hard work, we found that the rummage sale was one of our favorite ways of raising money. And whatever we were doing—catering weddings, touring factories, or selling twenty-five-cent sweaters—we found fellowship in working together. The Christian Service Class undoubtedly had more fun with fund raising than any other group anywhere.

Chapter 10

A Time To Grieve

After I had spent another six months writing and rewriting, Miss Brock suggested that my book was ready. She chided me for typing it so perfectly, pointing out that editors don't really care that much about neatness. But I typed it as carefully as I could—I intended to make a grand first impression on the publishing world!

I boxed up the manuscript and sent it to Miss Brock with high hopes and prayers. I could hardly wait for it to become a best seller.

For two months I prayed daily and hoped hourly for the book's success. Like the mother of a new baby, I told all my friends about it even while they kept trying to change the subject. Though God had prodded me and Miss Brock had helped me, I had come to feel that it was my work— my proudest accomplishment.

In Sunday School class, I also mentioned the book frequently. Whenever we got on the subject of doing God's will—or anything remotely related to it—I brought up my book and told again how God had guided me in the writing of it. I also suggested to the class that this whole business of doing God's will was not as complicated as people seem to think. It was really quite easy, I thought, and success was practically guaranteed.

Any day now I expected to receive in the mail a contract offering to buy the book rights, magazine rights, paperback rights, and the movie rights. And from there on it would be an easy step to fame and fortune. I had heard of movie rights selling for many thousands of dollars—and the tithe from that could certainly buy the pipe organ.

The current plans were for an electronic organ, but the architect had designed the new church so there would be room for a pipe organ if the money were found to provide it. With God making the arrangements, I could have the money in time to install the pipe organ right away.

The blow came—not in the conventional mailed rejection slip—but on the six o'clock news. Three Apollo astronauts had been killed in a fire at the Cape while preparing for a flight. My husband, who had helped train the men, was very upset; one brief burst of flame had snuffed out the lives of three unique men. Several days later I received a note from Miss Brock, accompanying the box containing the returned manuscript.

"It's well done," the note said, crisply professional, "but nobody is interested now in a humorous book about a space scientist. After the Apollo fire, there is nothing humorous about it."

I cried for several days for the astronauts and their families. Then I cried for a week over my book. After that I lapsed into a kind of perennial mourning. I was crushed. Bereft. Humiliated. Embarrassed. Betrayed!

I was a bride, deserted at the altar—a young mother burying her first-born. But most ravaging of all, I was a child whose Father had just slammed the door in her face. I had written a book—against my better judgment, against all reasonable odds—because I had been convinced that God had wanted me to do it. I had submitted the book to the publishing world, making myself vulnerable to rejection and criticism that my sensitive nature had never learned to tolerate. And this was my reward. It was no wonder, I moaned, that few people even try to do God's will.

Many of the members of my class had chronic problems which made their lives miserable. Last year Kathleen Barry had finally committed her moronic son to an institution so that she and her husband could create some sort of home life for their younger one. I had helped her to reach that difficult decision, and I knew that even now she was still agonizing over it.

Gerry Bass's husband was a problem drinker. She never complained much about this, but when she failed to show up for one of our activities, we knew: Carl Bass was on a spree again. At these times, poor Gerry visited his favorite haunts, trying to find him so that she could bring him home before he got hurt.

Patty Bedford served as president of the class for several years and did all sorts of good things for everyone she met, yet she had a domestic problem of long standing. Her brother-in-law was always in trouble and looked to Patty's husband to bail him out. When she went home, Patty never knew whether she would find her sister-in-law and three small children homeless and hungry, or her brother-in-law pouring out the details of his latest escapade.

I had always been grateful—had even thanked God—that I had no such perennial problems casting long shadows over my home. My marriage was extremely happy, and my children were bright and healthy. But I did have one insoluble problem. This had been recurring for years and had just reared its ugly head again: the feeling of being one of God's unemployed. This could be, I told myself bitterly, the most demoralizing problem of them all.

After having bragged so much about the book, I was loathe to admit that it had been rejected. Whenever anyone asked if I had heard anything, I hedged. Finally, humiliated beyond words, I admitted that it wasn't going to be published—that I wasn't going to have the money to buy the pipe organ.

We were in the church kitchen, making tea sandwiches for a wedding, when I told the girls the news. I didn't know whether to be relieved or insulted—they didn't seem to care very much.

"Nobody's dead," guffawed Martha. "I don't know why you're taking it so hard."

These good-hearted souls, who rushed to the aid of all kinds of people in distress, had no feeling for the intensity

105

of my suffering. The idea that anybody should be in agony over 132 pages of manuscript paper was beyond their comprehension. They simply brushed it off.

"Think about poor Vicky," urged Gerry. "I went to see her yesterday, and she is really taking it hard."

Though I had heard the news a week or so earlier, I had been too absorbed with my own sorrow even to think about it. Vicky's baby, a girl, had been so deformed at birth that the doctors had urged them to put her in an institution. Babies of this type usually die with the first infection, they told her, and they felt their recommendation was the kindest way. I would have cried for Vicky if I had had any tears left.

Two weeks later, after deciding for the hundredth time that I would simply have to get hold of myself, the final blow fell. An elderly friend of Jonathan Day died in his retirement home in Florida and left $60,000 to the church to be used for a pipe organ. He was a bachelor and a non-church man, but he had been impressed by Jon Day's devoted service as music chairman and, at Mr. Day's invitation, had heard the choir sing several times. So he had chosen the church as one of the beneficiaries of his sizable estate. God had given him the privilege of contributing the organ.

I cast off my self-control like an old coat. Underneath I discovered a person I had never met before—a crazed woman who tore at her hair and sobbed from somewhere deep inside, crying out against God's unreasonableness.

Then she grabbed up a wastebasket, ran outside, and dumped its contents into our stone fireplace. She sprinkled the trash with lighter fluid, and soon tall flames were shooting out in all directions. This wild woman then went upstairs, emptied my desk drawer, and began gathering up the notes, rough drafts, carbon copies, and revisions of my book. I knew what she was going to do, but I made no move to stop her. The problem of trying to use my abilities to do God's will had persisted since I was eleven years old. I was now thirty-nine and had to face the fact that it was a lost cause. There was no point in allowing this to blight the rest of my life. Together we began tossing pages of manuscript onto the funeral pyre of dreams.

106

Finally, I ran upstairs and picked up the only remaining copy of the book—the flawlessly-typed original manuscript which I had prepared so lovingly. Calmer now, I stood and watched the fire for several minutes, the manuscript cradled in my arms. Then I thrust my arms forward, poised ready to toss it into the flames. But I couldn't do it—and my mad alter-ego had disappeared. Instinctively I knew what should have been apparent all along: Roles assigned by God cannot be cast off at will.

Feeling foolish, I crept upstairs and gently placed the manuscript back into the desk drawer. I would keep it as a souvenir of my heroic effort to serve God.

One thing puzzled me about my failure to interpret God's will: my success as a Sunday School teacher. I clearly heard his call for me to teach Sunday School and for over seven years I had been serving him happily in that way. Why had this one summons worked out so well—and the subsequent one, just as clear and convincing, failed so miserably?

I couldn't make any sense out of it, but that night I decided one thing: I would go on serving God as a Sunday School teacher, but I would stop even calling myself a writer. If God wanted a writer for some reason or other, he could get somebody else.

I closed up my desk and placed the cover on my typewriter. From now on, I would be a happy dilettante.

Chapter 11

But I Chose You

Problems were also developing at the church. Actually most of them were traceable, in one way or another, to the Reverend Matthew Pearce, our associate minister. The trouble with Reverend Pearce had been brewing for nearly two years—ever since he and his wife and family had arrived at the parsonage. We all liked Donna Pearce at once and she became a welcome, active member of the Christian Service Class. But Matt Pearce was a puzzle.

I had always thought that ministers were very special people called by God to do his work—and that all of them possessed all of the virtues. I had also felt that the church revolved around the minister—that he was, in fact, the church.

However, from the beginning Matt Pearce seemed to display none of these saintly qualities. He was a handsome, Greek-god of a man, standing over six feet tall with wavy blond hair, deep blue eyes, and teeth as perfect as matched pearls. The outside of him was practically perfect—but inside there seemed to be flaws. There were reports that his abrupt, disagreeable disposition often sent choir boys home in tears. When he visited patients in the hospital, he left them feeling worse than when he arrived. In fact, he didn't even want to visit the hospital and had to be prodded by the official board.

Since the church had two ministers, the younger one only preached one Sunday a month, except when the senior minister was ill or on vacation. Nobody could really analyze what was wrong with the sermons—on the third Sunday of every month they were the riddle of the day. For a time, I thought my difficulties in understanding Reverend Pearce might be merely a personal thing—one of those quirks of personality which finds two people continually at odds with each other. But soon I discovered that I was not alone in viewing the young associate minister with misgiving.

Regardless of the title of his sermon, Reverend Pearce launched into discussions or anecdotes seemingly unrelated either to the title or to each other—or to God. Besides that, he seemed to avoid the significant events or ideas of the day —or of any day, for that matter. During one of Matt Pearce's interminable ramblings, a teen-aged boy, an outstanding science student at the local high school, leaned over and asked a friend in a loud whisper, "What's that got to do with anything?"

The third-Sunday sermons were so uninspiring that before long there was a noticeable drop in attendance. And those who had determined to stick it out paid dearly for this decision. One rainy Sunday when the sermon was as dull as the skies, a five-year-old girl admonished in a loud voice, "Wake up, Daddy. You're sleeping!"

After several months, these performances had widespread manifestations. The congregation soon divided itself into factions. There was the anti-Pearce group which either stayed at home or attended services elsewhere. Then there was a group which agreed that the sermons were a disaster, but felt that no one has the right to criticize a minister for any reason. There were some who said that the morning worship service wasn't that important. (These brave words were usually spoken by someone who came to church only frequently.) And there were a handful who claimed that God must have had some purpose in sending him to us—although they frankly couldn't think of any.

I found myself in this last group, particularly when I discovered how Reverend Pearce's ministry was affecting our efforts to raise funds for the new building. With other members of the building committee, I had visited the homes of various church members, canvassing for funds. A number of people who had pledged to support the project had become remiss in their pledges and we decided to find out why.

One of the members I visited was an outspoken blue-collar type who didn't even invite me into his house.

"I'm not giving you a nickel of my hard-earned dough to build a new church as long as guys like Pearce are on the payroll. When my wife was in the hospital," he continued, "he came over, looked at her, and said, 'You don't look very sick to me.' I felt like busting him right in his pearly teeth!"

Another of the delinquent donors on my list was a retired school teacher, a sweet-faced, silver-haired little woman.

"They keep telling me that the morning worship service isn't that important," she said. "Well, I admit that we can grow spiritually through prayer, Bible reading, meditation, and so forth—but we don't need a new sanctuary for that! It seems to me that if we're going to spend $400,000 to build a new sanctuary, then we have to say that the quality of the morning worship service is important—that it is the most important hour of our church week."

I couldn't argue with this logic and made a mental note to discuss the importance of formal worship services with the Christian Service Class.

This "contributors' rebellion" was particularly disturbing in light of the fact that the building project itself was not going well. A shortage of materials and the tardy arrival of the laminated arches to support the roof had played havoc with the construction schedule. A strike of the local plumbers had delayed the construction even further, and to make matters worse, a workman fell off the scaffolding and broke both of his legs.

The building committee members also had a hassle over the color scheme for the sanctuary. After about three hours of "I like blue" or "I think red would be lovely," we finally chose a practical green tweed. I thought this was a good choice because it was the most prominent color in God's

111

outdoors. However, when the rug samples arrived, some of the committee members thought that the sample was not the pattern we had ordered. Another argument ensued.

The choir was also in an upheaval. The fact that a pipe organ was now assured should have raised the group's morale. However, the new organ only served to make the job of soprano soloist more of a prize, and practically the whole soprano section began vying for the honor. Jackie Willard finally took her husband—and their letters of transfer—and moved on to another church "where I'll be more appreciated," she said.

And it was no surpise to most members that the choir director, when he saw the final plans for a choir loft without a podium, took his talents elsewhere.

In the midst of the confusion, Reverend Marsden had a showdown with Reverend Pearce. Our class heard a firsthand report of this from Joy, who was working in the church library when the confrontation occurred. The ministers evidently met in the hall and Reverend Marsden asked Reverend Pearce how much time he had spent on the sermon he had preached the previous Sunday.

"It's none of your business!" Reverend Pearce had snapped. "The trouble with you," he continued, "is that you pay too much attention to what the people say. I don't intend to preach just to please them."

"You know, some of our people have stopped giving to the building fund because of you," Reverend Marsden stated.

"That's just an excuse—they don't want to give anyway," Matt Pearce sneered. "You're afraid that I'll rock the boat and you won't get that church built, aren't you?"

It was a poorly-kept secret that after that scene Reverend Marsden had gone to see the district superintendent concerning his associate's attitude. Many people of the congregation had asked Reverend Marsden why he turned the pulpit over to Matt Pearce on the third Sunday, since it was always such a disaster. Actually, the district superintendent had set down this rule for associate ministers, and Reverend Marsden was reluctant to violate it—even when his own judgment dictated otherwise.

"Well, I cried for several weeks—I'm not going to deny it. But we all come to a time when we have to stop crying and accept the reality of our situation. God never promised that we would always have everything just the way we wanted it. As it says in the fifteenth chapter of John, *You did not choose me, but I chose you* . . . .

"If I didn't believe that, I'd be bitter every time I saw a child skipping rope or climbing a tree."

Vicky was not a tall young woman, and her long brown hair gave her the look of a school girl. But as she spoke she was standing tall, like someone with a lot of responsibility who feels capable of handling it.

"Don and I both feel that we have to stop bemoaning our fate and do whatever we can for our child. We can't second-guess God and we've got to stop trying," she added thoughtfully.

On the way home I pondered that verse. *You did not choose me, but I chose you* . . . . I wondered if this was Reverend Pearce's whole problem. Donna had told us one time that he had never had a divine calling to be a minister; he had gone into it because his mother had urged him to do so.

This discovery had shattered my illusions about the ministry. Of all the people in the world, I expected a minister to seek the will of God for his life. It was indeed shocking to find a minister who claimed no such mandate—who had only an intellectual acknowledgment of God.

Evidently I had different standards for Reverend Pearce from those I had for myself. At the time, I didn't see that this verse applied to me at all; I didn't even consider that it might.

Chapter 12

Julie's Bible

My search for a workable faith always seemed to progress two steps forward, then one giant step backward. I had been so busy bemoaning the backward steps that I had not noticed the great breakthrough: Somewhere along the way I had really begun to believe in the Christian doctrine concerning eternal life. A dying stranger named Julie Cochran first made me aware of it.

Julie Cochran was thirty-five years old and, barring a miracle, would never see thirty-six. What had started as a small lump in her breast two years earlier had now become a monster, thrusting deadly tentacles in all directions, feeding upon the frail body, slowly destroying blood, bones, and tissue. After several periods of hospitalization, Julie had been sent home to await death. Her husband, Steve, a truck driver, seemed helpless and uncomfortable with the pitiful shell that had replaced his wife. He solved the problem by hiring a nurse to stay with Julie and signing on for extra runs to pay the cost. Julie was largely alone, except for the nurse, who seemed to remain professionally aloof.

Patty Bedford described Julie's plight to the Christian Service Class at our March business meeting.

"She's a neighbor of mine," Patty told us, "and she's never had any church affiliation at all—not since her childhood Sunday School days. But now she keeps talking about a Bible—about having one of her very own with her name on it. I thought maybe this class would see its way clear to buy her one."

"I've already got one!" exclaimed Martha, who suddenly jumped up and ran out into the hall. She reappeared shortly with a new Bible, still in its box.

"My cousin just sent this to me and I don't really need it. I've got one just like it—so we can give her this."

"I've got another idea," added Joy. "Let's each write down our favorite words of comfort for her."

I was famous for the small white file cards which I used in a dozen ways while teaching the class. I produced a brand new pack from my purse and distributed them to the girls. Each one wrote her favorite verses on a card, along with a little note, and then put it in the appropriate place in the Bible as a bookmark. On the fly-leaf Patty wrote: "Presented to Julie Whitehead Cochran, an honorary member of the Christian Service Class of Wesley United Methodist Church."

We were all very pleased with our efforts. Patty promised to have Julie's name stamped on the cover and to deliver our gift promptly.

Three weeks later it was Easter, with all of its hope and promises. Our new sanctuary was still months from completion, so we would have our Easter services in the old church. Three identical services had been scheduled to handle the overflow crowds.

The congregation sang "Jesus Christ Is Risen Today" as the processional. The choir, its membership enlarged, sang the anthem like a host of angels. Reverend Marsden spoke eloquently about the resurrection and its promise. But these activities were completely eclipsed by the Easter-lily cross on the altar.

The cross, which had become a tradition in that church, was about ten feet high and was comprised of potted Easter lilies resting on a wooden frame, stair-step fashion. The frame was designed so that the cross looked as though it were made solely of flowers.

Easter had never meant much to me—either as a religious holiday or a day to display new spring finery. But that cross of lilies was the most beautiful and most meaningful decoration I had ever seen. It was not merely an Easter decoration—it was Easter.

The lilies—nearly 100 of them—were purchased by members of the congregation in honor or in memory of someone dear to them. Randy and I had bought one in memory of our mothers. When the cross was dismantled after the last service, the donors were asked to pick up their lilies.

Several days later I decided to give my lily away. I felt it should go to someone for whom it would have a special meaning: Julie Cochran.

The nurse was slow to answer my knock. She admitted me into a bungalow that was tidy, not so much from care as from the fact that it was no longer lived in fully. She motioned me in the direction of Julie's room.

The stranger on the bed turned slightly toward the door as I entered. Her pale skin, hanging loosely over her bones, had a strangely transparent quality about it. The soft brown eyes, reflecting the pain of too many torturous needles and tubes, flickered like candles about to be snuffed out. Her thatch of bright hair—the color of new copper—cascaded over the pillow and seemed to be the only thing about her that was still alive.

"I'm Mary Jane Chambers," I began. "Here's an Easter lily from our church. Since you couldn't come to the church, I brought some of it to you," I announced with false cheerfulness.

I placed the lily on the night table next to the gift Bible. I was amazed to see something I had never noticed before. This one lily contained the essence of Easter, the promise of eternal life, just as surely as the cross of 100 lilies. I prayed that this dying woman on the bed would see it too.

"My Bible," the girl-woman pointed out, "that's my Bible —it has my name on it."

"Would you like me to read the messages?" I asked, explaining that I belonged to the class which sent it.

She nodded. "I know I don't have long. The Bible is helping me very much, and I understand the meaning of the lily—resurrection."

First I read the Lord's Prayer and the 23rd Psalm. Then

119

I found the card from Miriam Jackson: "Dear Julie, I have always liked these verses from John 14."

I will not leave you desolate; I will come to you. Yet a little while, and the world will see me no more, but you will see me; because I live, you will live also.

Martha Koontz, always practical and to the point, had written the familiar John 3:16, the Easter story in miniature.

For God so loved the world that he gave his only Son, that whoever believes in him should not perish but have eternal life.

Vicky Peterson had chosen Psalm 121.

I lift up my eyes to the hills. From whence does my help come?
My help comes from the Lord, who made heaven and earth.
He will not let your foot be moved, he who keeps you will not slumber.
Behold, he who keeps Israel will neither slumber nor sleep.
The Lord is your keeper; the Lord is your shade on your right hand.
The sun shall not smite you by day, nor the moon by night.
The Lord will keep you from all evil; he will keep your life.
The Lord will keep your going out and your coming in from this time forth and for evermore.

The pain-filled eyes were closed now, and the breathing showed signs of heavy sedation. I didn't know whether Julie could hear me or not, but I continued reading. My class—that wonderful assortment of personalities in various stages of Christian development—had, in effect, sent to Julie Cochran a crash course in faith. It could have been called a spiritual transfusion.

Joanna Neilsen had written: "Julie, dear. I hope these words will mean as much to you as they have to me."

Come to me, all who labor and are heavy laden, and I will give you rest.
Take my yoke upon you, and learn from me; for I am gentle and lowly in heart, and you will find rest for your souls.

—Matthew 11:28-29

"Dear Julie," wrote Donna Pearce, "I hope you will like these words of the Apostle Paul."

. . . the time of my departure has come. I have fought the good fight, I have finished the race, I have kept the faith.

—2 Timothy 4:6-7

As always, Joy Werner proved herself to be the most spiritually advanced member of the class—several steps ahead of the teacher, for that matter. She had chosen verses 38 and 39 from the 8th chapter of Paul's letter to the Romans.

For I am sure that neither death, nor life, nor angels, nor principalities, nor things present, nor things to come, nor powers, nor height, nor depth, nor anything else in all creation, will be able to separate us from the love of God in Christ Jesus our Lord.

Julie seemed to be sleeping peacefully, almost childlike now. I carefully returned the Bible to its place of honor on the night table and tiptoed out of the room.

On a gloomy day a week later, Julie Cochran, age thirty-five years, two months, and fourteen days, crossed the threshold that divides the living dead from the eternally living. Like any traveler beginning an important journey, she left early in the morning.

The nurse, who had been moved by Julie's situation more than she liked to admit, told Patty about Julie's last moments.

121

"She seemed to pause for a moment on the brink," the nurse said, "and then she nodded ever so slightly in the direction of her Bible. She repeated the words that had made the last days of her earthly life bearable, 'My name is written there.' Then she smiled for the first time in months —a radiant smile free of pain, hypodermic needles and catheters." We all felt there was no doubt about it: Julie Cochran had moved to a sunnier climate.

Julie's death raised some questions in my mind. Why had I regarded her passing so much differently than Hobe Crandall's? For one thing, I hadn't really known Julie and so was able to look at her death more objectively. For another, she had lingered long and had suffered much, so death was plainly a release from torture. Perhaps the long-expected death is easier to accept than the sudden one, like Hobe's.

The class raised other questions. We were studying a lesson about the laborers in the vineyard in Matthew 20. The parable uses the example of a householder who is trying to recruit workers for his vineyard. He hired some workers early in the morning. Then he went out again at the third, sixth, and ninth hours and recruited more helpers. He even hired others at the eleventh hour to come and work. At the end of the day, the householder paid all the workers the same.

The workers who had been toiling long, bearing the burden of the day and the scorching heat, were incensed over what they considered to be an injustice. However, it is doubtful that they were more indignant than the Christian Service Class.

"It's just not fair," complained Bernice with a scowl. "It's no wonder workers began organizing themselves into unions after that."

I tried to explain that this was not a question of economics—this was a parable where the householder was God and the workers were being rewarded with eternal life.

"The case of Julie Cochran was like that," volunteered Patty, leaning forward in her seat as though she herself had just made an exciting discovery.

"Julie had never sung in the choir," Patty continued. "She had never contributed her money. She had never served on a council or a committee—or worked in the church kitchen. . . ."

"Then what am I doing, knocking myself out in the kitchen?" interrupted Martha with a mischievous grin.

Patty was thrown off balance only momentarily. Then she glanced around the sanctuary and added dramatically: "In fact, Julie hadn't even been inside a church since she was a small child!"

"Why then are we so convinced that she found eternal life?" I asked.

Vicky waved her hand in the air like an eager sixth grader who knows the answer. "She believed!" said Vicky in a firm, confident voice. "Jesus promised that belief was the only requirement. We have only to believe!"

These words were barely out when Bernice half rose to her feet and exclaimed, "She sure seems to have found a short cut!"

Laughter engulfed the class for what seemed like a full minute.

"We can't look at it that way," said Joy, pointing to the Bible verses in the printed lesson leaflet. 'If you'll notice in verse fifteen, the householder answers the complaints by saying, 'Is it not lawful for me to do what I will with mine own?' I think the parable is trying to tell us that service in God's vineyard is rewarding and that the ones who began early in the morning were the lucky ones."

"Sweating and toiling because they were short-handed! Sounds great," complained Bernice, amid groans from several of the others.

Patty reentered the discussion. "If Julie had lived, she would have been expected to demonstrate her faith by serving God in some way. She would have wanted to. If you really believe, you voluntarily contribute your time and money."

"But why do we need a church at all—if believing and serving are all it takes?" Bernice persisted, reminding me of a bulldog hanging onto a bone.

I had none of the answers to these questions. But, as usual, some of my pupils were spiritual prodigies.

"Think about it for a minute," urged Patty. "We helped

123

Julie during the last month of her life because of our own convictions. Having spent all of her adult life outside the church, she was not prepared for death."

"That's true," Miriam Jackson affirmed. "When we wrote our verses of comfort for her, some of us were giving her the benefit of twenty years of Bible reading."

Vicky clasped her hands together as though she had just caught an idea. "Maybe in this one instance, at least, we were doing what Christians are supposed to do all the time —make their church into a redeeming fellowship."

"That's very well put," replied Joy. "The church is a fellowship of believers, and it is much easier to grow spiritually *within* the church than outside of it."

I had learned a great deal from my class through that lesson, but I didn't really realize how much until a few weeks later. Once more I was on a stretcher headed for surgery. It was one of those catastrophes that befalls the wary and unwary alike.

I had gone to the doctor merely for a checkup. I was feeling fine and had no symptoms to complain about. But he had discovered a tiny limp in my neck—barely perceptible to him and not noticeable at all to me. Subsequent tests had pointed to the strong possibility that my thyroid gland was full of tumors. There were many unasked questions and answers hovering around me that morning as Randy kissed me goodbye at the door of my hospital room.

Reverend Marsden pressed my hand reassuringly as I was being wheeled down the long hall. There wasn't time for him to pray with me as the Christian Science chaplain had done during that memorable surgery years before. As I neared the operating room, I recited the 23rd Psalm as I had done in my previous crisis. This time, I could say it all the way through.

Hours later, I awoke with tubes in my throat, tubes in my nose, tubes in my arm. And I was breathing with the help of a machine. However, before I had time to ponder the extent of my problems, my surgeon burst into the room waving a report.

"I've got good news, Mrs. Chambers—your tumors were *not* malignant. Everything is going to be fine!"

Then I realized that I hadn't even been worrying about

124

it! I had put myself in God's hands so completely that there seemed to be nothing to worry about. Whatever the outcome, I had nothing to fear.

The Christian Service Class had offerd a redeeming fellowship to a dying stranger. It had taken much longer, but they also had helped to enlighten their backward teacher.

I had chosen the verse for Julie's Bible with great care. Since I was the teacher, I wanted verses that sounded good —that would measure up to what was expected of me. I found them in the 14th chapter of John, verses 1 and 2.

> *Let not your hearts be troubled; believe in God, believe also in me. In my Father's house are many rooms; if it were not so, would I have told you that I go to prepare a place for you?*

I had come to believe this from the depths of my soul.

Chapter 13

The Harvest Is Plentiful

"The newspapers are full of the space program again." Lenore Brock's words came to me over the telephone.

She began calling me as soon as the new Apollo missions were scheduled.

"Why don't you send your book manuscript to one of the publishers on the list that I sent you?"

I started to tell her that I had given up writing, but she was so enthusiastic that I couldn't say the words.

"Well, I may send it in," I hedged, "as soon as I get the time."

I hoped she wasn't going to hold her breath because I had no plans for submitting my manuscript—or myself—to the possibility of criticism or rejection. The manuscript was tucked away in a drawer, safe from critical eyes. I intended to leave it there.

Two weeks later she called again. This time I was more than a little annoyed. As much as I liked and respected her, I was beginning to regard her as a pest. She was a retired editor—and I wondered why she didn't just retire into her bookstore instead of nagging me. She always seemed to call when I was in the midst of doing something else, and I couldn't convince her that the book was a lost cause.

Finally, one day she called just as I was on my way to a

building committee meeting to discuss dedication plans.

"Jane," she insisted, "I don't know why you keep putting it off. On the news this morning they announced that they're going forward with plans to land a man on the moon next summer. This will make your book very timely!"

I was about to say, "I've given it up, Miss Brock, so let's forget it," when she knocked down that argument.

"I know you were wounded when it was rejected after the Apollo fire, but that was only circumstantial. You can't just give up. It looks to me as though the time is right for it now."

"Well, all right, Miss Brock, I'll send it off."

"This afternoon?"

"I don't think I can do it this afternoon—but I will do it tomorrow."

The next day I bundled it up for mailing just to appease Miss Brock. I had known a great many beginning writers who had tried to get books published and had received no attention from the editors. I thought my manuscript probably would be buried under an avalanche of mail and it would be months before I heard from the publisher, if ever. They might even lose it, I mused—and then I would be rid of the problem permanently.

As the postal clerk piled the neatly-wrapped manuscript on a mail cart and wheeled it away, I said a silent prayer. "Dear God, I have said many prayers for this book. I wrote it because I thought you wanted me to—but maybe I was wrong. I know that if you want it published, some editor will race to the printers with it. I place it in your hands."

After I mailed it, I promptly forgot about it. This was probably just as well. I was no longer physically or emotionally capable of sitting on the edge of my chair awaiting the outcome of such a nebulous project.

The building committee decided that the new sanctuary should be dedicated in November, right before Thanksgiving. Somehow the problems that had seemed so insoluble just a few months back had worked out. Reverend Pearce was still with us and was still, I thought, as uninspiring as ever. His ineffectiveness in the pulpit, however, had served as a catalyst in the church. One group had been trying to organize a prayer group, and another had been trying to get a Bible-reading class started. Strangely enough, the need for these activities was not realized until we came away frustrated from Reverend Pearce's sermons. Reverend Marsden was such an inspiring preacher that most of the congregation had just listened to him and made no attempt to develop themselves spiritually. Reverend Pearce's shortcomings had spurred more people into action.

Some of the members did leave as they had threatened to do, and others still skipped church on the third Sunday. But new people came in to pledge support to the building fund, which had been set up in three phases of three years each. For three years before breaking ground we had collected money. We were now in the second year of the second phase and slightly ahead of schedule. Frank Finley and some of the other business executives had done a good job of planning and managing the money.

We acquired an organist-choir director who thought the new church was beautiful—even without a podium. He was not as talented as his predecessor, but neither was he as temperamental—so it balanced out.

The Sunday before Thanksgiving was clear with a bright sun and a brisk breeze. The new sanctuary was constructed of white brick and natural wood that, with the grass-green carpeting, gave it the atmosphere of a pleasant woodland dell. Gold, crown-shaped chandeliers added a touch of elegance befitting a king's house. Rays of sunshine beaming through the high, plain windows seemed to come directly from God. Behind the wide altar gleamed the golden pipes of the new organ, enhancing the green, white, gold, and brown color scheme. The effect was lovelier than any of us had dared hope.

The sanctuary was filled with members and guests long before the dedication service began. Frank Finley had arrived shortly after the sexton and spent the morning testing all of the light switches, thermostats, and parts of the loudspeaker system. With the air of a homeowner preparing for a housewarming party, he placed three doormats outside the front doors.

Joy Werner arrived early also and served as a guide to numerous visitors.

Just before the dedication was to begin, Martha completed the job of decorating the refreshment tables in the social hall. She had piled homemade cookies on trays and made quantities of punch. Most of the cookies were from her own kitchen because a great many women had been too busy to bake.

Martha and her husband found seats beside Gerry Bass, who was alone. Two weeks earlier Carl Bass had gone on a five-day drunken spree. This surpassed any of his previous escapades, and he resisted Gerry's efforts to bring him home. Since he refused to go to a doctor for help, Gerry sought medical advice for herself. The doctor said there was no use in giving her medicine to calm her nerves as long as Carl continued to upset her. He advised her to move into an apartment.

Reluctantly, she had followed the doctor's advice. Now sadness replaced the mischievous twinkle I had seen in her eyes when she was the huge mouse in our christmas play. All of her friends were praying that she could endure the separation long enough to bring Carl to admit he was an alcoholic.

Vicky Peterson and her husband caused a murmur when they arrived with Cindy strapped into a specially-designed infant seat. Both Vicky and Don Peterson had matured since the birth of their deformed child more than a year earlier. They had organized a parents' group for people with handicapped children. Don, who was an engineer, had also tried his skill at designing equipment for use by these special children. He told everybody that he was equipping Cindy for camping, a recreation both he and Vicky enjoyed.

I wondered if Allison would come to the service. This building was here, in large part, because of Hobe's insistence —for he, more than anyone else, had prodded it into being. If it had not been for Hobe, the project might still be on the drawing boards.

Some of the building committee members were seated together in a special pew, but I chose to sit with Randy and our sons. For the first time, I realized my decision to teach had made a profound difference in their lives, too. Mark was now a tall, thin boy of ten with missing front teeth, and

Craig was a chubby, curly-haired seven. Both had grown up in the church—the nursery, the library, the kitchen, the Sunday School class, the Scout troop, and the sanctuary itself—until they felt very much at home there. And after I started teaching, Randy attended the Men's Bible Class. He also had served frequently as its teacher, thus helping to dispel the idea that all scientists are atheists.

As we took our seats, I got a glimpse of Allison in the back row. She didn't seem to be looking in our direction and I turned my head to avoid meeting her eyes. However, our boys waved a greeting to Andrea and Hobie. In spite of everything I felt sorry for Allison, sitting in the back as though she didn't feel quite welcome—even though she had donated a pulpit Bible in memory of Hobe.

At the last moment Pete and Bernice Oglethorpe sat down beside us. Bernice's face was a bit kinder these days. She actually smiled as she leaned over and whispered, "It doesn't look nearly as much like a barn as I thought it would." She had been exhibiting pictures of her two almond-eyed granddaughters in recent weeks. But she had never given any indication that she had reconciled with her daughter.

The dedication service began with a processional, "Holy, Holy, Holy." First came the green-robed choir, walking in pairs. Then followed an assortment of at least twenty-five visiting churchmen in a variety of dress. There were several in black clerical robes and several more in monk-like garb. I decided the one wearing a white lace surplice over a black robe must be the Catholic priest who was to give the call to worship. Then came our bishop, accompanied by a dozen of his cabinet members. They wore black ceremonial robes with stoles of white satin, denoting the festive nature of the occasion.

Praise the Lord. I will give thanks to the Lord with my whole heart, in the company of the upright, in the congregation. Great are the works of the Lord, studied by all who have pleasure in them. Full of honor and majesty is his work, and his righteousness endures for ever.

131

The priest had begun the call to worship, using Psalm 111. As it turned out, he was not the fancily dressed one at all. The clergyman with the lace surplice was the Lutheran minister from the church around the corner.

Our bishop, wearing a heavy gold cross around his neck and looking for all the world like the pope, delivered the sermon. "We are dedicating this church to the glory of God because this is his house. . . ."

I don't remember much of what he said after that because the scene was speaking so eloquently for itself.

The ecumenical service conveyed the feeling that this church was a link to the past. In every generation the faithful have built sanctuaries in which to worship God. And the denominational differences seemed so superficial they had become almost negligible.

Our beautiful new church was also a link to the future. I turned my head and glanced at Allison. She was looking down at Hobie and Andrea with a faint smile. I wondered if she, too, could hear an echo of the words Hobe had spoken on the last day of his life.

"A new church is a witness to our faith, a legacy to future generations," Hobe had said.

Most importantly, perhaps, the new church was also a statement of faith in the present. It had taken money to build this sanctuary, but it had required much more than that: faith, hope, love, and prayer—along with the planning, designing, building, and decorating. A diverse, imperfect congregation of mere human beings had—for once in their lives—worked together with God. And the results were magnificent!

We concluded the service by singing "How Great Thou Art." I'm sure everyone saw God's house through eyes blurred with tears by the time the last verse was finished.

I've wondered since if I lingered in the pew to greet the other members of the building committee as they came down the aisle or to avoid meeting Allison Crandall.

About two weeks after the dedication service—when I least expected it—the letter came from the publisher, expressing an interest in my manuscript. Even after they sent me a check, I found the situation difficult to believe. In a year when nudity and profanity saturated books, plays, and movies, a publisher took a chance on a wholesome, family-type story—a first book—from an unknown author who didn't even have an agent. I had entitled my book *Don't Launch Him—He's Mine!* because it depicted Randy's participation in the early phases of training the astronauts. The editors had, indeed, raced to the printer with it so that its publication would coincide with Neil Armstrong's walk on the moon. The only explanation that made any sense to me was from Romans: *If God is for us, who is against us?*

The problem all along had been that I had failed to apply the parable of the householder to my own life. And, even though Vicky had spelled it out—*You did not choose me, but I chose you*—I had continued to try to mastermind God. I could have saved myself much grief if I hadn't taken it upon myself to work out a timetable.

Suddenly, I had it all—the life of a successful author. I appeared on television and radio. I had a box of fan mail from people all over the world. Stories about me appeared in at least a dozen newspapers. I appeared as guest speaker for numerous organizations. Admirers sent me flowers and gifts. It was clear to me now that God wanted me to be a writer, but it was still a puzzling assignment. Nevertheless, I played the role of celebrity to the hilt and enjoyed it immensely.

Feeling like a philanthropist, I contributed a tithe of the publisher's check to the church building fund. And I discovered that I was no longer bitter that God had not seen fit to let me donate the organ. It's not the amount of money a person contributes that is important. It's the relationship between the donor and God. The person who gives a tithe of his earnings—freely and joyfully—is richly blessed by his personal relationship to God. The man who had willed the $60,000 for the organ had missed the joy of giving it personally.

I don't know when this realization came to me. I first became aware of it during a lesson we had on the subject of achievements. When someone asked me what my greatest accomplishment had been, I forgot all about my role of celebrity and I also forgot that I had helped to build a church. My greatest accomplishment? I replied spontaneously—to my own surprise—"I have found God!"

For years I had pitied the faithful handful who do virtually all of the church work. Indeed, this tiny group toils short-handed in the heat of the day while the uninvolved majority sits glassy-eyed in the shade. But the Christian Service Class taught me more than I ever taught them. I know now that the Joy Werners, the Martha Koontzes, Vicky Petersons, and Frank Finleys of every congregation are toiling because they have met the Keeper of the vineyard and he has changed their lives.

My search for God took me half a lifetime. This may seem a high price to pay, but if I hadn't found a personal relationship with God, my entire life would have been meaningless. Although it was afternoon when I joined the workers in the vineyard, the harvest of fellowship and service is truly plentiful.

Chapter 14

Judge Not That You Be Not Judged

I became reacquainted with the Sermon on the Mount and with Allison Crandall the same week. We began the study of the Sermon on Sunday morning and I found it to be just as I had remembered: full of lofty, unattainable goals, interspersed with nebulous instructions. However, I didn't have to worry much about teaching it because Bernice Oglethorpe took over.

Bernice long had been the bane of my existence as a Sunday School teacher—the largest obstacle on my road to sainthood. Negativism was embedded in her personality like the pattern in inlaid linoleum. She had been offered many roles in the church and Sunday School. And she had refused them all (except class treasurer), preferring to point out flaws in the plans of those who assumed the responsibilities. If someone suggested participation in world missions, Bernice would respond that we ought to take care of our own first. But if someone suggested that we sponsor a girl at the Methodist Home, Bernice retorted that there are millions of Methodists: Therefore, these children are well taken care of. Suggest we help a local child and Bernice would point out that the family would be embarrassed to accept our help.

I often hoped that Bernice would not be so regular in attendance, but she was seldom absent. She was always on hand to correct my pronunciation of biblical names or to deflat the proponent of some worthy cause.

The Sermon on the Mount begins with the fifth chapter of Matthew. But Bernice didn't give us a chance to talk about chapters five and six. She launched into a discussion of Matthew seven, verse one: *Judge not that you be not judged.*

"I've had more trouble with that verse than with any of the others in the Bible," she told us. "I think I've told you about that neighbor of mine and how we finally made up after several years. Well, she had been cheating her employer for quite awhile and I felt it was wrong. I told her so and we had a big fight. I was so upset that I couldn't even go to Communion. Remember the part that says, 'ye who do truly and earnestly repent of your sins and are in love and charity with your neighbors'? Most people don't take that seriously—but I do.

"Finally, the company auditor caught up with her. She lost her job and I realized something I should have been able to see earlier: I am not her judge."

"It seems to me that you *had* to decide that cheating her employer was wrong," Joy interrupted. "You can't go around pretending that you approve."

"I know that," Bernice replied, "but I should have hated the sin without hating the sinner. I've always been too quick to judge."

Everybody knew that Bernice's last statement had more to do with her rebellious daughter than with her neighbor. But those who wanted more details were destined to be disappointed. She obviously had accepted her grandchildren —but she never told anyone whether it was she or Brenda who made the first move toward reconciliation.

The deep philosophical entanglement regarding hating the sin without hating the sinner kept the class occupied until well after the dismissal bell. I was still reminiscing about the discussion on Monday morning while I raced through the supermarket trying to find a few items I had forgotten during my weekly shopping trip. As I rushed around a pile of canned goods, I found myself facing Allison.

There was a moment of embarrassed silence and then, in

her inimitable way, Allison said, "I can see we're both well organized this morning."

We both laughed—our personalities blending as in earlier days. With her grocery cart piled high with fresh vegetables, she looked like an industrious homemaker.

"You're looking much happier," I said, carefully selecting a box of salt.

"Well, yes and no," she said. "Doug got a divorce out of state and he wants me to marry him. But I don't know. . . ."

I was surprised at her words.

"Isn't that what you wanted?"

"I thought so, yes." Her long hands rearranged the contents of her shopping cart. "Heather has volunteered to go to an institution if Doug and I will take care of their girls. But the problem is that we both want to get married in church, and neither his church nor mine will allow it."

"Have you checked?"

"Yes, we have," she said. "He's an Episcopalian and his rector said there was absolutely no chance. Reverend Marsden didn't flatly reject it—he's still thinking about it. He said he would go to the district superintendent about it if some prominent church leader supports us. Fat chance of that! I don't think the church actually has any hard and fast rules about it—the problem is that Reverend Marsden is reluctant to go ahead without the district superintendent's approval."

"Well, I hope it works out," I said and retreated to the check-out stand.

The Sermon on the Mount and my encounter with Allison kept merging together in my mind, and I wanted to go home and think. What was it that was bothering me?

I turned the whole question of Allison and Doug over and over in my mind, as I had done many times before. I had examined every aspect of it, and I was still convinced that it had been wrong for them even to begin seeing each other. Also I still felt that I, myself, would not have respected a man who could desert an invalid wife. But then Bernice's words echoed in my memory, as did Jesus' clear instruction: *Judge not that you be not judged.*

I was not Allison's judge—that was the privilege of God!

Then I remembered my prayers for Allison over the past six years: "Dear God, help her to be a good example to her children." In this day of "the new morality," some people would not have bothered to get married at all—but Allison wanted a church wedding. Maybe my prayers for her were being answered after all.

I had learned valuable lessons from Joy, Martha, and Vicky. But ironically enough, it was unlovable Bernice who had taught me the important difference between hating the sin and judging the sinner.

I ran to the phone and, with tears streaming down my face, I said the hardest words any of us has to say: "Allison, I'm sorry." Then I added, "May I come over? I need to talk to you!"

When she met me at the door a few minutes later, I was aware for the first time of the agonies she must have suffered. I had realized that widowhood would be a hard role for her—but the part of town pariah was even more difficult for fun-loving Allison, who had once basked in the community's affection and approval.

We looked into each other's eyes for a long moment—then both of us burst into tears. She was the first to reach out her arms.

"Allison, I'm sorry, I'm sorry," I kept repeating. Then I offered to go and talk to Reverend Marsden with her.

That good man was more than a little surprised when Allison and I came to his office together. It had been a difficult week for him—even before our arrival. The twins tried unsuccessfully to color their hair: Joanie had shown up at Sunday School with her hair the color of an overripe pumpkin, while Janet's had a sort of muddy carrot look. And gossip about the parsonage family had reached a new crescendo with the news that Meredith was going to the senior prom with a member of the college varsity wrestling team.

Allison Crandall and Doug Bryant had been the subject of gossip for so many years that Reverend Marsden had not dared agree to marry them. But now he seemed relieved at the prospect of having the leader of the eighty-member Christian Service Class supporting him in this matter. He smiled appreciatively when I told him I had recently discovered it was not weakness that made the modern church

138

bend and break some of its rules. Perhaps, I suggested, it was a sign of strength, the recognition that God is the judge.

"That's a good way of putting it," he said. "I intend to borrow your words when I talk to the district superintendent."

Apparently these were good words to borrow, for within a week Allison called to tell me that she and Doug would have a wedding in our church.

The following week, I found I had taken a position from which there was no retreat—I defended this position at every turn. I also helped Allison plan the wedding and the reception—and shop for her clothes. Evidently, I was the only friend who would stick her neck out quite that far.

Allison was nearly forty years old, but she was as shy as a young girl about becoming a bride. When we went into the various dress shops, I told the salesgirls what we wanted while Allison stood, dark eyes downcast, almost ready to blush.

After visiting at least five stores, she came out of a dressing room modeling *the* dress: a pale pink silk with lace sleeves and a gracefully-draped skirt. Like many tall girls, Allison still had a good figure. The pink dress not only fit well it also complemented her dark hair. After much discussion and consultation regarding a hat, we found a pink silk cloche with just a wisp of a veil. Her college roommate from New Jersey had agreed to be the matron of honor; we suggested that she wear a dress of lilac-colored silk and lace, if possible.

The wedding was scheduled for 11:30 a.m. on Saturday, August 22. It was to be held in the new chapel.

I picked up Andrea and Hobie at eleven o'clock that morning and drove them to the church where Randy and our boys were waiting. Andrea, now a young lady of twelve, was wearing a dress in the same shade as her mother's, with a corsage of pink carnations. Hobie wore a new navy blue blazer with white slacks and a white carnation boutonniere.

Across the aisle on the groom's side of the chapel, Doug's three daughters, each wearing a pink corsage, had taken their places. Their aunt, Doug's sister, had a hard job keeping them in their seats, and when their father, looking handsome and solemn, walked up to the altar, they nearly burst with excitement.

The organist had been playing background music on the chapel's small electronic organ, but now he struck the chords of the wedding march. Joanne Franklin, the matron of honor, entered at the side door and walked slowly up to the altar. She was followed by Allison, wearing the pink dress and carrying a bouquet of pink roses and purple orchids in her trembling hands. She did not have the innocent freshness of the twenty-year-old brides whose weddings we had so often catered, but she was lovely, nevertheless. She had a sweetness which had somehow emerged from suffering, like a full-blown rose that has survived the rain and the wind.

As she took her place at Doug's side, he gave her a glance filled with tenderness, the tenderness of one who has found a treasure after having almost given up the search.

It is customary for the wedding guests to remain in their places after the ceremony so that the relatives can go out and greet the couple first. It is doubtful that this has ever been accomplished more quickly. No sooner had Doug and Allison walked down the aisle than all five children literally ran after them. They greeted the other guests as a family, hugging and kissing everybody.

My feelings during the ceremony were ambivalent. I was glad that Allison was so happy and that Doug seemed to be so devoted and sincere. And the children appeared to be overjoyed at the prospect of belonging to a whole family again. Doug's girls kept calling Allison "Mother," and Andrea and Hobie squeezed Doug's hands as though they were never going to release him. But hanging over this happy scene was a shadow—a poor woman in a wheelchair, broken in body and spirit, unloved, and deserted.

Was it better to have one complete family—with a pitiful leftover—or to have two broken families with eight miserable members?

I was glad that God is the judge.

Chapter 15

Two Viewpoints

I would like to end this story here—and to say that we all lived happily ever after, basking in the warmth of Christian fellowship and enjoying our beautiful new building. However, I have told the turth thus far and I cannot bring myself to compromise now.

The truth is that the terrible events of a winter's night have forever shattered the "happily ever after" image and, for a time, even rocked the very foundations of our trust in a just and loving God.

During the period following the dedication of the new sanctuary, I noticed a subtle change coming over the leaders of the congregation, particularly the board of trustees and property committee. If they had been housewives with brand new homes, they would have been called "house-proud."

It is only fair to point out that these people held positions of responsibility. It was natural for them to want to preserve the building and its furnishings and to see it properly insured. Unfortunately, there is a fine line between being responsible and becoming proprietary.

That the property committee had crossed this line was apparent at one of the church board meetings. I was chairman of the commission on Christian social concerns and had enlisted the aid of about fifteen people who wanted to "feed the hungry, clothe the naked, comfort the dying, etc." in a personal, non-institutional way.

We had helped several families who had lost everything in fires that swept through their barracks-like homes. And we had spent a great deal of time collecting wearable children's clothing. So I had hit upon the idea of setting up a collection center for children's clothing. This plan would expedite our efforts, and we wouldn't have to solicit clothes each time they were needed.

The property committee, however, said there was no room anywhere in the new building for such a project—unless I could talk the choir out of some of their space. The choir said absolutely not. Joy Werner offered to pick up the clothing and store it in her attic, but no matter how many trips she made to the church there always seemed to be a box, brimming with coats or snowsuits, in the narthex.

At the memorable board meeting Johnson Gray, who was chairman of the property committee, complained.

"We have a nice-looking church here—except somebody's always dumping used clothes by the door. I would like to ask Mrs. Chambers and her committee if they would stop cluttering up our beautiful new building with junk."

"Mr. Chairman," I said, "we're trying to do what Jesus commanded when he said, 'Feed the hungry and clothe the naked.' We do the best we can to keep the clothing picked up, but donors bring it at all times of the week. I wish we had a place to store it here—and a cupboard to start an emergency food pantry as well."

"I've already told you we don't have the room for that," Mr. Gray snapped. "I think this mess is a serious matter. The bishop was very eager to see us build a new church. I would hate for the word to get back to him that it looks so sloppy."

I probably should not have said it, but I could not control myself.

"Who's head of this church—Jesus Christ or the bishop?" I shouted.

This was a shocking discussion to many of the board members, but in the end my commission and I were asked to move the clothing box out of the church. This, of course, put an end to the entire project.

At a later meeting, the commission on education faced similar opposition concerning the nursery school project. The school, utilizing the Sunday School rooms on weekday mornings, paid a nominal rent for the use of the building. The previous board had agreed that it would be a community service to mothers who were forced to go out and work. However, the property committee didn't agree.

"The nursery school is the biggest liability we've had around here in years," Johnson Gray announced.

"Don't they pay for their utilities?" someone asked.

"Well, yes, but they don't pay us for the wear and tear on the building and for the extra garbage pick-up."

"That Unitarian Church over on Century Road runs a day care center in their church—paying for it themselves," someone else pointed out.

"They're not even Christians," judged Gray, "so I don't see why we should compare ourselves with them. Besides, they don't have such an expensive building."

"Do you think it's right to have the building standing empty six and a half days a week?" I asked.

"It's better to leave it empty than to have seventy-five kids stomping through it," Gray answered.

A vote was taken and the nursery school project was upheld—by a slim majority. But a frightening picture came to my mind. We had dedicated that church building to the glory of God, but we were really using it to suit ourselves. We were like the caretakers of an estate who throw a party in the main ballroom when the owner is out of town.

As our attention focused more upon our expensive new building, our outreach into the community seemed to grow narrower and narrower. Strangely enough, this was not true of our missionary giving. Frank Finley had taken over the job as head of the commission on missions, and our participation in that field had increased each year. We had even received a special citation for giving more than our share. No, the problem was not in our pocketbooks. The problem was very localized—in the hearts of our congregation.

The property committee even questioned the use of the

143

building by a group of deaf mutes. In the course of working with handicapped children. Vicky Peterson had discovered that the deaf have specific problems. A group wanted to organize, and they needed a place to meet once a month to exchange information and to socialize. Vicky felt this would raise their morale greatly and she determined to help them find a meeting place—preferably in the church.

After going through layers of red tape, she finally brought the question of permission to that church board. She explained the situation, her voice trembling slightly.

"Are any of these people members of this church?" Johnson Gray asked.

"Well, no, I'm afraid not," Vicky said. "Most of them are not members of any church—they have a hard time fitting themselves into ordinary groups."

"Are they willing to pay for their utilities?"

"I don't think they're planning to charge dues and have a treasury. Would the utilities for a two-hour meeting once a month be all that much?"

"What about the wear and tear—and the noise?"

Vicky gave Gray a look of quiet disdain as she said, "I doubt that they're going to hurt the chairs—and they certainly aren't going to make any noise."

The board voted to allow the deaf group to use one of the small meeting rooms once a month—on a trial basis. The vote was a narrow one.

Another item of controversy at the board meeting was the young people's modern worship service.

"Is it true," asked Annalee Farrell, spokesman for the Women's Bible Class, "that they plan to have *guitars*—and *dancing*—right in the sanctuary?" Without even waiting for confirmation of these terrible evils, she continued, "What, may I ask, is wrong with the music in the Methodist hymnal—why can't they stick to that?"

The board members were divided down the middle on this issue—largely along the lines of age and background. Some people seemed to feel that there was something sacrilegious about those spirited songs the young people wanted to sing. Others raised the question of what was so sacred about the Methodist hymnal.

"After all, it's not the Bible," said one of the younger

144

board members. I thought Annalee Farrell was going to faint.

The board finally allowed the group to have its modern worship service early Sunday morning—and conveniently neglected to announce it in the church bulletin. Reverend Marsden, ever mindful of the district superintendent's watchful eye, could not bring himself to support such a service formally.

I dragged myself out of bed at what seemed like dawn in order to get a firsthand look at this modern worship service.

As we walked into the church, five or six young people were lounging in the choir loft. Two guitars with amplifiers reposed near the pulpit, with electrical wires crawling all over. The "Call to Worship," which they had written and mimeographed, had for its theme, "Let us worship God. He has called us to love one another."

They had also handed out mimeographed copies of the words to the songs: "He's not Heavy, He's My Brother," "Blowing in the Wind," and "He's Got the Whole World in His Hands." Most of the adults stumbled over the words, but it didn't matter because the amplified guitar music was so loud that nothing else could be heard anyway.

The climax of the service caused the adults to gasp. While "The Lord's Prayer" was played softly in the background, six young girls wearing green robes borrowed from the choir came dancing up the aisle. And, scandal of scandals, they were barefooted!

Worse yet, they danced right up to the altar—and even onto its hallowed green carpet.

By this time we adults were staring at this spectacle with a kind of fascinated disbelief. But as we watched, it became apparent that this dance was an act of worship. Moving as gracefully as butterflies, the dancers reached their hands toward the heavens—and then bowed deeply with their heads, their knees—their whole beings. I saw something else, too. In addition to this total reverence, there was joy —the joy of being young and alive in God's world. They were doing something we middle-aged types unfortunately have never done—they were *celebrating* the Presence of God.

It was so beautiful I cried.

Then, as if to offer conciliation to their elders, the young people concluded with "Holy, Holy, Holy" right out of the Methodist hymnal. They had the message—even though they didn't have the form. And they had done what was meaningful to them.

Not long after the church had "survived" the modern worship service, controversy raged again. The target was a project which, although it had nothing to do with the new church building, revealed our growing exclusiveness. Patty Medford and I had responded to a cry for help in a nearby pocket of poverty: The breadwinner of one family had disappeared on a drunken spree, leaving his dependents without food, fuel, or decent clothes.

Patty soon learned that the father of the family was a chronic alcoholic. Furthermore, the family was Catholic and had already received much help from their own church. Their church evidently had lost patience with them, so the mother had just started calling the churches in the yellow pages—until we responded.

Despite that information, we knew that a six-year-old boy and a three-year-old girl were living on bread and milk —and even that was running low. Patty and I hesitated only for a moment. Then we used money from the class treasury to buy basic food supples. We paid for having the heat turned on and bought a new pair of shoes for the little boy so that he could continue in school.

This did not even come under the heading of church business, but the word got around. For days the financial types kept bringing it up as an example of the foolish generosity of the church's do-gooders. It was hard to know which they considered to be worse—the fact the family was Catholic— or that they were related to an alcoholic.

A month later the church board revealed how far apart the property group and the Christian social concerns group had grown. Johnson Gray presented a lengthy report outlining the need for better church housekeeping and the need to "protect our investment." His proposal included firing old Gilbert "Pops" Carter and hiring services of a professional housekeeping firm.

It was true the Gilbert Carter was growing old and was not very good at seeing the dirt in the corners anymore. But he enjoyed his work and was very faithful about setting up chairs and preparing the rooms for special events.

"Don't you think we would be unkind to Pops if we let him go—just like that?" Frank Finley asked.

"It's nothing personal," Gray replied. "It's a practical matter and this is a practical world. All Mr. Carter does these days is to push that electric floor polisher around. He likes that job, so he pushes it all day long. But he seldom cleans the bathrooms and he ignores cobwebs, too." Gray seemed pleased with his analysis.

"The housekeeping service would cost a little more than what we pay the sexton, but they would guarantee that the building would always be thoroughly clean. As many of you know, a place which is allowed to get dirty depreciates faster."

Once again the board grouped itself along philosophical lines. The financial group made a very convincing case for preserving property. On the other hand, the greatly-outnumbered opposition asked highly impractical questions about comparing a few cobwebs to a man's self-esteem.

In addition to the professional housecleaning crew, a part-time sexton would be needed to set up chairs and tables, lock up after meetings, etc.—one fact that "Mr. Efficient Planner" forgot to consider in his original estimate.

Each week the worship committee purchased a huge bouquet of fresh flowers from the florist, supplementing the potted palms that were permanent decorations. The oversized chandeliers were beautiful, but they boosted the electric bill tremendously. All of this brought the cost of building maintenance to well over $250 a week. I felt very uncomfortable about these expenditures, and I said as much. However, I was very mild and polite about it and few of the others supported my objections.

"You 'social concerns types' forget that we have to preserve our investment," Johnson Gray chided. So, not wishing to be the one who always opposed everything, I dropped the argument. The housekeeping service was approved, and a younger man was hired as part-time sexton.

I don't want to whitewash myself and imply that I felt I was the only Christian in the room. Actually, I loved that church building as much as anyone and was very proud to have been a part of the committee that initiated its construction. However, I felt then—as I do now—that putting so much into building maintenance is unacceptable from the standpoint of Christian stewardship. I will always regret that I was too cowardly to defend this point of view at the meeting.

As I look back, I can see that these attitudes were symptomatic of deeper problems. I had almost excluded Allison from our fellowship—indeed, I had done so for several years—on the grounds that she was an overt sinner. Then the board had voted down our clothing collection drive, and many had shown disapproval of our other projects. I was beginning to wonder what kind of church we would have if we excluded the overt sinners, the poor, the nursery school children who leave fingermarks, the young people with their guitars and tambourines, those of other denominations, the handicapped, and the elderly.

I said as much to Rachel Anderson, who belonged to the Christian Service Class and was also newly-appointed to the board of trustees.

"It all depends upon which side you're on," she told me. "When you find yourself responsible for such an expensive piece of property, you feel like locking it up and keeping everybody out."

This attitude was discouraging to me. I had been a Sunday School teacher of adults for ten years and had tried to set forth Bible-based ideas of what a church should do—and be. But the finance and property committees were leading the congregation in a different direction—and their philosophy seemed to prevail.

Chapter 16

You, Therefore, Must Be Perfect

We were just finishing dinner on an evening in early December when Allison rushed into the house.

"Jane, Jane!" she shouted. "The church is on fire!"

"You can't be serious!" I cried, but she was very serious, indeed. Our whole family threw on coats, dashed out the front door, and piled into Allison's car. We saw clouds of smoke while we were still several blocks away from the church.

As we joined the rapidly-growing crowd at the edge of the church parking lot, we learned what had happened. Frank Finley, passing the church on his way home from a nearby shopping center, had seen a wisp of smoke coming from the new sanctuary. Knowing that the church was empty, he turned in a fire alarm immediately. The town fire department responded in less than two minutes.

The church was practically all brick. The fire department, located only two blocks away, was one of the finest in the state. The fire was discovered early and the firemen responded promptly. We thought, along with most of the spectators, that the fire would soon be extinguished.

Instead, alarm after alarm went out to other fire companies in the area. But as the force of fire fighters expanded,

149

the fire grew also. Finally, 100 fire fighters fought the blaze, but flames shoot 200 feet into the sky.

Valiant men, with fine equipment, fought fiercely all through the night, while the crowd of half-frozen spectators watched in stunned silence. When morning came, a few mounds of scorched bricks marked the site where the stucture had stood. The magnificent church, so lovingly planned, so painstakingly built—and so conscientiously maintained—had disappeared before the very eyes of many of its leaders. The beautiful new sanctuary with its pipe organ, hand-embroidered altar cloths, new pulpit Bible, silver service, new hymnals, and countless other items—even the lovely little chapel—had disappeared as suddenly and as completely as a house made of ice deposited on a desert. We had built it for posterity—and it had lasted a little more than four years.

By the time we reach our fouth decade of life, most of us have sampled a variety of tragedies, failures, and disappointments. We have learned that we are all transients on this earth—mortals whose lives are fragile and fleeting. But until that horror-struck night, I had not considered that buildings are also temporal. I never once imagined that our beautiful new sanctuary, so sturdily constructed and solid under foot, could disappear between darkness and dawn. It was one of the most profound shocks of my life.

I do not wish to imply that the fire was God's judgment upon that church. No congregation has ever been more sincere about building "to the glory of God." In spite of its proprietary attitude regarding the new church, our congregation, I am certain, had as much concern and compassion for our fellow man as most suburban churches. Indeed, the good works of the Christian Service Class alone would put many larger congregations to shame. If God burned down all of the churches that disappoint him, the fire engines of the world would respond, bumper to bumper, to one gigantic fire alarm.

But those of us whose names were inscribed in the cornerstone of that church have learned many universal lessons from the tragedy. Most important of all we have learned —oh, how thoroughly we have learned!—that the church is not the building.

The real church is a community of believers worshiping God in spirit and in truth. This was graphically demonstrated to that burned-out congregation as they conducted worship services in a nearby junior high school auditorium two days after the fire.

There was nothing the least bit church-like about the meeting place: Like all schools, it had the smell of glue, vegetable soup, and sweaty gym clothes. But Reverend Tom Cooper stood on the stage and gave the call to worship in a firm, confident voice: *Praise the Lord. Praise God in his sanctuary; praise him in his mighty firmament!*

His voice wavered a little, however, as he read the scripture lesson, Romans 8:28, from the Living Bible: *And we know that all that happens to us is working for our good if we love God and are fitting into his plans.*

Reverend Cooper had become our minister three years earlier when Reverend Marsden had been assigned to a large church in Allentown. The Marsdens hated to leave Jonestown, but accepted the move as the lot of a minister's family. They were also happy that Reverend Marsden had received a promotion. In his own good time, the district superintendent had also reassigned Reverend Pearce—to a small church in the coal country.

No associate minister had been appointed to serve with Reverend Cooper; instead, several lay workers had been added to the staff. This arrangement seemed to be working out well, and Reverend Cooper had become an effective leader. In fact, there were tears in his eyes as he stood on the stage in the school auditorium. He felt the loss of the sanctuary almost as deeply as those who had actually built it.

Slowly that heartbroken congregation began to see that many good feelings and new understandings were a result of the tragedy. For one thing, the congregation that morning was swelled by members who had been alienated for some reason and had suddenly realized the pettiness of their grievances. There were also the apathetic who had never known how much attending church had meant until the opportunity was lost.

Using some borrowed Baptist hymnals, we sang old fa-

151

miliar songs such as "Jesus Loves Me" and "Blest Be the Tie That Binds." The words were reassuring.

We also rediscovered ties with other denominations. That morning at least a dozen nearby congregations—most of which had sent representatives to the dedication service—sent contributions. The practical Presbyterians sent two collection plates—along with their offering. But the nearby Catholic church outdid all of the others: They took up offerings at early masses and presented a check for $1,000 at our eleven o'clock service.

Still another bridge of understanding was built. Members of the youth groups announced that they were planning some fund-raising projects.

Even those who thought they would never recover came away from that service full of love, peace, and hope.

Within a month, the congregation was worshiping in its hastily refurbished old sanctuary, and plans were under way for rebuilding. Because of the pragmatism of men like Johnson Gray, the building had been adequately insured. But when it is restored, things will never be the same. The perspective of this congregation has been changed forever.

My own perspective has altered too. I love all kinds of church buildings—from small white New England boxes to massive, gold-encrusted cathedrals. I love processionals, formal worship services, sixty-voice choirs, pipe organs, and all the rest of it. But I have learned that we should not dedicate a church to the glory of God, plaster it with crosses, and then go ahead and do as we please.

Many of today's traditional churches appear to be staid, over-organized, impersonal, ritualistic, and uninspired. Young people by the thousands—and others not so young—defect because they sought in vain for that loving, inclusive, redeeming fellowship which the church should be.

Nobody has given me a license to preach, and I doubt that anyone ever will. However, by this time I am a battle-scarred veteran of practically every aspect of lay participation in the church. I have done some very serious contemplation about its future. It seems to me that the answer for congregations is the same as for individuals: To find what is the "good, acceptable, and perfect will of God" for their lives. God must be restored to his rightful position as head of the church. He ought to be the acknowledged head of every church board, council, committee, and commission, right up to and including the bishop's cabinet.

At the risk of sounding dogmatic, I would like to point out that any congregation daring to make God the head of all matters might find the following conditions:

No longer would we have board meetings where two hours are spent discussing the use of the kitchen while the precious souls who have dropped out of Sunday School are ignored completely.

Less attention would be paid to the wall-to-wall carpeting and more to the walking-wounded in the pews. This doesn't mean the building should not be attractive and well maintained. The philosophy of the property committee should be like that of those floor wax commercials which welcome all manner of traffic.

All boards would pray more and talk less.

Meetings would be vital and challenging, not dull, routine sessions held because it happens to be the second Tuesday, the fourth Thursday, or whatever.

No longer would there be church groups meeting for the primary purpose of eating. I'm not against eating or against group fellowship at dinner. I'm talking about the people I have seen who are more interested in the menu than in the person seated next to them—groups in which people talk during the devotions and leave before the program begins. There actually are groups—of both men and women— afraid to dispense with refreshments for fear nobody will come!

All groups would welcome visitors and new members without being prodded. The congregation would be an inclusive fellowship—not a country club or an overage fraternity.

Attendance at Sunday School and church would swell and there would be more volunteers than jobs. And no one would accept a job without trying to perform it.

Money would be no problem. The believers would "give as unto the Lord," which ought to mean that they would contribute at least as much as they spend on recreation.

Christian social concerns projects would not be artificial, forced efforts, handed down from a distant board. They would be spontaneous, heart-to-heart good works in which money would be raised and spent locally.

There would be celebrations as well as solemn rites.

Any minister of Reverend Pearce's type, who might discover he was in the wrong profession, would find something else to do, instead of hanging around for the retirement benefits. And a congregation with a truly ineffective minister would try to love him and forgive his shortcomings. They would also love the parsonage family and refain from petty criticism.

The minister would not bow down to the district superintendent. In turn, the district superintendent would not cater to the bishop, and the bishop would not surrender to pressure groups. Each, then, would be responsive to the needs of the people and responsible only to God.

Jesus said that those who love only their friends are not outstanding. The same could very well be said of the church. If the hierarchy seeks primarily to serve and perpetuate itself, what good is that? The heathen do as much.

Finding God's will for your life is not a one-time, sometime commitment. It must be a developing, growing, renewable covenant, as expressed in Matthew 5:48: *You, therefore, must be perfect, as your heavenly Father is perfect.*

I used to think this verse was only another example of the impossible standards set up in the Sermon on the Mount. If there is anything more impossible than loving your enemies and turning the other cheek, it is for a human being to be flawless.

However, a more apt definition of the word "perfect" is not "flawless," but "accomplished in knowledge or performance; expert, proficient." So a commitment of God involves learning and growing in faith and service until we become proficient. The person who volunteers to teach a Sunday School class, for example, and then teaches it the same way for twenty-five years, has not grown in the job.

A friend of mine bought a new stereo record player and committed herself to learn appreciation for classical music. I bought her a symphony album I thought she would like. It was a great success—she liked it so much she went out and bought three identical albums to have on hand in case the first record became worn. Instead of learning to appre-

154

ciate classical music, she committed herself to playing one composition over and over.

Many of us are like that with our commitment to God.

A developing, maturing, lifelong commitment to God takes each of us along a different pathway—none of them easy. For "Miss Know-It-All," the road has been a jungle path, overgrown with doubt and rebellion, through which I hacked my way. I have been sick and tired and lost. I have tripped and fallen on my face. I have shivered—and sweated —with fear. My heart has been broken, my will bridled, my spirit battered and bruised. What's more, I am still growing and I have no doubt that there are many more bruises in store for me.

But all this has validated my statement of faith: I know that my Redeemer lives! I know that he is the omniscient, ever-present, eternal, almighty God, and that he demands obedience from those who would serve him. I have learned that nothing less than the simple trust of a child holding his father's hand and following without question will be acceptable to him.

I know now that I will never be a choir soloist. Indeed, my voice is even weaker since my throat surgery. Nor will I ever play the organ. But these things no longer matter to me. God's plans are much better than mine. He has given me the honor—the great honor—of presenting this true story, which is written so that you, too, may believe—and serve.

Warm and Down-to-Earth...

That describes perfectly both the personality and the writings of

Dale Evans Rogers

Americans came to know and love her as the wife of Roy Rogers and a star in her own right. But there's another side: her trials and tribulations as a mother and foster mother, and her jubilation as a witnessing Christian.

Share her joys and sorrows in these wonderful books brimming with radiant faith and love:

_____ANGEL UNAWARE 95¢ paper

_____DEAREST DEBBIE 95¢ paper

_____TIME OUT, LADIES! 95¢ paper

_____THE WOMAN AT THE WELL 95¢ paper

And books *about* Dale:

_____THE ANSWER IS GOD *Davis* $1.25 paper

_____TWO STARS FOR GOD *Petersen* $1.25 paper

ORDER FROM YOUR BOOKSTORE

If your bookstore does not stock these books, order from

SPIRE BOOKS

Box 150, Old Tappan, New Jersey 07675

Please send me the books I've checked above. Enclosed is my payment plus 25¢ mailing charge on first book ordered, 10¢ each additional book.

NAME_____

STREET_____

CITY_____ STATE_____ ZIP_____

_____Amount enclosed. _____Cash. _____Check. _____Money order. (No c.o.d.'s)

S-11

If you yearn
for wholesome reading enjoyment
with a *"happy ever after"* ending...

you won't want to miss any of these tried and true favorites:

by Grace Livingston Hill:
___Crimson Roses 95¢

___Happiness Hill 75¢

___Maris 95¢

___Matched Pearls 75¢

___Partners 95¢

___The Patch of Blue 75¢

___Patricia 95¢

___The Strange Proposal 75¢

___Stranger Within the Gates 95¢

___White Orchids 75¢

by Eugenia Price:
___The Beloved Invader 95¢

___Lighthouse $1.25

___New Moon Rising 95¢

by Thyra Ferré Bjorn:
___Papa's Daughter 95¢

___Papa's Wife 95¢

by Marjorie Holmes:
___Two from Galilee $1.50

Order From Your Bookstore

If your bookstore does not stock these books, order from
SPIRE BOOKS
Box 150, Old Tappan, New Jersey 07675

Please send me the books I've checked above. Enclosed is my payment plus 25¢ mailing charge on the first book ordered, 10¢ each additional book.

Name _____

Street _____

City _____ State _____ Zip _____

___Amount enclosed. ___Cash. ___Check. ___Money order. (No c.o.d.'s)

S-16

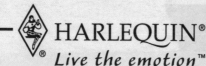

Harlequin® Historical
Historical Romantic Adventure!

Imagine a time of chivalrous knights and unconventional ladies, roguish rakes and impetuous heiresses, rugged cowboys and spirited frontierswomen— these rich and vivid tales will capture your imagination!

Harlequin Historical . . . they're too good to miss!

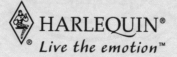

HARLEQUIN®
INTRIGUE®

BREATHTAKING ROMANTIC SUSPENSE

Shared dangers and passions lead to electrifying romance and heart-stopping suspense!

Every month, you'll meet six new heroes who are guaranteed to make your spine tingle and your pulse pound. With them you'll enter into the exciting world of Harlequin Intrigue— where your life is on the line and so is your heart!

THAT'S INTRIGUE— ROMANTIC SUSPENSE AT ITS BEST!

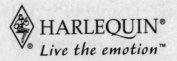

HARLEQUIN®
Live the emotion™

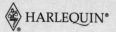

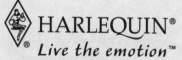

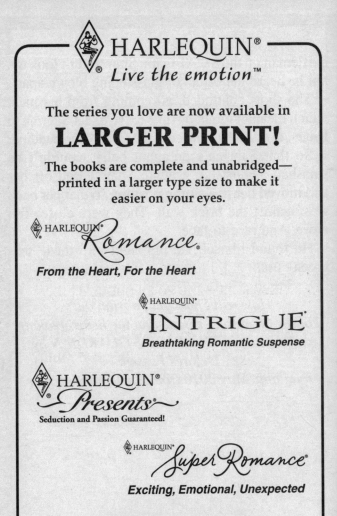

"Why will you never marry?"

"What?"

She'd surprised him with that question. He leaned over, his face close enough to hers she felt the warmth of his breath. She could barely see his eyes in the dark. "As I said, you saw my scars this morning. What woman would ever want to marry me?" he asked very softly.

Ella closed her eyes, blocking out the brilliant blanket of stars in the sky and kissed him sweetly.

Time lost all meaning. For endless minutes Ella was wrapped in sensation. She could have halted time and lived forever in this one moment. It was exquisite.

JEWELS of the DESERT

Deserts, diamonds and destiny!

In the Kingdom of Quishari, two rulers with hearts
as hard as the rugged landscape they reign over
are in need of desert queens....

When they offer convenient proposals,
will they discover doing your duty
doesn't have to mean ignoring your heart?

*Find out
in Barbara McMahon's fabulous duet!*

BARBARA McMAHON

Marrying the Scarred Sheikh

JEWELS *of the* **DESERT**

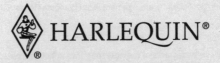

HARLEQUIN®

TORONTO • NEW YORK • LONDON
AMSTERDAM • PARIS • SYDNEY • HAMBURG
STOCKHOLM • ATHENS • TOKYO • MILAN • MADRID
PRAGUE • WARSAW • BUDAPEST • AUCKLAND

Recycling programs
for this product may
not exist in your area.

ISBN-13: 978-0-373-74020-8

MARRYING THE SCARRED SHEIKH

First North American Publication 2010

Copyright © 2010 by Barbara McMahon

Barbara McMahon was born and raised in the southern United States, but settled in California after spending a year flying around the world for an international airline. After settling down to raise a family and work for a computer firm, she began writing when her children started school. Now, feeling fortunate in being able to realize the long-held dream of quitting her "day job" and writing full-time, she and her husband have moved to the Sierra Nevada mountains of California, where she finds her desire to write is stronger than ever. With the beauty of the mountains visible from her windows, and the pace of life slower than that of the hectic San Francisco Bay Area where they previously resided, she finds more time than ever to think up stories and characters and share them with others through writing. Barbara loves to hear from readers. You can reach her at P.O. Box 977, Pioneer, CA 95666-0977, U.S.A. Readers can also contact Barbara at her Web site, www.barbaramcmahon.com.

To Kelly-Anne, Jeff, Justin, Dylan and Bridgette:
Family is always best. Love from me.

Dear Reader,

Twins as adults are different from twins as kids. Switching places and fooling people are undoubtedly fun as children. However, as they mature, childish antics are put away. Still—from time to time they are undoubtedly misidentified.

In Khalid's story, he is unlikely to be mistaken for his brother, due to a scar obtained when fighting oil fires. His choice of career is unlike his brother's as well. He likes to be in the desert working in actual oil fields, vetting equipment and drilling procedures—or putting out dangerous conflagrations that most men never even consider facing.

It was one such fire that damaged his face and led him to believe no one would ever want to be close to him. So when he meets a stranger at the beach after midnight, he's struck with the novelty of being accepted solely for what he says, not for how he looks.

If you had loved and lost the one man you thought was for you, would you search for another? Or even be open to the possibility if one showed up unexpectedly? Ella considers any thought of marriage pointless. She'd already loved a wonderful man, and after his death planned her future alone. Running into a stranger on the beach was exciting— as long as they kept their meetings brief.

It's when they come face to face in the harsh light of day each realizes things are going to change in a big way. Two brothers—twins to boot—find love and happy futures in totally unexpected ways.

All the best,

Barbara

CHAPTER ONE

ELLA PONTI walked along the shore. The night was dark. The only illumination came from the stars overhead. No moon tonight. The wavelets gurgled as they spent themselves on the sand. Alexander had loved walking in the dark and she felt a closer tie than any other time.

He'd been dead for over a year. The crushing pain of his death had eased, as others had told her it would. Only a lingering ache where her heart was reminded her constantly that she would never see him again.

Sighing, she looked to the sky. The stars sparkled and shimmered through the heat of the night. Turning slowly, she looked at the black expanse that was the Persian Gulf. Nothing was visible. Some nights she saw ships sailing silently through the night, their lights gliding slowly across the horizon. Nothing there tonight. Turning toward home, she began walking, splashing lightly through the warm water at land's edge.

What a contrast this land was, she mused as she

enjoyed the silence. Here at the seashore it was as beautiful as any Mediterranean resort; lush plants grew in abundance. She loved the leafy palms, the broad-leaf ferns and the flowers were nothing short of breath-taking. Each house around the estate she lived on seemed to flourish with a horticulturist's delight.

She enjoyed sitting out in the afternoons in the shady nooks of the garden, smelling the blend of fragrances that perfumed the air. While only a short distance from the capital city of Alkaahdar, it felt like worlds away from the soaring skyscrapers of the modern city.

She would go to bed when she reached her place. It was already after midnight. She liked to work late, as she had tonight, then wind down by a walk on the deserted beach—alone with only the sand, sky and sea.

With few homes along this stretch of beach, only those who knew the place well knew where to turn away from the water to follow winding paths through lush foliage that led home. Ella knew exactly where to turn even in the dark.

From a distance, as she walked along, she saw a silhouette of another person. A man, standing at the edge of the water. He was almost in front of where her path opened to the beach. In all the months she'd lived here, she'd never seen another soul after dark.

Slowing her pace, she tried to figure out who he might be. Another person who had trouble sleeping

through the night? A stranger exploring the beach? Or someone intent on nefarious activities?

Ella almost laughed at her imagination. The homes along this stretch of beach belonged to the fabulously wealthy of Quishari. There were guards and patrols and all sorts of deterrents to crime. Which was why she always felt safe enough to walk alone after dark. Had that changed? She had only nodding acquaintances with her neighbors. Ella kept to herself. Still, one of the servants at the main house would have told her if there were danger.

She could cut diagonally from where she was to where the path left the beach, avoid the stranger entirely. But her curiosity rose. She continued along splashing in the water. The flowing skirt she wore that hit her midcalf was already wet along the hem. The light material moved with the slight breeze, shifting and swaying as she walked.

"Is it safe for a woman to walk alone at night?" the man asked when she was close enough to hear his voice.

"Unless you mean me harm, it is," she replied. Resolutely, she continued walking toward him.

"I mean no harm to you or anyone. Just curious. Live around here?" he asked.

As she walked closer, she estimated his height to be several inches over six feet. Taller than Alexander had been. The darkness made it impossible to see any features; even his eyes were hidden as he

tilted his head down to look at her. No glimmer of light reflected from them. The traditional white robes he wore were highlighted by the starlight, but beyond that, he was a man of shadow.

"I live nearby," she replied. "But you do not. I don't know you."

"No. I'm here on a visit. I think." He looked back out to sea. "Quite a contrast from where I've been for the last few weeks."

She turned to look at the sea, keeping a safe twelve feet or so of space between them.

"Rough waters?"

"Desert. I wanted to see the sea as soon as I got here. I've been traveling for almost twenty-four hours straight, am dead tired, but wanted to feel the cool breeze. I considered going for a swim."

"Not the safest thing to do alone, especially after dark. If you got into trouble, who would see or hear?" Though Ella had gone swimming alone after dark. That had been back shortly after Alexander's death when she hadn't thought she cared if something happened or not. Now she knew life was so precious she would not wish harm on herself or anyone.

"You're here," he said whimsically.

"So I am. And if you run into trouble, do you think I could rescue you?"

"Or at least go for help." With that, he shed the robe, kicked off the shoes he wore.

Startled, Ella watched. Was he stripping down to nothing to go for a swim?

It was too dark to know, but in a moment, he plunged into the cool waters of the Gulf and began swimming. She had trouble following him with her eyes; only the sounds of his powerful arms cleaving the water could be heard.

"So I'm the designated life guard," she murmured, sitting down on the sand. It was still warm from the afternoon sun. Sugar-white and fine, at night it nurtured by its warmth, soft to touch. She picked up a fistful letting it run between her fingers. Idly she watched where she knew him to be. She hoped he would enjoy his swim and not need any help from anyone. She hadn't a clue who he was. For tonight, it was enough he had not had to swim alone. Tomorrow, maybe she'd meet him or maybe not.

Ella lost track of time, staring out to sea. So he came from the desert. She had ventured into the vast expanse that made up more of Quishari than any other topography. Its beauty was haunting. A harsh land, unforgiving in many instances, but also hiding delights, like small flowers that bloomed for such a short time after a rare rainstorm. Or the undulating ground a mixture of dirt and sand that reminded her of water. The colors were muted, until lit by the spectacular sunsets that favored the land. Once she'd seen an oasis, lost and lonely in the vast expanse of

the desert. But her fervent imagination found it magical. Water in the midst of such arid harshness.

She wished she could capture that in her own work. Show the world there was more to the desert than endless acres of nothing. She began considering plans for such a collection. Maybe she'd try it after finishing her current project. Tomorrow was the day she tried the new technique. She had the shape in mind of the bowl she wanted to make. Now she had to see if she could pull it off. Colors would be tricky, but she wanted them to swirl in glass, ethereal, hinting and tantalizing.

She felt relaxed as the moment ticked by. It was pleasant in the warmth of the night, with the soft sound of the sea at her feet and the splashing in the distance. Would the man ever get tired?

Finally she heard him approach. Then he seemed to rise up out of the water when he stood in the gradual slope. She rose and stepped back as he went directly to where his robes lay and scooped them up.

"You still here?" he asked.

"As designated life guard. Enjoy your swim?"

"Yes, life giving after the heat of the desert." He dried himself with the robes, then shrugged into them.

She turned. "Good night."

"Thanks for keeping watch."

"I don't know that I would have been any help had you gotten into trouble," she said, turning and half walking backward to continue along the shore.

"Shall I walk you home? It would be easy enough for me to do." He stood where he was, not threatening.

"No." She did draw the line there. She knew nothing about the man. It was one thing to run into a stranger on the beach, something else again to let him know where she lived—alone.

"I might be here tomorrow," he said.

"I might be, as well," she replied, then quickly walked away. She went farther down the beach and then cut into a neighbor's yard. She didn't want to telegraph her location. Hopefully he couldn't see enough in the darkness to know which path she'd taken. She walked softly on the edge of the neighbor's estate and soon reached the edge of the property she rented. Seconds later she was home.

Khalid watched until he could no longer see her. He had no idea who the woman was or why she was out after midnight on a deserted beach. He was dripping. Taking a last look at the sea, or the dark void where it was, with only a glimmer of reflected starlight here and there, he turned and went back to the house his grandmother had left him last summer. Her death had hit him hard. She'd been such a source of strength. She'd listened to his problems, always supportive of his solutions. And she had chided him often enough to get out into society. He drew the line there. Still, he cher-

ished her wisdom and her sense of fun. He would always miss her.

He thought about the woman on the beach. He could only guess she wasn't all that old from the sound of her voice. But aside from estimating her height to be about five feet two inches or so, he didn't know a thing about her. The darkness had hidden more than it revealed. Was she old or young? Slender, he thought, but the dress she wore moved in the breeze, not revealing many details.

Which was probably a good thing. He had no business being interested in anyone. He knew the scars that ran down his side were hideous. More than one person had displayed shock and repulsion when seeing them. Like his fiancée. Damara had not been able to cope at all and had fled the first day the bandages had been removed and she'd seen him in the hospital after the fire.

His brother, Rashid, had told him more than once he was better off without her if she couldn't stick after a tragedy. But it didn't help the hole he'd felt had been shot through his heart when the woman he'd planned to marry had taken off like he was a horrible monster.

He'd seen similar reactions ever since. He knew he was better off working with men in environments too harsh for women to venture into. Those same men accepted him on his merits, not his looks.

He had his life just as he wanted it now. Except—

he had to decide what to do with the house his grandmother left him. It had been a year. He had put off any decisions until the fresh ache of her dying had subsided. But a house should not sit empty.

He walked swiftly across the sand to the start of the wide path that led straight to the house. It was a home suited for families. Close to the beach, it was large with beautiful landscaping, a guesthouse and plenty of privacy. The lawns should have children running around as he and his brother had done. As his father and uncles had done.

The flowers should be plucked and displayed in the home. And the house itself should ring with love and laughter as it had when he and Rashid had been boys visiting their father's parents.

But the house had been empty and silent for a year. And would remain that way unless he sold it. It would be hard to part with the house so cherished by him and his family. Especially with the memories of his beloved grandmother filling every room. But he had no need for it. His flat in Alkaahdar suited him. There when he needed it, waiting while he was away.

As he brushed against an overgrown shrub, his senses were assaulted by the scents of the garden. Star jasmine dominated the night. Other, more subtle fragrances sweetened the still air. So different from the dry, acrid air of the desert. Instantly he was transported back to when he and Rashid had run and played. His father had been alive then, and of

course his grandmother. Who knew the odd quirks of fate, or that he'd end up forever on the outside looking in at happy couples and laughing families. That elusive happiness of families denied him.

Not that he had major regrets. He had done what he thought right. He had saved lives. A scar was a small price to pay.

He entered the house through the door he'd left open from the veranda. Bed sounded really good. He'd been traveling far too long. Once he awoke, he could see what needed to be done to get the house ready for sale.

Ella woke late the next morning. She'd had a hard time falling asleep after meeting the stranger on the beach. She lay in bed wondering who he was and why he'd been traveling so long. Most people stopped when they were tired. No matter, she would probably never see him again. Though, she thought as she rose, just maybe she'd take another walk after midnight tonight. He said he'd be there. Her interest was definitely sparked.

But that was later. Today, she wanted to try to make the new glass piece that had been taking shape in her mind for days.

After a quick breakfast at the nook in the kitchen, Ella went to her studio. As always when entering, she remembered the wonderful woman who had sponsored her chance at developing her skill as a

glassblower and who had offered to help her sell her pieces when they were ready. She missed her. She pursued her passion two-fold now—for herself and for her benefactor.

In only moments, she was totally absorbed in the challenge of blending colors and shapes in the bowl she was creating.

It was only when her back screamed in pain that Ella arched it and glanced at the clock. It was late afternoon—she'd been working for seven hours straight. Examining the piece she'd produced, she nodded in satisfaction. It wasn't brilliant by any means, but it had captured the ethereal feel she wanted. For a first attempt at this technique, it passed. A couple more stages to complete before the glass bowl was ready for a gallery or for sale. A good day's work.

She rubbed her back and wished there was some way she could pace herself. But once caught up in the creative process, it was hard to stop. Especially with glass. Once it was at the molten stage, she had to work swiftly to form the pieces before it cooled. Now it needed to go into the annealer that would slowly cool it so no cracks formed. This was often the tricky part. Especially when she had used different glass and different color mediums that cooled at different rates.

It would end up as it ended up. She tried to keep to that philosophy so she didn't angst over every piece.

Once the bowl was in the oven, she went back to her kitchen, prepared a light meal and carried it to the small terrace on the shady side of the house. The air was cooling down, but it was still almost uncomfortably warm. She nibbled her fruit as she gazed at the flowers that grew so profusely. Where else in the world would she be so comfortable while working on her art? This house was truly a refuge for her. The one place she felt safe and comfortable and almost happy. She'd made it a home for one.

Thinking about the flat she'd given up after Alexander's death, she knew she had traded their happy home for her own. It had taken her a while to realize it, but now she felt a part of the estate. She knew every flower in the garden, every hidden nook that offered shade in the day. And she could walk the paths at night without a light. It was as if the cottage and estate had welcomed her with comforting arms and drawn her in.

So not like the home of her childhood, that was for sure. She shied away from thinking about the last months there. She would focus on the present—or even the future, but not the past.

Taking a deep breath, she held it for a moment, listening. Was that a car? She wasn't expecting any friends. No one else knew where she was. Who would be coming to the empty estate? The gardener's day was later in the week. For a moment she didn't move. The car sounded as if it were going

away. Soon the sound faded completely. Only then did Ella relax.

After she ate, she rose and walked around the cottage. Nothing seemed disturbed. How odd that the car sounded so near. Had the sound been amplified from the road, or had it been in the drive for some reason?

The late-afternoon sun was hot. She debated taking a quick swim, but reconsidered. She wanted to walk along the beach tonight to see if the stranger returned. For the first time in over a year, she was curious about something—someone. Not many people shared her love of the night. Did he? Or had last night been only an aberration because of his long trip? Where in the desert had he been? She'd like to visit an oasis or drive a few hours into the desert, lose sight of any signs of man and just relish the solitude and stark beauty that would surround her.

She needed a car for that. Sighing softly, she considered renting a vehicle for such an expedition. Maybe one day in the fall.

Ella could scarcely wait until midnight. Very unusual, her impatience to see if the man was there again. For a year she'd felt like she was wrapped in plastic, seeing, but not really connected with the rest of the world. Yet a chance encounter in the dark had ignited her curiosity. She knew nothing about him, except he liked the sea and wasn't afraid to swim after dark. Was he old or young? Did he live

nearby or was he sneaking through the estates to gain access to the private beach?

Would he be there tonight?

Promptly at the stroke of twelve, Ella left her home to walk quickly through the path to the beach. Quickly scanning from left to right, she felt a bump of disappointment. He was not there. Sighing softly for her foolishness, she walked to the water's edge and turned to retrace last night's steps.

"I wondered if you would appear," the familiar voice said behind her. She turned and saw him walking swiftly toward her. His longer legs cut the distance in a short time. No robes tonight, just dark trousers and a white shirt.

"I often walk at midnight," she said, not wishing him to suspect she'd come tonight especially to see if he were here.

"As do I, but mainly due to the heat of the day."

"And because you don't sleep?" she asked.

He fell into step with her.

"That can be a problem," he said. "For you, too?"

"Sometimes." Now that he was here, she felt awkward and shy. Her heart beat a bit faster and she wondered at the exhilaration that swept through her. "Did you catch up on your sleep after your trip?"

"Got a few hours in."

"Holidays are meant for sleeping in late and

lazing around," she said, trying to figure out exactly how to ask questions that wouldn't sound as if she were prying.

"If I were on holiday, which I'm not, I still require little sleep."

"Oh, from what you said…" She closed her mouth.

"I did come off a job at an oil field west of here. But I'm here on business. Personal business, I guess you'd say."

"Oh." What kind of business? How long would it take? Would she see him again after tonight? Not that she could see him exactly. But it was nice to share the walk with someone, if only for one night.

"I have some thinking to do and a decision to make," he added a moment later.

"Mmm." She splashed through the water. There was a slight breeze tonight from the sea which made the air seem cooler than normal. It felt refreshing after the heat of her workshop.

"You speak Arabic, but you're not from here, are you?" he asked.

She looked up and shook her head. Not that he could likely see the gesture. "I've studied for years, I can understand it well. Do I not speak it well?"

"Yes, but there is still a slight accent. Where are you from?"

"Italy. But not for a while. I live here now."

"With family?"

She hesitated. Once again safety concerns reared

up. "Do you think I need a chaperone?" she asked, shying away from his question.

"I have no idea. How old are you?"

"Old enough." She stopped and turned, looking up at him, wishing she could see him clearly. "I am a widow. I am long past the stage of needing someone to watch out for me."

"You don't sound old enough to be a widow."

"Sometimes I feel a hundred years old." No one should lose her husband when only twenty-eight. But, as she had been told before, life was not always fair.

"I'm sorry for your loss," he said softly.

She began walking again, not wanting to remember. She tried to concentrate on each foot stepping on the wet sand. Listen to the sea to her right which kissed the shore with wavelets. Feel the energy radiating from the man beside her. So now he'd think she was an older woman, widowed and alone. How old was he? She had no idea, but he sounded like a dynamic man in his prime.

"Thank you." She never knew how to respond to the comment. He hadn't known her husband. He hadn't loved him as she had. No one would ever feel the loss as she did. Still, it was nice he made the comment. Had he ever lost a loved one?

They walked in silence for a few moments. Then she asked, "So what did you do at the oil field?"

"I consult on the pumps and rigs. My company

has a retainer with Bashiri Oil among others to assist when new fields are discovered. And to put out fires when they erupt."

"You put out oil fires?" She was astonished. She had seen the pictures of oil wells burning. Flames shot a hundred feet or more in the air. The intense heat melted and twisted metal even yards from the fire. She found it hard to work with the heat in her own studio with appropriate protective gear. How could anyone extinguish an oil well fire? "Is there any job more dangerous on earth?"

He laughed softly. "I imagine there are. It's tricky sometimes, but someone has to do it."

"And how did you get interested in putting out conflagrations? Wasn't being a regular fireman enough?"

"I'm fascinated by the entire process of oil extraction. From discovering reserves, to drilling and capping. And part of the entire scenario is the possibility of fire. Most are accidents. Some are deliberately set. But the important thing is to get them extinguished as quickly as possible. That's why we do consultation work with new sites and review existing sites for safety measures. Anything to keep a well from catching fire is a good thing. It's an interest I've always had. And since I could choose my profession, I chose this one."

"I just can't imagine. Isn't it hot? Actually it must be exceedingly hot. Is there a word beyond hot?"

He laughed again. She liked the sound of it. She

smiled in reaction, not at all miffed that he was laughing at her questions.

"Oh, it's hot. Even with the special suits we wear."

He explained briefly how they dealt with fire.

Ella listened, fascinated in a horrified way. "You could get killed doing that," she exclaimed at one point.

"Haven't yet," he said.

She detected the subtle difference in his voice. He was no longer laughing. Had someone been injured or killed fighting one of those fires? Probably. The entire process sounded extremely dangerous.

"They don't erupt often," he said.

"I hope there is never another oil fire in the world," she said fervently. "No wonder you wanted to go swimming last night. I'd want to live *in* the sea if I ever survived one of those."

"That is an appeal. But I'd get restless staying here all the time. Something always draws me back to the oil fields. A need to keep the rigs safe. And a sense of need to return burning wells to productivity. Duty, passion. I'm not totally sure myself."

"So it's the kind of thing you'd do even if you didn't need to work?"

He laughed again. "Exactly."

She stopped. "This is as far as I usually go," she said.

"Ben al Saliqi lives here, or he used to," Khalid said, turning slowly to see the house from the beach. Only the peaks of the roof were visible above the

trees that lined the estate, a soft glow from the lamps in the windows illuminating the garden.

"How do you know that?" she asked. There was hardly any identifying features in the dark.

He turned back to her. "I spent many summers here. At my grandmother's house," he said. "I know every family on the beach—except yours."

"Ohmygod, you're one of the al Harum men, aren't you? I'm your tenant, Ella Ponti."

CHAPTER TWO

"My TENANT?" Khalid said.

"I rent the guesthouse on your grandmother's estate. She was my patron—or something. I miss her so much. I'm so sorry she died."

"She rented out the guesthouse? I had no idea."

"I have a lease. You can check it. She insisted on drawing one up. Said it would be better for us both to get the business part out of the way and enjoy each other's company. She was wonderful. I'm so sorry she died when she did. I miss her."

"I miss her, as well. I didn't know about this," Khalid said.

"Well, I don't know why you don't. Haven't you been running the estate? I mean, the gardener comes every week, the maids at the house keep it clean and ready."

"This is the first I've visited since her death. The servants know how to do their job. They don't need an overseer on site."

"It's the first visit in a long while. You didn't

visit her the last few months she lived here. She talked about her grandsons. Which are you, Rashid or Khalid?"

"Khalid."

"Ah, the restless one."

"Restless?"

"She said you hadn't found your place yet. You were seeking, traveling to the interior, along the coast, everywhere, looking for your place."

"Indeed. And Rashid?"

"He's the consumed one—trying to improve the business beyond what his father and uncles did. She worried about you both. Afraid—" Ella stopped suddenly. She was not going to tell him all his grandmother had said. It was not her business if neither man ever married and had children. Or her place to tell him of the longing the older woman had had to hold a new generation. Which never happened and now never would.

"Afraid of what?" he asked.

"Nothing. I have to go back now." She began walking quickly toward home. How was she to know the mysterious stranger on the beach was her new landlord? She almost laughed. He might hold the lease, but he was nothing like a landlord. He hadn't even visited the estate in more than a year. She knew, because she'd never seen him there and she'd live here for over a year and had heard from his grandmother how much she

wished to see him beyond fleeting visits in the capital city.

He easily caught up with her. Reaching out to take her arm, he stopped her and swung her around.

"Tell me."

"Good grief, it's not that big a deal. She was afraid neither of her grandsons would marry and have children. She was convinced both of you were too caught up in your own lives to look around for someone to marry. She wanted to hold a great-grandchild. Now she never can."

"She told you this? A stranger."

Ella nodded. "Yes. We became friends and had a lot of time to visit and talk. She came to the guest cottage often, interested in what I was doing." And had been a rock to lean against when Ella was grieving the most. Her gentle wisdom had helped so much in those first few months. Her love had helped in healing. And the rental cottage had been a welcomed refuge. One guarded by the old money and security of the al Harum family. Ella had found a true home in the cottage and was forever grateful to Alia al Harum for providing the perfect spot for her.

Sheikh Khalid al Harum came from that same old money. She hadn't known exactly what he did but it certainly wasn't for money. No wonder his grandmother had complained. It was a lucky thing he was still alive.

"And what were you doing?" he asked, still holding her arm.

"Working. You could call her a patron of the arts."

"You're a painter?"

"No, glassblower. Could you let me go?"

Ella felt his hold ease. His hand dropped to his side. She stepped back and then headed for home. So much for the excitement of meeting the stranger. She could have just waited until she heard him at the main house and gone over to introduce herself.

Now she wanted to get home and close the door. This was the grandson who was always roaming. Was he thinking of using the house when in the capital city?

"Oh." She stopped and turned. Khalid bumped into her. She hadn't known he was right behind her. His hands caught her so she didn't fall.

"Are you planning to sell the estate?" she asked.

"It's something I'm considering."

"Your grandmother wanted you to have it. She'd be so hurt if you just sold it away."

"I'm not selling it away. It's too big for one man. And I'm not in Alkaahdar often. When I am, I have a flat that suits me."

"Think of the future. You could marry and have a huge family someday. You'll need a big house like that one. And the location is perfect—right on the Gulf."

"I'm not planning to ever marry. Obviously my grandmother didn't tell you all about me or you'd

know the thought of marriage is ludicrous. So why would I want a big house to rattle around in?"

Ella tried to remember all her sponsor had said about her grandsons. Not betraying any confidences, not going into detail about their lives, she still had given Ella a good feel for the men's personalities. And a strong sense that neither man was likely to make her a great-grandmother. The longing she'd experienced for the days passed when they'd been children and had loved to come to her home had touched Ella's heart. Alia had hoped to recapture those happy times with their children.

"Don't make hasty decisions," she said. Alia had died thinking this beloved grandson would live in her home. Ella hated the thought he could casually discard it when it had meant so much to the older woman.

"My grandmother died last July. It's now the end of May. I don't consider that a hasty move."

Ella didn't know what tack to use. If he wanted to sell, the house was his to do so with as he wanted. But she felt sad for the woman who had died thinking Khalid would find happiness in the house she'd loved.

"Come, I'll walk you back. You didn't use the path last night that leads to the house or guesthouse," he said.

"I didn't know who you were. I didn't want to indicate where I lived," she said, walking back. The night seemed darker and colder. She wanted to be

home. So much for looking forward to the evening walk. Now she wished she'd stayed in the cottage and gone to bed.

"Wise. You don't know who might be out on the beach so late at night."

"I've been taking care of myself for a long time. I know this beach well." She was withdrawing. There was something liberating about walking with a stranger, talking, sharing. But something else again once actually knowing the person. She'd be dealing with him in the near future. She didn't know this man. And until she did, she was not giving out any personal information.

A blip of panic settled in. If he sold the estate, where would she go? She had made a home here. Thought she'd be living in the cottage for years to come. She had to review the lease. Did it address the possibility of the estate being sold? She knew Madame al Harum had never considered that likelihood.

As soon as she reached the path, she walked even faster. "Good night," she said. She wasn't even sure what to call him. Sheikh al Harum sounded right, or did she use his first name, as well, to differentiate him from his brother who also was a sheikh? She was not used to dealing with such lofty families.

When she reached her house, she flipped on the lights and headed for the desk. Her expenses were minimum: food, electricity and her nominal rent. It

wasn't as if the al Harum family needed her money. But she had needed to pay her way. She was not a charity case. It wasn't a question of money; it was a question of belonging. Of carrying out her dreams. Madame al Harum had understood. Ella doubted the sheikh would.

She read the Arabic script, finding it harder to understand than newspapers. She could converse well, read newspapers comfortably. But this was proving more difficult than she expected. Why hadn't she asked for a copy translated into Italian?

Throwing it down in disgust, she paced the room for a long time. If she had to leave, where would she go? She studied the cream-colored walls, the soft draperies that made the room so welcoming. Just beyond the dark windows was a view of the gardens. She loved every inch of the cottage and grounds. Where else would she find a home?

The next morning Ella was finishing her breakfast when one of the maids from the main house knocked on the door. It was Jalilah, one who had also served Alia al Harum for so many years.

"His Excellency would like to see you," she said. "I'm to escort you to the main house."

So now he summoned her—probably to discuss her leaving. "Wait until I change." She'd donned worn jeans and an oversize shirt to work around the studio. Not the sort of apparel one wore to

meet with a sheikh. Especially if doing battle to keep her home.

Quickly she donned a dress that flattered her dark looks. It was a bit big; she'd lost weight over the last few months. Still, the rose color brought a tinge of pink to her cheeks.

Her dark eyes looked sad—as they had ever since losing Alexander. She would never again be the laughing girl who had grown up thinking everything good about people. Now she knew heartache and betrayal. She was wiser, but at a price.

Running a brush through her hair, she turned to face the future. Was there a clause in the lease that would nullify her claim if the estate was sold? As they walked across the gardens, she tried to remember every detail about the terms Madame al Harum had discussed.

She entered the house and immediately remembered her one-time hostess. Nothing had changed since the last time she'd visited. It was cool and pleasant. The same pictures hung on the walls. Her first vase from her new studio still held a place of honor on the small table in the foyer, holding a cascading array of blossoms. She'd been so happy it had been loved.

The maid went straight to the study. Ella paused at the doorway for a moment, her eyes widening in shock as she got a good look at Sheikh Khalid al Harum. He looked up at her, catching the startled

horror in her expression. His own features hardened slightly and she felt embarrassed she'd reacted as she had. No one had told her he'd been horribly burned. The distorted and puckered skin on his right cheek, down his neck and obviously beneath his shirt, disfigured what were otherwise the features of a gorgeous man. She'd been right about his age—he looked to be in his prime, maybe early thirties. And he was tall as she noted when he rose to face her.

"You wanted to see me?" she said, stepping inside. She held his gaze, determined not to comment on the burn, or show how sympathetic she felt at the pain he must have endured. She'd had enough burns herself in working with molten glass to know the pain. Never as big a patch as he had. What was a fabulously wealthy man like he had to be risking his life to fight oil fires?

Her heart beat faster. Despite the burn scar, he was the best-looking guy she'd ever seen. Even including Alexander. She frowned. She was not comparing the two. There was no need. The sheikh was merely her new landlord. The flurry of attraction was a fluke. He could mean nothing to her.

"Please." He gestured to a chair opposite the desk. "You're considerably younger than I thought. Are you really a widow?"

She nodded as she slipped onto the edge of the chair. "My husband died April a year ago. What did you wish to see me about?"

He sat and picked up a copy of the lease. "This. The lease for the guesthouse you signed with my grandmother."

She nodded. It was what she expected. He held her future in his hands. Why didn't she have a good feeling about this?

"How did you coerce her to making this?" he asked, frowning at the papers.

Ella blinked. "I did not coerce her into doing anything. How dare you suggest such a thing!" She leaned forward, debating whether to leave or not at his disparaging remark. "She offered me a place to live and work and then came up with the lease herself so I wouldn't have to worry about living arrangements until I got a following."

"A following?"

"I told you, I blow glass. I need to make enough pieces to sell to earn her livelihood. Until that time, she was—I guess you'd say like a patroness—a sponsor if you would. I rented the studio to make my glass pieces and she helped out by making the rent so low. Did you read the clause where she gets a percentage of my sales when I start making money?"

"And if you never sell anything? Seems you got a very cushy deal here. But my grandmother's gone now. This is my estate and if I chose to sell it, I'm within my rights. I don't know how you got her to sign such a lopsided lease but I'm not her. You need

to leave. Vacate the guest quarters so I can renovate if necessary to sell."

Ella stared at him. "Where does it say I have to leave before the end of the five years?" she asked, stalling for time, trying to think about what she could do. Panic flared again. It has seemed too good to be true that she'd have a place to live and work while building an inventory. But as the months had gone on, she'd become complaisant with her home. She couldn't possibly find another place right away—and she didn't have the money to build another studio. And not enough glass pieces ready to sell to raise the money. She was an unknown. The plans she and his grandmother had discussed had been for the future—not the present.

"I do not want you as a tenant. What amount do you want to leave?"

She didn't get his meaning at first, then anger flared. "Nothing. I wish to stay." She felt the full force of his gaze when he stared at her. She would not be intimidated. This was her *home*. He might see it as merely property, but it was more to her. Raising her chin slightly, she continued. "You'll see on the last page once I begin to sell, she gets ten percent of all sales. Or she would have. I guess you do, now." She didn't like the idea of having a long-term connection with this man. He obviously couldn't care less about her or her future. Madame al Harum had loved her work, had encouraged her so much.

She appreciated what Ella did and would have reveled in her success—if it came.

Sheikh Khalid al Harum saw her as an impediment to selling the estate.

Tough.

"I can make it very worth your while," he said softly.

She kept her gaze locked with his. "No."

"You don't know how much," he said.

"Doesn't matter. I have the lease, I have the house for another four years. That will be enough time to make it or not. If not, I'll find something else to do." And she'd keep her precious home until the last moment.

"Or find a rich husband to support you. The estate is luxurious. You would hate to leave it. But if I give you enough money, you'll be able to support yourself in similar luxury for a time."

She rose and leaned on the desk, her eyes narrowed as she stared into his.

"I'm not leaving. The lease gives me a right to stay. Deal with it."

She turned and left, ignoring her shaky knees, her pounding heart. She didn't want his money. She wanted to stay exactly where she was. Remain until those looking for her gave up. Until she could build her own future the way she wanted. Until she could prove her art was worth something and that people would pay to own pieces.

* * *

Khalid listened to the sound of her hurried foot-steps, then the closing of the front door. She refused to leave. He glanced at the lease again. As far as he could tell, it was iron tight. But he'd have the company attorneys review. There had to be a way. He did not want to sit on the house for another four years and he suspected no one would buy the place with a tenant in residence. What had his grand-mother been thinking?

He leaned back in his chair and looked at the chair his unwanted tenant had used. Ella Ponti, widow. She looked like she was in her midtwenties. How had her husband died? She was far too young to be a widow, living alone. Yet the sadness that had shone in her eyes until the fire of anger replaced it, showed him she truly mourned her loss. And he felt a twinge of regret to be bringing a change to her life.

Yet he couldn't reconcile her being in the cottage. Had his grandmother been taken in? Was Ella nothing more than a gold digger looking for an easy way in life? Latch on to an old woman and talk her into practically giving her the cottage.

He was on the fence about selling. He remem-bered his grandmother in every room. All the visits they'd shared over the years. Glancing around the study, he hated to let it go. But he would never live in such a big house. Which left selling the estate as the best option.

He should have visited his grandmother more

often. He missed her. They'd had dinners together in Alkaahdar when he was in town. Sometimes he escorted her to receptions or parties. But long weekends at the estate doing nothing were in the past. And in retrospect she'd asked after him and what was going on in his life more than he'd asked after hers. Regrets were hard to live with.

Though if she'd seen Ella's reactions, maybe she would have stopped chiding him that he made too much of the scar. Ella's initial reaction had been an echo of his one-time fiancée's own look of horror. He knew it disgusted women. That was one reason he spent most of his time on the oil fields or in the desert. He saw the scar himself every morning when he shaved. He knew what it looked like.

Shaking himself out of the momentary reverie, he picked up the phone to call the headquarters of Bashiri Oil. The sooner he found a way to get rid of his unwanted tenant, the better.

Ella stormed home. She did not want to be bought out. Why had Khalid al Harum come to the estate at this time? He'd never visited in all the months she'd live here, why now? She had her life just as she wanted it and he was going to mess it up.

And how dare he offer her money to move? She was not going anywhere. She needed this tranquil setting. She'd gradually gotten over the fierce intensity of her grief. She owed it to Alia al Harum. The

older woman had such faith in her talent and her ability to be able to command top money for her creations. She had strongly encouraged Ella to prove it to herself. And she would for the memory of the woman who had helped her so much.

And no restless grandson was going to drive her away.

She shrugged off the dress and tossed it on the bed. So much for dressing up for him. He only wanted her gone. She pulled on her jeans and oversize shirt. Tying her hair back as she walked, she went to the studio. The glass bowl she'd created yesterday still had hours of graduated cooling to complete before she could take it from the oven. She was impatient to know if it would be as beautiful as she imagined. And flawless with no cracks from irregular cooling, or mixing different types and textures of glass that cooled at different rates. Fingers crossed. Patience was definitely needed for glasswork.

In the meantime, she picked up her sketchbook and went to sit by the window. She could do an entire series in the same technique if the bowl came out perfect. She stared at the blank page. She was not seeing other glass artwork, but the face of Khalid al Harum. What a contrast—gorgeous man, hideous scar. His grandmother had never mentioned that. She'd talked of her grandchildren's lives, her worry they'd never find happiness and other memories of their childhood.

When had the fire happened? He could have been killed. She didn't know him, nor did she care to now that he'd tried to bribe her to leave. But still, how tragic to have been burned so severely. She looked at the couple of small scars on her arms and fingers from long-ago childhood scrapes. Fire was dangerous and damaging to delicate human skin. Every burn, no matter how small, hurt like crazy. She shivered trying to imagine a huge expanse of her body burned.

Had it happened recently? It didn't have that red look that came with recent healing. But with all the money the al Harums had, surely he could have had plastic surgery to mitigate the worst of the damage.

Impatient with her thoughts, she rose and paced the studio. She needed to be focused on the next idea, the next piece of art. She had to build a collection that would be worthy of an exhibit and then of exorbitant prices. Had Madame al Harum spoken to the gallery owners as she had said she would do when the time was right? Probably not. Why speak of something that was years away from happening.

"Great. It's bad enough he'll try to get me off the property. I truly have no place to go and no chance of getting a showing if I don't have someone to vouch for me," she said aloud. She could scream.

But it would do no good.

"Deal with it," she said to herself. She'd take the advice she'd given him and make sure she made

every moment count. He might try to evict her, but until she was carried kicking and screaming from the studio, she'd work on her collection.

The day proved interminable. Every time she'd start thinking about Khalid al Harum, she'd force her mind to focus on designing pieces using the swirling of blues and reds. It would work for a few moments, then gradually something would drift in that had her thinking about him again.

She didn't like it one bit.

After dinner, she debated taking a walk on the beach. That usually cleared her mind. But after the last two nights, the last thing she wanted was to run into *him* again.

She sat on her terrace for a while, trying to relax. The more she tried to ignore his image, the more it seemed to dance in front of her. She was not going to be intimidated by him. Jumping to her feet, she headed down the path to the beach. She'd been walking along the shore for months. Just because he showed up was no reason to change her routine.

When she stepped on the sand, she looked both ways. No sign of anyone. Slowly she walked to the water, then turned south. If he did come out, chances he would head north as she had the last two nights. She'd be safe from his company.

It didn't take long for the walk to begin to soothe. She let go of cares and worries and tried to make herself one with the night.

"I took a guess," a voice came from her right.

Khalid rose from the sand and walked the few yards to where she was. "I thought you might go a different way tonight and I was right." The smug satisfaction in his tone made her want to hit him.

"Then I'll turn and go north," she said, stopping and facing him. She'd tried an earlier time and a different direction. Had he come out to the beach a while ago to wait for her? She ignored the fluttery feeling in her stomach. So he came out. It probably was only to harangue her again about leaving.

"I am not stopping you from going in either direction," he said. He stood next to her, almost too close. She stepped back as a wavelet washed over her feet. The cool water broke the spell.

"You are of course welcomed to walk wherever you wish," she said. She began to walk again along the edge of the water.

Khalid walked beside her.

The silence stretched out moment by moment. Ella had lost all sense of serenity. Her nerves were on full alert. She was extremely conscious of the man beside her. Her skin almost tingled. She could see him from the corner of her eye—tall, silhouetted against the dark sky. She didn't need this sense of awareness. This feeling of wanting to know more. The desire to defend herself to him and make him change his mind and want her to stay in the guesthouse until the lease expired.

She kept silent with effort, wondering if she could outlast him. It grew harder and harder to keep silent as they went along.

"I called an attorney," he said at last.

She didn't reply, waiting for the bad news. Was there an escape clause?

"You'll be happy to know the lease is airtight. You have the right to stay as long as you wish. The interesting part is, you have the right to terminate before the end but my grandmother—and now me—didn't have the same right."

She'd forgotten. Madame al Harum had insisted Ella might wish to leave before five years and didn't want her to feel compelled to remain. At the time Ella had not been able to imagine ever leaving. She still didn't want to think about it. Would four more years be enough time?

"So if you wished to leave, I'd still make it lucrative for you."

"I don't live here for the money," she said.

"Why do you live here? You're not from here. No family. No husband. What holds you to the guesthouse, to Alkaahdar?"

"A safe place to live," she said. "A beautiful setting in a beautiful country. I also have friends here. Quishari is my home."

"Safe? Is there danger elsewhere?" he countered, focusing in on that comment.

She stopped to look at him. She wanted to get this

through to him once and for all. "Look, I came here at a very hard time in my life—just after my husband died. Your grandmother did more for me than anyone, including making sure I had a place to live, to work, sheltered from problems and a chance to grieve. I will forever be in her debt. One I can now never repay. It hit me hard when she died. I grieve for her, as well. Now I'm coming to a place of peace and don't wish to have my life disrupted because you want to get rid of a home she loved and left to you in hopes you'd use it. Do not involve me in your life. I have no interest in taking a gazillion dollars to leave. I have no interest in disrupting my life to suit yours. I want to be left alone to continue as I have been doing these last months. Is that clear enough for you?"

"Life changes. Nothing is as it was last year. My grandmother is dead. Yes, she left me the estate in hopes I would settle there. You saw me this morning. You know why I'll never marry. Why should I hold on to a house for sentimental reasons, visiting it once or twice a year when some other family could enjoy living in it daily? Do you think it is easy for me to sell? I have so many memories of my family visiting. I know I'll face pressure from others in the family to hold on to it. But it's more of a crime to let it sit vacant year after year. What good does that do?"

"Why will you never marry? Did the fire

damage other parts of you?" she asked, startled by his comment.

"What?"

She'd surprised him with that question.

Oh, this was just great. Why had she opened her mouth? Now she had to clarify herself. "I mean, can you not father children or something?"

He burst out laughing.

Ella frowned. It had not been a funny question.

"So you're all right in that department, I guess," she said, narrowing her eyes. "So what's the problem?"

He leaned over, his face close enough to hers she felt the warmth of his breath. She could barely see his eyes in the dark. "As I said, you saw me this morning. What woman would get close enough for me to use those other parts?" he asked very softly.

She stared into his eyes, as dark as her own, hard to see in the dim light of the stars. "Are you stupid or do you think I am? You're gorgeous except for a slight disfiguration on one side. You sound articulate. I expect you are well educated and have pots of money. Why wouldn't someone fall for you? Your grandmother thought you should be married. Surely she'd have known if there was a major impediment."

"I do not wish to be married for my money. I have a temper that could scare anyone and, I assure you, looks count a lot when people are looking for mates. And my grandmother saw only her own

happy marriage that she wished replicated for her grandsons."

"So again I say what's the problem?"

"Maybe you are stupid. This scar," he said, reaching for her hand and trailing her fingers down his cheek, pressing against the puckered skin.

He let her hand go and she left it against the side of his face. The skin was warm, though distorted. Lightly, she brushed her thumb against it, drifted to his lips which had escaped the flame. Her heart pounded, but she was mesmerized. His warmth seemed to touch her heart. She felt heartbreak for his reasoning. He was consigning himself to a long, lonely life. She knew what that was like. Since Alexander's death, hadn't she resigned herself to the same?

But the circumstances were different. She had loved and lost. Khalid needed to feel someone's love, to know he was special. And to keep the dream his grandmother had so wanted for him.

Khalid was shocked. Her touch was soft, gentle, sweet. Her thumb traced a trail of fire and ice against his skin. No one had touched him since the doctors had removed the last of the bandages. When he released her, he expected her to snatch her hand away. It was still there. The touch was both unexpected and erotic. He could feel himself respond as he hadn't in years.

"Enough." He knocked her hand away and took

a step back. "Tell me what it would take to get you to leave the guesthouse."

"Four years," she replied, and turned to resume her walk.

He watched as she walked away along the sea's edge. She was serious. At least at this moment. She didn't want money. She wanted time.

Why was she here? Was there anything in his grandmother's things that explained why she'd befriended Ella Ponti and made that one-sided deal with her? He hadn't gone through all her papers, but that would be his next step first thing in the morning.

He remained standing, watching. She didn't care if he walked beside her or not. If this was her regular routine, she'd been coming for nightly walks for a year. She didn't need his company.

Why had he come out tonight? He usually kept to himself. He couldn't remember the last time he'd sought out a woman's company. Probably because it would have been an exercise in futility. Ella had seen him in broad daylight. Tonight it had been like the last two: wrapped in darkness he could almost forget the burn scar. She had treated him the same all three nights.

Except for her touch tonight.

Shaking his head, he almost smiled. She shocked him in more ways than one. Was the reaction just that of a man too long without a woman? It had to be. She had done nothing to encourage him. In fact,

he couldn't remember another woman standing up to him as she had, both tonight and earlier this morning. Deal with it, she'd said, dismissing his demand she leave as if it were of no account.

Which legally it proved to be. Maybe he'd stop pushing and learn a bit more about his unwanted tenant before pursuing other avenues. She intrigued him. Why was she really here? Maybe it was time to find out more about Ella Ponti, young widow living so far from her native land.

CHAPTER THREE

MAYBE she had finally gotten through to him, she thought as she walked alone. He had not followed her. Good. Well, maybe there was a touch of disappointment, but not enough to wish he was with her.

She clenched her hand into a fist. His skin had been warm, she'd felt the strong line of his jaw, the chiseled outline of his lips. Not that she wanted to think about his lips—that led to thoughts of kisses and she had no intention of ever kissing anyone else. It almost felt like a betrayal of her love for Alexander. It wasn't. Her mind knew that, it would take her heart a bit longer to figure that out. She still mourned her lost love.

"Alexander," she whispered. It took a second for her to recall his dear face. She panicked. She couldn't forget him. She loved him still. He'd been the heart beating in her. But his image wavered and faded to be replaced by the face of Khalid al Harum.

"No!" she said firmly. She would dismiss the man from her thoughts and concentrate on something else, anything else.

Wildly, she looked around. Out to sea she spotted a ship, gliding along soundlessly in the distance. Was it a cruise ship? Were couples and families enjoying the calm waters of the Gulf? Would they be stopping in one of the countries lining the coast? Maybe buy pearls from the shops or enjoy the traditional Arab cuisine. Maybe couples would be dancing. For a moment she regretted she'd never dance again. She was young to have loved and lost. But that was the way life was sometimes.

She had her art.

Stopping at last, she gazed at the ship for a long moment, then glanced back up the beach. Khalid al Harum stood where she'd left him. Was he brooding? Or just awaiting her return. She studied his silhouette and then began walking toward him. She had to return home. It was late and she'd had enough turmoil to last awhile.

When she drew even she stopped. "Now what?"

"Now we wait four years," he replied.

That surprised her. Was he really going to stop pressuring her? Somehow she had not thought he'd give up that easily. Yet, maybe he was pragmatic. The lease was valid. She had the law on her side—even against a sheikh. Dare she let her guard down and believe him?

"Since we'll be neighbors for the time, might as well make the best of things," he said.

That had her on instant alert. He didn't strike her

as someone who settled for making the best of any situation unless it suited his needs and demands.

"And how do we do that?"

"Be neighborly, of course." He walked beside her. "Surely you visited with my grandmother from time to time."

"Almost every day," she said. "She was delightful. And very encouraging about my work. Did you know you have one of my early pieces in your house?"

"What and where?"

"The shallow vase in the foyer. It's a starburst bowl. Your grandmother liked it and I gave it to her. I was thrilled when she displayed it in such a prominent place."

"Maybe I'll come by one day and see your work."

Ella wasn't sure she wanted him in her studio or her house. But she probably had to concede that much. If he truly stopped pushing her to leave, she could accept a visit or two.

"Let me know when," she said.

Khalid caught up on some e-mail the next morning and then called his brother. Rashid was the head of Bashiri Oil. Khalid was technically equal owner in the company, along with an uncle and some cousins, but Rashid ran the business. Which suited Khalid perfectly. He much preferred the oil fields to the offices in the high-rise building downtown.

"What's up?" Rashid asked when he heard his brother's voice. "Are you still in Hari?"

"No, I'm at Grandmother's estate. Did you know she rented out the guesthouse last year?"

"No. Who to?"

"An artist. Now I'm wondering why the secrecy. I didn't know, either." Another reason to find out more about Ella Ponti.

"Good grief, did he convince her to sponsor him or something? What hard-luck story did he spin?"

"Not a he, a she. And I'm not sure about the story, which is the reason for the call. Can you have someone there run a background check? Apparently Ella has an airtight lease to the premises and has no intention of leaving before the lease expires—in four more years."

"A five-year lease? Have someone here look at it."

"Already done. It's solid. And she's one deter-mined woman. I offered her as big a bribe as I could and she still says no."

"So, look for dirt to get her out that way." Rashid suggested.

"No, I think I'll go along with it for a while. I just want to know more about her. I respect Grand-mother's judgment. She obviously liked the woman. But she also knew her and I don't."

There was a silent moment before his brother spoke again. "Is she pretty?"

"What does that have to do with a background check? She's a widow."

"Oh. Sure, I'll have one of the men call you later and you can give him what you have to start with. Bethanne and I are dining with Mother tonight… care to join us?"

"I'll take a rain check. I'm going through Grandmother's things. I still can't believe she's gone. It's as if she stepped out for a little while. Only, she's never coming back."

"Planning to move there?"

"I was thinking of selling the place, until I found I have an unbudgeable tenant."

"Then good for the widow. None of us wants you to sell."

"It's not your place. You got the villa south of the city."

"Where I think Bethanne and I will live. You love the sea. Why not keep it?"

"It's a big house. You don't need it—you have your own villa by the sea. Why let it sit idle for decades?"

"Get married and fill it up," his brother suggested.

"Give Mother my love and have someone call me soon," he said, sidestepping the suggestion. Rashid should know as well as he did that would never happen. But his brother had recently become engaged and now had changed his tune about staying single. He was not going to get a convert with Khalid.

Ella's words last night echoed. He shook his head. Easy to say the words in the dark. Harder to say when face-to-face with the scars.

He hung up the phone and looked again at the vase sitting on his desk. He'd taken it last night from the foyer to the study. It was lovely. Almost a perfect oval, it flared at the edges. From the center radiating outward was a yellow design that did look like a sunburst. Toward the edges the yellow thinned to gossamer threads. How had she done it? It was sturdy and solid yet looked fragile and enchanted. He knew his grandmother håd loved it.

Seeing the vase gave validity to Ella's assertion she was an artist. Was she truly producing other works of art like this? Maybe his grandmother had seen the potential and arranged to keep her protégée close by while she created. She'd been friendly and helpful to others, but was an astute woman. She must have seen real talent to encourage Ella so much. So why not tell the rest of the family?

Khalid rose and headed next door. It was time he saw the artist in her studio, and assessed exactly what she was doing.

He walked to the guest cottage in only seconds. Though it was close, because of the lush garden between it and the main house there was a feeling of distance. He saw a new addition, obviously the studio. How much had his grandmother done for this tenant?

He stepped to the door, which stood wide-open. He could feel the heat roiling out from the space. He looked in. Ella was concentrating on her project and didn't notice him. For a long moment Khalid

watched her. She wore a large leather apron and what looked like leather gloves that reached up to her elbows. She had dark glasses on and straddled a long wooden bench. At one end a metal sheet was affixed upon which she turned molten glass at the end of a long tube. As he watched, the glass began to take shape as she turned it against the metal. A few feet beyond was a furnace, the door open, pouring out heat.

Her dark hair was pulled back into a ponytail. He studied her. Even attired as she was, she looked feminine and pretty. How had she become interested in this almost lost art? It took a lot of stamina to work in such an adverse environment. It had to be close to thirty-seven degrees in the room. Yet she looked as cool as if she were sitting in the salon of his grandmother's house.

Slowly ,she rotated the tube. She blew again and the shape elongated. He was afraid to break her concentration lest it cause her to damage the glass globule.

She looked up and frowned, then turned back to her work. "What do you want?" she asked, before blowing gently into the tube again.

"To see where you worked." He stepped inside. "It's hot in here."

"Duh, I'm working with fire."

He looked at the glowing molten glass. She pushed it into the furnace. No wonder it was so hot; everything inside the furnace glowed orange.

She pulled out the molten glass and worked on it some more.

Khalid began to see the shape, a tall vase perhaps. The color was hard to determine as it was translucent and still glowed with heat.

He walked closer, his scar tissue reacting to the heat. He crossed to the other side, so his undamaged cheek faced the heat. How did she stand it so close for hours on end?

"Do you mind if I watch?"

"Not much I can do about it, is there?" she asked with asperity.

Khalid hid a smile. She was not giving an inch. Novel in his experience. Before he'd been burned, women had fawned over him. He and Rashid. He'd bet Ella wouldn't have, no matter what.

"Did my grandmother build this for you?"

"Mmm," she mumbled, her lips still around the tube.

"State of the art?"

"Mmm."

He looked around. Other equipment lined one wall, one looked like an oven. There were jars of crushed glass in various colors. On one table were several finished pieces. He walked over and looked at them. Picking up a vase, he noted the curving shape, almost hourglasslike. The color was pastel—when held up so the white wall served as a background, it looked pale green.

When on the table, it grew darker in color contrasting with the wood.

He wondered how much all this cost and would his grandmother ever have made any money as a return on her investment. She must have thought highly of Ella to have expended so much on an aspiring artist.

He looked at the other pieces. He wasn't a connoisseur of art, but they were quite beautiful. It was obvious his grandmother had recognized her talent and had encouraged it.

When he glanced back at Ella, she was using a metal spatula to shape the piece even further. He watched as she flattened the bottom and then began molding the top to break away from the tube. Setting the piece on the flat bottom, she ran the spatula over the top, gradually curving down the edge. He watched her study it from a couple of angles, then slide it onto a paddle and carefully carry it to the oven. She opened the top doors and slid it in, closing the doors quickly and setting a dial.

Turning, she looked at him, taking off her dark glasses.

"So?" she said. Her skin glowed with a sheen of perspiration.

"Interesting. These are lovely," he said, gesturing to the collection behind him. Trying to take his eyes off her. She looked even more beautiful with that color in her cheeks.

"I hope so. That's the intent. Build an inventory and hit the deck running. Do you know any art dealers?" she asked hopefully.

Khalid shook his head. His family donated to the arts, but at the corporate level. He had no personal acquaintance with art dealers.

She sighed and untied her apron, sliding it off and onto the bench. "Me, neither. That was another thing your grandmother was going to do—introduce me to several gallery owners in Europe. Guess I'll have to forge ahead on my own."

"Too bad you can't ride in on the al Harum name," he murmured.

Her eyes flared at that. Was he deliberately baiting her to see her reaction? He liked the fire in her eyes. It beat the hint of sadness he saw otherwise.

"I was not planning to ride in on anyone's name. I expect my work to stand on its own merits. Your grandmother was merely going to introduce me."

"Still, an introduction from her would have assured owners took a long look before saying yea or nay, and think long and hard about turning down a protégée of Alia al Harum. She spent a lot of money in some galleries on her visits to France and Italy."

"I don't plan on showing in Italy," she said hastily.

Khalid's suspicions shot up. She was from Italy—why not show in her home country? He'd given what information he had to a person at the oil company to research her background. Now he

wanted more than ever to know what brought her to Quishari, and how she'd met his grandmother.

"Do you think you can sell enough to earn a living?" he asked.

"Your grandmother thought so. I believe her, so yes, I do. I don't expect to become hugely wealthy, but I have simple needs, and love doing this creative work, so should be content if I ever start selling."

"Have you sent items out for consideration?"

"No. I wanted to wait until I had inventory. If the pieces sell quickly, I want more in the pipeline and can only produce a few each month. I have a five-year plan."

He met her eyes. Sincerity shone in them. It seemed odd to have this pretty woman talk about five-year plans. But the longer he gazed at her, the more he wanted to help. Which was totally out of character for him. He broke the contact and gave a final glance around the studio. Heading for the door, he paused before leaving. "I say give it a test run, send out some of your best pieces and see if they'll sell. No sense wasting five years if nothing is worth anything."

Ella stared out into the garden long after Khalid had left. He made it sound so simple. But it wasn't. What if she didn't sell? What if her pieces were mundane and mediocre? She could live on hope for the next few years—or have reality slap her in the face and crush her. She was still too vulnerable to venture

forth to see if her work had merit. Madame al Harum had been so supportive. Now she ran into a critic. She had to toughen up if she wanted to compete in the competitive art world. Could she do it?

She cleaned up, resisting the temptation to peer into the lower part of the annealer to check the progress of the piece she'd done yesterday. She hoped it would be spectacular. Maybe Khalid al Harum was right. She should not waste time creating glass pieces if they would never sell. The slight income from Alexander's insurance would not carry her forever. If she couldn't make a living with glass, she should find another means to earn her livelihood.

Only, she didn't want another means. She loved making glass.

Once she finished cleaning the studio, she grabbed her notebook and went to sit on the terrace. The arbor overhead sheltered it from the hot sun. She enjoyed sitting outside when planning. It was so much more pleasant than the hot studio. She opened the pages and began to study the pictures she'd taken of the different pieces she had already made. She had more than one hundred. Some were quite good, others were attempts at a new technique that hadn't panned out. Dare she select a few pieces to offer for sale?

What if no one bought them?

What if they skyrocketed her to fame?

She did not want to rock the boat. She liked life the way it was. Or the way it had been before Khalid al Harum had arrived.

Idly she wondered what it would take to get rid of him. The only thing she could think of was moving out so he could sell the estate. She wasn't going to do that, so it looked as if she were stuck with him.

He was so different from his grandmother. Distracting, for one thing. She'd known instantly when he appeared in the doorway, but had ignored him as long as she could. Of course he had the right to visit his property, but his grandmother had always arranged times to come see what she was working on. There was something almost primordial about the man. He obviously was healthy and virile. She was so not interested in another relationship, yet her body seemed totally aware of his whenever he was near. It was disconcerting to say the least.

And distracting.

Ella stayed away from the beach that night. She listened to music while cataloging the pieces she thought might do for a first showing. She only had a couple of photos of the first batch of vases and bowls she'd made when she moved here. She needed to take more pictures, maybe showcase them in one of the salons in the main house. It was an idea she and Madame al Harum had discussed.

Good grief, she'd have to ask Khalid and she could imagine exactly what he'd say to her pro-

posal. Or maybe she could sneak in when he wasn't there. Surely there was an oil field somewhere in the world that needed consulting. If he'd take off for a few days, she was sure Jalilah would let her in to photograph the pieces sitting in prominent display in the main salon. It would add a certain cachet to her catalog and maybe garner more interest when she was ready to go.

She went to bed that night full of ideas of how to best display the pieces she would put in her first catalog. The only question was if she dare ask Khalid for permission to use his salon for the photographs.

By the time morning arrived, Ella regretted her decision to forego her walk. She had slept badly, tossing and turning and picturing various scenarios when asking Khalid for his help. Maybe she should have been a bit more conciliatory when discussing her lease. She planned to stand fast on staying, but she could have handled it better.

Only she disliked subterfuge and manipulation; she refused to practice it in her own life.

After a hasty breakfast, she again dressed up a bit and headed for the villa. Walking through the gardens, she tried to quell her nerves. The worst he could do was refuse. The guesthouse had a small sitting area, not as lavish as the main dwelling. She could use that, but she longed for the more elegant salon as backdrop for her art.

Jalilah opened the door when she knocked.

"I'd like to see Sheikh al Harum," Ella said, hoping she looked far more composed than she felt.

"He has someone visiting. Wait here."

Ella stood in the foyer. Her vase was gone. She peered into the salon; it wasn't there, either. Had something happened to it? Or had Khalid removed it once he'd learned she made it? That made her feel bad.

"Come." The maid beckoned from the door to the study.

When Ella entered, she stopped in surprise. Two men looked at her. Except for their clothing, and the scar on Khalid's cheek, they were identical.

"Twins?" she said.

Khalid frowned. "Did you want something?"

"Introduce us," the other man said, crossing the room and offering his hand.

"My brother," Khalid said.

"Well, that's obvious." Ella extended her hand and smiled. "I'm Ella Ponti."

"I am Rashid al Harum. You're the tenant, I take it."

She nodded. "Unwanted to boot."

"Only because I want to sell," Khalid grumbled. "Rashid is trying to talk me out of it, too."

"Good for you. I told him your grandmother wanted him to have the house. She could have left it to a charity or something if she hadn't hoped he'd live here," she said.

"It's a too big for one man," Khalid said.

"So—"

He raised his hand. "We've been over that. What do you want?"

Rashid glanced at his twin. "Am I in the way?"

Ella shook her head, bemused to see her vase in the center of Khalid's desk.

"Not at all. I came to ask permission to photograph some of my work in the salon. Give it a proper showing—elegant and refined. The guest cottage just doesn't have the same ambiance."

"You want to take pictures of my house?" Khalid asked. "Out of the question."

"Not the house, just some of my special pieces sitting on a table or something which would display them and give an idea of how they would look in another home. The background would be slightly blurred, the focus would be on my work."

"Use the table in your workroom."

"That's elegant."

He frowned. "I don't see—"

"—any problem with it," Rashid finished before his twin could finish. "I was admiring your vase when you arrived. Khalid explained how you made it. I'd like to see more of your work. I bet Bethanne would, as well."

"She'd do anything you say," Khalid grumbled.

"Bethanne?" Ella asked.

"My fiancée. She's making some changes to

my villa in preparation of our marriage and moving in there."

"So the consumed one is getting married— wouldn't my grandmother love to know that?" Khalid asked.

"What are you talking about?" Rashid asked, glancing at his twin.

"Nothing, only something your grandmother said to me once. I'm happy for you and your fiancée. You might tell your brother how happy you are so he could go find someone to make a life with and leave me alone," Ella said hastily.

Rashid looked at her and then Khalid.

"Forget it. We've been over this before. I'm not marrying," Khalid growled.

Rashid looked thoughtful as he again looked back and forth between the two others in the room.

"I, uh, have to be leaving. I'll bring Bethanne by tomorrow if that suits you, Ella. She'd love to see the glass objects. Khalid, you have what you asked for. Let me know if you need more." He nodded to both and left, a small smile tugging at his lips.

Ella hated to see him go. He was much easier to be around than his brother.

"So I can use the salon?" she asked. Rashid had indicated yes, but it was still Khalid's place and his decision she needed.

"What if I say no?" he asked, leaning casually against the side of the desk.

"Then I'll pester you until you say yes," she replied daringly. "Maybe it'll help sell some of my work earlier than originally planned and I could move away sooner."

"How much sooner?"

"I don't know, five days?"

A gleam of amusement lit his eyes. "For such an early move, how can I refuse?"

"Thank you. I'll give credit in my brochure so everyone will know you helped."

"No. No credit, no publicity."

She started to protest but wisely agreed. "Okay. I'm cooling a couple of pieces now and once they are ready, I will begin taking pictures. I appreciate this."

"You weren't on the beach last night," he said.

He had been, obviously.

"I, uh, needed to get to sleep early. Big day today."

"Doing what?"

"Coming to ask you about the salon" sounded dumb. What else could she come up with?

He watched her. Ella fidgeted and looked around the room. "Just a big day. Why is my vase in here?"

"I was looking at it. I thought it was mine."

"I guess. I should have said why is the vase I made in here instead of the foyer."

"I wanted to look at it. I like it."

She blinked in surprise. "You do?"

Amusement lurked in his eyes again. "You sound surprised. Isn't it good?"

She nodded. "I just can't imagine you—"

"Having an eye for beauty?"

"I wasn't exactly going to say that."

"You haven't held back on anything else."

"You are very exasperating, do you know that?" she asked.

"Makes a change from other names I've been called."

If he drove the other people he knew as crazy as he did her, she wasn't surprised.

Khalid stood and moved around to sit at the desk. "So, you'll be on the beach tonight?" he asked casually.

Ella shrugged. "Thanks for letting me use the salon for the photographs."

"One caveat," he said, glancing up.

She sighed. It had been too good to be true. "What?"

"I get to give final approval. I don't want certain prize possessions to be part of your sales catalog. No need to give anyone the idea that more than your glass is available."

"Done." She nodded and turned. At the door she stopped and looked at him over her shoulder. "I do expect to take a walk tonight as it happens."

She wasn't sure, but she suspected the expression on his face was as close to a smile as she'd seen.

CHAPTER FOUR

ELLA and Khalid fell into a tentative friendship. Each night she went for a walk along the beach. Most evenings Khalid was already on the sand, as if waiting for her. They fell into an easy conversation walking in the dark at the water's edge. Sometimes they spoke of what they'd done that day. Other times the walks were primarily silent. Ella noted he was quieter than other men she'd known. Was that his personality or a result of the accident? She gathered the courage to ask about it on the third evening after he said she could use the salon.

"How did you get burned?" she asked as they were turning to head for home. She hadn't wanted to cut the walk short if he got snippy about her question.

"We were capping a fire in Egypt. Just as the dynamite went off, another part of the well exploded. The shrapnel shredded part of my suit, instant burn. Hurt like hell."

"I can imagine. I've had enough burns to imagine

how such a big area would be almost unbearable. Were you long in hospital?"

"A few months."

And in pain for much of that time, she was sure. "Did you get full mobility back?"

"Yes. And other parts were unaffected."

She smiled at his reminder of her attempt at being tactful when he said he wouldn't marry. A burned patch of skin wouldn't be enough to keep her from falling for a man. She suspected Khalid was too sensitive to the scar. There were many woman who would enjoy being with him.

"Good. What I don't get is why you do it?"

"Do what?"

"Put your life at risk. You don't even need to work, do you? Don't you have enough money to live without risking life and limb?"

He was quiet a moment, then said, "I don't have to work for money. I do want to do what I can to make oil production safe. Over the last fifty years or so many men have died because of faulty equipment or fires. Our company has reaped the benefit. But in doing that we have an obligation to make sure the men who have helped in our endeavors have as much safety guarding them as we can provide. If I can provide that, then it's for the good."

"An office job would be safer," she murmured.

"Rashid has that covered. I like being in the field. I like the desert, the challenge of capturing the liquid

crude beneath the land, or the sea. I like knowing I'm pitting my skills and experience against the capricious nature of drilling—and coming out on top more than not."

"Still seems ridiculously dangerous. Get someone else to do it."

"It's my calling, you might say."

Ella was silent at that. It still seemed too dangerous for him—witness the burn that had changed his life. But she was not someone to argue against a calling. She felt that with her art.

She turned and he caught her hand, pulling her to a stop. She looked up at him. The moon was a sliver on the horizon, the light still dim, but she could see him silhouetted against the stars.

"What?"

"My mother is hosting a reception on Saturday. I need to make an appearance. I want you to go with me."

Ella shook her head. "I don't do receptions," she said. "Actually I don't go away from the estate much."

"Why?"

"Just don't," she murmured, turning to walk toward home.

He still held her hand and fell into step with her.

"Consider it payment for using the salon," he said.

"You already agreed to my using the salon. You can't add conditions now."

"Sure I can—it's my salon. You want to use it,

consider this part of the payment. It's just a reception. Some people from the oil company, some from the government, some personal friends. We circulate, make my mother happy by being seen by everyone, then leave. No big deal."

"Get someone else."

He was silent for several steps.

"There is no one else," he said slowly.

"Why not?"

"I've been down that road, all right? I'm not going to set myself up again. Either it's you, or I don't go. My grandmother helped you out—your turn to pay back."

"Jeeze, talk about coercion. You're sure it'll only be people who live here in Quishari?"

"Yes. What would it matter if foreigners came? You're one yourself."

"I am trying to keep a low profile, that's why," she said, hating to reveal anything, but not wanting to find out her hiding place had been found.

"Why?"

"I have reasons."

"Are you hiding?" he asked incredulously.

"Not exactly."

"Exactly what, then?" He pulled her to a stop again. "I want to hear this."

"I'm in seclusion because of the death of my husband."

"That was over a year ago."

"There's a time limit on grieving? I hadn't heard that."

"There's no time limit, but by now the worst should be behind you and you should be going out and seeing friends. Maybe finding a new man in your life."

"I see my friends," she protested. "And I'm not going down that road again. You're a funny one to even suggest it."

"When do you see friends?"

"When they come to visit. I'm working now and it's not convenient to have people over. But when I'm not in the midst of something, they come for swimming in the sea and alfresco meals on my terrace. Did you think I was a hermit?"

"I hadn't thought about it. I never see these friends."

"You've lived here for what, almost a week? No one has come in that time. Stick around if you're so concerned about my social life."

"Mostly I'm concerned about your going with me to the reception this weekend."

"No."

"Yes. Or no salon photos."

Ella glared at him. It missed the mark. He couldn't see her that well. And she suspected her puny attempts at putting him in the wrong wouldn't work. He did own the estate. And she did need permission to use the salon. Rats, he was going to win on this one. She did not want to go.

She was content in her cottage, with her work and with the solitude.

Only sometimes did it feel lonely.

Not once since Khalid had arrived.

Dangerous thoughts, those. She was fine.

"All right, we'll go, greet everyone and then leave."

"Thank you."

They resumed the walk, but Ella pulled her hand from his. They were friends, not lovers. No need to hold hands.

But her hand had felt right in his larger one. She missed the physical contact of others. She hadn't been kissed in ages, held with passion in as long. Why did her husband have to die?

"I'll pick you up at seven on Saturday," he said.

"Fine. And first thing tomorrow, I'm coming to take photographs. I don't want to miss my chance in case you come up with other conditions that I can't meet."

He laughed.

Ella looked at him. She'd never even seen him smile and now he was laughing in the darkness! Was that the only time he laughed?

"I expect I need to wear something very elegant," she mumbled, mentally reviewing the gowns she'd worn at university events. There were a couple that might do. She hadn't thought about dressing up in a long time. A glimmer of excitement took hold. She had enjoyed meeting other people at the university,

speaking about topics far removed from glass making. Would the reception be as much fun? She felt a frisson of anticipation to be going with Khalid. She always seemed more alive when around him.

"You'll look fine in anything you wear," he said easily.

Just like a man, she thought, still reviewing the gowns she owned.

The next morning Ella carefully took two of her pieces, wrapped securely in a travel case, and went to the main house. Ringing the doorbell, she was greeted by Jalilah.

"I've come to take pictures," she said.

"In the salon, His Excellency has told me. Come." The maid led the way and then bowed slightly before leaving.

Ella put the starburst bowl on one of the polished mahogany tables.

Khalid appeared in the doorway. He leaned against the jamb and watched.

"What do you want?" she asked, feeling her heartbeat increase. Fussing, she tried pictures from different angles. She could hardly focus the lens with him watching her.

"Just wanted to see how the photo shoot went."

"Don't you have work to do?"

"No."

She tried to ignore him, but it was impossible. She

lifted the camera and framed the bowl. She snapped the picture just as the doorbell sounded. She looked at Khalid. "Company?" she asked. Maybe someone who would take him away from the salon.

He looked into the foyer and nodded. "Rashid and Bethanne. Good timing. They can help."

"Help what?"

"You get the best pictures. You want to appeal to the largest number of buyers, right?"

"Of course." The sooner she started earning money, the sooner she might move.

"Hello," Rashid said, coming into the room with a tall blond woman. "Ella, this is my fiancée, Bethanne Sanders. Bethanne, this is Ella Ponti. Now, can you two talk?" he asked in Arabic.

"I also speak Italian and French and English," Ella said, crossing the room to greet the pair.

Switching to English, Rashid said, "Good, Ella speaks English."

"I'm so delighted to meet you," Bethanne said, offering her hand.

Ella shook it and smiled. "I'm happy to meet you. My English is not so good, so excuse me if I get things mixed."

"At least we can communicate. And you speak Arabic. I'm learning from a professor at the university. That's not easy."

"And the maid," Rashid said softly.

Bethanne laughed. "Her, too."

"Would that be Professor Hampstead?" Ella asked.

"Yes, do you know him?" Bethanne asked with a pleased smile.

"My husband worked at the university in language studies. I know the professor and his wife quite well. He's an excellent teacher."

"We came to see your work," Rashid said. "I see you've started on the pictures."

"Photographing some pieces for a preliminary catalog. I'd like to see if I can move up my time-table for a showing. Once I have enough pictures, I can make a small catalog and circulate it."

"Why are you taking pictures here?" Bethanne asked, walking over to look at the bowl. "Oh, this is exquisite. You made this? How amazing!" She leaned over and touched the edge lightly but made no move to pick it up.

"I think the ambiance of the other furnishings here will show it off better. I want the background to be blurry, with only the glass piece in clear focus, but to give the feel that it would fit in any elegant salon."

"And Khalid was all for the project, obviously," Rashid said with a glance at his twin.

"Obviously—she's here, isn't she?" Khalid said. "You two can help with the project. Give us an unbiased perspective and select the best pictures."

"I'd like to see the other pieces you've made," Bethanne said.

"I'm happy to show you. Shall we go now?"

"Finish the pictures of these, then when you go to your studio, you can bring some more over," Khalid suggested.

The next couple of hours were spent with everyone giving opinions about the best angle for pictures and which of the different art pieces Ella had created should be included. Rashid said he'd see if his mother had some recommendations on art galleries who would help.

Ella felt as if things were spinning out of control. She and Alia al Harum had discussed the plans, but they'd been for years down the road. Now so much was happening at once.

Khalid looked over at her at one point and said, "Enough. We will return to the main house and have lunch on the terrace. Bethanne, you haven't told Ella what you do. I think she'll be interested."

Ella threw him a grateful smile. "I'll just tidy up a bit and join you."

Rashid and Bethanne headed out, but Khalid remained behind for a moment.

"They only wanted to help," he said.

"I'm glad they did."

"But you're feeling overwhelmed. You set the pace. This is your work, your future. Don't let anyone roll over you."

"Good advice. Remember that next time you want your way," she said, sitting down on her

bench, touched he'd picked up on her mild panic and dealt with it. She hadn't expected such sensitivity from the man.

"You are coming for lunch?"

"Yes. I just need a few minutes to myself."

"I'll come back for you if you don't show up in twenty minutes."

"Did anyone tell you you're a bit bossy?" she asked.

"Twenty minutes," he said, and left.

Ella took less than the twenty minutes. After a quick splash of cool water against her face, she brushed her hair and lay down for ten minutes. Then hurried to the main house. Khalid and the others were on the terrace and she walked straight there without going through the house.

Lunch was delicious and fun. It was a bit of a struggle to remember to speak English during the meal, but she was confident she held her own in the conversation that ranged from Bethanne's career as a pilot to Rashid's recent trip to Texas to the reception on Saturday night.

"Are you coming?" Rashid asked his brother at one point.

"Yes," Khalid said.

Rashid and Bethanne exchanged surprised looks. "Great."

"I'm bringing Ella," Khalid continued.

Both guests turned to stare at her. She smiled

brightly. Was this such an amazing thing? Surely Khalid had brought other women to receptions before.

"Condition of using the salon for the pictures," she murmured.

"Of course," Rashid said with another quick glance at his fiancée.

"Great. Maybe you could go shopping with me before then," Bethanne said. "I'm not sure I have anything suitable to wear."

Ella hesitated. She hadn't been shopping except for groceries since her husband's funeral. Dare she go? Surely it would be okay for one afternoon. It wasn't as if anyone was hanging around the main streets of the city looking for her.

"I don't know if I would be much help." She felt Khalid's gaze on her and glanced his way.

"Help or not, don't women love to buy beautiful dresses?"

"I don't need one. I have several," Ella said.

"Come help me find several," Bethanne urged.

Rashid watched the interaction and then looked at his brother. He narrowed his eyes when Khalid never looked away from Ella.

"Okay, I'll go tomorrow afternoon," Ella said fast, as if afraid she'd change her mind.

When lunch finished, Ella thanked her host and fled for her cottage. She'd had more activity today than any time since Alexander had died. And she'd agreed to go shopping—out along the main district

of Alkaahdar. Surely after all this time it would be safe. She had a right to her own life. And to live it on her terms.

That night she debated going for a walk. She was getting too used to them. Enjoying them too much. What happened when Khalid moved on? When he went to another oil field to consult on well equipment, or had to go fight a fire. That thought scared her. He was trained; obviously an expert in the field. He knew what to do. It was dangerous, but as he'd explained, except for that one accident, he'd come through unscathed many times.

But that one could have killed him. Didn't he realize that? Or another one similar that might rip the helmet and protection totally off. She shivered thinking about it.

She went for her walk, hoping he'd be there. It was better than imaging awful things that could happen.

He sat on the sand near the garden.

"It's warm," he said when she appeared, letting some sand drift from his hand.

"Sometimes I sit on the beach in the night, relishing the heat held from the day."

"Sand makes glass," he commented.

"Yes. I've heard that lightning strikes on beaches produces glass—irregular in shape and not usually functional. I'd like to see some." She sat beside him.

"I like the fact I'll know your brother and Bethanne at the reception."

"And me."

"Yes, and you. We aren't staying long, right."

"I said not long. Why are you nervous? You've been to university receptions—this would be sort of the same, just a different group of people. You'll be bored out of your mind with all the talk about oil."

She smiled at his grumbling. "Is that the normal topic?"

"With a heavy presence of Bashiri executives it usually is. The minister of finance is not in charity with us right now. Rashid closed a deal he didn't like. But I'm sure a few million for pet projects will sweeten his disposition."

Ella didn't want to talk about money or family. She jumped up. "I'm going to walk."

He rose effortlessly beside her and kept pace.

"Tell me more about the oil fields you've been to," she said, looking for a way to keep her thoughts at bay. She liked listening to Khalid talk. Might as well give him something to talk about.

The next afternoon Ella had a good time shopping. Once inside boutiques, she didn't glance outside. While in the car she had seen no one that appeared to be paying the two of them any attention. Bethanne was fun to shop with. She looked beautiful in the elegant cool colors that went so well with

her blond hair. Twice, salesclerks offered jewel-tone dresses and Bethanne had suggested Ella try them on. Of course the sizes were wrong. Ella was slight, almost petite, not nearly as tall as the American. She was tempted, but conscious of her limited funds, cheerfully refused. She had dresses that would suit. She wasn't going to spend a week's worth of groceries on a dress she'd wear for about an hour.

Bethanne decided on a lovely blue that mimicked the color of her eyes.

"Done. Let's get some coffee. And candied walnuts. They're my favorites," she said when she received the dress in a box.

Having the chauffeur stow the dress in the limo's trunk, Bethanne asked him to take them to an outside café. When they found a coffee house with outside seating on a side street, she had him wait while she and Ella went for coffee.

"This was fun," Bethanne said. "I hope we can become friends. I will be marrying Rashid in a few months and don't know but a handful of people in Quishari. And most of them don't speak English. So until I master this language, I'm left out of conversations."

"I would like another friend. Tell me about Texas. I've never been to the United States."

"Where have you been that you learned so many different languages? And that's not even your career, like the professor's is."

"I went to school in Switzerland for a few years and in England."

"And the Arabic?"

"That I learned because Alexander was learning it and planned to come to an Arabian country to work."

"Alexander was your husband?" Bethanne asked gently.

Ella nodded. "We knew each other from when we were small. I loved him it seems all my life."

"I'm sorry for your loss," Bethanne said.

"Me, too." Ella didn't want to think about it. Every time she grew sad and angry. It had happened. Nothing could change the past. She had to go on. Today she was with a new friend. And beginning to look forward to the reception on Saturday.

Ella worked through the next two days culling her collection, deciding which pieces to display and which to hold in reserve.

She tried on the dresses she'd worn to university events, dismayed to find she had lost more weight than she'd thought. They all were loose. Finally she decided on a dark blue long gown that shimmered in the light and almost looked black. If she wore her hair loose, and the pearls she received when she was eighteen, she'd do. It wasn't as if it were a real date or anything. But she wanted to look nice for Khalid's sake. If he broke his normal habit of nonattendance, it behooved her to look her best.

* * *

Saturday evening, Ella prepared for the reception with care. She had some trepidation about venturing forth into such a large gathering, but felt safe enough since the guests would most likely all be from Quishari. Her hair was longer than she usually wore. The waves gleamed in the light. She hoped she would pass muster as a guest of a sheikh. Her heart tripped faster when she thought of spending the evening with his family and friends. And some of the leaders of the country. She planned to stay right by Khalid's side and remind him how soon they would leave.

Promptly at seven he knocked on the door of the cottage. She picked up a small purse with her keys and went to greet him.

"You look lovely," he said when she opened the door.

She thought he looked fantastic. A man should always wear a tux, she decided.

"I could say the same. Wow, you clean up good."

"Ready?"

"Yes." She pulled the door shut behind her. To her surprise, Khalid had a small sports car waiting. She had expected a limousine as Rashid used. She liked the smaller car; less intimidating. More intimate.

"If we were going for a spin in the afternoon, I'd put the top down. But not tonight."

"Thank you. I spent hours on my hair."

"Literally?"

She laughed, feeling almost carefree for the first time in months. "No, I just washed and brushed it."

He reached over and took some strands in his fingers. "It feels soft and silky. I wondered if it would."

She caught her breath. His touch was scarcely felt, yet her insides were roiling. She looked out the windshield, trying to calm her nerves. It was Khalid, cranky neighbor, reluctant landlord. She tried to quell the racing of her heart.

When they arrived at the reception, Ella was surprised to find it held in a large hotel. "I thought your mother would have it at her home," she commented when he helped her from the car. A valet drove the sports car away.

"Too many people, too much fuss. She prefers to have it taken care of here."

"Mmm." Ella looked around. She hadn't been to such an elegant event in years. Suddenly she felt like a teen again, proud to be going to the grown-up's affair. Excited. She could do this, had done so many times before. But she preferred smaller gatherings, friends to share good times. Like she and—

No, she was not going there. Tonight was about Khalid. She owed him for his reluctant help. So she'd do her best to be the perfect date for a man of his influence and power.

"Khalid, I'm so glad you came. Rashid said you would—but your track record isn't the best." A beautiful woman came up and embraced him. She

smiled at him, patted his good cheek then turned to look at Ella.

"Salimeia, may I present Ella Ponti. Salimeia is my cousin," Khalid said, looking somewhat self-conscious.

Ella couldn't imagine he felt that way. She was aware of his self-confidence—almost arrogance when around her. She watched as he gave a quick glance around the gathering.

An older woman, dressed in a very fashionable gown came over, her eyes fixed on Khalid.

"I am so glad you came," she said, reaching out to grab his hands in hers.

"Mother, may I present Ella Ponti. Ella, my mother, Sabria al Harum."

"Madame, my pleasure," Ella said with formal deference.

"How do you do?" Khalid's mother looked at him in question, practically ignoring Ella.

"I'm glad he came, too. Mo is here. I'll find him and tell him you're here," his cousin said. She smiled and walked away.

"Ella is my tenant," he clarified.

She looked horrified. "Tenant? You are renting her the house your grandmother left you?"

"No, she has the cottage on the estate and has lived there for a year. Didn't you know about her, either?"

Ella expected the woman to shoo her out the door.

She was not the warm, friendly woman her mother-in-law had been.

Sabria al Harum thought for a moment. "The artist Alia was helping?" she guessed.

Ella nodded once. She felt like some charity case the way the woman said it.

"I did not know she had her living on the premises." She said it as if Ella was a kind of infestation.

"I do live there and have an airtight lease that gives me the right to stay for another four years," Ella said with an imp of mischief. She did not like haughty people.

"Nonsense. Khalid, have our attorneys check it out." His mother sounded as if any inconvenience could be handled by someone else.

Ella hid a smile as she looked at Khalid.

"Already done, Mother. Ella's right, she has the right to live there for another four years."

Other guests were arriving. Khalid took Ella's arm and gently moved her around his mother. "We'll talk later," he said. "You have other guests to greet."

"Gee, is she always so welcoming?" Ella said softly, only for his ears.

"No. She is very conscious of the position our family holds in the country. Perhaps because she came to the family as an adult, not raised as we were. Come, I see someone I think you'll enjoy meeting."

She went willingly, growing more conscious of the wave of comments that were softly exchanged

as they passed. She caught one woman staring at Khalid, then looking at Ella. Giving in to impulse, she reached out to take his arm. It automatically bent, so she could have her hand in the crook of the elbow. He pressed her against his side. She moved closer, head raised.

Khalid introduced her to a friend and his wife. They chatted for a few moments, Khalid mentioning Ella's art. Both were interested.

"My uncle has a gallery in the city. Do send me your catalog so I can send it to him," the wife said.

"I would love to. Thank you." Ella replied.

They mingled through the crowd. Once the complete circuit of the ballroom had almost been made, she tugged on Khalid. He leaned closer to hear her over the noise. "Once we've made the circle, we leave, right?"

"If you're ready."

"Ah, Khalid, I heard you came tonight." A florid faced, overweight man stepped in front of them. "Tell your brother to stop sending our business outside of the country. There are others who could have handled the deal he just consummated with the Moroccans." He looked at Ella. "Hello, I don't believe we've met."

"Ella, the finance minister, Ibrahim bin Saali. This is Ella Ponti."

The minister took her hand and held it longer than needed. "A new lovely face to grace our gatherings. Tell me, Miss Ponti, are you from Quishari?"

She tugged her hand free and stepped closer to Khalid. "I've lived here for years. I love this city."

"As do I. Perhaps we can see some of the beauty of the city together sometime," he said suavely.

Ella smiled politely. "Perhaps."

"Excuse us," Khalid said, placing his hand at the small of her back and gently nudging her.

They walked away.

"That was rude," she said quietly in English.

"He was hitting on you."

"He's too old. He was merely being polite."

"He does not think he's too old and polite is not something we think of when we think of Ibrahim."

She laughed. "I don't plan to take him up on his offer, so you're safe."

Khalid looked at her. "Safe?"

She looked back, and their eyes locked for a moment. She looked away first. "Never mind. It was just a comment."

Khalid nodded, scanning the room. "I think we've done our duty tonight. Shall we leave?"

"Yes."

He escorted her out and signaled the valet for his car. When it arrived, he waited until Ella was in before going to the driver's side. "Home?"

"Where else?" she asked.

"I know a small, out-of-the-way tavern that has good music."

"I love good music," she said.

He drove swiftly through the night. What had possessed him to invite her to stay out longer? She had attended the reception, he got some points with his mother, though she hadn't seemed that excited to meet Ella. They could be home in ten minutes.

Instead he was prolonging the evening. He'd never known anyone as interesting to be around as his passenger. She intrigued him. Not afraid to stand up to his bossiness, she nevertheless defended Ibrahim's boorish behavior. He smiled. Never could stand the man. He had been afraid for a moment Ella might be tempted by Ibrahim's power and position. Not his Ella.

He had to give her credit. No one there had guessed she'd come as part of a bargain. No one made comments about how such a pretty woman was wasting her time with him.

The tavern was crowded, as it always was on Saturday nights. It was one place few people recognized him. He could be more like anyone else here, unlike the more formal events his mother hosted. There were several men he knew and waved to when they called to him. Shepherding Ella to the back, they found an empty table and sat, knees touching.

Ella looked around and then at Khalid. "I hear talk and laughter, but no music."

He nodded. "It starts around eleven. We're a bit early. Want something to eat or drink?"

"A snack would be good. We hardly got a

chance to sample the delicacies your mother had available."

"Want to go back?"

"No. This suits me better."

"Why is that?" he asked. He knew why he preferred the dim light of the tavern, the easy camaraderie of the patrons. The periodic escape from responsibilities and position. But why did she think it was better?

"I don't know anyone."

"That doesn't make sense. Wouldn't it be better to know friends when going to a place like this?"

She shrugged. "Not at this time."

"Did you have a favorite spot you and your husband liked to frequent?" he asked. He wanted to know more about her. Even if he had to hear about the man who must have been such a paragon she would never find anyone to replace him.

She nodded. "But I don't go there anymore. It's not the same."

"Where do you and your friends go?" he asked.

"Nowhere." She looked at him.

Her eyes were bright and her face seemed to light up the dark area they sat in.

"This is the first I've been out since my husband's death. Friends come to visit me, but I haven't been exactly in a party mood. But this isn't like a real date or anything, is it? Just paying you back for letting me use the salon for my pictures."

"Exactly. You wouldn't want to go on a real date with me. I know about that from my ex-fiancée."

"What are you talking about?"

"This." He gestured to the scar on the side of his face.

"Don't be dumb, Khalid. That has nothing to do with it. I still feel married to Alexander and am faithful."

Khalid nodded and looked away, feeling her words like a physical blow. Even if they got beyond the scar, she would never be interested in him. She loved a dead man. He wished they'd gone straight home. She could be with her memories, and he could get back to the reality of his life. Only her words had seemed so wrong.

CHAPTER FIVE

HE LOOKED back at her. "You're not serious? You are not married—that ended when your husband died. And you are far too young and pretty to stay single the rest of your life."

She blinked in surprise. "I'm not that young."

"I'd guess twenty-five at the most," he said.

"Add four years. Do you really think I look twenty-five?" She smiled in obvious pleasure.

Khalid felt as if she'd kicked him in the heart. "At most, I said. Even twenty-nine is too young to remain a widow the rest of your life. You could be talking another sixty years."

"I'll never find anyone to love like I did Alexander," she said, looking around the room. For a moment he glimpsed the sorrow that seemed so much a part of her. He much preferred when she looked happy.

"My grandmother said that after her husband died. But she was in her late sixties at the time. They'd had a good marriage. Raised a family, enjoyed grandchildren."

"I had a great marriage," she said.

"You could again."

She looked back. "You're a fine one to talk. Where's your wife and family?"

"Come on, Ella, who would marry me?"

"No one, with that attitude. How many women have you asked out in the last year?"

"If I don't count you, none."

"So how do you even know, then."

"The woman I was planning to spend my life with told me in no uncertain terms what a hardship that would be. Why would I set myself up for more of the same?"

The waiter came and asked for drink orders. Khalid ordered a bowl of nuts in addition.

"She was an idiot," Ella said, leaning closer after the man left.

"Who?"

"Your ex-fiancée. Did she expect life to be all roses and sunshine?"

"Apparently." He felt bemused at her defense. "Shouldn't it be?"

"It would be nice if it worked that way. I don't think it does. Everyone has problems. Some are on the inside, others outside."

"We know where mine is," he said.

She shocked him again when she got up and switched chairs to sit on his right side. "I've noticed, you know," she said, glaring at him in defiance.

"Noticed what?" He was growing uncomfortable. He tried to shelter others from the ugly slash of burned skin.

"That you always try to have me on your left. Are you afraid I'll go off in shock or something if I catch sight of the scar?"

"No, not you."

"What does that mean?"

"Just, no, not you. You wouldn't do that, even if you wanted to. I'd say your parents raised you very well."

"Leave my parents out of any discussion," she said bitterly.

"Touch a nerve?"

She shrugged. "They and I are not exactly on good terms. They didn't want me to marry Alexander."

"And why was that?"

"None of your business."

The waiter returned with the beverages and plate of nuts. Ella scooped up a few and popped them into her mouth.

"Mmm, good." She took a sip of the cold drink and looked at the small stage.

"I think your musicians are arriving."

So his tenant was at odds with her parents. He hadn't considered she had parents living, or he would have expected her to return home after her husband's death. Now that he knew they were alive, it seemed strange that she was still in Quishari and not at their place. His curiosity rose another notch.

He would nudge the researcher at the oil company to complete the background check on his tenant.

Khalid spent more time watching Ella as the evening went on than the musicians. She seemed to be enjoying the music and the tavern. He enjoyed watching her. They stayed until after one before driving home.

"Planning to take a walk on the beach tonight?" he asked.

"Why not?" she asked. "I'm still buoyed up by that last set. Weren't they good?"

"I have enjoyed going there for years. We'll have to go again sometime."

"Mmm, maybe."

He didn't expect her to jump at the chance. But he would have liked a better response.

"Meet you at the beach in ten minutes," she said when she got out of the car.

"No walking straight through?" he asked.

"I don't know about you, but I don't want to get saltwater and sand on this gown. And I'd think it wouldn't be recommended for tuxedos, either."

Khalid changed into comfortable trousers and a loose shirt and arrived at the beach seconds ahead of Ella.

They started north. The moon was fuller tonight and spread a silvery light over everything. Without much thought, he reached for her hand, lacing their fingers together. She didn't comment, nor pull away.

Taking a deep breath, he felt alive as he hadn't in a long while.

"I appreciate your going with me tonight. My mother is always after me to attend those things for the sake of the family," he said.

"She would have been happier without me accompanying you," Ella said.

"She doesn't like anyone who shows an interest in her sons. Unless it's the woman she's picked out. Did you know Rashid almost had an arranged marriage?"

"No, what happened?"

"His supposed fiancée was to be flown in on the plane Bethanne delivered. Only she never left Morocco. When he fell for Bethanne, Mother was furious. I think they are getting along better now, but I wouldn't say Mother opened her arms to Bethanne."

"I bet your grandmother would have loved her."

"She would have loved knowing Rashid was getting married."

For a moment Khalid felt a tinge of envy for his brother. He had found a woman he adored and who seemed to love him equally. They planned a life in Quishari at the other home their grandmother had left and had twice in his hearing mentioned children. He'd be an uncle before the first year was out, he'd bet.

"Bethanne doesn't strike me as someone who cares a lot about what others think of her," Ella said.

"I'm sure Mother will come around once she sees how happy Rashid is. And once she's a grandmother."

Ella fell silent. They walked for several minutes. Khalid wondered what she was thinking. Had she wanted to be a mother? Would her life be vastly different if she had a small child to raise? She should get married again.

She was right—that was easy enough for him to say. They were a pair, neither wanting marriage for different reasons. Maybe one day another man would come along for her to marry. Once she was out, showing off her creations, she'd run into men from all over the world.

Khalid refused to examine why he didn't like that idea.

"Ready to head back?" she asked.

He nodded, but felt curiously reluctant to end the evening. He liked being with Ella.

The return walk was also in silence, but not without awareness. Khalid could breathe the sweet scent she wore, enjoy the softness of her hands, scarred here and there by burns from her work. She wore a skirt again. He didn't think he'd seen her in pants except when working at her studio. It made her seem all the more feminine. He didn't want the evening to end. Tomorrow would bring back the barriers and status of tenant and landlord. He had no more reasons to seek her out or take her out again. But he wanted to.

"I can get home from here," she said when they reached the path.

"I'll walk that short distance." He was not ready to say good-night.

When they reached the cottage, she tugged her hand free. "Good night. I enjoyed the tavern. And am glad I got to meet your mother even if she wasn't as glad to meet me."

He reached for her, holding her by her shoulders and drawing her closer. "I'm glad you went with me."

"We're even now, right?" Her voice sounded breathless. He could see her dimly in the light from the moon, her eyes wide, her mouth parted slightly.

With a soft groan, he leaned over and kissed her. He felt her start of surprise. He expected her to draw away in a huff. Instead, after a moment, she leaned against him and returned his kiss. Their mouths opened and tongues danced. Her arms hugged him closer and his embraced her. For a long moment they kissed, learning, tasting, touching, feeling.

She was sweet, soft, enticing. He could have stood all night on the doorstep, kissing Ella.

But she pushed away a moment later.

"Good night, Khalid," she said, darting into the house and shutting the door.

"Good night," he said to the wooden door.

This was not going to be their last date, no matter what Ella thought.

Ella leaned against the door, breathing hard. She closed her eyes. She'd kissed Sheikh Khalid al

Harum! Oh, and what a kiss. Unlike anything she'd ever had before.

"No!" she said, pushing away and walking back to the kitchen. She wanted water, and a clear head. She loved Alexander. He was barely gone a year and she was caught up in the sensuousness of another man. How loyal was that? How could she have responded so strongly. Good grief, he'd probably think she was some sex-starved widow out to snare the first man who came along.

How could she have kissed him?

She took a long drink of water, her mind warring with her body. The kiss had been fantastic. Every cell in her tingled with awareness and yearning. She wanted more.

"No!" she said again. She had her life just as she wanted it. She did not need to become the slightest bit involved with a man who wanted her to leave so he could sell a family home.

On the other hand, maybe she should do just that. Put an end to time with Khalid by moving away.

She went to her bedroom and dressed for bed, thoughts jumbled as she brushed her teeth. She had a good place here, safe and perfect for making new pieces of art. She wasn't going anywhere. She just had to wait a little while; he'd get tired of being here and be off on some other oil field consultation and she'd be left alone. She just had to hold out until then. No more night walks. No more kisses.

Though as she fell asleep, she brushed her lips with her fingertips, remembering their first kiss.

The next morning Ella went to her studio, ready to work. She had to focus on her plans for the future and forget a kiss that threatened to turn her world upside down.

Easier said than done. Her dreams last night had been positively erotic. Her first thought this morning was that kiss. And now she was growing warm merely thinking about Khalid and his talented mouth. Why had he showed up? Why not go consult at some oil field and leave her in peace.

Try as she might, as the morning wore on, she couldn't get last night off her mind. Finally putting a small dish into the annealer to cool down, she decided to go see Khalid and make sure he knew she was not interested in getting involved.

She cleaned up, had a light lunch and then went to broach him at his home.

When she rang the bell, Jalilah opened the door, looking flustered. "Come in, things are hectic. His Excellency is leaving in a few minutes."

"Leaving?" This was perfect. He was leaving even earlier than she planned. He'd probably been as horrified by their kiss as she had been. He'd leave and if he ever came back, they'd have gotten over whatever awareness shimmered between them and they could resume the tenant-landlord relationship.

"A fire. He and his team are gathering at the airport in an hour."

Fear shot through Ella. He was going to another fire. For a moment she remembered Alexander, bloodied and burned from the car crash. He'd been coming after her. He hadn't deserved to die so young. She didn't like that memory any more than the one that flashed into her mind of Khalid burned beyond recognition. Nothing as unforgiving as flames.

She walked swiftly to the study, where Khalid was speaking on the phone. Entering, she crossed to the desk.

"See you then," he said, his eyes on her. "Got to go now."

"You can't go put out a fire," she said.

He rose and came around the desk. Lightly brushing the back of his fingers against her cheek, he asked, "Why not. It's what I do."

"It's too dangerous. Don't you have others who can handle that?"

"Others work with me on these projects. It's another one at a well Bashiri Oil has down on the southern coast. It blew a few months ago and it's burning again. Something's wrong with the pump or operators. Once this is capped, I plan to find out why it keeps igniting."

"It's dangerous."

"A bit. Are you all right? You have circles beneath your eyes."

She brushed his hand away. "I'm fine. It's you I'm worried about. What if something goes wrong? You don't have to do this. Send someone else."

"Something has gone wrong—a well is on fire. My team and I will put it out and do our best to make sure it doesn't happen again. I have to do this. It's what I do."

"It's too dangerous."

"I like the danger. Besides, what does it matter who does it as long as it gets put out? If not me, another man would be in danger. Maybe one who has a wife and children waiting at home."

She couldn't reach him. He would go off and probably get injured again. Or worse.

"Don't go," she said, reaching out to clutch his arms. She could feel his strength beneath the material, feel the determination.

"I have to—it's what I do."

"Find another job, something safer."

"Not today," he said, and leaned over to brush his lips against hers. "Come on, you can walk me out."

She stepped back, fear rising even more. What if something happened to him? She'd planned to tell him to stay away, but not like this.

When they reached the foyer, she noticed the duffel bags and heavy boots. He lifted them easily and nodded to Jalilah to open the door. A moment later they were stowed into the back of the small sports car. Ella followed him like a puppy, wishing

she had the words to stop him. The seconds flew by. She could not slow time, much less stop it. But if she could, she would. Until she could talk him out of this plan. What if something happened to him?

"See you in a few days," he said easily.

"I hope so," she replied. But what if she didn't? What if she never saw him again? The feelings that thought triggered staggered her. She didn't want to care. That way lay heartache when tragedy struck.

She rounded the car and stood by him as he opened the driver's door. "Come back safely," she said, reaching up to kiss him. All thoughts of putting distance between them vanished. She couldn't let him go off without showing just a hint of what she felt. She would not think of all that could go wrong, but concentrate on all that could go right.

He let go the car door and kissed her back, cupping her face gently in his hands. His lips were warm but in only a moment she felt cold when he pulled away.

"I'll be back when the job's done," he said, climbing into the car. "Stay out of trouble," he said, and pulled away.

She watched for a moment, then with an ominous sense of foreboding, returned to her cottage. She felt as if she was in a daze. Fear warred with common sense. He knew what he was doing. Granted it was dangerous. But he'd done it before. And he did not have a death wish. He would take all necessary precautions.

Changing into work clothes, she went to the studio. She could always lose herself in art.

But not, it appeared, today. She tried to blow a traditional bowl, but the glass wasn't cooperating. Or her technique was off. Or it was just a bad day. Or she couldn't concentrate for thinking of Khalid. Glancing at her watch, she wondered where he was. She should have asked questions, found out where the fire was. How long he thought he'd be gone.

After two hours of trying to get one small project done, she gave up. Her thoughts were too consumed with Khalid. If he'd left the airport an hour ago, he could already be in harm's way. She paced her small studio, wondering how she could find out information about the fire. She did not have a television. She tried a radio, but the only programs she found were music.

Finally she went to the main house. When the maid answered the door, Ella asked to use the phone. She had done so a couple of times when Madame al Harum had lived here, so Jalilah was used to the request. Ella hoped Khalid had not given instructions to the contrary.

Jalilah showed her into the study and left. Ella stayed in the doorway for a moment. Everything inside instantly reminded her of Khalid. How odd. She'd visited Madame al Harum in this room many more times than she had her grandson. But he'd stamped his impression on the room in her mind forever.

She went to the phone. Who could she call but his brother. She hunted around for the phone number of Bashiri Oil and when she found it on a letterhead, she tried the number. It took her almost ten minutes to get to Rashid's assistant.

"I'm calling for Sheikh Rashid al Harum," she said for about the twentieth time.

"Who is calling?"

"Ella Ponti. I'm his brother's tenant in the house his grandmother once owned," she repeated.

"One moment, please."

On hold again, Ella held on to her composure. What would she do if Rashid wasn't there? Or wouldn't take her call? She had no idea how to reach Bethanne, who might be an ally.

"Al Harum." Rashid's voice came across the line sounding like Khalid's. She closed her eyes for a second, wishing it were Khalid.

"It's Ella Ponti. Khalid left this morning to put out a fire. Do you know anything about that?"

"I do. It's on one of the wells in the southern part of the country. Why?"

"I, uh…" She didn't know how to answer that. "I wanted to make sure he's all right," she said, wondering if Rashid would think her daft to be asking after his brother with such a short acquaintance.

"So far. The team arrived a short time ago. They assess the situation then plan their attack. It could be a day or two before they actually cap it."

Two days he could be in danger and she wouldn't know? This was so not the answer she wanted.

"Um, could you have someone keep me updated?" she asked tentatively. She didn't know if Sheikh al Harum would be bothered, but she had to ask. Surely there was some clerk there who could call her once something happened.

"I worry about him, too," Rashid said gently. "I'll let you know the minute I hear anything."

"Thank you. I'm using his phone. I don't have one. Jalilah can get me." She hung up, a bit reassured. She didn't want to question her need to make sure he was safe. She'd feel the same about anyone she knew who had such a dangerous job.

Ella sat in the desk chair for several moments. She studied the room, wondering what Khalid thought about when he sat here. She suspected he missed his grandmother more than he might have expected. The older woman had spoken so lovingly about her grandsons. Their family sounded close.

Except perhaps their mother. Or was her hesitancy welcoming women into the fold mere self-protection. It would be too bad to have someone pretend affection if they were only after money. How would she become convinced? Nothing had convinced her parents Alexander had not been after their money. They hadn't seemed to care that their only daughter was very happy in her marriage. The constant attempts to end the union had only alien-

ated them. Ella hoped Madame al Harum never resorted to such tactics, but accepted Rashid's choice and wished him happiness.

She stood up and went back to her place. She didn't want to think about her parents, or Alexander, or anything in the past. She didn't want to worry about a man she hardly knew. And she didn't want to worry about the future. For today she'd try to just make it through without turmoil and complications, fear and dread.

Shortly after lunch there was a knock at the door. When Ella opened it, she was surprised to see Bethanne.

"Hi, I thought you might wish for some company," she said.

"Come in. I'm glad for company. I couldn't work today."

"I wouldn't be able to, either, if Rashid was doing something foolishly dangerous."

When they were on the terrace with ice-cold beverages, Ella smiled at her new friend. "What you said earlier, about Rashid being in a dangerous position—ever happen?"

"Not that I know about. And I would be sick with worry if he went off to put out an oil well fire."

"You and he are close, as it should be since you will be marrying him. Khalid is my landlord."

Bethanne laughed. "Right. And Madame al Harum and I are best friends."

Ella wrinkled her nose slightly. "I don't think she thinks in terms of friends."

"Well, not with the women who might marry her sons."

"I heard she helped arrange a marriage, but it didn't take place."

"Good thing for me. Rashid was going along with it for business reasons. Honestly, who wants to get married for business reasons? I'm glad he caught on."

"And the other woman?"

"She ran off with a lover and I have no idea what happened after that. But she obviously had more sense than my future husband. Much as I adore him, I do wonder what he was thinking considering an arranged marriage. I can't imagine all that passion— Oops, never mind."

Ella looked away, hiding a smile. She remembered passion with Alexander when their marriage was new. The image of Khalid kissing her sprang to mind. Her heart raced. She experienced even more passion that night. She did not want to think about it, but couldn't erase the image, nor the yearning for another kiss. Would that pass before he returned?

She had not helped her stance by kissing him goodbye. She should have wished him well and kept her distance.

"If they don't get the well capped today, they'll try tomorrow," Bethanne said, sipping her drink. "And if that doesn't work, Rashid wants to go there.

If we do, want to fly with us? I took the crew down. They spent the entire flight going over schematics of the oil rig. It's in the water, you know. You'd think with the entire Persian Gulf at their feet it would be easy enough to put out a fire."

Ella laughed, but inside she stayed worried.

Bethanne was wonderful company and the two them spent the afternoon with laughter. Ella was glad she'd come to visit. Except for a very few friends from the university, she didn't have many people she saw often. She had wanted it that way when Alexander first died. Now she could see the advantage of going out more with her friends. It took her mind off other things. Like if Khalid was safe or not.

The next morning she took an early walk along the beach. She never tired of the changing sea, some days incredibly blue other days steely-gray. She loved the solitude and beauty. During the day other people used the beach and she waved to a family she knew by sight. Watching the children as they played in the water gave her a pang. She and Alexander never had children. They thought they had years to start a family. They had wanted to spend time together as a couple before embarking on the next stage of family life.

His death cut everything short. She wished she'd had a baby with him. Would a child have brought her more comfort? Or more pain as every day she saw her husband in its face? She'd never know.

When she returned to the cottage, she saw a black car parked in front of the main house. Staying partially hidden behind the shrubs, she watched for a moment. It was not Khalid's sleek sports car. Was Madame al Harum visiting? Surely she knew her son was gone. Unless—had something happened. She could scarcely breathe. If Khalid had been injured, would Rashid send someone to tell her?

A moment later a man came from the house and got into the car, swiftly driving away.

Ella caught her breath at the recognition. She pulled back and waited until the car was gone before moving. In only seconds she was home, the door firmly locked behind her. How had they found her? She paced the living room. Obviously the maid had not given out where she lived or he would have camped on her doorstep. But it was only a matter of time now before he returned. Maybe he wanted to speak to the sheikh. Good grief, Khalid didn't know not to give out the information. His grandmother had been a staunch ally, but Khalid was looking for a way to get her to leave early. Had he any clue? Could she convince him not to divulge her whereabouts if her brother came calling again?

He had no reason to keep her home a secret. In fact, she could see it as his benefit to give out the information and stand aside while he tried to get her to return home.

Pacing did little but burn up energy, which seemed

to pour through her as she fretted about this turn of events. She had grown comfortable here. She liked living here, liked her life as she'd made it since Alexander's death. She was not going home, no matter what. But she did not want the pressure Antonio would assert. Should she leave before Khalid returned? If he didn't know where she was, he couldn't give the location away.

But she didn't want to leave. Not until she knew if he was all right. What if the fire damaged more than equipment? Men could die trying to put out an oil fire. She so did not need any of this. She'd worked hard the last year to get her life under control.

Drawing a deep breath, she went to her desk and pulled out a sheet of paper. She'd make a list of her choices, calmly, rationally. She'd see what she could do to escape this situation—

Escape. That's what she wanted. Could Bethanne help? She could fly her to a secret location and never tell anyone.

Only, would she? And how much would it cost to hire the plane? Maybe she should have sold some of her work to give herself more capital. She had enough for her needs if she was careful. But a huge chunk spent on a plane trip could wreak the financial stability she had. Did she have the luxury of time? She could find a bus to take her some-where in the interior. But not her equipment. Not her studio.

She couldn't leave that behind. It was her only way to make the glass art that she hoped was her future.

Jumping up, she began to walk around, gazing out the window, touching a piece of glass here and there that she'd made. What was she going to do?

There was a knock on the door. Ella froze. Had he found her already? Slowly she crossed the room and peeked out of the small glass in the door. It was Jalilah.

Ella opened the door.

"Hello," the maid said. "I came to tell you someone was at the house earlier, asking after you. He said the sheikh had sent inquiries to Italy. I remember Madame's comments when you first came here to live. She wanted you to have all the privacy you wanted. I told the man the sheikh was away from home and did not know when he would return."

"Thank you!" Ella breathed a sigh of relief. She had a respite. No fear of discovery today.

But—Khalid had sent inquiries to Italy? Why?

Jalilah bowed slightly and left.

Had Khalid sought to find other ways to get her to leave? Anger rose. How dare he put out inquiries? Who did he think he was? And more importantly, who did he think she was? He couldn't take her word?

After a hasty lunch Ella could barely eat, she went to the studio, trying to assess how much it would take to move her ovens, bench and all the accoutrements she had for glassblowing. More than a quick plane ride west.

Maybe she could leave for a short while, let her brother grow tired of looking for her again and when he left, she'd return. Only, what if Khalid then told him when she returned. She'd never be safe.

She heard a car and went to the window, peering out at the glimpse of the driveway she had. It was Khalid's car. He was home.

Without thinking, she stormed over to the main house. The door was shut, so she knocked, her anger at his actions growing with every breath.

Jalilah opened the door, but before she could say a word of greeting, Ella stepped inside.

"Where is he?" she demanded.

"In the study," the maid said, looking startled.

Ella almost ran to the study door. Khalid was standing behind the desk, leafing through messages. He hadn't shaved in a couple of days, the dark beard made him look almost like a pirate—especially when viewed with the slash of scar tissue. His clothes were dirty and she could smell the smoke from where she stood. None of it mattered.

"What have you done to my life?" she asked.

CHAPTER SIX

HE LOOKED up. "Hello, Ella."

"I mean it. What gives you the right to meddle in things that don't concern you? You have ruined everything!"

"What are you talking about?" he asked.

"You sent inquiries to Italy, right?"

He lifted a note. "Garibaldi?"

"If you wanted to know something, why not ask me? I told you all you needed to know. I told you more than I've told anyone else."

"Who is Antonio Garibaldi?" he asked, studying the note a moment, then looking at her. His eyes narrowed as he took in her anger.

"He's my brother. And the reason my husband is dead. I do not wish to have anything to do with him. How could you have contacted them? How could you have led them right to me? I've tried so hard to stay below the radar and with one careless inquiry you lead them right to me. I can't believe this!"

"Wait a second. I don't know what you're

talking about. Your family didn't know you were living here?"

"If I had wanted them to know, I would have told them."

"How did your brother cause your husband's death? Didn't you say it was a car crash? Was your brother in the other car?"

"No. He practically kidnapped me. He lured me to the airport with the intent of getting me on the private jet he'd hired. Only someone told Alexander. He was coming to get me before Antonio could take me out of the country. He crashed on the way to the airport. The police, thankfully, stepped in and stopped our departure." She looked away, remembering. "So I could identify Alexander's body."

She burst into tears.

Khalid looked at her dumbfounded. In only a second he was around the desk and holding her as she sobbed against his chest.

"He had a class. He should have been safely inside, teaching, instead he was trying to come to my rescue," she said between sobs. She clutched a fistful of his shirt, her face pressed against the material, her tears soaking the cotton. She scarcely noticed the smoke. "He would still be alive today if Antonio hadn't forced me. *Alexander.*" She cried harder.

Khalid held her close, her pain went straight to his heart. He'd felt the anguish of losing a woman he

thought he would build his life with. But his anger soon overcame any heartache. This woman was still devastated by the loss of her husband. What would it be like to mean so much to someone? He thought about his brother and the woman he was going to marry. Bethanne loved him; there was no doubt to anyone who saw them together. She'd be as devastated if something happened to Rashid.

Khalid knew that kind of attachment, that kind of love, was rare and special. Her husband had been dead for more than a year. Ella should have moved on. But the strength of her sobs told him she still mourned with an intensity that was amazing. The emotions told of a strong bond, a love that was deeply felt.

He had never known that kind of love. And never would.

Finally she began to subside. He didn't know what to do but hold her. He'd caused this outburst by his demand to know more. Had the man at Bashiri Oil been clumsy in his research? Or was the family on alert for information about their daughter? Was her brother's involvement the cause of the estrangement, or did it go deeper? Khalid wanted answers to all the questions swirling around in his mind.

But now, his first priority was to make things right with Ella.

Slowly he felt her hands ease on the clutching of his shirt. A moment later she pushed against his chest. He let her go, catching her face in his palms

and brushing away the lingering tears with his thumbs. Her skin was warm and flushed. He registered the softness and the vulnerability she had with her sorrowful eyes, red and puffy.

"I did not know making an inquiry would cause all this," he said. "You are safe here. I will not let anyone kidnap you. Tell me what happened."

She pushed away and stepped back. "I'm not telling you anything. You tell my brother when he contacts you again that you have no idea where I'm living. Make him go away. Make sure he never finds me."

"You think he'll come again?" Khalid asked.

"Of course. He's tenacious."

"Why should he come for you?"

"My family wants me home. I want to stay here. If you can't guarantee I can stay, I'll have to disappear and won't tell you where I go."

Two weeks ago Khalid would have jumped at the offer. He wanted his tenant gone so he could put the estate up for sale. But two weeks changed a lot. He wasn't as anxious to sell as he had once been. He liked living near the sea. He liked the after dark walks along the shore. He did not want his tenant to leave and not give a forwarding address.

More importantly, he wanted to know the full story of what was going on. How could she be so afraid of her family?

"How old are you?" he asked, stepping back to give her more space.

"Twenty-nine. You know that. What does that have to do with anything?"

"As far as I understand the laws in most countries, that makes you an adult, capable of making your own decisions on where to live."

"You'd think so," she said bitterly, brushing the last of the tears from her face. She walked to the window and peered out, but Khalid didn't think she saw the colorful blossoms.

She rubbed her chest, as if pressing against pain. "Alexander and I were childhood sweethearts. My parents thought we'd outgrow that foolishness. Their words. They had a marriage in mind for me that would probably rival what your mother had for Rashid. Combining two old Italian families, and merging two fortunes that would only grow even larger over the years."

Khalid frowned. He made a mental note to get in touch with the man at the company who had been doing the research for him. What had he discovered?

"So you and Alexander married against parental wishes. It happens."

"When they discovered where we were living, Antonio came and said I had to return home. There would be an annulment and the arranged marriage would go forth. I laughed at him, but he was stronger than I was and soon I was in a car heading for the airport. The rest you know. I managed to dodge him at the police station and then hid until I

thought he'd left Quishari. Mutual friends contacted your grandmother who offered me a place to live. I'm forever grateful to her. I miss her a lot. She really liked my work, and I think she liked me. But more importantly—she gave me a safe haven. I'll never forget that."

"I'm sure she did," Khalid said, stunned to learn this. Had his actions threatened the haven Ella clung to? He would have to take steps to remedy the situation.

Ella turned and looked at him.

"If my actions caused this, I will fix it," he said.

"If? Of course they did. No one has ever come here before. Why did you have to ask about me. I told you about me."

"I wanted to know more. My grandmother never mentioned you. My family doesn't know about you. What you told me was limited."

"You're my landlord—you know all you need to know about me. I pay my rent on time and I have a lease. I don't trash the place. End of story."

"I want more."

"Well, we don't always get what we want in life," she snapped.

Khalid stared at her, seeing an unhappy, sad woman. One to whom he'd brought more pain and suffering. It didn't come easy, but he had to apologize. "I'm sorry."

She shrugged. "Sorry doesn't change anything."

"It lets you know I didn't deliberately cause you this grief. I said I'd fix it and I shall."

"How? Erase my brother's memory? Put up guards so no one can get on the estate? Wouldn't that also mean no one goes off, either? I had things going just fine until you showed up."

"Sit down and we'll get to the bottom of this." He went around the desk and called Bashiri Oil. In less than a minute he was speaking to the researcher in the office who had been asked to find out more about Ella Ponti. He listened for a solid five minutes, his expression impassive as the man recited what he'd discovered, ending with…

"One of her brothers was in the office yesterday, trying his best to get more information. We know better than to give that kind of information. He accosted people in the halls and in the parking area. Finally we had security remove him from the premises. But I'd watch out—he's looking for his sister and seems most determined."

"I, also, can be determined," Khalid said softly.

"True, Excellency. And I'd put my money on you."

Khalid ended the call.

"It appears the inquiries I had made did cause your brother to return to Quishari. He is staying at the Imperial Hotel. He has made a pest of himself at the company headquarters, questioning everyone trying to locate you. Why is it so important that you marry the man your parents picked out? Surely that

was years ago. You said you'd been married for four years, and Alexander has been dead for one. What is so compelling?"

"To further the dynasty, of course. And ensure the money doesn't go outside the family or the family business—wine. I have a trust, that I can't access for another couple of years. But my father was convinced Alexander wanted only my money. He was wrong. Alexander loved me. We lived modestly on his income from the university. We were so happy."

Tears filled her eyes again, and Khalid quickly sought a way to divert them. He was not at all capable of dealing with a woman's tears. He wished he'd never thought to find out more about the woman his grandmother had rented the cottage to.

"I'll go see your brother and make sure he leaves you alone."

She blinked away the tears, hope shining from her eyes.

"You will?"

Khalid nodded, loath to involve himself in her family dynamics, but he felt responsible for causing the problem. "I'll shower, change and go to the hotel myself."

Ella thought about it for a moment, then nodded once. "Fine, then. You take care of it." She turned and went to the door, pausing a moment and looking back at him. "I'm glad you got home safely. The fire out?"

"Yes."

"Did you find out what caused it?"

"I believe so. We have taken steps to make sure there won't be another one at that rig."

"Good." She left.

Khalid rubbed the back of his neck. He had better get changed and to the hotel before her brother annoyed even more people. Or came back and found Ella.

Ella kept her house locked up all day. She knew her brother. He would not likely be sidetracked from his goal just on Khalid's say-so. Not that she would buck the power of the sheikh. He could probably buy and sell her brother without batting an eye. And it was his country. His family was most prominent. Antonio would find no allies in Quishari. Served him right. She couldn't forget the last time she'd seen him. If he had never come last year, Alexander would be alive today.

As the afternoon waned, Ella wondered if Khalid had truly gone to see her brother. She had not seen him return. What if he'd changed his mind? Upon further consideration, he had to know this would be the perfect way to rid himself of the tenant he didn't want. The more Ella thought about it, the more certain she was that was what happened. It could not take Khalid hours to go tell Antonio to go home.

Restless, she set off for her walk when it was barely dark. She doubted she'd sleep tonight. In

fact, she might best be served by packing essentials and contacting Bethanne to ask for a ride someplace. At this point, Ella would take anyplace away from Alkaahdar.

She walked farther than normal, still keyed up. When she came to a more populated area, she sat near the water. There were others still on the beach. A small party had a fire near the water, and were sitting around it, laughing and talking. She watched from the distance. How long had it been since she felt so carefree and happy?

When that party began breaking up, Ella realized how late it was—and she still had a very long walk home. She rose and walked along the water, the moon a bright disk in the sky. She was resigned to having to leave. There didn't seem to be any choice unless she wanted her family to take over her life. And that she vowed would never happen. She was not some pawn for her father's use. She liked being on her own. Loved living in Quishari. She'd have to find a way.

She slowed when she drew closer to the estate. Would Khalid be on the beach? She wasn't up to dealing with him tonight. She'd made a fool of herself crying in his study. She didn't want to deal with any more emotion. She was content with her decisions and her walk. A good night's sleep was all she wanted now. Tomorrow she'd begin packing and slip away before Antonio found her. She'd contact

her friend Marissa to come after she was gone to pack up her glass art. Once she was settled somewhere, she'd see about resuming the glassblowing.

Khalid saw Ella slip through the garden on her way to the cottage. He had tried her place earlier, but she was already gone. Now she was back. It was late, however. He needed to tell her how the meeting with her brother had gone, but maybe it would be best handled in the morning.

He sat in the dark on the veranda, watching her go to her home. A moment later the lights came on in one room, then another. Before a half hour passed, the cottage was dark again. He hoped she had a good night's sleep, to better face tomorrow. He knew she would not be pleased with what he had to tell her.

The next day it rained. The dreary day seemed perfect to Ella as she packed her clothes in one large suitcase. She put her cosmetics in a smaller suitcase and stripped the bed, dumping the sheets into the washer behind the kitchen. She'd leave the place as immaculate as it had been when she moved in. The only part she couldn't do much with would be her studio. She hoped Khalid would permit her friend to come to clear away her things. If not, so be it. It wouldn't be the first time she'd started over. She was better equipped now than she had been a year ago.

The knock on the door put her on instant alert.

She would not open to Antonio no matter what. Slowly she approached the door, looking through the glass, relieved to see it was Khalid.

Opening the door a crack, she stood, blocking the view into the living room. "Yes?" she said.

"I need to talk with you," he said. Today he wore a white shirt opened at the throat. His dark pants were obviously part of a suit. Was he going somewhere for business later?

"About?"

"Your brother, what do you think?"

"You saw him?'

"I did. Are you going to let me in or are we going to talk like this?"

She hesitated. "Is it going to take long? Either you got rid of him or you didn't."

He pushed against the door and she gave in, stepping back to allow him to enter.

She shut the door behind him and crossed to the small sofa, sitting on the edge. He took a chair near the sofa.

Wiping suddenly damp palms against her skirt, she waited with what patience she could muster.

"I saw your brother at the hotel. He is very anxious to talk with you. Seems there's a problem with your family that you only can help with."

"Sure, marry the man they picked out."

Khalid nodded. "Apparently there have been some financial setbacks and your family needs

an influx of cash that the wedding settlement would bring."

She frowned. "What setbacks? The wine business is doing well. We've owned the land for generations, so there's no danger from that aspect. I don't understand."

Khalid shrugged. "Apparently your younger brother has a gambling habit. He's squandered money gambling, incurring steep debts which your father paid for. That didn't stop him. Unless they get another influx of cash, and soon, they will have to sell some of the land. It's mortgaged. They've been stringing creditors along, but it's all coming due soon and they are desperate."

"Giacomo has a gambling problem?" It was the first she'd heard about it. She frowned. For a moment she pictured her charming brother when she had last seen him. He had still been at university, wild and carefree and charming every girl in sight. They'd had fun as children. What had gone wrong?

"While I'm sorry to hear that, I don't see myself as sacrificial lamb to his problem. Let my father get him to marry some wealthy woman and get the cash that way." She could see her patriarchal father assuming she would be the sacrifice to restore the family fortunes.

"Both your brothers are already married."

Ella was startled at the news. She realized cutting herself off from the family when she married

Alexander had meant she wasn't kept up-to-date on their activities. When had her brothers married? Recently? Obviously during the years she and Alexander had lived in Quishari.

"Apparently Antonio feels it is your duty to the family to help in this dire circumstance," Khalid said dryly.

"He's echoing my father. I have no desire to help them out. And I certainly am not going to be forced into marrying some man for his money to bail Giacomo out of a tight place." Antonio had always looked out for her and Giacomo. Looks as if he was still looking out for their younger brother. What about her?

Khalid nodded. "I knew you would feel that way."

"Does he know I live here?" she asked.

Khalid shook his head. "He could end up coming here to see me again and discover you around. But I did not tell him where you lived."

"I'm leaving."

He looked surprised at that.

"Going where?"

"I don't know yet. But I'm not telling anyone. That way they can't find me again."

"Would it be so bad to be in touch with your family? I can't imagine being cut off from Rashid."

"That's different. Your mother isn't trying to marry you off to the woman she wants. Just listen to what Antonio said—I'm to come home and marry

some man for his fortune. You don't want to be married for money, why would you support that?"

"You know I wouldn't. Would it hurt to listen to what he has to say?"

"I'm not going back to Italy."

He shook his head. "I'm not suggesting that. Parents can't arrange marriages for their offsprings."

"Your mother tried with Rashid."

"And it came to nought. I don't see her doing anything now but eventually accepting Bethanne will be his wife."

"She tried it, that's the point. She may try with you."

"I doubt it. She doesn't like the scars any more than another woman would."

"Honestly, I can't believe you harp on that. So you have a scar. Try plastic surgery if you don't like it. In truth, it makes you look more interesting than some rich playboy sheikh who rides by on his looks."

"Playboy sheikh?" he said.

Ella leaned forward. "This is about my problem, not yours."

"Of course." The amusement in his eyes told her he was not taking this as seriously as she was. Why should he? He had power, prestige, money. She had nothing—not even a family to support her.

"So did Antonio leave?" she asked.

"Not yet. He wants to see you. Hear from you that everything is fine."

"And try to kidnap me again to take me home."

"No. I, uh, made it clear he could not do that."

"How?"

Khalid looked uncomfortable. "Actually by the time the meeting was drawing to an end, I was a bit exasperated with your brother."

Ella laughed shortly. "I can imagine. He's like a bulldog when he's after something. So what did you tell him?"

"That you and I were engaged."

Ella stared at him for a long moment, certain she had misheard him. "Excuse me?" she said finally, not believing what echoed in her mind.

"It seemed like a good idea at the time."

"You told my brother we were engaged? You don't even like me. We are not engaged. Not even friends, from what I can tell. Why in the world would you say such a thing?"

"To get him to back down."

"I don't believe this. You're a sheikh in this kingdom. You could order people to escort him to the country borders and kick him out. You could get his visa denied, declare him persona non grata. You could have—"

"Well, I didn't do any of that."

She blinked. "So Antonio thinks we're engaged."

Khalid nodded.

"And that's it? He's going home now?"

"After he's met you and is satisfied you are happy with this arrangement."

For a moment Ella felt a wave of affection for her brother. She didn't always agree with him, but for him to make sure she was happy sounded like the brother she remembered with love. However—

"No."

"No what?"

"I'm not taking that chance. I don't want to see Antonio. I don't want him to know where I live." She looked at him with incredulity. "You don't think they expect you to give the family money if I were really going to marry you, do you? He's probably just as happy with you as candidate as whomever they had picked out in Italy."

"I mentioned that I have a few thousand qateries put away for the future."

"Utterly stupid," she said, jumping to her feet. "I cannot believe you said that. You go back and tell him you were joking or something."

Khalid rose, as well, and came over to her. "Ella, think for a moment. This gets you off the hook. We'll meet him for dinner or something. Show we are devoted to each other. And that you have no intention of returning to Italy. Then he'll be satisfied and take off in the morning. You'll be safely ensconced here and that's an end to it. Once your family finds another way to deal with the debt, you can write and say the engagement ended."

She considered the plan. It sounded dishonest. But it also sounded like it might work. If she could

convince Antonio she was committed to Khalid. Glancing out the window, she wondered if she could look as if she loved the man to distraction when her heart was buried with Alexander.

Yet, he knew her. He could believe she'd fallen in love. He'd often teased her for being a romantic. And her family would welcome Khalid like they never had Alexander. This time they had no reason to suspect he was interested in her money. Next to him, she was almost a pauper.

"Do you think it'll work?" she asked, grasping the idea with faint hope.

"What could go wrong?" he asked. "You'll convince your brother you're deliriously happy. He'll go home and you'll go back to making glass art."

"What do you get out of this?" she asked cynically.

"No more tears?" he said.

She flushed. "Sorry about that."

"No, I didn't mean to make light of it. Just make sure you don't have another meltdown. I'll be gone again soon so you'll have the place to yourself again, like before."

"So you're not planning to sell?"

"Maybe not for a while. I find I'm enjoying living by the water."

"Okay. We'll try your plan. But if he doesn't leave, or tries anything, I'm taking off."

Khalid arranged dinner at a restaurant near the hotel. He picked Ella up at seven and in less than twenty

minutes they arrived at the restaurant. She saw her brother waiting for them once they entered.

"Ella," he said in Italian, coming to kiss both cheeks.

"Antonio," she replied. It had been almost a year since she'd seen him. He looked the same. She smiled and hugged him tightly. No matter what— he was still her older brother.

He shook hands with Khalid. Soon all three were seated in a table near the window that looked over a garden.

"We've been worried about you," Antonio said.

"I'm fine."

"More than fine. Engaged to be married again." He gave her a hard look.

She looked at him. "And?"

"It will come as a surprise to our parents."

"As learning about Giacomo's gambling problem surprised me."

Antonio flicked a glance at Khalid and shrugged. "A way will be found to get the money. Family needs to support each other, don't you think?"

When the waiter came for the order, conversation was suspended for a moment. "Khalid doesn't speak Italian. He speaks English or French, so you choose," Ella said in English.

"English is not so good for me. But for, um, good feelings between us, I speak it," Antonio said.

"Ella tells me your family has been in the wine-

making business for generations," Khalid said. "You are a part of that operation?"

Antonio nodded. "I sell wine. Giacomo helps father with the vineyard and the make. My father wants Ella to come home. She goes a long time."

"Maybe in a while. She cannot come now," Khalid said flatly.

Antonio looked surprised that anyone would tell him no. Ella hid a smile and took a moment to glance around the restaurant. The tables were given plenty of space to insure a quiet atmosphere and offer a degree of privacy for the customers. Her eye caught a glimpse of the minister of finance just as he spotted her.

"Uh-oh," she said softly in Arabic. "The minister is here."

Antonio frowned. "If we speak English, all speak," he said.

"Sorry, I forgot," she replied, looking at Khalid for guidance.

A moment later the minister was at their table.

"Ah, the lovely Madame Ponti," he said with a smile, reaching out to capture her hand and kiss the back. "Rashid, I didn't expect to see you with Madame Ponti," he said with a quick glance at Khalid.

Khalid stood, towering over the older man, exposing the scar when he faced him. "Minister," he said.

"Ah, my mistake. Khalid. No need to get up. I'm

on my way out and saw you dining." He smiled affably at Antonio. "Another guest?"

"Ella's brother." Good manners dictated an introduction which Khalid made swiftly. Explaining Antonio was Italian and didn't speak Arabic.

"English?" he asked.

Antonio nodded.

"Welcome to Quishari," the minister said with a heavy accent.

"Happy to be here. We are celebrating good news—Ella's engagement."

CHAPTER SEVEN

ELLA was struck dumb. She wished she could stuff a sock in her brother's mouth. Her horrified gaze must have shown, as Khalid reached out and touched her shoulder.

"Congratulate us, Minister. You are the first outside the family to know," he said easily.

His grip tightened and she tried to smile. What a disaster this was turning out to be. Khalid must be furious. That's what they got for trying to put something over on Antonio.

"My felicitations. I have to say I am not surprised after seeing you at your mother's event the other evening."

Khalid nodded, releasing his hold on Ella's shoulder as if convinced she would not jump up and flee—which she strongly felt like.

"Don't let me keep you from dinner," the minister said as the waiter approached with their meals on a tray.

When he left, Ella gave a sigh of relief. Maybe

Khalid could catch him later and explain. She needed to concentrate on getting her brother on the next plane to Italy.

"Mother and father will want to meet your fiancé," Antonio said as they began to eat. "You two should visit soon. I can wait here a few days and return with you."

"Unfortunately I am unable to get away for a while and Ella must work on her art," Khalid said.

"Art?" Her brother looked puzzled.

"You have not seen the beautiful glass pieces she makes?" Khalid asked in surprise.

"Oh, those." Antonio gave a shrug. "I've seen bowls and such. Nice enough."

Ella knew better than to take offense at her brother's casual dismissal of her work. He had thought it an odd hobby when she'd been younger. But she'd come a long way since those early attempts. Not that she needed to show him. If Khalid was successful in getting him to leave, she'd be grateful. If not, then maybe Plan B would work better—get Bethanne to fly her somewhere far away and tell no one.

The meal seemed interminable. Ella wanted to scream at her brother to leave her alone. She couldn't forget his part in Alexander's death. If he had not tried to take her home last year, Alexander would still be alive.

Everything was different. When they finished

eating, Khalid escorted them to the curb where the limo was waiting. Ushering them both inside, he gave instructions for Antonio's hotel and settled back.

"We will drop you at your hotel and in the morning I will arrange for the limousine to pick you up to take you to the airport. Ella will contact your parents when it is convenient to visit."

Never underestimate the power of money, status and arrogant male, she thought as she watched her brother struggle with something that would assert his own position. But one look from the dark eyes of the sheikh had Antonio subsiding quietly.

"As you wish. My father will be delighted to learn his daughter is engaged to one of the leading families in Quishari. I hope you both can visit soon."

The ride home from the hotel was in silence. Ella didn't know whether to be grateful to Khalid or annoyed at his outlandish handling of the situation. If the minister hadn't learned of the bogus engagement, they could have muddled through without any bother.

"What if the minister says something?" she asked.

"Who's he going to tell? We are not that important in his scheme of things. You worry about things too much," he said, studying the scenery as they were driven home.

"At least I didn't go off half-cocked and say we were engaged. Too bad he speaks English. The language barrier could have prevented it. I doubt he speaks Italian."

Khalid looked at her. "Your brother will return home, tell your parents you are safe and go on with his life. Once things settle down, you can tell them things didn't work out."

She laughed nervously. "I doubt things will settle down. They will push for marriage."

"Tell them I am not ready."

"Oh, Khalid, if they really need money for Giacomo, then my guess is the next step is get me safely married to you and hit me up for some money. If you were poor as Alexander was, they would never be satisfied with a marriage between us."

"You're an adult. Just tell them no."

"Antonio tried to force me from the country last time. Just say no doesn't work with my family."

"He won't try you in the future, not as long as you live in Quishari."

"Then I may never leave," she said, still worried about the entire scenario.

Khalid had the limousine stop by Ella's cottage and dismissed the man. He escorted her to her door.

"Thanks for dinner, and for standing up for me," she said, opening it.

"That's what fiancés are for," he said, brushing back her hair and kissing her lightly on the lips.

He turned and walked to the villa, wishing he had stayed for a longer good-night kiss. He had hidden it from Ella, but he was worried the minister could stir up trouble that would be hard to suppress.

When he entered the study a few moment later, the answering machine was flashing. He pressed the button.

"What's this I hear about your engagement? You couldn't tell me before the minister?" Rashid's voice came across loud and clear—with a hint of amusement. "Or did he get it wrong? Call me."

Khalid sighed and sank onto the chair. Dialing his brother, he wondered if he could finesse this somehow. It was hard sometimes to have a twin who knew him so well.

"Hello."

"Rashid, it's Khalid."

"Ah, the newly engaged man. I didn't have a clue."

"It's not what you think?"

"So what is it?"

Khalid explained and heard Rashid's laughter. "Sounds almost like Bethanne and me. We pretended she was my intended to close the deal I was working on when the woman I expected didn't show up. Watch it, brother—fake engagements have a way of turning real."

"Not this time. In fact, I wasn't going to tell anyone beyond Ella's brother. Once he was back Italy, she'd be left alone."

"Now you have the minister calling me and undoubtedly Mother to congratulate us on your engagement. And I know from experience, Mother isn't going to be happy."

"She should be glad anyone would even consider marrying me with this face."

"Not if it isn't someone she picked out—which I'm coming to believe means someone she can boss around. Bethanne isn't exactly docile. So what's the plan?"

"I haven't a clue. It would have gone smoothly if the minister hadn't come over. Her brother would have left and things would have returned to normal."

"Whatever that is these days." Rashid was quiet for a moment, then said, "Any chance…"

"What, that she'd want to marry me? Get real. First off, I'm not planning to marry. Your kids will carry on the line. And second, she's still hung up on her dead husband. And I see no signs of that abating. She was crying over him today."

"Fine, you've played the role of hero, rescuing her from her brother. Would that make her feel she owes you? Maybe vacate the cottage so you can sell the place sooner?"

"I wouldn't use that to get her gone."

Rashid was silent.

"Anyway, things will work out."

"Call me if you need me," Rashid said.

When he hung up, Khalid contemplated finding a job ten thousand miles away and staying as long as he could. Who would think inheriting a beautiful estate could end up making him so confused.

The phone rang again.

When he answered, he sighed hearing his mother's greeting.

"I just had an interesting call," she began.

"I know." For a split second he considered telling her the truth. But that fled when he thought of her calling to set the minister straight. He would not like having been lied to.

"Is it true? Honestly, if I had thought you were planning to marry, which you have stated many time you are not, I know several nice women who would have suited much better than a widow of dubious background."

"I know her background."

"I don't. Where is she from? Are you certain she wants to marry you to build a life together, or is she in it to keep the cottage? Once her career takes off, will she leave for greener fields?"

"Who knows what the future holds," he said.

"Your father used to say that all the time. Honestly, men. I suppose I have to have another party to introduce her formally to everyone like I did with Bethanne."

"Hold off on that, Mother."

"Why?"

His mother was sharp; anything out of a normal progression would raise doubts. And he didn't want Ella talked about, or word to reach her family that the engagement wasn't going strong.

"You just had a party…we can wait a few weeks."

Maybe by then something would occur to him that would get him out of the situation. He'd thought it the perfect answer to getting rid of Ella's brother. The first time in recent months he did anything spontaneous and it grew more complicated by the moment. Give him a raging oil fire any day.

"Nonsense. I'll call your aunt. She'll be thrilled to hear you are getting married and want to help. We had given up on you, you know."

Hold that thought, he wanted to say. But for the time being, he'd go along with her idea. He wondered if Ella would. Or if she'd put an end to it the minute her brother took off in the morning. She hadn't welcomed the idea when he first told her.

He went to change into casual clothes and headed for the beach. He didn't know if she'd join him on a walk tonight. He could gauge her reaction by her manner if she did show up.

When he reached the beach, there was no sign of her. He'd wait a bit. It wasn't that late.

Sitting on the still warm sand, he watched the moonlight dance on the water. The soft night breeze caressed. The silence was peaceful, tranquil. Why did men make things so complicated. A quiet night surrounded by nature—that's what he needed. That's what he liked about the desert. The solitude and stillness.

He heard her walking through the garden. Satisfaction filled him. She was coming again. Despite

their differences, he felt closer to her in the dark than he did anyone except Rashid. Theirs was an odd friendship; one that probably wouldn't last through the years, but perfect for now.

"I wondered if you'd want to go walk," she said, walking over and sitting beside him. "You were right, you know. I overreacted, but this was a perfect scheme to get rid of Antonio. You know, of course, that had this been real, the minute we married, he'd be hitting you up for money."

"It crossed my mind," Khalid said. Antonio didn't know him well—nor ever would. But giving money away to people who wasted it was not something he did. Though he could understand family solidarity. Wonder if there were a different way to handle the situation.

He rose and reached out his hand to help her up. With one accord, they left their shoes and began walking to the water. Once on hard-packed sand, they turned north.

Khalid liked the end of the evening this way. Ella was comfortable to be around. With the darkness to cloak the scar, he had no hesitation in having her with him. She didn't have to see the horrible deformity and he didn't have to endure the looks of horror so often seen in people when they were around him. Not that he'd caught even a glimpse of that with Ella after that first day. She seemed to see right through the scar to the man beneath.

"At least we don't have to worry about that. I'm still working on a catalog and will see if I can get a showing earlier than originally planned. Once I have a way to earn a living, I'll be out of your way."

"There is one complication," he said.

"What?"

"My mother thinks we are engaged and is planning a party to announce it to the world."

"What? You've got to be kidding? How did your mother find out?" She stopped walking and stared at him.

"She called me tonight. The minister wasted no time. He has it in for Rashid and I expect is trying to gain an ally with mother in getting insider info or something."

Ella shook her head. "I can imagine how delighted she is to think we're engaged. Did you set her straight?"

"No."

"Why not?"

He refused to examine the reason. He felt protective toward Ella. He didn't want anything to mar her happiness—especially her family. It seemed she'd had enough grief to last a lifetime.

"Seemed better not to."

"Well, tell her in the morning."

"Or, let her think that for a while. What does it hurt?"

Ella thought about it for a moment. "Maybe no one," she said reluctantly.

"If people think you are engaged to me, it'll give you a bit of a step up when going to galleries."

"I wouldn't pretend for that reason."

"But you would to keep your family out of your life."

"I didn't know my younger brother had a gambling problem. He was the cutest little boy. So charming."

He took her hand and tugged her along and resumed walking. "I know. Family pressure can be unrelenting, however. If they think you are already out of reach, they have to look elsewhere for financial help. Personally I'd kick the man out and tell him to make a go of it on his own."

"You talk a hard line, but I bet you would try to work something out if it were Rashid," she said.

Khalid knew that to be true.

"I'm not sure it's fair to you," she continued.

"Why not? I'm the one who started the entire convoluted mess."

"I know, which I think is totally off the wall. But no one who knew us would believe we could fall in love and plan to marry."

"Because of the scar," he bit out.

She whacked him on his arm with her free hand. "Will you stop! That has nothing to do with anything. I'm still grieving for my husband. I don't want to ever go through something like that again.

It's safer to go through life alone, making friends, having a great career, but not putting my heart on the line again. It hurts too much when it's shattered."

"Safer but lonely, isn't it?"

Ella glanced at him. Was he lonely? On the surface he had it all: good looks, money, family behind him. The downside would be the job he did. Yet because of the scarring on his face, he pulled away from social events, hadn't had a friend come to visit since he'd been in the main house. And to hear him talk, he was shunned by others.

She'd seen some looks at the reception, fascinated horror. Her regret was he had to deal with rude, obnoxious people who didn't seem to have the manners necessary to deal with real life.

"Come on," she said, pulling her hand free. "I'll race you to that piece of driftwood." With that, Ella took off at a run for the large log that had washed up on shore during the last storm. She knew she couldn't beat Khalid; he'd win by a long margin. But maybe it would get them out of gloomy thoughts. She felt she'd been on a roller coaster all day. It was time to regain her equilibrium and have some fun.

She'd taken him by surprise, she could tell as he hesitated a moment before starting to run. She had enough of a head start she thought for a few seconds she might win. Then Khalid raced past her, making it look easy and effortless.

Ella was gasping for breath when she reached

the log. He was a bit winded, which helped her own self-respect.

"Do you often race at night?" he asked.

"No one can see me and I can race the wind. It's better than racing you, for I can convince myself I win."

He laughed and picked her up by her waist and twirled them both around. "I win tonight," he said, and lowered her gently to the ground, drawing her closer until they were touching from chest to knees. He leaned over and kissed her sweetly.

Ella closed her eyes, blocking out the brilliant blanket of stars in the sky. Hearing only her own racing heartbeat and the soft sighing of the spent waves. Soon even they were lost to sound as the blood roared through her veins, heating every inch of her. She gave herself up to the wonderful feelings that coursed through her. His mouth was magic. His lips like nectar. His strong body made her feel safe and secure, and wildly desirable.

Time lost all meaning. For endless minutes, Ella was wrapped in sensation. She could have halted time and lived forever in this one moment. It was exquisite.

Then reality intruded. Slowly the kiss eased and soon Khalid had put several inches between them. She stepped forward not wanting to end the contact. His hands rested on her shoulders and gently pushed her away.

"We need to get back before things get out of hand," he said.

She cringed and turned, glad for the darkness to hide her embarrassment. How could she so wantonly throw herself at him when he made it perfectly clear he was not interested in her that way. His gesture with the fake engagement was merely a means to offer some protection to her. If her brother had never shown up, never threatened her, Khalid would never in a million years have pretended that they were involved.

And that was fine by her.

She increased her pace.

"Are we racing back?" he asked, easily keeping pace.

"No." She slowed, but longed to break into another run and beat him home, shut the door and pull the shades. She was an adult. She could handle this—it was only for the length of time to get to her cottage. Then she'd do her best from now on to stay away from Khalid al Harum!

That vow lasted until the next day. Ella spent the early hours working on a small bowl that would be the first of a set, each slightly larger than the previous. She concentrated and was pleased to note she could ignore everything else and focus on the work at hand.

It was past time for lunch when she stopped to get

something to eat. In the midst of a project, she became caught up in the process. But once it was safely in the annealer, thoughts of last night surfaced.

Jalilah knocked on the door before Ella had a chance to fix something to eat.

"His Excellency would like to see you," she said.

"I'm getting ready to eat," Ella said. "Tell him I'll be over later."

Jalilah looked shocked. "I think he wants you now," she said.

"Well, he can't always have what he wants," Ella said. "Thanks for delivering his message. Tell him what I said. Maybe around three." She closed the door.

Who did he think he was, expecting her to drop everything just because he summoned her? He had delusions if he thought she'd drop everything to run to him.

In fact, she might not go at all.

Except her curiosity was roused. What did he want?

She prepared a light lunch and ate on her small veranda. The hot sun was blocked by the grape-covered arbor. The breeze was hot, blowing from the land and not the sea. She wouldn't stay outside long.

Sipping the last of her iced tea, Ella heard the banging on the front door. Sighing, she rose. It didn't take a psychic to know who was there. Dumping her dishes in the sink on her way to the front of the cottage, she wondered if she dare ignore him.

Opening the door, she glared at him instead. "What do you want?"

"To talk to you," he said easily, stepping inside.

She moved to allow him. It was that or be run over. He was quite a bit larger than she was.

Closing the door, she turned and put her hands on her hips. "About what?"

"My mother is hosting another party. This time to formally announce our engagement. We need to go."

"Are you crazy? This has gone on long enough. Tell her the truth."

"Not yet. You need to make sure your family turns elsewhere for relief from your brother's gambling. It's only one evening. You'll meet people, smile and look as if you like me."

"I'm not sure I do," she said, narrowing her eyes. "This gets more complicated by the moment."

"We need to invite some of your friends to make it seem real."

She crossed her arms over her chest. This was unexpected. "I'm not involving my friends. Besides, no one would believe it. They all know how much I loved Alexander. And do you really think they'd believe you'd fall for me?"

"So pretend."

"We don't have to pretend anymore. Antonio's gone and it was for his benefit, right?"

He was silent for a moment.

"Right?" she repeated.

"He did not leave as we thought."

"Why not?" She frowned. What was her brother doing? He wasn't waiting for the wedding, for heaven's sake, was he?

"Now how would I know what your brother thinks…I just met him. But the limo showed up at the hotel in time to get him to the airport for the first flight to Rome and he said he'd changed his plans and would be remaining in Quishari a bit longer."

"Great." She walked across the room and turned, walked back, trying to think of how to get out of the mess the men in her life had caused.

"I'll go away," she said.

"After the announcement," he replied.

She looked at him. He was calm. There was a hint of amusement in his eyes. Which made her all the more annoyed. "This is not a joke."

"No, but it's almost turning into a farce. I thought telling him would shut him up. Do you think I want the world to think I got engaged again and then a second fiancée breaks the engagement?"

She had not thought about that at all.

"Then you break it," she said.

"That'll look good."

"Well, one of us has to end it, so you decide. In the meantime, I do not want to go to your mother's. I do not want the entire city to think we are engaged. I do not—"

He raised a hand to stop her.

"Then you come up with something."

"I wouldn't have to if you hadn't told my brother."

"You could have told him the truth at dinner last night."

She bit her lip. She did not want to return to Italy. She would not be pressured day and night by parents trying to talk her into a marriage with some wealthy Italian to shore up her brother's losses. The days when daughters were sacrificed for the good of the family were long past. If only her father would accept that.

"Okay, so we pretend until Antonio leaves. Can we hurry him on his way?" she asked, already envisioning her mother's tearful pleas; Giacomo's little boy lost entreaties; Antonio begging her to think of the family reputation. She loved her family, but she wasn't responsible for them all.

"He's your brother. I could never hurry Rashid. The more I'd push, the more he'd resist."

She nodded. "Okay, so brothers are universal. Somehow we have to get him to leave me alone."

"So we'll convince him tonight that it's an arrangement meant to be and maybe he'll leave."

"Or hit you up for a loan."

Khalid frowned. "Do you really think that's the reason for the delay?"

"I don't know." Maybe her brother just wanted to make sure she was happy. Yet he'd been right there when her parents had railed against her for marrying

Alexander and never said a word in her behalf. She had no intention of letting any of her family dictate her life.

"What time do we go to your mother's?"

"I'll pick you up at seven."

"How dressy?"

"About like last time. Do you need a new dress?"

She looked at him oddly. "I have enough clothes, thank you. What—do you expect everyone to hit you up for money?"

"No. But women always seem to need new clothes. I can help out if you need it."

"I do not." She studied him for a moment. Thinking about her own family, she knew there were some shirt-tail relatives who had asked her father for handouts. He'd refused and when she was a child, she wondered why he didn't share. Once she was older, she realized some people always have their hands out.

For a moment she wished she had brought some of her clothes from home. She and her mother had shopped at the most fashionable couturiers in Rome. She'd left them behind when joining her husband in Quishari. The dresses for receptions were more conservative. She wished at least one would make Khalid proud to be escorting her.

Then she remembered the red dress she'd bought from a shop near campus. Her friend Samantha had urged her to buy it. She'd never worn it. It was too daring for a professor's wife. But for tonight, it might just be the thing. Sophisticated and elegant,

it was far more cosmopolitan than anything else she now owned. She smiled almost daringly at Khalid. If he insisted they continue, she'd show him more than he bargained for.

He studied her for a moment, a hint of wariness creeping into his expression.

"Until tonight," he said.

She nodded, opening the door wide and watching him as he started to leave.

"I don't think I trust your expression," he said.

She feigned a look of total innocence. "I'm sure I have no idea what you're talking about, darling."

He tapped her chin with his forefinger. "Behave."

She laughed and shooed him out the door. Tonight might prove fun. She was not out to impress anyone, nor kowtow to them. Madame al Harum would be horrified. The minister might wish he'd kept his mouth shut. And her brother would learn not to mess with his sister's life anymore.

Ella was ready before the appointed time. She'd tapped Jalilah's expertise in doing up her hair. She remembered the maid had a talent for that which her former employer had used. The dress was daring in comparison to the gowns Ella had worn to the university functions. The thin crimson straps showed brilliantly against her skin, the fitted bodice hugged every curve down to where the skirt flared slightly below the knees. The satiny material gleamed in the

light, shifting highlights as she walked. She had her one set of pearls she again wore. The dress really cried out for diamonds or rubies, but Ella had neither. The high heel shoes gave her several inches in height, which would add to her confidence. She was ready to face the world on her terms.

Khalid arrived at seven. He stared at her for a moment, which had Ella feeling almost giddy with delight. She knew she'd surprised him.

"You look beautiful," he said softly.

She felt a glow begin deep inside. She felt beautiful. The dress was a dream, but the color in her cheeks came from being near Khalid. She knew she would do him proud at the reception, and give others something to think about. All too soon this pretend engagement would end, but until midnight struck, she'd enjoy herself to the fullest. And make sure he did, as well. He deserved lots for helping her out without question.

"Thank you. So do you," she said with a flirtatious smile.

He gave a harsh laugh. "Don't carry the pretense too far," he said. "This is a dumb idea."

"It was yours," she reminded him.

He laughed again, in amusement this time. "Don't remind me. I say we ditch the reception and go off on our own. You look too beautiful to be stuck in a room full of my mother's friends."

"You're not thinking. What would your mother

say. She went to all the trouble to celebrate what she thinks is a happy occasion. You can't disappoint her."

"You got it right first time—it's hard to think around you the way you look right now."

Ella smiled, delighted he was so obviously taken with how she looked. The dress was really something and she didn't ever remember feeling so sexy or feminine. The hot look in Khalid's eyes spiked her own temperature. Maybe his idea of not going out had merit.

"Let's go wow them all. And when we've put in our appearance, we'll dash back here and take a walk on the beach. Much more fun that the ordeal ahead." Filled with confidence from his reaction, she could hold her own with his mother and anyone else who showed up.

CHAPTER EIGHT

WHEN they arrived at his mother's apartment building, Ella was impressed. It looked like a palace. They were admitted by the uniformed doorman and quickly whisked to the top floor by a private elevator.

"The family home, no hotel," she murmured.

"Only a few intimate friends, like maybe a hundred. You never gave me a list of your friends, so I had one of my assistants contact the university and find out who your friends were. Told them it was a surprise."

Ella gave a loud sigh. "You just can't leave things alone, can you? Did you drive everyone insane while growing up?"

"Hey, I had Rashid to help me then."

"But not now?"

"He knows, but he is the only one besides you and me. Unless he told Bethanne. I forget there is a new intimate confidant with my brother. That'll be interesting—learning how to deal with that aspect."

Entering the large flat that overlooked Alkaahdar,

Ella was struck by the large salon, ceilings at least twelve feet high. A wall of windows opened to a large terrace. The room held dozens of people yet did not appear crowded. Classical artwork hung on the walls. The chandelier sparkled with a thousand facets. The furniture looked more Western than Arabian, chosen for elegance and style.

"Khalid, you should have been here before the first guests," his mother chided, coming to greet them. She looked at Ella, her eyes widening slightly. "You look different tonight," she said taking in the lovely dress and the sophisticated hairstyle.

Ella inclined her head slightly. "I've been told I clean up good," she said cheekily.

Sabria al Harum didn't know how to respond.

Khalid gave his mother a kiss on her cheek. "We're here, that's the important thing. I can't believe you managed such a crowd on less than a day's notice.

"Everyone here wishes you well, son," she said, eyeing Ella as if she wasn't sure how to react to her.

Ella slipped her arm through Khalid's and leaned closer. "We are honored you did this for us on such short notice, aren't we, darling?" she said, smiling up at him.

"Indeed we are, *darling*," he said back, his eyes promising retribution.

"Mingle, let people congratulation you," Sabria said. She gave Ella an uncertain look.

Rashid crossed the room with Bethanne. He

grinned at Khalid and Ella. "Congratulations, Brother," he said, then leaned in and gave Ella a kiss on the cheek. "Keep him in check," he said.

"I couldn't believe it when Rashid told me," Bethanne said, glancing around. She hugged Ella, and said in English. "I think it's fabulous."

Ella giggled a little. "Outlandish, I thought," she replied, one arm still looped with Khalid's.

Antonio came over, bowing stiffly.

"I thought you went home," Ella said when he stopped beside them.

"There were one or two things to deal with before I left. I spoke to our parents. They wish you both happiness in your marriage," he said. "If I had left, I would have missed this."

"And wouldn't that have been too bad," she murmured in Arabic.

"Come," Khalid said, "let me introduce you to some friends."

As they stepped away from the entry, they were surrounded by people who were mostly strangers to Ella. However one or two familiar faces had her smiling in delight to see again, though inside she felt guilty to be deceiving everyone.

Conscious she needed to convince her brother nothing would deter her from marrying Khalid, she stayed within touching distance all evening, reaching out sometimes to touch his arm as if to ground herself. Once when she did, he clasped her

hand, lacing their fingers together and holding it all the while he carried on a conversation with a friend.

The finance minister saw Khalid with Ella and broke away from the small group he was talking with and came over to them.

"Your mother must be so pleased, both her sons are taking the next step to insure the family continues."

"There's more to marriage than having children," Khalid said dryly.

"Ah, but nothing like small ones around to keep you young."

"Do you have children?" Ella asked.

"Not yet."

"Yet you and your wife have been married for many years," Khalid said.

For a moment the minister looked uncomfortable, then he changed the subject. "So are you and your brother marrying at the same time? Or as Rashid is the elder, will you defer to him?"

"Our plans are not yet firm," Khalid responded. "Excuse us, please, I see some friends of Ella's have arrived." Khalid moved them toward the door where two couples were standing, looking around in bewilderment.

"How do you know they are my friends?" she asked recognizing her friends.

"They look out of place. They obviously don't know anyone else here."

Greetings were soon exchanged. Though Ella's

university friends were startled by the scar on Khalid's face, they quickly hid it and greeted him as warmly as they did her.

"I had no idea," Jannine said. "Though we haven't seen much of you this last year. I guess a lot has happened that I don't know about."

"It has been a hectic and busy year," Ella said vaguely. If this had been a true engagement, she would have shared the news with her friends immediately. She knew they'd wish only happiness for her.

"So, how are you doing with your glassmaking?" Joseph asked. He looked at Khalid. "You've seen her work, of course."

"Yes. Exquisite. She's planning a showing before too much longer. I predict a spectacular future for our artist."

"Do tell us all," Monique said.

Ella was pleased her friends had come on such short notice and silently vowed to keep in touch better. They'd been part of her life for several years and were each interesting people. She talked about the tentative plans for getting into a gallery someplace. They listened attentively, only now and again darting a glance at Khalid.

A moment later, he touched Ella's shoulder.

"Someone I must speak to. I'll leave you with your friends." He left and she watched as he crossed over to an elderly man. Turning back to her friends, she found all eyes on her.

"He's one of the richest men in the country, you know," Jannine said. "How in the world did you land him?"

"Good grief, Jannine, is that how you refer to me? I feel like a large-mouth bass," her husband said.

Everyone laughed.

"Okay, maybe that was not quite what I meant."

"So did you mean how did Ella attract him? She's pretty, young and talented. What's not to like?" Monique said.

"You all are twisting my words and you know it. Tell all, Ella."

She glossed over details mentioning simply that she had been renting a cottage on a family estate and they met that way. The rest they knew. "Tell me what's going on at the university. I've been so out of touch."

Joseph began telling her about professors and students she might remember. She enjoyed catching up on the news, but felt distant, as if that part of her life was over and she was no longer connected as she once had been. It felt a bit lonely.

Glancing around at one point, she saw Khalid and Rashid both talking with the elderly man. They were in profile, left sides showing. Stunning men, she thought. Then Khalid turned and caught her eye. Once again the ruined side of his face showed. She swallowed a pang of regret for the damage and smiled. That was easily overlooked when his dark

eyes focused on her. Then she felt as if everything else faded away and left only the two of them in a world of their own.

"She's got it bad," Jannine said, laughing.

"What?" Ella asked, turning back to her friend.

"He's gone five minutes and you're already looking for him. How long until the wedding?"

"I'm not sure. We haven't made plans yet."

Antonio came over at that point. Ella made introductions and the group began talking in English, a common language for them all.

"This is a night of firsts," Jannine said. "I didn't even know Ella had family. She never spoke of you."

Her husband nudged her.

"Oh, sorry. Was that not the thing to say?"

Antonio looked at her. "You never spoke of us? Ella, we are your family."

"Who wouldn't accept my husband," she replied.

As the others looked on, she wished she could march her brother away and find Khalid. She was tired of the pretense, tired of trying to smile all the time when she wanted to rail against Antonio for getting her into this mess.

"But you like al Harum better, scar notwithstanding" Joseph muttered in Arabic.

Ella narrowed her eyes. "Khalid is a wonderful man. He puts out oil fires. Do you know how dangerous that is? He was injured trying to stop a conflagration. There are very few people in the world

who can do something like that. And did you ever stop to think how much pain and agony he went through with such severe burns?"

Khalid put his hand on her shoulder. "Defending me?"

"There's no need," she said, glaring at Joseph.

Antonio watched, glancing between Joseph, Ella and Khalid.

"No offence meant, Ella," Joseph said.

"None taken," Khalid said. "Please, help yourselves to refreshments. I want to borrow Ella a moment to introduce her to an old friend."

He took her hand in his and they moved toward the man she'd seen before. Rashid and Bethanne were talking with him.

"He was a friend of my grandparents, Hauk bin Arissi. Unfortunately he is thrilled with our engagement. It is awkward, to say the least. I do not like deceiving people."

"You should have thought of that."

"Or left you to your brother?"

Before Ella could respond, they were beside Hauk bin Arissi. Introductions were made.

"Ah, Khalid, you and your brother have once again surprised me. The antics you used to do. Your grandmother would be so happy today—both her precious grandsons embarking on a lifelong partnership with such beautiful women."

"You are most kind," Ella said.

"Ah, and you my dear, already speak our language."

"I've lived in Alkaahdar for several years. Studied the language before that."

"You speak it well."

"Thank you. My reading is not as proficient."

He waved his hand dismissively. "Have Khalid read to you. The evenings my wife and I enjoyed reading from the classics. I do miss that."

She glanced at Khalid, a question in her eyes.

"We all miss her, Hauk."

"So how did you two meet. I've heard about Bethanne's piloting."

"She lives on Grandmother's estate, the one I inherited."

"So he inherited me," Ella said.

"Are you the artist? The glassmaker? Alia told me about your excellent work. I saw the vase you made for her. It looks like captured sunshine."

Ella smiled. "Thank you for telling me. I miss her so much."

Hauk studied her a moment, then looked at Khalid. "You, also, have found a treasure. See you treat her appropriately."

Khalid bowed slightly. Ella saw the amusement in his eyes. For a moment she wished this was real. That he would treasure her and treat her appropriately. The thought startled her. This was one evening to get through, not let their pretense slip. Soon things would go back to normal.

* * *

By the end of the evening, Khalid's temper was held by a thread. His mother was pushing for a wedding date, pushing to learn more, pushing period. The minister watched Ella more than Khalid thought wise. His wife had been unable to attend, and Khalid did not like the way he eyed Ella. Rashid teased him, which normally he'd accept in good stead. But tonight, it rubbed him wrong.

He and Ella spent most of the evening together, except when she was visiting with her friends. It was growing late when she came over to him and smiled sweetly at the couple he was talking with.

"Will you please excuse us?" she asked, drawing Khalid away.

With the same smile on her face, she leaned closer, to speak only to him.

"My feet hurt, my cheeks hurt, I'm getting very cranky so suggest we leave very soon."

He leaned forward, breathing in the scent of her perfume, something flowery that he had grown familiar with over the last few weeks.

"I was ready to leave about two hours ago."

"I could have gone then. We've been here long enough, right? Your mother can't complain."

"She will, but that's her way. Come, follow me."

He led the way down a corridor and in moments they were in the primary hallway of the building. In seconds they descended in the elevator and were outside.

Ella leaned her head back and drew in a deep breath. It was all he could do to resist leaning over and kissing her. But standing in front of the building with the doorman and valet parking attendants standing mere feet away wasn't conducive for such activities.

Ella was tired. The strain of pretending she was wildly happy with a new engagement, and the anxiety over her brother, was wearing on her. To make matters worse, she almost wished she and Khalid were engaged. He had been most attentive tonight, hovering over her like he couldn't stay away. He even seemed the tiniest bit jealous when he spoke to the finance minister. He was so good in his role he almost had her convinced.

What would it be like to be engaged to him? Fabulous. She knew that without a doubt. He would lavish attention on the woman he chose for wife. She sighed softly, wishing she could imagine herself as his wife. To share their lives, to have his support of her art would be beyond wonderful.

Suddenly she was jealous of the unknown woman who would one day see past his own barriers and find a way into his heart. She would be the one to receive his kisses and caresses. She would be the one to share nights of passion and days of happiness. Ella could see them living on the estate his grandmother had left him—with a half dozen children running around, laughing and shouting with glee.

"Are you all right?" Khalid asked.

Ella hoped he couldn't read minds. "Of course. Just tired."

"So no walk along the beach tonight?"

Did he enjoy their shared time as much as she did? Unlikely. He probably liked walking and didn't mind if she accompanied him. The darkness hid all things. Was that special for him?

"Not tonight." She'd have to decide how to handle this. Everything was complicated. She was drawing closer and closer to Khalid and while he seemed to enjoy her company, she wasn't sure he was seeing her as anything but the woman who leased his cottage. Who was an impediment to his selling the estate.

When they reached home, Ella dashed into the cottage even before Khalid got out of the car. She closed the door and hurried to her bedroom, already unfastening the necklace. She didn't want to be thinking about kisses and caresses and dark nights alone with the man. He tantalized her with things she had thought lost forever.

Her life with Alexander had been all she ever expected. And when he died, she thought a part of her had, as well. But could she find another life, one unexpected but fulfilling nevertheless? Khalid was so different from Alexander it was amazing to her she could think of him in such terms. Alexander had been kind, gentle, thoughtful. Khalid was exciting, provocative, dynamic and intense. Yet she felt more

alive around him than any other time in life. Colors seemed more vivid. Experiences savored longer. Nebulous longing rose, solidifying into a desire to be with him.

She put the pearls on the dresser and peeked out of her curtains. She could only see a small corner of the main villa from this room. Nothing to show Khalid had gone to the study or his bedroom. Or, would he take a walk on the beach tonight without her. That first night he'd not known she was there. Did he often swim alone after dark?

Suddenly she felt daring. Taking off her dress, she slipped on her bathing suit. Just maybe she'd go swimming in the dark. So much the better if he were there, as well.

Pulling on a cover-up, she hurried to the beach. The moon was waning, but still cast enough light over the beach to see a pile of material near the water. Scanning the sea, she thought she saw him swimming several yards offshore. Smiling at the thought of reading his mind, she dropped her own things by his and plunged into the warm water. It felt energizing and buoyant. Swimming toward him, she saw when he first realized she was there.

Treading water, he waited for her to get closer.

"What are you doing here?" he asked.

"I didn't want a walk. But a swim sounded nice," she replied. When she drew closer, she also tread water. "Do you swim every night?"

"Not every night. But many. I like it."

"Always after dark."

"Easier that way."

"How far do the scars go?"

Khalid stared at her for a long moment, then motioned her closer. When she paddled nearer, he reached out and caught one hand, drawing her up to him. Tracing the ruined skin down his right side, he tried to gauge her reaction in the dim light. Most women would be horrified. The scarring went across part of his chest and his upper arm. It no longer pained him, except to look at.

She kicked closer and brushed against him. Instant heat. It had been a long time since he'd slept with a woman. He was already attracted to Ella, but her touch sent him over the edge. He pulled her into his arms and kissed her, kicking gently to keep them both above water. Then he forgot everything except the feel of her in his arms. Her silky skin was warm in the water. Her hair floated on the surface, tangling with one hand as he held her closer. Her kiss spiked desire for more—much more.

The water covering them both brought him back to sanity.

She broke away and laughed, shaking her head. Water flew from her hair, splashing against him.

"Romantic," she said, pushing up against him again, wrapping her arms around his neck. "Unless

you drown us." Her lips were close, then she brushed against him, teasing, tantalizing. She trailed light kisses along his lips, across to his left cheek, then to his right one. He pulled away.

"Don't," she said softly, cupping his ruined cheek with her hand. "Khalid, you make me forget everything. Don't pull away and bring reality back. This is a night just for us." Again she kissed him and this time he didn't hold back. He relished the feel of her in his arms, the length of her petite body pressed against his, banishing the loneliness of the last few years. He felt more aware of every aspect of life than ever before. All because she kissed him.

They were both breathing hard when the kiss ended. Khalid wanted to sweep her ashore and make love to her on the sand. He even began swimming that way, but stopped when he realized she was swimming parallel to the shore.

"It's a glorious night for a swim," she called out, swimming away with each stroke.

He'd been fooling himself. He knew what women saw when they looked at him. The night hid the scars, but light would expose them for the awful things they were. He'd take what he could get and ignore the vague yearning for even more.

He swiftly caught up with her.

"I thought you said it was unsafe to swim after dark," he said, keeping pace with her.

"If one is alone, it is. I'm not alone, I have you."

Together they swam along the coast, only turning back when Khalid began to fear she would tire out before reaching their things. Ella seemed as full of energy at the end as when they started. And once their towels and clothes were in sight, she stopped and tread water again. Curious, he stopped, too, and was greeted with a wave of water. A tap on his shoulder as he shook his head to clear the water from his eyes was followed immediately by "You're it!"

Ella dove under the water and for a moment he didn't know which direction she'd gone. When she resurfaced some yards away, he struck out. She laughed and dove beneath the water again. This time she appeared near the shore. Khalid laughed and reversed direction. By the time he reached her, she was already standing and hurrying up the shallow shelf to reach the beach.

Snatching up her towel, she wrung out her hair and then dried herself, all the while moving back, watching him.

"Dangerous games you play, Ella," he said, walking steadily toward her.

"It was fun." She laughed, but kept backing away.

Khalid pursued, gaining ground with every step.

"It was. But you don't play fair. Why leave the water?"

"I'm tired. That was a long swim." She giggled

and stepped back. "I'm leaving my cover-up behind," she said.

"Come and get it."

"I'm not that dumb."

"No one said you were dumb," he said, reaching out to catch her.

She laughed but came willingly into his arms. "Khalid, you are the dangerous one," she said just before he kissed her.

The next morning Khalid stood on the veranda on the side of the house nearest Ella's cottage, looking toward the sea. He'd had breakfast early, checked in with the office and debated taking a consulting job that had been offered or sending his second in command. The time away would give him some perspective. Last night replayed itself like an endless film. He should have pushed for more. But his respect for Ella wouldn't allow him to press for more than she wanted. And it appeared as if kisses were the limit of her willingness.

He should take the job.

"The maid said I'd find you here," Rashid said behind him.

Khalid turned. His casual clothes contrasted with the Western suit and tie that Rashid wore.

"And she was right. What's up?" he asked his brother.

"Just came by to see you." Rashid pulled a chair

away from the small table and removed his suit jacket, hanging it across the back. Sitting, he looked at his brother, eyebrows raised in silent question.

Khalid came across and pulled out another chair, sitting opposite his twin.

"I heard from an oil company in Egypt. They want us to come vet their new well."

"Are you going?" Rashid asked.

Khalid shrugged. "Don't know."

"You usually jump at foreign assignments."

"I've been to Egypt before."

"More than once. Maybe your new fiancée is keeping you closer to home."

"I don't need that from you. You know the entire thing escalated out of hand. Damn, I was only trying to help out my tenant. I told you."

Rashid smiled at that. "Right. Somehow I guess I forgot."

"Like you ever would. Is that why you're here? To rehash the entire affair?"

"Ah, you've moved on to an affair now."

"No, I have not. I stepped in to try to keep her family from pressuring her. Once her brother leaves, end of story." He rose and paced to the edge of the stone floor, then turned back.

"What would you have done?" he asked.

"The same thing, I'm sure. Actually I came by to see if you were at all interested in her. She seemed

devoted to you last night. Maybe this could develop into something good."

The scene in the water and on the sand flashed into mind. Khalid wasn't sharing that with his brother, twin bond or not. "An act." Had it all been an act? He hoped not.

"A suggestion only—" Rashid began.

"What?" Khalid felt his barriers rise.

"Give the relationship a chance. She's a nice woman. Talented, pretty. She loved the country, gave up her family for her first husband. Is loyal."

"Makes her sound like a dog or something."

"I'm trying to get through to you that not everyone is Damara. She was shallow and superficial and at the first setback fled. In retrospect, you got a lucky break. What if you were married and she couldn't stay for the long haul."

"I'm sure she felt she caught the lucky break." He turned back to gaze at the sea, remembering the scene in the hospital—he so doped up because of the searing pain and the one person beside his twin he thought he could count on instead shredding their relationship. As he watched the water sparkle beneath the sun, that image was replaced with a scene from last night: Ella's splashing him and then laughing.

Ella kissing his damaged skin. Ella.

More than anything, he loved her laugh.

Scowling at his thoughts, he turned back to Rashid.

"I'm taking off. The job in Egypt will last a couple of weeks at least."

"Give my suggestion some thought."

"There's nothing like that between us. She needed help. I gave it. She's locked into the cottage legally—nothing I can do to get rid of her before the lease expires. We'll muddle through. Not everyone is like you. Enjoy what you have with Bethanne. Don't try to find a happy ending here."

Rashid rose, slung his jacket over his shoulder and looked at his brother. "Okay. I gave it a shot. Your life is yours. Just don't screw it up any more than you can help."

Khalid laughed. "Thanks for the vote of confidence."

Once Rashid left, he went to the study and called his office. "Make the arrangements…I'll leave this afternoon," he told his assistant.

Ella had expected to hear from Khalid, but he had not sent word for her to come to the main house, nor visited. She kept busy sorting the glass pieces, pleased to study some and find they were better quality than she remembered. Stepping back a bit helped her gain perspective. The piece might not have attained her vision for it, but it was still good.

She had early pieces grouped together. Later ones separated. Definitely an improvement in the later ones. Maybe she should have a seconds sale—

knock off the prices of the earlier less-than-perfect pieces. But only after she had started selling.

The pictures she had taken in the house looked great. She'd see about contacting a printer to make them into a booklet.

As much as she tried to concentrate on work, she was on tenterhooks for Khalid. Last night had been amazing. She'd hated to go home alone.

But this morning—nothing.

Finally she took a light lunch on her veranda. Maybe she should just go over and find out what he was doing. Or if he had gone into his office today. It was a workday after all. She'd gotten used to his being available whenever she wanted. How spoiled was that?

She refused to hang around like some lovelorn idiot. She had her own life. If it coincided with his once in a while, so much the better.

The day seemed to last forever. She cleaned her small cottage. Did a load of laundry, even cooked dinner which was not something she often did. Finally—it was dark. Normally she walked after eleven, but even though it was scarcely past nine, she couldn't wait.

She headed for the beach. No sign of Khalid. She knew she was early. Slowly she walked to the water's edge. She'd wait.

Which wasn't easy to do when every nerve clamored for him. She sat on the warm sand, the

water lapping the beach a few feet from her toes. Picking up handfuls of sand, she let it slip between her fingers. Last night had been surreal. One part at the party Khalid's mother had given. The other—the real part—had been swimming in the warm sea. She smiled remembering how much fun she'd had. How much she liked being with Khalid.

Glancing over her shoulder, she wondered what time it was. How long before he came?

CHAPTER NINE

THE next morning Ella headed to her studio, firmly intending to push all thoughts of a certain sheikh from her mind. It did not take a two-by-four hitting her on the side of the head to get it. He had not shown at the beach last night. When she finally gave up and returned home, all lights in the main house were off. Had he gone out?

It didn't matter. He was merely her landlord. Nothing else. She would not let herself believe there was something special between them. If there was any special feelings, they were obviously one-sided—on her side.

Now she was going to focus on her career and leave all men out of the equation until she was firmly on the path to money. Next place she lived, she wanted to own. To be able to come and go when she pleased and not worry about someone trying to evict her because of their own agenda.

Firing up the oven, she chose the glass shards carefully, then melted the different colors, picking

them up one at a time on her wand. Slowly the glasses melded and when she began shaping the blob, she was pleased with the greens and blues and turquoise that began to show through. Taking her time, concentrating on the task at hand, Ella fashioned a large flat plate.

It was early afternoon when she was satisfied and put the art piece in her annealer. Stretching to work out the kinks in knotted muscles, she went to the cottage for lunch. For the first time in hours her mind flipped to Khalid. Where was he? Despite her vow to refrain from thinking about him, now she could think of nothing else.

She wished he'd stroll around the corner of the veranda on which she sat and smile that lopsided smile that crinkled the skin around his eyes and caused her to catch her breath. Saunter over and sit casually in the chair, his dark eyes sending shivers down her spine as she lost herself in them.

She was becoming too involved with the man. He'd made it clear he was not interested in any relationship—short or long-term—and she'd do best to remember that.

Yet when she remembered the fun they'd had playing in the water, the drugging kisses that had her clamoring for more, it was hard to believe. Didn't actions speak louder than words? His actions showed he liked her. She wanted to spend more time with him. It was the first time since Alexan-

der's death she'd had such an interest in anyone. Khalid was special. She felt stirred up every time they were together. When apart, she longed to see him again. Even if he never did more than talk about his work, she relished the moments together.

Frowning, she sat back in her chair and gazed toward the sea. She had a small glimpse of it from this place on her veranda. Normally it soothed. Today, however, she was more worried than before. She could not be falling for the man. She could list a dozen reasons why that would be such a bad idea—starting with she could get her heart broken.

Yet, testing her feelings as she might test a toothache, she had to admit there were a lot of similarities to falling in love. She wanted to be with him. Felt alive in his presence. Knew he was very special. Yet she didn't believe he was perfect. He could be short-tempered at times. And his idea that no one would ever find him attractive because of the scar was dumb. Sure, it was disfiguring, but he was more than a swatch of skin on the right side of his face and neck.

When he spoke to her, she felt like she was the only person in the world. The flare of attraction wasn't dying down. His kisses spiked her senses like nothing else had. And his protective view was intriguing. Her own family didn't feel that obligation, yet he'd stepped in without being asked to try to thwart her brother's goal.

She leaned back in the chair, trying to relax. She should just go along with things—pretend to be engaged and see what happened. Only it was hard to play that part when half the couple had vanished.

Perhaps vanished was a bit strong, she argued. He had not come to the beach last night nor stopped by today. He had no need to. Except she wanted him to.

She jumped up and cleared her dishes. After rinsing them off, she changed into a cool sundress, brushed her hair and headed for the main house.

Jalilah answered the door to her ring.

"Madame Ponti," she said politely.

"Is His Excellency in?" Ella asked.

"No. He has flown to Egypt."

"Egypt?" Ella hadn't expected that. "When will he be home?"

"I cannot say. He took a large suitcase, so I suspect a few days at least."

Ella thanked the maid and turned to return home. Walking slowly through the garden, she wondered why he hadn't told her. She almost went back to see if he had responded to a fire. That would cause every moment to be precious as he packed and left and he might not think to let his fake fiancée know of his plans. But the maid had said he had a large suitcase and might be gone awhile. No sense of urgency in her tone. Had he just left?

Ella debated calling Bethanne to ask if she knew what Khalid was doing, but decided she would not.

Still at the front of the main house, Ella turned when a car drove down the driveway. She recognized her brother even before he got out of the vehicle.

"Ella," he said.

"Antonio. What are you doing here?"

"I came to speak to Khalid al Harum. I've spoken with father and he entrusts me to handle things. Are you visiting, as well?"

"What things?" Did he not know she lived on the estate? If not, she didn't plan to tell him. She was more interested in what her father wanted Antonio to handle.

"Marriage settlements," Antonio said after a moment's hesitation.

"Dowery?" she asked, walking closer to her brother.

He looked uncomfortable. "Not exactly."

"Exactly what? I've moved away from home. I was married several years to another man. I can't imagine why there would be any talk of settlements unless you plan to see if Khalid would give something to get out of the mess Giacomo caused. Which I absolutely forbid."

"Forbid? You can't do that—it's between me and your future husband."

"If you even speak to him about that, I'll refuse to marry him," she said recklessly. She would not put Khalid in such a situation. She was embarrassed to even think of her family asking the man for money. It would be bad enough if they were madly

in love and truly engaged. But this was humiliating. She would not let Antonio do it.

He studied her for a moment. "If you don't marry him, you can come home and marry someone else."

"I may never marry again," she said, stepping up to her brother and tapping his chest with her forefinger. "But I sure will never marry someone I don't love. Giacomo got himself into this mess, let him get himself out of it. I am not a pawn to be used like in feudal days. I can't believe even our father would consider such a thing."

"Your family needs you," Antonio said, capturing her hand and pushing it away. "The sheikh has more money than anyone we know. He wouldn't miss a few thousand euros. Let him help us."

"No! I mean it, if you talk to him about this, I'll vanish and it'll be years before you find me next time."

Her brother stared at her for a long moment. "We need help, Ella," he said softly. "Where else can we go? We cannot make it known in Italy or the business will suffer. If we don't get an infusion of cash soon, it will come out. A company in dire straits loses business which could help it get out of trouble. Then take-overs are bandied about. The business has been in our family for generations, for centuries. Would you see all that gone?"

"No, of course not. Look for other ways. Mother's jewelry—"

"Most already copied in paste and the originals sold."

That surprised Ella. Things were worse than she envisioned.

"Is Giacomo still gambling?" Ella asked, horrified at the lengths her family had already gone. She felt herself softening to them. They had practically excommunicated her when she married Alexander. But they were still her family. The problem seemed larger than she'd realized from what Antonio said.

"No. But the fallout is lasting."

"Go home, Antonio. If I can, I'll send some money." It was too bad her trust fund was not available until she turned thirty. Maybe she could borrow against that. Or she could see about selling some of her artwork. Madame al Harum had thought it had merit. Would others?

He looked at the house.

"Khalid is not home. He had a business trip to Egypt. I don't know when he'll be back."

Antonio nodded. "Very well, then. Come visit, Ella. Your mother misses you."

"One day." It was hard to overlook the obstacles her parents had thrown in her way when she had married Alexander. But she knew her husband never wanted her to be parted from her family. He would not want her holding on to wrongs of the past.

She watched Antonio drive away and began to walk back to the cottage. Alexander would not have

wanted her to be a widow all her life, either. He had loved life, loved her and would always want the best for her. Including another husband who could bring her happiness.

Wistfully, she wished Khalid had the same thoughts.

It was amazing the absence of one slightly stand-offish man made. As the days went by, Ella gradually resumed her former routine. Working during the day, long walks after dark. Always alone. Only her enjoyment of being alone had been disturbed. She missed Khalid. Which only went to reinforce her belief she had to get on with her life and not grow attached to him.

The bright spot in the week was a visit by Bethanne. She was driving a new car Rashid had just bought for her and wanted to take Ella for a spin.

"It's no fun to have a brand-new convertible and have no one to share it with," she said as the two began driving away from the estate.

"And Rashid doesn't want to go?"

"He has one of his own. I'm sure he's not as enchanted with the convertible as I am. Isn't it great?" She drove to the coast highway and flew along the sea. Ella glanced at the speedometer once and then quickly looked away. Obviously the pilot in Bethanne had no qualms about flying low. Instead of worrying, Ella relaxed and enjoyed the ride. The

blue of the Persian Gulf was on their right. The road was straight and smooth. The wind through her hair made her feel carefree and happy. With sudden insight, she realized she was happy. In this day, in this moment. Worries were gone. Plans and projects on hold. Nothing held her back. She could enjoy this time and not feel sad or guilty.

It had taken a long time, but she knew she was ready to embrace life again. To find all it had to offer and enjoy every speck of the journey—even the heartbreaks and hardships.

"You're quiet," Bethanne said with a smile. "What are you thinking?"

Ella told her and Bethanne nodded. "I know the feeling. But I have an excuse. I'm in love. The colors in the sea seem brighter because Rashid's in my life. The flowers more delicate and lovely, especially when I'm in the garden with him. But I bet coming out of grieving is like falling in love with life again. I'm so sorry for your loss, but time does heal wounds. I was so devastated when I learned my dad was really dead. I grieved both before and after I found out. Then I realized he had loved life. He had done exactly as he had wanted throughout and had no regrets at the end. That's what I want."

"No regrets?"

"No regrets and feeling I lived life to the fullest. Which means even more than I expected before I met Rashid. He's so fabulous."

Ella laughed. "So says a woman in love."

"I know, and I'm so proud of him I could burst, and happy he loves me as much." She flicked Ella a glance. "How is Khalid these days?"

She gazed at the sea. "I wouldn't know. He's on a business trip."

"Still in Egypt?" Bethanne asked.

Ella nodded. "I have no idea when he'll be back."

"I'll ask Rashid if you like."

She hesitated. She didn't want to make demands or have him think she had any expectations. But she did want to know how he was, what he was doing, when she'd get to see him again. Ella almost groaned. She had it bad.

"Please." Khalid need never know she'd asked after him. When he returned, she'd play it cool, not going for walks, not expecting him to spend time with her. But for now—she wanted any information she could get.

Trying to change the subject, Ella asked about how much flying Bethanne was doing these days and the subject of Khalid was dropped.

That evening Ella was summoned to the main house by the maid for a phone call. It was Bethanne.

"Rashid said Khalid is still in Egypt. He called him to see when he was coming home. Turns out he's thinking about visiting some of the oil fields in the interior of Quishari before coming home. Stalling do you think?"

"Why would he?" Ella said, her heart dropping at the news he would be gone even longer.

"I could fly you inland, if you like," Bethanne said.

Ella blinked.

"You know, you could get some great ideas from seeing some of the nomadic people and the colors they use in weaving cloth. And there is an austere beauty of the desert that I find enchanting at all times of the day, from cool sunrise to the spectacular sunsets."

"It's tempting."

"I'll ask my darling fiancé if we can go tomorrow. That way, when Khalid shows up, you'll already be there."

Ella wanted to protest, but she closed her mouth before the words would spill out. She longed to be with him again. Here was a chance to see him in the kind of environments he worked. Not in fire suppression, but as a consultant to oil fields. She'd never seen an oil pump and had only the vaguest idea of how everything worked from discovery to gasoline in her car. It would be educational.

She laughed at her foolishness. She was going to see Khalid! "You're on. And tell Rashid thank you very much!"

The next morning Bethanne picked Ella up and drove them to the airport in her new car.

The gleaming jet sat in solitary splendor in a private section of the airport. Service personnel

scrambled around, making sure the jet was ready to fly. Ella watched with fascination as Bethanne changed her personality into a competent pilot, double-checking all aspects of the plane before being satisfied. She invited Ella into the cockpit, and talked as she went through the preflight routine. In only moments they were airborne. Ella leaned forward to better see the landscape below them. The crowded developed land near the sea gradually grew less and less populated until they were flying over desert sand. In the distance, toward the west, she saw hills, valleys and mountains. The flight didn't take long, and went even faster fascinated as she was by the sights below.

She knew Bethanne had been half joking when talking about getting new ideas, but Ella already had a bunch of them crowding in her mind. She had brought her sketchbook, but it was in her bag. Her fingers itched to get down the ideas. She would love to capture the feeling of the burning sand, the starkness of the open land. The contrast with the sea and distant mountains.

"Nice, huh?" Bethanne said.

"Beautiful. It's so lush where I'm from in Italy. And I've lived in Alkaahdar since arriving. I had no idea the desert could be beautiful."

"It's not to all. But I love it. Rashid tells me if I wish, he will build us a villa by an oasis surrounded by endless desert. I'm still too new at everything in

Quishari to wish to change a thing. But the thought tantalizes."

"I think I should like that, as well. As long as there was enough water at the oasis."

They circled the town of Quraim Wadi Samil on the edge of an oil field and then Bethanne landed.

Ella watched the pumps on the field with their steady rise and fall as they made their approach. She regretted losing them from view as they landed.

"That's where Khalid will be tomorrow," Bethanne said. "Rashid arranged for someone to pick us up and drive us to the hotel. Once I know Khalid's arrived, I'll return home."

"Stranding me here?" Ella said. She hadn't expected that.

"Hey, he's good for helping a damsel in distress."

Ella laughed, growing nervous. What if he was more annoyed than anxious to help? And she wasn't exactly stranded. She'd be able to take a bus back to the capital city, or even one of the daily commercial planes.

Bethanne arranged for them to go to the hotel that Khalid would use when he arrived. She and Ella checked in and agreed to meet for lunch, then take a short tour of the town.

By dinnertime, they'd both showered, changed and were sitting in the lobby.

Bethanne watched the double doors to the street while Ella sat with her back to them.

"He just walked in," Bethanne said, smiling. She looked at Ella. "Go say hi and ask him to join us for dinner. We'll want to hear all about Egypt."

Ella rose and turned, her heart kicking up a notch when she saw him. He wore a dark suit and white shirt with blue and silver tie. He looked fantastic. She took a breath and crossed the lobby, her eyes never leaving him. She saw when he turned slightly and saw her. For a moment she thought she saw welcome in his eyes. Then he closed down.

"Ella, is everything all right?" he asked, crossing the short distance to meet her.

"Everything is fine. Did you have a good trip to Egypt?"

Khalid's eyes narrowed slightly, then he looked beyond her and saw Bethanne. She raised one hand in a short wave and grinned.

Khalid looked back at Ella. He hadn't expected to see her. One reason he'd decided to stop off at Quraim Wadi Samil was to delay returning home. But she was standing right in front of him, her eyes dark and mysterious, shadowed with a hint of uncertainty. He clenched his fists at his sides to keep from reaching out and pulling her into a hug that he might not ever let go.

"We wondered if you'd like to join us for dinner," she said quickly. "Tell us about your trip."

"You didn't come all this way to have dinner and hear about my trip," he said.

"Actually I'm getting new ideas for more glass pieces. You should see the sketches I've done since I've arrived. I'm hoping to go to the oil fields tomorrow." She stopped abruptly.

"With whom?" he asked, feeling a flare of jealousy that someone would show her around.

"You?" she said.

Khalid relaxed a fraction. His voluntary exile for the last week hadn't done anything to kill his desire for this woman. Now she was right here.

"I don't usually eat dinner in restaurants," he said slowly.

She nodded. "I know, eating alone is awkward in public places. But you'll have me and Bethanne so it'll be fun."

Fun? The stares of the other customers? The whispers that ran rampant as speculation abounded?

"I'm glad to see you again," she was saying. "I've missed you at night when I walk along the beach." Her eyes were shining with more happiness than he'd ever seen before. For another smile, he'd face the horror of others at the restaurant. He'd make sure he was seated by a wall, with the damaged side of his face away from other diners.

"I need to check in, then it will be my pleasure to escort two such lovely ladies to dinner."

She reached out and touched his arm, pulling her hand back quickly as if unsure of a welcome.

"We'll be waiting." With another smile, she turned and walked back to Bethanne.

Dinner did not prove to be the ordeal Khalid had expected. As if in one agreement, the seating went as he wanted. With fewer people having to see the scar, they were more ignored than he normally experienced. For the first time in years, he enjoyed dining out. The food was excellent. The conversation lively. The more he grew to know Bethanne, the more he understood his brother's love for the woman. Yet his eyes kept turning to Ella. She was feminine and sweet. He detected a difference but couldn't put his finger on it. Was she more confident? Had the sadness diminished around her eyes?

"So Rashid called and doesn't want me to wait until tomorrow to return home. I'm leaving right after dinner," Bethanne said.

Ella looked startled. Khalid watched her as she turned to the other woman. "I thought we'd stay a day so I can see everything here."

Bethanne looked at Khalid. "You can show her around, can't you? She wants to see an oil field. You could explain things. And show her the sunrise. I think the colors in the sky are amazing."

Khalid knew a setup when he saw one. But instead of arguing, he looked at Ella. Another day

together suited him. "Fine. We'll watch the sunrise together, I'll take you to the oil fields."

"And see she gets home safely?" Bethanne said.

Amusement warred with irritation. He suspected this was not Ella's plan but one of his soon to be sister-in-law's. Yet why not give in with good grace. He had to admit he'd missed Ella while in Egypt. More than once he'd seen something he'd wanted to share with her. Had almost called her a couple of times.

Dangerous territory, but he was a man who lived with danger. He liked being with her. There was no harm in that. It was only if he let himself dream of a future that could never be that he risked more than he wanted to pay.

Ella couldn't fall asleep after returning to her room. She was too much a night person to go to bed early. Yet Khalid had made no suggestion about spending time with her in the evening. Bethanne had now taken off for Alkaahdar. Ella sat at the window, watching the dark sky display the sparkles of lights from a million stars. There was no beach to walk along. It was too late to wander around town alone. There was nothing to do but think and that she didn't want to do.

She drew out her sketchpad, but instead of sketching various pieces of glass she wanted to try, she drew quick vignettes of Khalid—walking along the beach, swimming in the sea, leaning against his desk.

She also sketched him in traditional Arab robes, like he'd worn the first night she'd met him. She'd love to see him attired like that again. Did he wear the robes in the desert? Slowing in her drawing, she let her imagination drift as she thought about an oasis like Bethanne had talked of. What would it be like to have a small house in the scant shade of the palms surrounding a small pool of clear water? She envisioned a rooftop veranda that would provide a 360-degree view when the heat of the day dissipated. Quiet. Silent except for the wind sweeping across the sand. Sometimes the sand hummed in harmony. Would they feel cocooned together in a world apart?

She filled several pages with sketches, then tossed the tablet aside. Restlessness was getting her nowhere. She had best go to bed and hope to fall asleep quickly. She'd spend tomorrow with Khalid.

He was waiting for her when she stepped into the lobby the next morning. She greeted him and joined him in the small restaurant attached to the hotel for breakfast. The croissants were hot, the jam her favorite—grape. The coffee was dark and aromatic. She sipped the rich beverage, trying not to stare. Khalid looked fabulous. His dark eyes met hers.

"Ready for the scenic tour?" he asked.

"Ready. I have a hat, sunscreen and a long-sleeved shirt to put on at midday to protect against the sun."

"I have hired a Jeep for our use, and stocked it with a cooler and plenty of cold water. Even lunch."

She smiled in anticipation. "Lovely, a picnic, just the two of us."

"I know a place you'll love," he said.

She would love anyplace he showed her. Looking away before she made a fool of herself, she finished her meal.

In no time they were in the open Jeep, weaving their way through the streets of the old town. The sandstone walls blended with the color of the desert. Bright spots of blues and red punctuated the monotonous walls. Soon the crowded streets fell behind. The homes were farther and farther apart until they were left behind and she and Khalid continued straight for the oil field she could see in the distance.

Fascinated by the acres of oil pumpers slowly rising and falling as they drew the oil from deep in the ground, she ignored what was behind her, trying to see what was ahead.

"Amazing. How did anyone know there was oil here?" she asked. There was nothing in the sparse desert to differentiate it from any other area.

"Geologists can find it anywhere. My father is the one who started this field. For Bashiri Oil, of course."

She looked around. "Was the town this big when the oil was discovered?"

"No. First the drilling and now the activity of the wells boosted the population considerably. It was a

small, sleepy oasis way back when oil was first discovered. Inhabited by a few families who had lived here for generations. It was on the trade routes and the migration of nomadic people, so this was a resting place for caravans."

"Now it's another city, though small. With an airport."

Khalid laughed. "With an airport. Did Bethanne really bring you here to get ideas for your glass?"

"That was one reason," she said, staring straight ahead.

She caught a glimpse of him from the corner of her eye when he looked at her. "And another?"

"To see you."

He didn't respond, so Ella looked at him. "Surprised?"

"A bit."

"I think we need to get straight on what we're doing," she said.

He looked at her again, then back to the road. "We're going to see the wells, then have a picnic."

"About this fake engagement. I think Antonio has finally returned home. That should be the end of that matter. Interesting, don't you think, my parents are not against my being engaged to you a stranger, but objected to my marriage to Alexander whom they had known for years."

"Money is important to a lot of people. You are not one of them," he said.

"I think people are much more important. And experiences in life. I'm enjoying today. I have never gone very far into the desert. And I've never been to an oil field." She gave him a shy look, "Nor with a sheikh."

"Hey, I'm a man like any other."

Oh, no, she thought privately. *You are unlike anyone else in the world.* For a moment she wanted to reach over and touch him, grasp his hand and hold on and never let go. Her heart beat faster and colors seemed brighter. She loved him. Closing her eyes for a moment, she wondered when it had happened. How it could have happened. And what she could do to make sure he never knew.

Khalid was the perfect guide when they reached the oil field. He introduced her to the foreman and then gave her an abbreviated tour, explaining how the wells were drilled, capped and put into production. He even told her how something minor could go wrong and cause a fire. She had a healthy respect for the men who worked the fields, their lives in danger if any one of a myriad of things went wrong.

After their visit to the oil field, he drove them straight into the desert. It was just past noon. The sun glared overhead. The air was hot, the breeze from the moving car not doing much to cool. Ella had donned her hat and long-sleeved shirt and was sweltering. She was about to suggest they give up this expedition and return to the air-conditioned

comfort of the hotel when she saw the faint suggestion of green in the distance. She stared at the spot
gradually seeing the palms as they drove close. A
cluster of trees offering a respite to the monotonous
brown of the sand.

"The oasis?" she asked, pointing to the spot.

"Yes. A small wadi that holds enough water for
a few humans or animals, it can't support a settlement. But there is plenty of water for the trees and
shrubs that grow around it. And it provides a nice
shady spot in a hot afternoon."

Ella studied the contrast of the golden-brown of the
desert with the surprise of green from the trees. It gave
her an idea for a new art piece. Could she do a palm,
leaning slightly as if wishing to touch the earth?
Maybe a small collage with blue glass at the base surrounded by a smoky golden glass with the palm rising.

Khalid stopped in the shade and turned off the
engine. For a moment only silence reigned. Ella felt
the heat encompass them, then a slight cooling from
the shade. She turned and smiled at him.

"It's beautiful here. I know now why Bethanne
says she'd like a home in the desert with water nearby.
It would be lovely. I could live in such a place."

"Sometimes when things get too much, I come
here for a few days." Khalid studied the water, the
pond a scant four feet in diameter. The palms were
spread out, their roots able to find enough moisture
to support them even some distance from the pool.

"Surprisingly the water is cool," he said.

"In this heat?" she asked.

"Come."

He got out of the Jeep and waited for her at the front. When she joined him, he reached over to take her hand, leading her to the water's edge. They sat on the warm sand. Ella trailed her fingers in the water.

"It is cool!" she said in amazement. The water felt silky and refreshing. "How did you find this place?"

"Exploring when I was a kid. Rashid and I spent lots of time exploring while my dad spent time in the town. We learned later it was to visit a woman who had had a child by him."

Ella looked at him in surprise.

He looked back. "We never met her. She died, the daughter. My father's only daughter. He kept her hidden from my mother, understandably. She died in a plane crash that claimed Bethanne's father's life. My father died only days later—we think of a broken heart. Rashid and I haven't mentioned it around Mother."

"Does she know?"

"We don't know. But out of respect we have not brought it up. If she does, it must hurt her and if she doesn't, we don't want to have her learn about it at this late date."

Ella nodded, understanding. She wished her family was as loving and concerned for each other

instead of always thinking of money and how to expand the vineyard or protect the family name.

"Your mother is lucky to have you two," she said wistfully. Would she ever have a child? A strong son who would look like his father? Or a beautiful little girl with dark eyes and a sparkle that telegraphed the mischief she might get into?

CHAPTER TEN

THE afternoon was pleasant in the shade. Khalid had brought blankets to spread on the sand. The picnic lunch was delicious. Ella ate with relish. The cool water from the pool completed the meal. Afterward, Khalid made sure the blankets were in the shade and lay down. Closing his eyes, he looked completely relaxed.

Ella watched him for a time, growing drowsy. Finally she lay down and closed her eyes. The quiet and peace of the oasis enveloped her and before long, she slept.

When she awoke, Khalid was nowhere to be seen. The Jeep was parked where he'd left it so she knew he hadn't gone far. She splashed cool water on her face and then rose, folding the blankets and putting them in the back of the Jeep.

"Khalid?" she called.

He appeared a moment later from behind a sand dune. "Just checking things out," he said, walking back to the shady area.

"Sandstorms can wreak havoc in this area. That's what brought down the plane my father's daughter was on. Yet time and again, this oasis reappears. I was trying to figure out why. Ready to return to town?"

Ella nodded, feeling reluctant to end the afternoon. She looked around, imprinting every bit of the scene in her mind. It would forever be special—because of Khalid.

The sooner they were back among others, the sooner she could get her emotions under control. She really wanted to stay. To camp out under the stars. To share feelings and thoughts on the vastness of the desert and the beauty found despite the harshness.

To tell him he was loved.

That she could not do. She hurried to the Jeep and jumped in.

Quraim Wadi Samil seemed to shimmer in the late sunshine as heat waves distorted the air. They drove into the town and straight to the hotel. Ella felt wrung-out with the heat. She would relish the coolness of the hotel. She began to long for the cottage by the sea. At least there seemed to always be a breeze by the Gulf.

"Dinner at seven?" Khalid asked as they entered the lobby.

"That's perfect." It would give her time to shower and change and cool down.

Her room was spacious with little furnishings to clutter the space. She lay down for a few moments,

wondering if there could be any future between her and Khalid. His fake engagement had been to help her out, made public by the minister. Since he already had it in for Khalid's family, they dare not end the engagement so soon without negative gossip. Yet the longer it lasted, the more people would expect to see them together, and expect plans for a wedding to be forthcoming.

She wished she was planning a wedding with Khalid. She would so love to spend the rest of her life with him. It would be very different from the life she had before. Khalid had a stronger intensity with life than she was used to. Was it because he flirted with death whenever dealing with oil fires?

The thought of him being injured again had her in a panic. Would he consider not doing that in the future?

As if they had a future.

Ella rose and went to take her shower. She had some serious thinking to do. She could not bear to fall more in love with the man and then have fate snatch him away. Maybe it was time to consider going back to Italy and finding a life she could live there. She'd already lost one man she loved. She could not go through that again.

At least if she left, she could always remember Khalid as he was today. And hope to never hear of his death. As long as he was living in the world, she could find contentment. Couldn't she?

* * *

Khalid met Ella at the elevator when she stepped off in the lobby at seven. He had been tempted to go to her room, but had mustered what patience he could to wait for her in a public place. She'd looked perfect that afternoon sleeping in the shade at the oasis. He'd wanted to touch her cheeks, faintly pink. Her hair looked silky and soft. He had touched her hair before and knew its texture.

He was playing a fool's game, tempting fate by spending time with her. What if he became attached? He knew what he could expect from life. He'd made his peace with being alone years ago. His work was interesting and challenging. Especially when fighting fires. He liked the men he worked with. Liked being consulted by Rashid from time to time.

But he couldn't change reality. A scarred and bitter man was not going to appeal to a pretty woman like Ella. He'd help her out because he disliked the way her brother was handling things. And her family sounded totally unlike his. Despite the scarring, his family rallied around when needed.

He moved away from the pillar where he'd been leaning when she stepped out. Her look of expectancy touched him. When she spotted him, she smiled. Khalid felt it like a punch in the gut. It always made him feel whole again. She didn't seem freaked out by the scar. He still remembered the night she had

cupped his cheeks, touching the damaged skin without revulsion. He'd never forget it.

"I thought I wouldn't want to eat again after that lavish lunch," she said as she hurried over to meet him. "But now that I've cooled down, I'm famished."

"Then let's hope they have enough food to fill you up."

She laughed. He almost groaned. Her laugher was like water sparkling and gurgling over rocks in the high country. Light and airy and pleasing. He wished he could hear it all his life.

"So tomorrow we return home?" she asked as they walked to the restaurant.

"Yes. We'll summon a plane if you like."

"I'd love to see the country between here and the coast, but not in a hot Jeep like today. It was fine for a short foray into the desert, but for the long drive home, I'd like more comfort."

"Your wish is my command," he said. He did wish he could do anything for her she wanted. An air-conditioned car would be easy. Could he help with selling her artwork? He knew nothing about that. But his mother did. If she'd just warm up to Ella a little, she'd be a tremendous help.

He had a life-size picture of that ever happening. Rashid was head over heels in love with Bethanne, and his mother still chided him for not seeking the woman she had wanted him to marry. He wasn't head over heels in love with Ella. But he liked being

with her. Liked hearing her take on things. It gave him a different perspective.

He loved hearing her talk period. Her voice carried a trace of accent. Her Arabic was quite fluent, but softer than most women's. He liked it.

"Khalid!"

He looked at her.

"What?"

"I asked how long it would take to drive back to the coast. Where were you?" She peered up at him.

"Woolgathering. It takes about eight hours. It's a long and boring drive. The road is straight as a stick and there's nothing but sand and scrub bushes as far as the eye can see. We can do it, but I'd rather fly home and spend the afternoon at the beach."

"That does sound nice."

The maître d' appeared and showed them to a secluded table. He presented the menus with a flourish then quietly bowed away.

"No argument? I thought you wanted to drive home," he said.

"Well, you've obviously been across the desert and if it looks all the same, maybe I don't need to experience it for eight hours. You can take me on another trip to the desert if I need more inspiration," she replied, looking at the menu.

"Maybe."

She looked up and grinned. "We are supposed to be engaged, remember?"

"I thought you wanted to talk about that," he said. He had not planned for things to get complicated when he'd told her brother they were engaged. How was he to know it would come out and his mother would make a big production about it?

"So I do. How do we get out of it?"

He stared at her—realizing for the first time he did not want to get out of it. He could understand her haste in ending the agreement. Hadn't his fiancée tossed him over because of the scar? But he wanted Ella to pretend a bit longer.

"We can say we fought on this trip and the deal is off," he said slowly.

She looked at him thoughtfully. "So whose fault was it?"

He met her gaze, almost smiling. "Does it matter?"

"People will ask. And if they don't, they will speculate."

"Have it be mine. It doesn't matter."

"Of course it does," she said passionately. "If you break it off, that's not very nice of you. And if I do, that doesn't reflect well on me."

"So I play the villain. It won't impact my life."

She shook her head slowly. "Not fair. You tried to help me out. And I appreciate it. Antonio would still be here trying to coerce me back to Italy if you hadn't."

"So if I can't break it off and you can't, we don't." Was that the solution? Keep the engagement going long enough for her to feel more comfortable

around him. Would she ever see beyond the exterior to what he thought and felt? Could she ever fall in love with him?

Unlikely. She still loved her dead husband. And he sounded like a paragon. Intellectual. A professor. What did an oil field roustabout have to offer in comparison? Granted he had position in the country, but she hadn't been very impressed being seen with a sheikh. He had money, but she came from money herself and was unimpressed. Not like other women he'd dated years ago. In fact, nothing seemed to impress Ella. That was one thing he loved—*liked*—about her. Money and stature and material items others were impressed by seemed inconsequential to her. She liked people—and it didn't seem to matter what they had or did; if they were of interest to her, she was friendly. If not, she was cordial. And someone who knew her well could easily tell the difference.

"So we stay engaged for a while longer," she mused. "Suits me." Her attention turned back to her menu.

Khalid felt a strange relief at her compliance. At least for a while longer, they continued being engaged.

And didn't engaged couples kiss?

The thought sprang to mind and wouldn't leave. He glanced at her. Her attention on the menu, he had ample time to study her lips, imaging them pressed against his again. Imagine feeling her soft body against his, passion rising between them.

If he didn't stop soon, he'd embarrass himself. He wanted dinner ordered eaten and over. They could walk to the square. The day's heat was abating. It would cool down soon as the desert did at night. They could find a secluded spot and watch the stars appear. And he'd hold her and kiss her and pretend for one night everything was normal.

It almost worked that way. They agreed to stroll through town when dinner finished. And when they found a parapet overlooking a city garden, they leaned against the still-warm stone and tried to make out the plants in the garden. But the light faded quickly. Turning, Ella looked up at the sky. "It's growing darker by the second. Soon a million stars will show."

He nodded and stepped closer, bringing her into his arms. "And you are more beautiful than all of them," he said, and kissed her.

Nothing was normal about that kiss. He felt every inch of his body come alive as he deepened the kiss. She responded like she had been waiting as long as he had. Her mouth was sweet and tender and provocative. Her curves met his muscles and tempted him even more. Her tongue danced with his, inflaming desire to a new level. The parapet disappeared. The stars were forgotten. There remained only the two of them, locked in an embrace that he wanted to go on forever.

Forgotten was the hideous scar that so repulsed

others. Gone was the fear he would never find a woman to overlook the distortion even for a night. Khalid felt he was soaring. And he loved every moment.

If only it could last forever.

But it was not fair to Ella to kiss her when he'd coerced her into this engagement. Slowly he broke off the kiss, pleased when she followed him as he pulled back—obviously not wanting to end the kiss.

He was breathing hard when they parted. She was, too.

"Wow," she said, then turned. "I think we should go back to the hotel."

He wanted to agree—if she meant they'd go to his room. He wanted to make love to her so badly he ached from head to toe. Yet nothing she'd said or done gave him any indication that was where her thoughts were heading.

They turned and walked back toward the hotel.

"Did you arrange for Bethanne to pick us up tomorrow?" she asked as they came into the light spilling into the street from the hotel.

"She'll be here at nine."

"Good."

When they entered the lobby, Ella quickened her pace. She punched the elevator button almost savagely. She hadn't looked at him once since they came into the light.

"Ella, if you're upset—"

"Why would I be upset?" she asked in a brittle tone. "Engaged couples kiss all the time."

The elevator arrived and she stepped in, punching the number for her floor.

Khalid hesitated, then remained where he was. She did look up as the doors began to close.

"See you in the morning," he said before she was lost from view.

Turning, he went back outside. A long walk—like maybe to Alkaahdar—was required. He hoped he had his head on straight come morning.

Stupid, stupid, *stupid!* How could she have responded so freely to Khalid's kiss. No wonder she drove him away. He didn't even want to escort her to her room. Probably thought she'd jump him and drag him inside. Ella paced her room, slapping the wall when she reached it. Turning, she paced to the other wall, slapped it. What could she do to make things come right? She knew he had only helped her out. There was nothing there. How could she have responded so ardently?

Because she loved him and knew he had been lacking in love for years. She wanted to hold him close, pour out her feelings, let him know she loved him beyond anything. But to do so would probably have him running for the nearest exit. A kindness to help her out of a jam didn't mean he was falling for her. He had his life, she had hers.

"Stupid!" she almost shouted the word.

Taking a deep breath, she crossed to the bed and sat down hard. Nothing was going right. She was at odds with her family, had lost her husband—whom she was having trouble remembering when every time she tried her mind saw Khalid. She felt a flare of panic. She couldn't forget Alexander. He'd been her childhood sweetheart. They'd had a nice marriage. At one time she thought he was the only man for her.

Only Khalid had a way of making her forget him. Forget the sweet love they'd shared for the hot and passionate feelings that sprang to life anytime she saw Khalid. Or even thought about him.

Daydreams about what life together could be like. And fears for his safety. She had to get away. Pack her things, face her parents and take complete charge of her life. She didn't have to marry anyone. It wasn't her fault her brother had a gambling problem. Time he faced the music and not expect her to martyr herself on his behalf.

And if she made it big in art, great. If not, maybe she could do stained glass work, or something to keep doing what she loved. It wasn't the same as sharing a life with a man she felt passionately about. But it would have to suffice.

If she could make it on her own. Somehow she must find a way to be self-supporting.

Which meant staying in the cottage was her best

bet—the lease was solid for another four years. Khalid would get tired of hanging around and move on. Or sell the estate with the cottage occupied. She could make sure she didn't walk along the beach at night. Or venture outside if she knew he was in residence.

She'd faced worse. She could do this.

"But I don't want to," she wailed, and burst into tears.

The next morning Ella felt more composed. She ate a small breakfast in her room. Made sure no traces of last night's tears showed and descended to the lobby promptly at nine. Khalid was nowhere to be seen. She hadn't gotten the time wrong, had she?

One of the porters saw her and came over. "I will take your bag. You should have called down. The taxi is waiting."

So he wasn't even going back with her. That should help. But Ella felt the loss to her toes. Much as she'd talked herself into staying away from him in the future, she still hoped to fly back with him this morning. Saying goodbye silently so he'd never know, but having a few more hours of his company. Now even that was denied her.

The gleaming white jet sat on the runway with a bevy of men working around it. The cab stopped near the plane and a man rushed over to get her bag. She felt like royalty. Tears stung as she tried to smile

and walked to the plane. She missed Khalid and it had been less than ten hours since she'd seen him.

Bethanne popped out of the opened doorway. "Hey, let's get a move on. I've got another run later," she said with a wide smile.

It must not be odd that Khalid wasn't with her, Ella thought as she ran lightly up the stairs.

"Where to later?" she asked, hoping Khalid would not be a topic of conversation.

"To take Khalid and his crew to that fire, of course. Didn't he tell you? Since I was already airborne when the call came in, he's staying here and I'm flying back to get the rest of his crew and then we'll head for Kuwait."

Ella felt her heart freeze. "Another fire?" she said. He had not told her. He had not contacted her at all that morning. Which should show her more than anything how nebulous their connection was. It was not her business after all. He saw no reason to inform her.

"A double from what I understand. Want to sit up in the cockpit? We can talk as I fly."

In a surprisingly short time they were airborne. Ella was so curious about the fire she could hardly sit still. Respecting Bethanne's need for concentration, she kept quiet until the pilot leveled out.

"There, all set. We're heading for the capital city now," Bethanne said.

Ella looked at her. "Tell me about the fire. Khalid didn't say a thing to me about it."

"It's in Kuwait and a bad one. Apparently two wells, connected somehow, ignited. Seven men are known dead and a couple of others are missing. They says it's burning millions of gallons of oil. And hot enough to be felt a half a mile away."

"He can't put it out," Ella said, staggered trying to imagine the puny efforts of men to extinguish such a raging inferno.

"You know Khalid, he'll do his best. And my money's on him."

"Someone should stop him," Ella said.

"What?" Bethanne looked at her. "He'll be okay. He always comes through."

"He got burned pretty badly one time," Ella reminded her.

"Freak accident."

"Which could happen again. Good grief, if the heat is felt so far away, what would it be like close enough to cap it? It's probably melting everything around it and there'd be nothing to cap."

"So they put out the flames, let the oil seep and figure out a way to get into production again. That's what Khalid does, and he's really good at it, according to Rashid. Who, by the way, also wishes he wouldn't do this job. But he knows Khalid is driven to do this and won't stand in his way."

Ella nodded, fear rising like a knot in her throat. She swallowed with difficulty, every fiber of her being wanting to see Khalid again.

She gazed out the window, wishing they'd arranged to ride back together in that air-conditioned car she'd wanted. They would have been out of contact, and someone else would be tapped to try to put out the oil fire. He'd be safe.

"When did the call come?" she asked.

"It happened last night. I suspect they called him once they saw what happened. He's the world's best, you know."

"He should retire."

Bethanne reached out and squeezed Ella's hand. "I know, I'd feel that way if it were Rashid. But women can't change men. My mother told me that fact years ago when explaining how she and my father married and then divorced. She had hoped having a family would be enough for him, but it never was. Some men are meant to do more adventurous things than others."

"I'd hardly call putting out raging oil fires adventurous—more like exceedingly dangerous. Why couldn't he have been a professor or accountant or something?"

Bethanne shrugged. "You might ask yourself why you're engaged to the man. You knew what he did. Yet you plan to marry. It's not going to get easier, but support is important."

Ella couldn't tell her why they were engaged. Apparently Rashid had kept Khalid's secret. Ella couldn't tell anyone she considered leaving Quishari because of Khalid. Maybe the decision

would be taken from her. There was nothing she could do now but pray for his safety. She wished they'd ended the evening differently. That she had told him how much she cared. That she'd dare risk everything to let him know she loved him. Would she ever get that chance?

The flight seemed endless. She wanted more information. Could she call Khalid when they landed? She knew Bethanne was flying his crew back to Quraim Wadi Samil to pick him up and fly them all to Kuwait. He'd still be at the hotel. For a moment her mind went blank. What was the name of the hotel? She had to call him, tell him to be careful.

"Rashid will meet the plane," Bethanne said after responding to flight control. She began descending. Ella could see the city, the blue of the Gulf beyond. But the beauty was lost, fear held her tightly. "He's not going, is he?" Ella asked.

"No, he's taking you home. I'll be back late tonight. He didn't want you to be alone."

"Maybe I can work to take my mind off things," she said. The truth was she couldn't think about anything except Khalid and the danger he was facing.

"Go with Rashid. He'll have the most current information about Khalid and the crew. Besides, he's swinging by his mother's place to update her. Dealing with Madame al Harum is enough to take anyone's mind off troubles. That woman is a piece of work."

Ella smiled despite her worry. "At least we have

that in common. Do you think she'll ever come around to accepting you?"

"My guess is once I have a baby or two."

Ella blinked and gazed out the window. What if she and Khalid married and she had a baby? She remembered thinking about a little dark-eyed little girl, or a couple of rambunctious boys that looked just like Khalid. How would she ever stand it if they wanted to grow up to be oil firefighters.

"Madame al Harum must be beside herself with worry," she said. "I would be if it were my son going to fight that fire."

"I would never let a son of mine grow up to do that," Bethanne said.

"Thought you said a woman can't change a man."

"Well, then I'd start with a little boy."

Ella laughed. Then almost cried when she thought more about the danger Khalid faced. How he'd once been an adorable little boy, running at the beach, playing with his twin. How quickly those years must have flown by.

Rashid was standing beside a limo when the plane taxied up to the hangar. There were a half dozen men near him with duffel bags and crates. As soon as the engines were shut down, men began swarming around the plane, loading everything. It was being refueled even as Ella stepped down the stairs. Bethanne followed, then hugged Rashid tightly.

"I wish you'd let someone else fly the plane," he said.

"I'm going. Don't argue. It's Khalid you should be worried about. I'll pick him up and then take them all to Kuwait. I'll be home late tonight. You take care of Ella. I think she's in shock."

"No, I'm fine. I think I should go home."

"You're coming with me," Rashid said.

She looked at him, almost seeing Khalid. Certainly hearing that autocratic tone of his. They looked so alike, yet so different.

"Any news?" she asked.

"Nothing beyond what we learned earlier. Once we reach home we'll call Khalid. He's been talking with the oil field people so will have the latest intel. This all you have?" he asked as one of the men put her bag in the trunk of the limo.

"Yes. It was a short trip." Too short if it was to be the last time she saw Khalid.

Ella went with Rashid to his mother's home. He did not speak on the ride except to try to reassure her that Khalid knew what he was doing and wouldn't take any foolish risks. "Especially now," Rashid said.

Ella nodded, wishing they'd never embarked on this stupid fake engagement. Everyone thought he'd be extra careful, but Rashid knew Khalid had no special reason to be extra cautious. She knew he wouldn't be foolhardy, but so many things could go

wrong. What if there was another explosion and his suit was torn again. She couldn't bear to think of the pain he'd go through while healing.

Or what if things went really, really wrong?

"My mother can be a bit difficult. We know she loves us. Sometimes I think it's hard for a mother to realize her children are grown and have their own lives."

Ella thought about her parents. "Sometimes they just want to control children forever."

"Or maybe they get used to it and find it hard to let go."

"Your mother doesn't have to like me," she said.

"No, but it would make family life so much more comfortable in the future, don't you think? We do celebrate happy occasions together—holidays, birthdays."

"Bethanne said once she was a grandmother, she'd come around."

Rashid laughed. "That's our hope. But not right away. I want her to myself for a while."

Would Khalid ever want someone to himself for a while? She wished it would be her.

Madame al Harum was distraught when they arrived. She rushed to the door. "Have you heard anything more?"

"No, Mother," Rashid said, giving her a hug. "He's still in Quraim Wadi Samil. Bethanne just took off to get him. It'll be a few hours before they're in Kuwait."

"Call him. I need to talk to him," she ordered.

"You and Ella."

The older woman looked at Ella as if seeing her for the first time. "Oh." She frowned. "Of course."

"We both want Khalid safely back," Ella said.

Madame al Harum nodded. "Come, we will call him."

Khalid had maps and charts spread around him when the phone rang.

"Al Harum," he said, hoping this was another call from the site, updating the situation.

"Khalid, it's your mother. I wanted to tell you to be careful."

"I always am, Mother." He leaned back in his chair, pressing his thumb and forefinger against his eyes. He'd been studying the layout of the oil field, where the pipes had been drilled and the safety protocols that were in place. He figured he could recite every fact about that field in his sleep.

Glancing at his watch, he noted the plane would be arriving in less than an hour. He had talked to his second in command before he boarded and all the gear they needed was either on the plane or being shipped directly to the fire.

"We will watch over Ella for you," she said.

Khalid's attention snapped back to his mother. Ella. He should have told her this morning before she left, but he'd already been involved in learning

all he could from the source. He hadn't wanted to interrupt the phone call to go tell her goodbye.

"She returned safely?" he asked.

"Yes. She's here. Take care of yourself, son."

Before Khalid could say anything, he heard Ella's soft voice.

"Khalid?"

"Yes. You got back all right, I see."

"I didn't know until we were on the plane what was going on. I wished you had told me. You will be careful, won't you?"

"I always am." He was warmed by the concern in her voice.

"From what I've heard, this one is really bad."

He heard a sound from his mother in the background.

"It does seem that way. I'll know more when I get there, but so far, this is probably the most challenging one we've tried."

"I guess I couldn't talk you out of going?" she asked hopefully.

He laughed, picturing her with her pretty brown eyes, hair blowing in the sea breeze. "No, but I wish I didn't have to leave you. Not that I'd take you to a fire. I enjoyed yesterday." He wished he could pull her into his arms this moment and kiss her again. If he hadn't already been on the phone, nothing would have stopped him from explaining this morning—and taking another kiss for luck.

"Me, too."

He waited, hoping she'd say more. The silence on the line was deafening.

"I better go. I'm expecting another call," he finally said. Nothing was going to be decided on the telephone.

"Okay. Take care of yourself. I'll be here when you get back."

He hung up, wondering where else she'd be but at the cottage. She had a lease for another four years. And at this moment, he was grateful for his grandmother's way of doing things.

The phone rang again and this time it was the field manager in Kuwait. Time to push personal agendas on the back burner. He had a conflagration to extinguish.

CHAPTER ELEVEN

ELLA chafed at the way time dragged by. Rashid stayed for a while, then claimed work needed him and took off. Leaving her with Madame al Harum. Ella knew she'd be better off at home. She could try to take her mind off her worry about Khalid with work. Here she had nothing. She rose from the sofa where she'd sat almost since she'd arrived and walked to the window which overlooked the city. It looked hot outside. She'd rather be at the beach.

"I think I'll go home," she said.

"Stay."

Turning, she looked at Khalid's mother. "There's nothing to do here. At home I have work that might distract me from worry."

Sabria al Harum tried to smile. "Nothing will make you forget. I had years of practice with my husband when he went on oil fields. Always worrying about his safety. And he did not try to put out fires. I now worry about Khalid. Rashid assures me he knows his job. But he cannot know what a fire will do."

"It makes it worse since he was injured once," Ella said, looking back out the window.

"Yet you don't seem to mind his scar."

Ella shrugged. "He is not his scar, any more than he is defined by being tall. It's what's inside that counts."

There was a short silence then Sabria said, "Many people don't grasp that concept. He was terribly hurt by the defection of his fiancée when he was still in hospital."

"She either freaked or was not strong enough to be his wife. Khalid is very intense. Not everyone could live with that."

"You could."

Ella nodded, tears filling her eyes. She could. She would love to be the one he picked to share his life. She would match him toe-to-toe if he got autocratic. And she would love to spend the nights in his arms.

"He was like that as a little boy," Sabria said softly.

When Ella turned, she was surprised at the look of love on her hostess's face. "Tell me," she invited. She was eager for every scrap of knowledge she could get of Khalid.

"I have some pictures. Come, I'll tell you all about my wild twins and show you what I had to put up with." The words were belied by the tone of affection and longing.

Ella was surprised at the number of photo albums in the sitting area of Sabria al Harum's bedroom.

The room was bright and airy, decorated in peach and cream colors, feminine and friendly. She would never have suspected the rather austere woman to have this side to her.

Pulling a fat album from the shelves behind the sofa, Sabria sat and patted the cushion next to her for Ella to sit. Placing the album in Ella's lap a moment later, she opened it. For the next hour, the two women looked at all the pictures—from when two adorable babies came home in lacy robes, to the smiling nannies who helped care for them, to the proud parents and on up to adulthood. There were fewer pictures of the two young men, too busy to spend lots of time with their parents. Then she paused over one last picture.

"This was the one taken just before the fire that scarred my son so badly. He has never had his picture taken since. People can be cruel when faced unexpectedly with abnormalities—whether scarring or handicaps. He was doubly injured with the loss of his fiancée. He has so much to offer."

Ella nodded. A mother always said that, but in Khalid's case, it was true.

The phone rang. Sabria rose swiftly and crossed to answer the extension in her sitting room.

"Thank you," she said a moment later.

"That was Rashid. The team has taken off from Quraim Wadi Samil. They'll be in Kuwait in a couple of hours. There's nothing to do but wait."

"Then come with me to my studio. I'll show you my work and you can advise me. Madame Alia al Harum thought I had promise. I want to earn a living by my work, but if it is really impossible, maybe I should find out now, rather than later."

"You will not need to work once married to Khalid."

Ella had no quick response. Only she and Khalid knew there would be no marriage.

"Come and see."

Sabria thought about it for a moment then nodded. "I believe I should like to see what you do."

The afternoon passed slowly. Sabria looked at all the work Ella had done, proclaiming with surprise how beautiful it was. "No wonder my mother-in-law thought you had such promise. You have rare talent. I know just where I'd like to see that rosy vase. It would be perfect in my friend's bedroom. Perhaps I shall buy it for her. When will you begin to sell?"

Ella explained the original plan and then her idea to start earlier. Soon she and Sabria were discussing advantages and disadvantages of going public too soon, yet without the public feedback, how would Ella know which ideas were the most marketable.

Ella wasn't sure if it was the situation, or the fact Sabria was finally receptive to seeing her as an individual—not someone out to capture her son's affections—but she felt the tentative beginning of a friendship. Not that Sabria would nec-

essarily wish to continue when the engagement was broken. Ella could see the dilemma—who took the blame? She didn't want to. Yet in fairness, she needed to be the one. Khalid had been helping her. He did not need any more grief in his life.

They called Rashid for news before eating dinner on the veranda. Nothing new. Ella made a quick spaghetti with sauce she'd prepared a while ago and frozen. The camaraderie in the kitchen was another surprise. Ella thought she could really get to like Khalid's mother.

"I'm going now," Sabria said after they'd enjoyed dinner and some more conversation. Ella could listen to stories about the twins all week. Darkness had fallen. It was getting late. Nothing would change tonight. Khalid had told Rashid they needed to plan carefully since the fire was involved with two wells.

When she took a walk on the beach before going to bed, Ella looked to the north. She could see nothing. The fire was too far away. But she could imagine it. She dealt with fire every day—controlled and beneficial. Raging out of control would be so different. She offered another prayer for Khalid's safety. Her decision to leave was best. She could see about selling what she'd already done and arrange shipping to Italy of her annealer and crucible and glass. She'd establish herself somewhere near enough to see her parents, but far enough

away to make sure they knew she was not coming back to the family. Not until her brother's situation was cleared up.

In the meantime, she did her best not to focus on Khalid, but everything from the beach to the house next door reminded her of him. She could picture him standing in her doorway. Looking at the art she had created. Holding the yellow vase in his house that his grandmother had loved. She ached with loneliness and yearning. Could she get by without him over the years ahead?

She had to. There was no future for her in Quishari. That part of her life was over.

Tomorrow she'd begin packing and making arrangements to move.

The next two days were difficult. Ella made Rashid promise to call her the moment he learned of anything—good or bad. There was nothing else she could do, so she began packing. She ordered shipping cartons and crates and enlisted the help of Jalilah to help her. Carefully they wrapped the fragile pieces in packing materials, then in boxes, then crates. It was slow work, but had to be done carefully to insure no breakage during transit.

Every time Khalid's cordless phone rang, Ella's heart dropped, then raced. She'd answer only to hear Rashid's calm voice giving her an update. The materials had arrived. The maps had been updated. The

plan was coming together. There was never a personal message for her. What did she expect? Khalid had far more important things to worry about.

But each time Rashid hung up, Ella's heart hurt a bit more. One word, one "tell Ella I'm okay," would have sufficed.

On the third day, Ella could see the progress. She had arranged for the shipping agent to pick up what was already packed. He would hold it at the depot until everything was ready and ship all at once. She and Jalilah were talking when Ella heard a car. Glancing out the window, she saw Rashid and Bethanne get out and hurry toward the cottage.

Fear swamped her as she rushed to the door. "What happened?" she called before they could speak.

Bethanne came to her first, hugging her tightly. "He'll be okay," she said.

"What?" Sick with fear, she looked at Rashid.

"Another well exploded. The fire is worse than ever. Khalid was hit by flying debris. One of the crew was killed, but Khalid's in hospital. He's going to be okay. We're going now. You come with us."

Ella wanted to refuse, but her need to see him was too strong. She had to make sure he was truly okay before leaving.

"I just need my purse and passport," she said. She dashed to the house, Bethanne with her. "Bring a change of clothes and sleepwear. We're planning to stay as long as we need to," she said.

Ella went through the motions, but her thoughts stuck on Khalid. "He's really all right?"

"No, but he will be. So far he's still unconscious. We hope we're there by the time he wakes up," Bethanne said, helping fold clothes and stuffing them in the small travel bag.

Time seemed to stop. Ella felt like she was walking through molasses. She remembered hurrying to Alexander's hospital bed—too late. He had died from the car crash injuries before she was there to see him. She couldn't be too late for Khalid.

She sat on the edge of the bed.

"I can't go," she said.

Bethanne stopped and looked at her. "What?"

"I can't go." She pressed her hands against her chest, wishing she could stop the tearing pain. Khalid. He had to be all right!

"Yes, you can. And will. And greet him with all the love in your heart. He cannot have another fiancée abandon him when he's in the hospital."

Ella looked at Bethanne. "I'm not—" Now was not the time to confess she wasn't really his fiancée. "I'm not abandoning him. But I don't think I can go into a hospital."

"We'll be right with you. Come on. That's all you need. Get your passport and let's go."

Four hours later they entered the hospital. Ella felt physically sick. The few updates Rashid had

obtained during the flight had not been encouraging. Entering the new hospital, Ella felt waves of nausea roil over her. "I need a restroom," she said, dashing to the nearest one. Bethanne followed.

After throwing up, Ella leaned limply against the stall wall. "I can't do this again," she said.

"He'll be okay, Ella. He's not Alexander. He'll pull through," Bethanne said, rubbing her back.

"Go on up. I know Rashid needs to see him instantly. I'll clean up and be right behind you." She wanted a few moments to herself. She could do this. She had to. The thought of Khalid lying helpless in bed was almost more than she could stand. But she also wanted to see him. At least one more time. And assure herself he was alive and would recover.

She tried hard to think of this as visiting a sick friend. But as she walked down the corridor, the smells that assailed her reminded her vividly of the frantic dash to see Alexander. Only the times got mixed up. She felt the fear and panic, but it was for Khalid. The door was ajar to the room she'd been directed to. She stood outside, drawing in a deep breath, hoping she wouldn't lose her composure.

Rashid stepped out, smiling when he saw her. "I'm calling Mother. He's awake. And probably wondering where you are." He flipped open his mobile phone and hit a speed-dial number. Walking down the corridor, he began to speak when his mother answered.

Ella turned back to the room, stepping inside. Immediately she saw Khalid, the hospital bed raised so he was sitting. His face was bandaged, both eyes looked blackened. His right shoulder was also bandaged. Bethanne was on the far side, talking a mile a minute in English. Khalid watched her; he hadn't seen Ella yet.

Which was a good thing. It gave her time to get over her shock, give a brief thanks he was awake and seemingly able to recover. Pasting a smile on her face she stepped into the room.

"You scared me to death!" she said.

Khalid swiveled around, groaned at the movement, but looked at her like she was some marvelous creation. Her heart raced. Nothing wrong with his eyes.

"You came," he said.

"You said you'd keep safe." She walked over to the bed. Conscious of Bethanne watching her, she leaned over and kissed him gently on the mouth. His hand came up and kept her head in place as he kissed her back.

"Don't hurt yourself," she said, pulling back a few inches, gazing deep into his eyes.

"I didn't think you'd come," he said, pulling her closer for another brush of lips.

"Why ever not?" Bethanne asked. "If Rashid were injured nothing could keep me away."

"And nothing could keep me away," Ella said. She

straightened and took his hand in hers, feeling his grip tighten. Studying him, she shook her head.

"You look horrible," she said.

He laughed, and squeezed her hand. "I feel like a truck ran me over. That was something we didn't expect—another explosion. I think they had the wells linked in a way that didn't show on the maps."

"I heard one of your men died. I'm so sorry."

"Me, too."

She leaned closer. "But I'm glad it wasn't you."

"I'm going to find Rashid. We'll be back." Bethanne waved and headed out of the room.

"When Rashid first came in, I thought you hadn't come," he said.

"Well, some of your fiancées might desert you in hospital, but not all," she said lightly, hating for him to know how much it had taken for her to come. She was so glad she had, but the fear she'd lived with wouldn't easily be forgotten.

He laughed again. Despite his injuries, he seemed the happiest she'd ever seen him.

"Did that blow to the head knock you silly?" she asked.

"Maybe knocked some sense in me. I lay here thinking, after I woke up, what if you didn't come? We haven't known each other that long. What if you didn't care enough to come."

"What if I knocked you up side the head again to stop those rattled brains. Of course I would come.

I had to see that you were all right. I couldn't just take Rashid's word for it."

"Why?"

She looked at their linked hands. "I care about you," she said.

"How much?"

She met his gaze. "What do you mean, how much?" she asked.

"I want to know how much you care about me—what's hard about that?"

"Like, more than spinach but less than chocolate?"

His gaze held hers, his demeanor going serious. "Like enough to marry me, stay in Quishari and make a life with me?"

Ella caught her breath. For a moment she forgot to breathe. Did he mean it? Seriously?

"Are you asking me to marry you?" she said. "I mean, for real?"

He nodded. "I am. I hated to say good-night to you in Quraim Wadi Samil. Hated even more leaving for Kuwait without having another kiss. Then I woke up here and realized, life is unexpected. I could die here today, or live for decades. But I knew instantly either way, I wanted you as part of my life. I love you, Ella. I think I have since you touched my cheek on the beach weeks ago. A woman who wasn't horrified by how I look. Who could see me clearer in the dark than anyone in the light. A woman who had been through a lot already,

and valued people for who they were, not what they could offer monetarily. Did I also mention who sets my entire body on fire with a single kiss?"

Warmth and love spread through her as she smiled at his words. "You didn't. Maybe we need another check on that." She leaned over and kissed him.

"Are you saying yes?" he prompted a few moments later.

"I am. I love you. I never expected to say those words again after Alexander's death. But you swept into my life, running roughshod over any obstacles I might throw up. I can't pinpoint the moment I fell in love, but I can the moment I realized it. I will love you forever."

"The fire is still going," he said.

"And are you planning to put it out?"

"Might be involved in the planning. But right now I don't feel up to standing to kiss you, so doubt if I'll be leading a foray close to the flames."

"This time," she murmured, remembering what Bethanne had said. She wouldn't want to change a thing about this man.

"This time. But I'm careful. I'm still here, right?"

"Right. Here's hoping there are no more fires in your future."

"Only the one you set with your kisses," he said.

Ella laughed, seeing an entirely different side of the man who had captured her heart. And to think, she almost missed this. She'd have some quick un-

packing to do when she got back to the cottage. She couldn't bear for him to think she was leaving. She'd tell him—after a while. After he was convinced of her love as she was already convinced of his.

"I love you, Ella, now and always."

"I love you, Khalid. Now and always."

EPILOGUE

"I'M GETTING car sick riding with my eyes closed," Ella said, still gripping the edge of the door to help with the bouncing. They'd left Quraim Wadi Samil a while ago. In the last ten minutes, Khalid had insisted she close her eyes—he had a surprise for her. It couldn't be the oasis; she'd already seen that. What else was out in this desert?

"Almost there," he said, reaching out to grasp her free hand in his, squeezing it a little.

She felt the car slowing. Then it stopped. The desert wind brought scents of sand, scant vegetation and—was it water?

"Open your eyes," he said.

She did and stared. They were at the oasis. The late afternoon sun cast long shadows against the tall palms, the small pool of water—and the sandstone house that looked as if it had miraculously sprung up from the ground.

"What? Is that a house?"

He left the Jeep and came around to her side,

taking her hand to help her out. "It's our house. Ours and Rashid's and Bethanne's. She doesn't know yet. He'll bring her out next week. We have it first."

Ella looked around in astonishment. "You built it here miles and miles from anywhere? How could you get all the materials, how—never mind, money can achieve anything. This is fantastic! I want to see."

He smiled and led her across a flagstone patio to the front door. Lounge chairs rested on the patio, which gave a perfect view of the pool and palms. Opening the door, he swept her into his arms and stepped inside. "Isn't this what newlyweds do?" he asked at her shriek of surprise.

"Yes, in Italy. I didn't know you did it in Quishari." She laughed, traced the new scar on his face and pulled his head down for a kiss. She was so full of love for this husband of hers. And so grateful for his full recovery—with one or two new scars which only made her love him more.

"Why not at our home when we married?" she asked.

"We had the reception there—how could I carry you over the threshold? You were already inside."

"Hmm, good point."

He set her on her feet and turned her around. The small room was furnished with comfortable items. Large windows gave expansive views. Two of her glass pieces were on display. Taking a quick tour,

Ella discovered the small kitchen, bath and two large bedrooms.

"This is so lovely," she said, returning to the center of the main room. Khalid had done all he could to make her life wonderful. He'd backed her art exhibit, which turned out wildly successful. She had orders lined up for new pieces.

They'd attended Bethanne and Rashid's wedding in Texas. And then done a quick tour of several larger cities in the United States which Ella had enjoyed with her new husband.

On their way back to Quishari, they'd stopped in Italy so he could meet her parents. Even settled Giacomo's remaining debts, with a stern warning to never gamble again—which only reiterated what her father had decreed. She'd protested, but Khalid had insisted he wanted to have harmonious relations with his new in-laws.

Which she still hoped for with his mother. One day at a time, she reminded herself. At least they'd been married in Quishari, which Madame al Harum liked better than Rashid and Bethanne's wedding.

"The best is outside. Come," Khalid said, drawing her out and around to the side of the house where stairs led to the flat roof.

When they reached the upper level, Ella exclaimed at the loveliness. Pots of flowers dotted the hip-high wall. Several outdoor chairs and sofas provided ample seating. The view was

amazing. Slowly she turned around, delight shining in her eyes.

"This is so perfect."

He smiled at her and drew her into his arms. "I wanted something special for us to get away to sometimes, just the two of us. To enjoy the quiet of the desert and the beauty of this oasis."

She smiled, then frowned a little.

"You don't like it?"

"I love it. It's just…" She bit her lower lip and glanced around, then back at Khalid. "It won't be just the two of us."

"Rashid and I plan to keep the other informed when we want to use the house. We won't be here when they are. Or I can just tell him forget it, we want it all ourselves."

"Don't you dare. It's not that. We're having a baby," she blurted out. "Darn, that was not the way I wanted to tell you," she said.

Staring at his stunned face, she almost laughed. "Well, we've been married for four months and not exactly celibate. What do you think?"

"I'm stunned. And thrilled." With a whoop, he lifted her up and spun her around. "How are you feeling? When is it due? Do we know if it's a boy or girl? How long have you known?"

She laughed, feeling light and free and giddy with happiness. She thought he'd be happy; this confirmed it.

"You know Bethanne and Rashid are expecting. She gave me a full rundown on the symptoms she was feeling, from morning sickness to constantly being tired. Only, I don't have any of those. I feel fine. But there are signs and I had it confirmed yesterday. I was going to tell you last night, but then you had that meeting, and then we flew to Quraim Wadi Samil and here we are. Really, this turns out to be the best place to tell you. I loved our picnic here months ago. I'm so thrilled with this new house. We'll have only happy memories here. Do you know we're probably going to have our baby within weeks of Rashid and Bethanne's?"

"So our child will grow up with theirs," he said with quiet satisfaction.

She nodded, already picturing two small children playing on the beach by their home. Or coming here with parents to explore the desert.

"Do you think we'll have twins?" she asked.

"Who cares—one at a time or multiples, we'll love them all."

"All?"

"Don't you want a dozen?" he teased.

She laughed. "No, I do not. A couple, maybe three or four, but not twelve."

"Whatever makes you happy. You have made me happy beyond belief. I love you, Ella." He drew her into his arms and kissed her gently. "You changed everything beyond what I ever expected."

She smiled at him, not seeing the scars, only the love shining from his eyes. "You are all I'll ever want," she said, reaching up to kiss him again on the rooftop of a house made for happy memories.

* * * * *

*Harlequin Intrigue top author Delores Fossen
presents a brand-new series of breathtaking
romantic suspense!*
TEXAS MATERNITY: HOSTAGES
*The first installment available May 2010:
THE BABY'S GUARDIAN*

Shaw cursed and hooked his arm around Sabrina.

Despite the urgency that the deadly gunfire created, he tried to be careful with her, and he took the brunt of the fall when he pulled her to the ground. His shoulder hit hard, but he held on tight to his gun so that it wouldn't be jarred from his hand.

Shaw didn't stop there. He crawled over Sabrina, sheltering her pregnant belly with his body, and he came up ready to return fire.

This was obviously a situation he'd wanted to avoid at all cost. He didn't want his baby in the middle of a fight with these armed fugitives, but when they fired that shot, they'd left him no choice. Now, the trick was to get Sabrina safely out of there.

"Get down," someone on the SWAT team yelled from the roof of the adjacent building.

Shaw did. He dropped lower, covering Sabrina as best he could.

There was another shot, but this one came from

a rifleman on the SWAT team. Shaw didn't look up, but he heard the sound of glass being blown apart.

The shots continued, all coming from his men, which meant it might be time to try to get Sabrina to better cover. Shaw glanced at the front of the building.

So that Sabrina's pregnant belly wouldn't be smashed against the ground, Shaw eased off her and moved her to a sitting position so that her back was against the brick wall. They were close. Too close. And face-to-face.

He found himself staring right into those sea-green eyes.

How will Shaw get Sabrina out?
Follow the daring rescue and the heartbreaking
aftermath in THE BABY'S GUARDIAN by
Delores Fossen,
available May 2010 from Harlequin Intrigue.